The Ostrich

A Tale of Flightless Adventure

by

Stephen William McNamee

Book One of the Qistone Trilogy

Chapter 1: Feathery Farewell?

Dust swirled everywhere. It was early afternoon, but it might as well have been the middle of the night for anyone standing below seven feet in this small area of prairie land in Texas. Had there been an observer, flashes of feathers would have been seen; angry "huffs" of exhaled air would have been heard, and a dozen pairs of dark, menacing eyes shooting daggers into their soon to be victim would have turned even the bravest onlooker into a sniveling brat. But, dear readers, no observer stood witness to what transpired next.

The ostriches flapped their flightless wings and slowly formed a circle. Inside this circle full of steam, dirt, and sweat, engulfed in a brown, sandy fog, stood this petite, 80-pound girl. Her hair was long, black, and unruly. Ringlets of curls swirled and twirled in all directions. Dirt covered her light, latte-colored face, and dried mud caked her once blue and pink sneakers. Dear readers, had this hypothetical observer been around to see this tiny girl surrounded by *extremely* angry ostriches who were ready to attack, he or she would have thought, "Oh no, this girl is toast!" And why wouldn't they think that? What could a scrawny, 12 year-old girl do against approximately 2000 lbs of feathery fury?

The birds towered over her, snapping their beaks open and shut, likely just deciding which bird would get to strike her first.

"Seriously guys?" Amira pleaded. "This is *not* cool. I'm late for practice! Don't you have *any* respect for my time?"

The birds squawked angrily. Any second and they'd begin their attack.

"Okay fine," she muttered...well "okay fine" is what she *would* have muttered, but really she only got out, "Okay f-" before five of the birds lunged at her. Suddenly, the fog of dust that surrounded her before was replaced by a dirt storm that engulfed her fully. Squawks and groans pierced the sky. "Stop that!" the girl screamed. But the birds did not comply. Every few seconds you might be able to see Amira's elbow cut through the dust or her sneaker touch the ground for a fraction of a second before it hopped back into the abyss. A concerned passerby may have felt like several minutes occurred watching this horrifying scene; however, in truth, it was over in 35 seconds.

Dirt soared through the air. It was as if 30 square feet of land just decided it didn't want to be part of the world anymore, so it left leaving a cloudy chaos behind. Nothing could be seen. Soon, surely the birds would tire of pecking at her corpse and would continue on their way, wherever that way took them. Once the dust finally blew away perhaps her body would be found by a hiker...or a rancher...or whoever enjoys walking around arid areas of Texas in the late summer: basically, fools. Maybe her family would cry over her body and wonder why, *WHY* would birds do this to such a sweet girl, *why* would the world be so cruel, *why*- oh wait, hold on. Some of the dust cloud dispersed showing one ostrich tied up and writhing on the ground. Oh, well at least she went down fighting. Her family could eulogize her as a brave soul, who fought with tiny fists of fury until she drew her last breath, until- oh, hold on...okay, more dust cleared away and yet another ostrich was tied up on the ground...and although it's most assuredly an optical illusion a pair of feet seemed to be firmly planted on the ground...well, maybe not *planted* since her left foot tapped the earth in a slow dignified manner, and sure maybe attached to those feet were legs, and as more dust fled, knees could be seen, and soon there stood a dirty, *dirty* girl, hands on hips, and a look of ice in her eyes. Several ringlets fell over her face, but she just pushed her lower lip out and puffed, and the ringlets realized she was in no mood to be trifled with, so they fell back behind her ears.

"Happy?" she asked. *Enough of this*, she thought. "HeYAHHHH! HEYAHHH!" she screamed as she began to jump up and down waving her arms frantically over her head. Horror flowed out of the ostriches' eye sockets as they fled in the direction of Amira's choosing. She then untied her former attackers and repeated the same screaming/jumping-jack routine, and the birds fled as well following their brethren far into the distance to what looked like a gated area with a rather reddish barn attached to one end. *Finally*, she thought, and then she thought about how she was going to exact her revenge on one of most challenging things any twelve year-old girl has to deal with: her little bro- Woops, light breathing from behind interrupted her thoughts. She turned around and there stood, Moha, her least favorite ostrich. The ostrich, standing close to ten feet tall, just stared down at her, but not with a menacing look, but rather with what could only be described as a joyful look. It was as if Moha's eyes were sparkling, but Amira was in no mood to see joy.

"You probably put them up to this, huh?" she asked.

The bird just stood there and seemed to shrug its wings slightly.

"Well do I have to fight with you too, or will you just go home?

Then, two strange moments occurred, although for a little while Amira convinced herself that she was tired and that the light was playing tricks on her, for the ostrich seemed to smile at her and even more bizarre, it then winked at her. Next, Moha, made a triumphant squawk and hopped along back in the direction of the barn. Moha, received his name because of that strange stripe of purple feathers that existed on top of its head. You see, Moha was short for Mohawk, but Amira's little brother couldn't say "Mohawk" when they first got Moha so- OH THAT'S RIGHT! Moha had interrupted Amira's thought process before, but now, during her walk home, Amira had plenty of time to reflect...where were we?...*right:* ostriches attack, Amira wins, blah, blah, blah, then she thought about how she was going to exact her revenge on one of most challenging things any twelve year-old girl has to deal with: a baby brother. Thus, as Moha, with his strange streak of purple feathers that ran down the center of his head, became smaller and smaller, Amira took a deep breath, put her hands in her front pockets, and lowered her head as she began her own trek back to the farm letting her imagination run wild with thoughts of malice toward her sibling.

***

The gate clanged shut behind her as Amira headed towards the white-wooded house.

"Amira! Amira!" a high-pitched voice screamed from behind her.

Without even looking behind her she asked, "Hashim, how many times do I have to tell you not to open the ostrich gate when I'm not around?"

Hashim, wearing dirty tanned shorts and a Dallas Cowboys t-shirt, skipped along to catch up to her. "But I had to open the gate. We were playing football!"

Amira looked around and didn't see any other children. "Who was playing football?"

"We were!" Hashim claimed excitedly as he tossed a football to himself.

"Who's we?" she asked.

"Me and the ostriches! And guess what?"

"What?"

"I scored a touchdown."

"You what?"

"I threw myself a pass and caught it, so I scored a touchdown!" he bellowed as he now hopped right along side of her.

"What does that have to do with you opening the gate?" she steamed.

"Right! Umm...right! Well, the end zone was on the other side of the fence, so I *had* to open the gate."

Amira had had enough. She stopped in her tracks, turned to her little pip squeak of a brother and slapped the ball out of his hands. "Hashim! You are the smallest boy in your class *by far*.

You are never going to play football! You're too small! So stop playing football and stop opening the gate!"

Hashim's eyes narrowed and watered as Amira glared at him. But instead of crying, he suddenly smiled and picked up his ball and said, "Well, I'm gonna have to grow some day. Maybe I'll end up being really big."

"I doubt it," she stated flatly before continuing to the house.

"Amira?"

"Yes Hashim?"

"Sorry."

"It's okay."

"Was it hard to get the ostriches back in our yard?"

"It wasn't too bad, although I think I swallowed a feather."

"Ewwww," he said while puckering his face.

As they reached the side door to their home, the screen door opened, and an attractive woman in her early forties, with a slight accent, peaked out. Like Amira, she had long, black, curly hair, but hers was pulled back into a tight bun. She wore a plain white blouse and black pants, and she had this air of professionalism and kindness about her, as if she would be comfortable in any situation. "Amira," her mother, Nara, stated, "there you are. Why do you always do this? Come inside and clean up. You're going to be late for practice. Hashim come inside too, I made you a sandwich."

"I'm starving!" Hashim exclaimed while zooming past Amira and squirting by his mother into the house.

By the time Amira reached the kitchen (about five seconds after Hashim), Hashim had already wolfed down three quarters of his lamb sandwich.

"Mawummm?" Hashim asked while chewing his sandwich.

"Mouth closed when you chew Hashim," she stated while smiling at the hyperactive boy.

Gulping the food down quickly, he then asked, "Is Amira going to eat?" while his sister walked through the kitchen into the hallway to grab a pink, Teenage Mutant Ninja Turtles backpack stuffed to the brim and beyond.

Patiently, Amira's mother replied to the boy, "No Hashim. We talked about this. Amira and I are fasting now. We can't eat until after sunset."

"Oh yeah!" Hashim said, while swinging his feet, which were too short to touch the green, linoleum floor while sitting on the kitchen table's chair. "Why are you fasting again?"

From the hallway, Amira yelled, "Because of Ramadan."

"But Ramadan was so *long* ago."

"Yes, Hashim but your sister was sick, remember? So she couldn't fast then, which is why she's fasting now."

"Oh yeah. What'd she have again?"

"Mono, little one."

"Oh yeah. Mom, Amira was *so* boring when she had mono, remember?"

Nara smiled thinking back to Hashim holding an action figure or Hot Wheels toy car and frowning as he'd watch over Amira from the upstairs hallway as she'd fall in and out of consciousness. "Yes Hashim, I remember."

"Hey Mom?"

Slightly less patiently, she replied, "Yes?"

"Amira swallowed an ostrich feather a few minutes ago, does that mean she broke her fast and Allah hates her?!"

"Hashim!" his mother exclaimed.

Amira reentered the kitchen dragging her backpack (which was unusually heavy for some reason) along the floor as she sidled into a chair next to Hashim at the table. "I wouldn't have swallowed an ostrich feather if you hadn't left the gate open again."

"I 'splained that already."

"Hashim, Allah does not hate your sister, and will forgive her for mistakenly swallowing a feather. Now hurry up Amira, you're going to be late for swimming practice."

"I wouldn't be running late if Dad was here to help with the ostriches."

"Amira, your father is in Egypt for work. He's not over there because he wants to be, but he loves us and needs to be over there for us," her mother stated while searching for something in her purse. She continued, "And besides, we have Charlie to help us out."

"Charlie? Charlie hasn't been here in over a week!" Amira whined.

"My beautiful banoota, you know that his daughter is going to give birth any day now. I told him to come over whenever he has time."

"Well then why can't we hire someone else to help out?"

"Because Allah believes in you Amira and believes that you are more than capable of handling them," she replied while pulling out a University ID card.

"Hey Mom, if Amira swallows water while swimming, does that mean she breaks her fast?" Hashim piped in.

"Only if she does so purposely dear, and your sister wouldn't do that."

"What if she swallowed a pool full of feathers *and* water?"

"Why on earth would I do that?" Amira asked.

Hashim shrugged his shoulders and said, "I don't know. Maybe you would if you were hungry."

"You're supposed to be hungry during a fast dummy. That's what makes it a fast," Amira retorted while squeezing his arm.

"Ow. Mom!" Hashim whined while pulling his arm away from his sister.

"Enough you two. Hashim, go grab your books, we need to get to school."

"But I'm on summer vacation!" he protested.

"Yes dear, but you know I'm teaching a class tonight and you need to come with me because Amira has to get to practice" she said, while picking Hashim up and putting him down in the direction of the staircase, which would lead to his room where one could find the aforementioned books he was supposed to take.

"Why'd you even sign me up for swimming; you know I don't want to be on the team this year," Amira said. This statement was not entirely true.

"Hush child. You love swimming, and you're so good at it. Now stop complaining and get on your bike and go!" her mother said as she pushed Amira out the door.

"I'm not even supposed to be here right now." This statement Amira believed was true, but it turns out, wasn't true at all.

"Have fun sweetie," her mother said as she smiled and slammed the door.

***

The road from Amira's house to the middle school's swimming pool was paved for unknown reasons...unknown because Amira passed a total of less than two-dozen houses during her 2-mile bike ride and nary a car passed by her. The road was straight and flat, which allowed Amira's mind to wander. *I hate going to practice,* she thought. Again, not a true statement. *Why did Dad leave us behind this year? Texas in the summer? Seriously!?* Amira had a point. The past ten summers, the family had spent in her parents' homeland, Egypt. There, she would get to play with her thirty or so cousins, and cook with her grandmother, and sing out of tune with her father at night. She'd run around Cairo with her favorite cousin, Aini. Aini was one year older than Amira, and although she lived in Cairo, Aini spoke English with a British accent because she spent half of her school day at a British school located in a neighborhood once completely colonized by the British. Aini and Amira loved running into Western tourists with cameras slung around their necks and fanny packs bulging from their waists, who just assumed these little Egyptian girls had no idea how to speak English.

"Exxxx-cuuuuse me love," the tourists would say. "Do youuuu know where (they'd gesture with arms) the Py-ra-mids' are?"

The girls would smile dumbly and not say a word.

"The PY-RA-MIDS. Weeee wantttt to seeee them and rent Caaaa-mels. You understand CA-MELS and PYRAMIDS, right?"

"Dear, they don't speak a word of English. They're probably just fascinated by your wristwatch," the wife would say. "It's sad really. Sad."

"Ohhhh, CAHHHH-MEEEELS" Aini would reply. "UMMM, Cahhh-meeels, yes?" she'd say while miming with her hand what looked to be two humps to signify she understood.

"Yes, yes!" the man would excitedly reply. "See honey, these kids understand," and then he would mimic her two-humps motion.

"Yeeees. CAHHH-MEEELS eeeen Ahhhrabic is (speaking Arabic) sooooo ummmm goooo to dat *beeelding and ahhsk for* (more Arabic)" she'd continue while miming the two-hump motion.

"Thank you darlings. Obviously, this city isn't classless after all," the wife would say as they walked down the street toward the building Aini pointed to.

Then the girls would giggle and run off because the Arabic word Aini gave them for "camels" was in fact the Arabic word for female "breasts" and the building she pointed them toward to rent "camels/breasts" was supposedly a brothel according to one of Aini's classmates.

Yes, spending a summer in Egypt far surpassed anything she could do during the summer in a small town outside of Dallas where...where, well, where nothing much happened. Thus, this 2-mile stretch of road gave her ample time to stew over her unfortunate circumstances. *Why am I even going to practice? I don't want to be there.* Again, this statement was false. Amira desperately wanted to be "there" as in the pool. She just hated being late, not because her swim coach would yell at her (she wouldn't), but rather because by being late, she would miss the end of the boys' practice, which meant she might miss seeing....Kyle.

***

As far as Amira was concerned, if the boundaries of Texas began at Kyle Ander's feet and ended at the top of his head, she'd be fine with that and apply for state citizenship immediately. Kyle, one year senior to Amira, was a god among boys. He captained the swim team, was president of the middle school's student council, stood tall, walked taller, and he even had several whiskers on his chin that would grow into an impeccable goatee given enough time...say 4 to 6 years, give or take. He had shaggy brown hair that always fell perfectly and magical, deep blue eyes that seemed to glow. Twice in the past three months, Amira amazingly conversed with Kyle after his practice and before hers. Granted one conversation consisted of Kyle saying, "Hello" and Amira grunting with a smile, and the other consisted of Kyle telling Amira her backpack was unzipped, which caused Amira to spin around to zip up her backpack, but since her backpack was still on her back, it spun with her and she ended up taking out a second grader whose only crime was being just tall enough to be hit in the forehead with it. But, from Amira's perspective their deep connection was unquestionable. She rehashed her conversations with Kyle as she rode toward the pool, and with each rehashing, she peddled faster and faster still, determined that today would be the day a third conversation would take place.

***

She practically leapt off her bike when she reached the school's parking lot and made it within five steps of the door before she remembered that she needed to lock her bike. Racing back to the bike, she pulled out her brand new lock from a side pocket in her backpack. She had meant to memorize the combination earlier in the day, but Hashim's football prowess prevented that from occurring. No matter though, she had the combo written down in her backpack; thus, she could memorize it tomorrow. Right now, there were more important things to attend to like impressing Kyle with her awesomeness. So, she quickly locked her bike and sprinted inside the school and continued to sprint down the yellowish-green linoleum, tiled floors, flying by lockers, and bulletin boards with posters describing things like why reading is cool (apparently because when you read you get to sit underneath a beautiful tree with a rainbow in the background while penguins dance and monsters sit at a kid's table drinking tea), Bunsen burner safety (goggles are a must...or else you too could end up like the girl on the poster and be blind...although to be honest, she was wearing cool sunglasses), and interestingly a bulletin board containing a collage listing accomplishments of modern minorities in America (more on this later). Soon, the swimming pool doors were in sight and thru thin, rectangular, shatter-resistant glass windows that all school doors seem to have, she swore she could see Kyle inside. She was now steps from the door. 12 steps, 8 steps, 7 steps, 4 steps- *WAIT!!!* she thought. She can't sprint in like a crazy girl. She needed to show Kyle that she exuded grace at all times. Sadly, the linoleum floor had been recently buffed, so Amira, lacking the ability to break, exuded a tremendous amount of grace as she slid on her butt until she slammed into the door with a loud *THUD!*

That's okay, she thought. No one saw, so all she had to do was crawl below the windows and past the nearest corner and just wait for 30 seconds to a minute and then get up and walk in and no one would ever know who or what made that sound. No harm, no foul...I mean sure, she would be sporting a rather dark blue bruise on her right shoulder which took the brunt of the impact for a week or so...so okay, there was *some* harm, but no real foul.

Fate shined kindly on her in this instance as Amira successfully crawled around the corner unseen. Amira used those thirty seconds well: she straightened her shorts, patted down her hair, and calmed down her heart rate by taking four long breaths. Then with the grace of a queen, Amira walked to the door and opened it...and...uh-oh, her heart sped up a bit because there stood Kyle next to the pool, his swim shorts still dripping chlorine filled droplets of pool water. There stood Kyle holding court as seven or eight other boy swimmers laughed after every sentence he spoke. Amira couldn't hear what he was saying but she was sure it was brave and sincere and honest and meaningful and thoughtful...and beautiful...and smart...and-OKAY AMIRA! WE GET IT. KYLE *rocks*. Can I continue with my narration now? Of course, Amira couldn't answer, but let's just pretend she said yes, and get on with it.

Okay Amira, it's your time to shine, she thought. *Just strut by him ever so slowly and then without even looking at him, just say "Hey Kyle" as you pass him by and then keep on walking without waiting for a reply,* she told herself.

There was about eight feet of space between the pool and where Kyle was holding court, so Amira chose to walk along the edge of the pool allowing her to be just under eight feet away from him; plus, the pool edge made sure she actually walked in a straight line because straight lines are cool. Each journey begins with a first step, so Amira stepped confidently forward with her right foot. With each step her confidence grew. Closer and closer she came to Kyle's group. Although she looked dead ahead, her peripheral vision told her that Kyle was glancing over at her. Within seconds, she'd be able to say "Hey Kyle," two simple words that would set her master plan in motion, a plan that would end with Kyle's unyielding love for her, a six-year courtship and a marriage atop a mid-level pyramid. In truth, Amira did look radiant at that moment, so her plan worked to perfection...well, worked to perfection up until the point where the water polo ball slammed into her face causing her and her backpack to go flying into the pool. Although she would argue differently, I like to think she fell *gracefully* into the pool, confidently if you will...one could say she confidently flailed her arms and with great poise under the circumstances, let out a dignified yelp of protest as gravity unmercifully pulled her down into four feet of watery abyss.

***

Every story needs a villain, someone for the readers to root against, a villain with horrible body odor, decaying teeth, whose skin is covered in warts, whose hair is full of dandruff, a villain with a screechy voice and an ear piercing cackle for a laugh. Unfortunately for Amira, this particular villain was none of those things. In fact Amber of Auburn hair was beautiful, striking, popular, had a perfect smile, and always smelled soooooo good. Whenever, Amira saw her, she could never think to herself, *Amber*, but rather she always thought to herself, *Amber of Auburn hair* because Amber's hair *was* perfect. Always perfect, both in shape and smell. Even after swim practice, when she'd pull off her swim cap, it was as if her hair had been resting in some hair salon-universal vortex that protected it completely from chlorine and swim-cap damage because it still looked beautiful *immediately* after practice.

However, Amira didn't hate her for her hair. Rather, she disliked her because Amber decided last year after Amira beat her in a swim meet that Amira was not worthy to breathe the same air as Amber and her friends. Thus, Amber took every opportunity she could to mess with Amira. So, as Amira floated underwater with her hair in a Medusa-like state, she thought about Amber and about the other surface dwellers like Kyle who were surely laughing at her pool flop, and she wondered, *could this day get worse?* Actually, it could, and it did, but let's get to that later. For now perhaps dear reader, you could imagine a pleasant field with tons of lilies and sunshine, so that Amira can have a few seconds to herself below the surface before the realities from above come crashing down on her...lilies and sunshine...lilies and sunshine. Ah, much better.

Amira rose to the surface to sounds of laughter and dozens of eyes directed at her. She scanned the crowd quickly to see how badly Kyle was laughing at her but she didn't see him. He was probably keeled over somewhere with a stomachache caused from laughing so hard she thought...oh well, no matter; she placed her palms on the raised, reddish tiles that marked the pool's edge and lifted herself and her waterlogged backpack out of the water.

***

Amber swore that she warned Amira about the projectile heading for her head, and in truth she did warn Amira...about one-fifth of a second before the ball impacted with Amira's forehead. But as Amber tried to explain later, Amira should thank her because you need to develop lightning quick reflexes in swimming because when the starting gun goes off, the fastest one off the block has the advantage.

All of Amber's opinions were lost on Amira as she climbed out of the pool. As Amira used both hands to push her sopping wet hair back and away from her face, she surveyed the contorted faces around her, the faces contorted from diverted blood flow and unique muscle configurations that laughter generally causes. Now, it's not easy to walk away with confidence while carrying approximately 20 pounds of added water weight that was currently distributed evenly throughout one's clothing and pack. However, Amira found that confidence, that inner strength that too few in this world possess. Thus, Amira smiled, took a deep breath and confidently put her right foot forward.

That wasn't so hard, she thought, so she put her left foot forward and realized that she'd walk away from this scene with no problem. So again she stepped forward and-hey now....hmm, a gentle tapping on her shoulder interrupted Amira's confident gait.

No problem, she thought as she confidently spun 180 degrees. To her surprise there stood Kyle with magical blue eyes staring at her.

"I think this fell out of your backpack," he said while extending his hand which held, not one but two wet, Transformers action figures.

Hashim! she hissed silently. "Thank you," she said taking the action figures from his hand. Okay, granted, her confidence had taken a hit due to the water "incident," action figures, and the fact that Kyle was staring at her, but who wouldn't be shaken? Besides, she still had enough confidence to walk out of-

"And this," he said as he handed her a Ziploc bag full of what appeared to be several folded pair of Amira's underwear...yup, there was a Care Bear pair, which unfortunately was populated by several, nay a *ton* of Care Bears that seemed to be shooting rainbows left and right for no apparent reason...well, they probably had a *caring* reason why they did so, but that thought offered little solace to Amira, and then of course there was her unicorn pair, a starry-astronomy pair, a pair with humorous Arabic sayings that would surely be lost on this crowd...well, you get the idea: several pair neatly folded into a Ziploc bag, which though dripping wet on the outside did seem to do it's job of keeping its contents clear from all external elements (such as pool water). Now, Amira had no idea *why* a sealed, plastic bag of her undergarments would be in her backpack, but she had little time to deal with that question since Kyle then quickly handed her a journal entitled, "Amira's Diary Of Dreams And Inspirations" which also happened to be sealed in a Ziploc bag, apparently dry as well (2 for 2 for Ziploc!).

So within the past two minutes our protagonist went from "smooth-walking Amira" to "sopping wet Amira" to apparently "an adolescent with a penchant for plastic bags and carrying around embarrassing articles in her backpack along with her favorite transforming toys-Amira". But, let's be honest: Transformers along with Ziploc sealed underwear and diaries *aren't* all that bad; she could bounce back from that kind of embarrassment, and she was right: she *could've* bounced back from the toys and whatnot...yes, she *could have*, but

18

unfortunately Kyle had one more "gift" to bestow upon Amira. Kyle bent down to pick up the last thing he had snagged from the pool: a poster-type object, but really more of a collage, a *home-made collage*...a home-made collage created by Amira and her friend Karen...containing photos of their "crushes" like certain popular teen movie stars and musicians...oh, and in the center with tons of hearts drawn around the photo happened to be a picture of one, Kyle Anders, the blue-eyed dreamboat who stood before her. Well, since collages are created using paper, markers, sparkles, glues, etc., Amira dodged a bullet because everyone knows that water destroys thin, flimsy paper products that are made using such ingredients, so- oh *right*, totally forgot: Karen thought it would be a *great* idea to *laminate* their wonderful, fun creation they made on a boring Saturday night last June. Well perhaps, Kyle didn't notice his photogr- oops, never mind since Kyle just glanced at the photo as Amira did, and then they locked eyes on each other and...well...

Now with a Middle Eastern background, Amira generally had a slightly darker color skin tone than the kids at her school, but since the blood in her face was too embarrassed to hang around her brain, it rushed out of her face leaving her paler than Casper the Friendly Ghost, and boy could she have used a friend right then and there. But the paleness didn't last long because then her body decided that blushing would be appropriate considering the circumstances, so the blood reversed course and rushed back up into her cheeks. So, Amira's cheeks reddened...and reddened...until tomatoes envied her skin color; however, blood flow hadn't returned to the rest of her face like her forehead or chin. This led to an extremely pale face with really, really red cheeks. Basically, she looked like a soaking wet, homicidal clown, which generally twelve year-old girls do not aspire to look like or take their fashion sense from (although she would be thirteen in a few months, so who can say for sure?). Now, some would claim that in the next few seconds, her eyes watered up in a humiliated dam of tears just waiting to burst, but to be fair, her blood shot eyes were probably first caused by the chlorinated water, and she was determined to walk away from this situation with her head held high, and- Wait, you know what? Screw walking away slowly with your pride: RUN AMIRA RUN! And that is exactly what she did. With her wet backpack flailing behind her, while clutching Transformers and Ziploc bags in her right hand and a wet collage in her left hand, she sloshing-ly sprinted out of the pool area, down the hallway, barreling through the school's side doors which led to the parking lot where her bike was locked...was locked...was locked...crap. Dear reader, part of me wishes I could have warned her that her- well, she'll figure it out in a second anyway.

As Amira reached her bike, she thought *freedom! Freedom from these immature kids, freedom from practice, freedom from Amber of Auburn hair, freedom from stupid Kyle with his stupid fallen-items-water-recovery system, freedom from- wait, a second*, she thought, *what's my combination?* It was then that it dawned on her, that her "freedom" depended on a piece of paper with a series of three numbers that was sitting somewhere in her backpack, likely in a "chlorine-enhanced" watery pulp. Over the next 110 seconds, the amount of syllables that erupted from her mouth was quite astounding. Fortunately, this narrator does not speak Arabic because rumor has it that halfway across the world the entire crew of a Dubai tanker blushed at the vocabulary

Amira utilized...you know, surely just yelling about sunshine and daffodils and such.

***

The late afternoon sun mostly dried Amira's clothing. The puddle she created while sitting on the curb next to her bike quickly evaporated leaving just an ovular piece of cement that was slightly darker from the rest of the surrounding concrete. Amira sat with her legs curled up tight by her arms and her head bent down so that all you could see really was a head of hair that obviously had hundreds of different opinions on which way the strands should fall. From this self-created closed little universe, Amira stared at the amber colored spherical charm that her grandmother had given her, which always hung around her neck and now dangled between Amira's head and damp lap. Amira stared at the charm watching it sway slightly back and forth as she pondered what to do next...walk home? Gnaw thru the metal bike rack? So many possibilities to consider.

"Amira? What are you doing?" said Karen Yu, a petite girl with straight black hair, which she often pulled back into a ponytail. Karen wore bright blue sandals with a matching blue shirt, yellow shorts, and chem lab goggles hanging from her neck to round out the outfit.

"What's it matter? My life's over."

"Why? I mean you look like a mess right now, but what's wrong?" Karen said smiling.

"A mess? That's how you plan on cheering me up?" Amira asked, glad that her friend was here.

Karen dragged her backpack-on-wheels over to Amira and plucked herself down next to her. "Do we need to have a singing moment?" Karen asked coquettishly.

"No, please no, I'm upset."

"Perfect!" Karen yelped and then proceeded to sing, *"Amira the stars are so bright. Oh Amira, why won't you come home tonight. Amira the owls are 'hoo-ing', wanna know what you been DO-ing."*

"God! You are such a dork! Stop!"

"Second verse!"

"Please stop. I'll tell you anything you want to know!" Amira pleaded in her best impersonation of a 1950's femme fatale. (Author's note: I've heard better.)

"Then tell me what's the good word, my bird?"

Amira collapsed backward onto the sidewalk and rehashed the incidents that led her to sitting outside of school, damp, and without a means of transportation home on this day.

"Amber's such a *birch* tree," Karen said. (Karen felt swearing showed a lack of imagination.) "You need to stand up to her once and for all Amira."

"You *know* I can't."

"Ugh, who cares about Kyle right now? This is about your self-respect. So what that he's Amber's brother!" Karen said. (Oh, did I forget to mention that fact to you dear reader? My bad.) You're cooler than she is, smarter, a better athlete, prettier."

Amira puffed her hair out of her face so that she could roll her eyes at Karen.

"Well, *generally* you're prettier than she is, at least when you're not all damp and flustered. Anyway, that's why she doesn't like you; she's scared of you. She's scared of your awesomeness."

"Yeah, yeah, yeah. Deep down I'm this beautiful princess, who like a flower is just waiting to bloom," Amira respond. (Interesting choice of words, by the way.)

"No, deep down, you're a *dork*, but I'm your friend, so it's my job to hide that part of you from the world, and believe me, you don't make it easy."

Amira smiled and said, "I'm not supposed to be laughing right now. I'm traumatized. Everyone's going to be laughing at me tomorrow!"

"No, they won't wait for tomorrow. They'll start tonight," Karen astutely pointed out.

"Ugh! Why are you at school anyway? You're the dork! We're on vacation!"

"Meredith and I had a student council meeting, planning stuff for the upcoming year and all, and then I had to go speak with Mr. Raspy because my parents want me to enter some student statewide science competition this fall. Why do they have to be so stereotypical? Why couldn't they be beatniks who wanted their daughter to be a Spoken Word artist or something...anything but a science dork?"

"What's a beatnik?" Amira asked.

"I don't know...someone who wears all black and snaps when they agree with you or something?"

"Where is Meredith anyway?"

"She's playing street hockey with Carlos behind the school," Karen replied. Meredith and Carlos, both close friends with Karen and Amira, both loved sports that were not "big" in Texas. Thus, they formed a club a year ago where one afternoon a week they would alternate playing hockey (for Meredith) and soccer (for Carlos). "They'll probably quit soon because Carlos was whining about the bruises he was getting from her slapshot...but whatever, they use a tennis ball. He should deal with it if he plans on being a man some day," Karen said.

"You sound like Meredith."

"Yeah totally, I stole that line from her," Karen said. "You know maybe we could get back at Amber more indirectly."

"What do you mean?"

"I don't know...maybe we can steal her diary and photocopy it and make tons of copies and spread them around school."

Amira tilt her head to the side and stared at Karen and said, "And we would get that how?"

"It's not my job to think of everything. I'm just a girl forced to wear chem. goggles on a summer day because my parents are afraid that if they give me too much free time, I'll end up pregnant and barefoot. Who would *choose* not to wear shoes?"

"Ew, I never want kids," Amira said as she slowly cheered up.

"Tell me about it. Like, oh my god: *you're* even more than I can handle," Karen said while sticking out her tongue.

"Whatever! You're the child!" Amira exclaimed while jokingly pushing Karen.

"Well, well, well" said a large eclipse that suddenly cast them into shadow. Sadly, the eclipse was not planetary in the making but rather was due to Brendan Jeffries standing in front of them. "What do we have here? Where's the other half of the MOP Squad?" he continued. "Did mommy separate you guys for being bad? Did the MOP Squad get into a fight over the transformer dolls you brought to school Amira? Did-"

"Is this going to take awhile?" Karen asked, "Because if so, then I want to sit in a more comfortable position."

Actually, dear readers, if you don't mind, let's all sit more comfortably for a minute, as I interrupt this exchange, for you see, I think now would be a good time to explain the *MOP Squad* comment.

MOP Squad Interruption

The "Mop" Squad as the fearsome foursome were called, did not achieve their nickname due to their janitorial talents. Forgive me dear reader, but to properly explain, we will need to take a short jaunt down memory lane, round the corner and walk through traumatization alley. Basically, we need to jump back a few years, back to a more "peaceful" time in this town's history. Yes, let's start with the town.

How should I put this? If Plaintown, Texas, were a brand of bread, it would be Wonder Bread. If Plaintown, Texas were a sandwich it would be Fluffernutter and mayonnaise *on* Wonder Bread. Get the point? Well, with that in mind...

Although Amira was born in Texas, her parents figured that they would speak to her solely in Arabic while at home, and when she was of school age, she could learn English at school. Well, shockingly the Fluffernutter sandwich of a town had never heard anyone speak Arabic before, especially a five year-old child, so the 42 year-old teacher, Mrs. Dawes, who wore a bright red pant-suit with huge shoulder pads and bigger hair to match did what any teacher would do in that situation: assumed Amira was mentally retarded, gave her a red ball, and placed her on a mat in the corner of the room. Little Amira, who had been in Egypt just two weeks prior, had been told by a cousin three years

25

older than she that American school teachers wrapped the knuckles of misbehaving students with metal rulers. Thus, a terrified five year-old Amira sat in the corner holding this red, rubber ball and just stared at it, not knowing what she was supposed to do or how to avoid being beaten.

Seeing this, the teacher muttered to herself, "That poor child, she doesn't even know what a ball is." The ball-corner-staring extravaganza took place for three days before Amira's mother asked Amira more specifically what she was learning at school. Anyway, let's not spend too much time down here in Memory Commonwealth. Let's just say her teachers recalibrated Amira's intelligence and she learned English, and actually excelled in all her classes. Grades K through 3 flew by, but then something strange happened to the town of Plaintown during Amira's 4th grade year: the school's minority population rose by 250%!...that is from one minority student (Amira) to three...well, maybe 3.5...just play along for a minute. Yes, in just one autumn day, the student body's Vitamin D absorption rates suddenly became mildly varied.

Fourth Grade: Amira stared at beige tiles broken up by metal chair legs, which led to uncomfortable, green plastic squares where 4th graders sat impatiently, waiting for Mrs. Kendall to take attendance. This was the first day of classes, but really Amira was ambivalent about it all since not much changed from year to year at Davy Crockett Elementary. Each classroom had a moss green chalkboard, which encompassed most of the front wall. The teacher's desk always sat to the left of the board at a 45-degree angle where Teacher "X" could sit during quizzes, tests, grammatical exercises, etc. To the left of the desk, there was an American flag hanging limply on a wooden pole looking as though it too wished it could be outside playing in the wind and sun. Above the chalkboard was a long poster displaying all the letters of the alphabet. A poster always hung to the right of the chalkboard with a picture of an Eagle and the Pledge of Allegiance underneath the picture, and to the right of that poster, before one reached the end of the wall and the beginning of the door, always hung a bulletin board with things stuck to it like, "The Food Pyramid!" or "Remember to turn in your permission slips for the Oil Refinery Field Trip" or some current news article about why the rest of the country shouldn't mess with Texas, etc. Really, the only thing that changed from year to year was the color of the seats the students sat in. Some years green, some years blue, one year red, but that only lasted a month before parents decided that the color red could cause aggressive tendencies in some of the students (yes, sometimes child psychology and steer psychology intermixed in this Texas town), and thus they were replaced by grey seats that year. Each year, in those colored seats sat 27 white students, some of whom were funny, some of whom were smart, some of whom were mean, some of whom ate string cheese everyday, *and* one student of Arabic descent. But something was afoot on day one of Amira's fourth grade year, for instead of 28 desk-chair sets, there were 31, and two of the new desks were situated, one on each side of Amira with the third put in the back corner. Amira had not realized the desks next to hers had been empty because she didn't really care, but they *were* empty. Then, something quite extraordinary happened. In walked Principal Green (who was white) with a tiny girl wearing jean shorts, a funky pink and green t-shirt and a wristband with dolphins on it. That, in itself,

27

isn't all that extraordinary, but what was quite interesting was that her skin tone was darker than Amira's.

"This is Karen Yu," Mr. Green stated matter-of-factly. "Her family just moved here from California, and this is, wait- where'd he go?" Mr. Green looked anxiously into the hallway. "Carlos, get in here please." A small boy holding a soccer ball, wearing a *Real Madrid* jersey that nearly covered his khaki shorts entirely, walked into the room. Mr. Green continued, "Yes, this is Carlos Ortega...Hmm, now where should we put you two?" he pondered aloud using his community theatre skills. You see the plan had already been set in motion by the school powers-that-be the night before. "Ahh, yes, there are two open desks right there, right next to Ms. Masri. Ms. Masri, please raise your hand." (as if Carlos and Karen wouldn't be able to figure that one out). Amira obliged though, and Karen and Carlos each took a seat next to Amira. You see, the school power brokers felt that perhaps the minorities would feel more at home sitting next to each other. Ahhh, yes because nothing makes an Arab feel more at home than when sitting next to a Korean and Mexican, and vice versa for the other two. The school board's logic, as always: flawless.

"Well, Mrs. Kendall, please continue with your-" Mr. Green began.

"Eh-hem, Mr. Green I believe you're *aboot* to forget someone," interrupted this perky little, pale-skin (but with rosy cheeks), freckled girl with brown, shoulder-length hair, wearing a *Rush* t-shirt, Birkenstocks, and dark, dark blue jeans that were far too big for her and would in fact be falling off of her but for the purple-studded belt which had been pulled taut around her waist.

"Oh, right," Principal Green stated, "This is...umm..."

"Thanks Chief," she continued, "I can take it from here. Hi, I'm Meredith Denton, there's a desk in the back corner, which is mine, and I'd like to sit down before I pass *oot*." She walked confidently to her desk, and as she passed by Karen, Carlos, and Amira, she smiled and rolled her eyes as if they had all been the best of friends ever since their make-believe meeting at Camp Winniehaha five summers back (of course no such camp exists, so that never happened...just wanted to be clear). Strangely, she had no backpack with her but rather just carried in her left hand what appeared to be a black banjo case with a red maple leaf sticker on it. Although Meredith, Karen, Carlos, and Amira did not know it at that moment, their fourth through twelfth grade fates would soon be intertwined.

Now reader, your narrator did promise something about explaining the origin and meaning of the "The Mop Squad," and whether you know it or not, you now have the requisite background needed to truly appreciate the madness behind the method...wait, maybe I reversed that...no, actually I think I got it right. So yes, in that fourth grade year where the minority population tripled and thereby threw the school's brain trust for a loop, the school thought it would be a good time to rethink its relations/interactions with the non-white student body. Thus, they met in the second week of the school year and decided to create the "Minority Outreach Program."

"You want us to do what?" Karen asked Ms. Kendall who had sequestered Karen, Amira, and Carlos in the classroom as theirs peers played outside during morning recess.

"Well," Ms. Kendall said while smiling broadly, "Mr. Green and I were talking and we thought how wonderful it would be for our umm, *diverse students* to share with the rest of the class your wonderful cultures...that you come from."

"I'm from Pasadena," Karen retorted.

"No, your Ayyy-shiiinnnn culture," Ms. Kendall replied, drawing out the word, "Asian" so that Karen would be sure to understand.

"Like my Asian culture as in how broke actors rent out cheap rooms in like Koreatown in L.A. or do you mean "Asian" as in like my two week vacation I took with my family to visit my great aunt in Korea?"

"Wait a second!," Carlos protested, "this is like homework!"

"I'm sure it won't feel like homework Carlos when you're working on it at home because it's such a wonderful gift you will be sharing with the class. And you know what? How about you each help each other with your projects? That will be grand!"

Amira just stared blankly ahead, not really sure how to react.

"What projects?" Meredith piped in after popping her head in from the hallway.

"Ms. Denton, shouldn't you be outside enjoying this glorious day with your classmates?" Ms. Kendall asked.

"No, this sounds much cooler. Can I join the club?" Meredith said.

"Well, this isn't really a club dear. This meeting is for the Minority Outreach Program, so it's really just for minor-" Ms. Kendall began before something dawned on her: *The Minority Outreach Program could, in some quarters, be considered racist itself.* Thus, she decided to finish her sentence differently than originally planned. "Ms. Denton, you are right. Of course you may join the program and share your Canadian culture with the rest of your classmates. That would be terrific. I apologize for not inviting you. Really, we at the school use the term, "minority," in a very loose manner. When we say, "minority," we really just mean people not from Texas, that's all."

"But *I'm* from Texas," Amira stated, mildly shocked at what was going on.

"You know what I mean dear," Ms. Kendall said while winking at Amira. "Anyway, I think we should begin next week. Ms. Masri, would you do the honor of giving the first talk since you are not technically a new student? We'll do it next Tuesday during recess, so you'll have an entire half-hour to share interesting facts about Iraq." (Author's note: yes, Amira's actually Egyptian).

"Seriously?!" Karen said (and admittedly, it was quite impressive how wide open her eyes were at that moment), "you are like making us do this during recess? So, we are supposed to share our culture, but all the kids are just going to be mad at us and blame us for *stealing* their recess. Won't that be what they remember about our cultures? That minorities steal recesses from white kids?"

"Ms. Yu, let's not be dramatic. If you make the project fun, your classmates will forget all about recess." (They wouldn't.)

"Homework? You're givin' us *homework*?" Carlos asked desperately again. Obviously racial injustices, prejudices, and stereotypes took a backseat in his mind to the prospect of doing additional work from the comfort of his home.

"Now, go on and enjoy the fresh air. You still have ten minutes of recess."

"But, we already have homework," Carlos said exasperatedly.

"Shoo, Mr. Ortega. Go have fun. I need to grade some quizzes." Actually, she needed to read her favorite gossip magazine while sipping lemonade *with just a dash of bourbon* from a flask she kept hidden away in her desk.

So, three defeated students and one chipper Canadian student walked out of the classroom into the shadowy hallway that was lit sporadically from natural light that bounced in from various windows.

"Why are you guys so sad?" Meredith queried.

"Why? This totally *sucks*!" Carlos claimed.

"I agree with Carlos. This is so unfair," Karen added.

"This might be worse than when I had to sit in the corner with that ball all day long," Amira mumbled to herself while slumping her shoulders forward and thrusting her thumbs into her front pocket

"Sucks? No way. What are you talking *aboot*? This is awesome. Do you realize that we can say whatever we want up there?" Meredith stated giddily. "The school is freaked out right now!"

"This school is *freaky* you mean," Karen said.

"No! The school is scared to death of offending us! So you can say whatever you want up there and you won't get in trouble because they don't want to seem like they're racist."

"Really?" Carlos asked, for the first time seeming like he might eventually snap out of his homework-induced funk. "I can say *anything*?"

"Oh yeah! I'm totally gonna go all oot and make mine really made up," Meredith almost screamed due to her excitement. "So stop pooting guys."

"Pudding?" Carlos asked.

"No. pooting. You know being all sad and whiny and stuff."

"Oh, you mean *pouting*. You need to work on your accent Meredith," Carlos stated matter-of-factly.

"Ooooh, accents, what a great idea!" Meredith exclaimed. "Yes, we need to do accents. Amira, can you do any accents?"

"I can do a Southern Belle accent, I guess," Amira replied.

"Cool...and oh yeah, what are you supposed to do the project on?" Meredith asked.

"Well, my family's Egyptian, so I guess Egypt," Amira sighed while squinting into the morning sun they all just walked into as they entered the playground.

Meredith closed her eyes for a second, and then said, "Y'all, there's a lot of sand in Egypt y'all...and mummies, and pyramids ya'll! Y'all are so sweet for listening. You're like honey glaze on ham sprinkled with sugar you are y'all," she finished while curtseying to her MOP counterparts. Then the four of them burst out laughing. The third grade girls who were playing foursquare nearby stared as Carlos tried on an Irish accent, and Meredith tried on a Long Island accent, while Karen found her inner Russian spirit.

"I think I know what I'm going to do now," Karen said.

"Awesome!" Meredith bellowed.

Well readers, I won't bore you with the entirety of all the projects, but I will let you read some of the highlights below in a bit of a montage, sans music:

"Pasadena does not allow overnight parking," Karen dryly stated.

"Mummies actually created the need for potpourri since during the mummification things could get stinky y'all like molasses on a paper plate full of sugar buns on a humid Georgia day," Amira explained.

"Commerson Dolphins are often called the 'zebras of the sea' due to their black and white bodies. Throughout the Southern Hemisphere the "Commerson Dolphin Circus" tours going from beach to beach...However, these dolphins cannot be found in Miami, Sevilla, or Mexico City," Carlos recited while staring down at his paper as Meredith played violin-inspired background music. (Author's note: since Carlos' grew up in numerous places, mainly: Miami, Sevilla, and Mexico City, he felt obligated at the end of every fact to state where things could and could not be found in each city...granted, the Commerson Dolphin Circus could not be found in *any* city since it was completely made up.)

"The drinking age in Ontario is only 19, so often girls can get into bars as early as 14," Meredith stated.

"Ms. Denton! I do not think that information is illuminating in the least," Ms. Kendall angrily said.

"Once in the bar, Canadian teenagers can watch the most important show on the BBC: Molson Hockey Night in Canada where during intermission you get to learn about why Europeans are wimps and why French Canadians should be more patriotic in a segment called, "Coach's Corner," which is hosted by Don Cherry, who often wears crazy sports coats," Meredith continued undaunted.

"Vanadzer, Armenia" is one of Pasadena's sister city's. Korean American culture in Vanadzer is like totally sparse at best," Karen said.

"Though rare y'all Common Dolphins are found in the Mediterranean Sea," Amira stated deciding to connect her "lesson" with Carlos' talk.

Although Amira, Karen, Carlos, and Meredith found all the talks quite amusing, the rest of the class was not as ecstatic. Karen's words about the students connecting minorities with the stealing of recess proved prophetic, for the four were shunned for several months afterward, where during those months, the rest of the student body called them the MOP Squad and would often ask them questions such as, "Hey, MOP Squad, my birthday is tomorrow; do you wanna ruin that too?" Or "Hey Mopheads, can you tell me how to be lame because I'm getting tired of being cool all the time." Or if one of their peers was running late, "Hey Moppernutters, you suck!" Succinct and to the point if you ask me, but try not to fret too much about them dear reader; their popularity purgatory did not last forever. Eventually they were all accepted back (to varying extents) into the good graces of their fellow students, so all those months really did was cement their friendships...and create a nickname for their group.

End of MOP Squad Interruption...back to bullying incident

Brendan Jeffries made up one third of the Jeffries trifecta, which consisted of his twin brother, Brandon, and younger brother by 11 months, Brad. Because of their natural size and strength (imagine a Rubik's Cube, now imagine that Rubik's Cube with arms and legs and a smaller Rubik's Cube with a brownish buzz cut sitting on top for a head...now imagine that Rubik's Cube, but much less colorful and much less complex, and voila: the Jeffries clan!), the Jeffries brothers also made up the linebacker unit for the school's football team. Now it would be rude to say that the three brothers were dumb, so instead let's just say that if Brendan, for instance, was wearing a ten gallon hat, well...he likely could only fill up 6 of those gallons...ditto for his brothers. The joke was that they always wore sports jerseys with their first names on the back, so they'd remember which one they were.

"Ohh, that hurt my feelings Yu Baboon. I might have to cry. I wish I had a hanky to wipe away my tears...oh wait, I guess this will do," he said pulling out a piece of cloth with an intricate drawing of what looked like a village surrounded by forests and mountains that had hieroglyphics, Sanskrit, *and* Chinese characters written at the bottom. In truth, Amira had seen the cloth painting before because it *belonged* to her or her family and not to Rubik's cube boy.

"Hey!" Amira yelled springing to her feet. "Where'd you get that?"

"Where else?" he said, "next to the school's pool, where you keep all your dork crap."

Though the events of the afternoon confused Amira to no end, one thing she did know was that the cloth Brendan held was a gift Amira's grandmother had given her. She kept it in a drawer in her room, and whenever, she felt sad or tired or alone, she would pick up the cloth, stare at the beautiful picture on it, run her fingers over the various writings and suddenly feel light, feel connected.

"Just give it back," she stated exasperatedly,

Brendan picked up a rock and wrapped the wet cloth around it (obviously it had not been in a Ziploc bag in her backpack or the bag had opened), "Sure baby, here ya go," he huffed while throwing the cloth wrapped rock to his brother, Brandon, who was standing a few feet away and wearing a Texas Rangers t-shirt with the name "Brandon" on its back.

Brandon nabbed the rock/cloth and quickly tossed it to Brad, who positioned himself so that the brothers formed a triangle around the girls. Amira considered using some ostrich wrangling techniques on the brothers, but decided against it because she thought her mother wouldn't approve, and she knew she'd already get in trouble with her mother for missing today's swim practice and for offering a poor explanation as to why her bike was currently locked at school, so she just tried to jump up and grab the orb from them, but this strategy failed over and over again.

Brad launched the orb and Brendan caught it and then immediately tossed it to Kyle who had just walked out of the school. Kyle caught the cloth-wad with ease, smiled, and then quickly tossed it back. His smile faded considerably when he noticed Amira glaring at him. He attempted a shoulder-shrug-half-smile-palms-turned-up-apology maneuver, but Amira seemed less than impressed. Then, Brandon tossed the wad of cloth back to Brendan, but as he did so, a loud "CRACK!" pierced the sky, and suddenly the cloth/rock was hit in midair by a tennis ball that knocked the rock free from the cloth. The cloth floated to the ground settling near a parked, white, rusted Ford pickup truck. While the Jeffries stood shocked at the projectile that had zoomed by them, Amira ran over and grabbed the cloth. Thus, quickly the game of "keep-away" ended.

"Wow!" Carlos said while staring at Meredith who had paused at the end of her slapshot's follow-through to watch her shot. "That was rad! How did you *hit* that in midair?"

"I...I was aiming at Brendan's head," Meredith replied with a dejected look on her face.

"Oh. Wow, you missed him by like 15 feet," Carlos responded through the goalie mask he adorned over his face.

"Yeah."

"That sucked."

"Thanks Carlos," Meredith said as she rollerbladed over to Amira and Karen.

"You guys are dorks yo," said Brad. "Let's go home before we get dork-infected." And with that, the Jeffries clan walked away from the MOP Squad.

A few moments later, Carlos, bogged down in goalie equipment, waddled over to the group. "What was that all about?" he asked.

"Just boys being stupid," Karen said while staring at the collage she and Amira had created. She then astutely tried to hide it behind her back.

"Why are you hiding Amira's laminated Kyle poster behind your back?" he then asked.

"Wait, how do you know it's Amira's, *Carlos*? Sneaking a peak in her closet when we're hanging out at her house?" Karen queried.

"Umm, dude the pool thing happened like 20 minutes ago...of course, I've already heard about it," Carlos claimed while stripping off his goalie pads.

"Does everyone at school already know?" Amira asked meekly.

"No," Meredith said, "just kids who were actually at school today, like the marching band, drama club, chess club. You know kids like that." Amira noticeably sagged. "But don't worry," Meredith continued, "I'm sure there'll be something equally traumatic that will happen to someone else in a week or so, and this will all blow over."

"What are you guys up to?" Karen asked Meredith and Carlos.

"Oh, Carlos and I have to drag this crap (pointing to her hockey gear) and the net back to my house, and then we thought we'd go to the mall. Want to come?"

"I can't. I need to get home and it's going to take me forever to get home because my stupid bike is locked and I forgot the stupid combination," Amira sighed.

Meredith walked over to Amira and hugged her. "You have not had a good day. I'll go ask Chris, the janitor, to grab some lock cutters. I'm sure he won't mind."

"Really?!" Amira asked. *That was Meredith,* she thought to herself. *The girl was friends with EVERYONE. She treated everyone the same, whether you were popular or a dork, the principal or the janitor, it didn't matter. Meredith was just Meredith, and thus she thought it only fair to accept you as you. You couldn't even be envious of Meredith's popularity,* Amira realized, *because she was well, cool AND kind, a rare combination.*

"Yeah, no problem. Chris and I are simpatico, which is a word I learned yesterday while beating Carlos at Scrabble."

"You're not supposed to look at the dictionary before playing a word. *You cheated,*" Carlos responded.

"If that's what you need to tell yourself to sleep at night Carlos, I'll understand," Meredith replied. "Now can you grab the net while I go talk to Chris?"

"Yeah, yeah. You know if you guys want to have a girly moment, you can just tell me, and I can go flex in a mirror or something," Carlos said while walking away, kicking loose gravel as he left.

"Oh, Carlos," Meredith said, "We know you love us and that we're all going to fight over you in the next couple of years because you're the only boy for us."

Carlos looked over his shoulder, grinned, and said, "I know...too bad for you guys that I'll only be dating older women."

"WHATEVAH!" Karen yelled and then rolled her eyes. She then handed the Kyle-collage over to Amira.

"Seriously, are you okay?" Meredith said while staring at Amira.

"Yes. I'm fine," she said as she rearranged things in her backpack. "Boys are so lame!" Amira yelled in a fit of disgust.

"Oh, don't worry, I'm sure they'll make our lives much worse over the next few years," replied Meredith. "Let me go get the janitor for you," she continued as she picked herself up and walked toward the school's entrance.

"Thank you Mer!" Amira said. Amira exhaled and stretched her arms as high above her head as she could. "Want to come to my house and hang out or do you not want to be seen with Ziploc-bag-freak girl?" she asked Karen.

"You mean ZBFG? Yeah, they already shortened your new nickname. I probably shouldn't be seen with *that* girl," Karen stated while smiling. But, I am going to your house, *but* I'm not sure I can hang out."

"What do you mean?"

"Well, I promised your brother that I'd come over and play tonight," Karen explained.

"*What?* When did you two make this plan?"

"He answered the phone when I called you the other day, and we talked for a minute, and he asked I could come play tonight since your mom is going to be teaching, so it will just be you and your brother."

"Why would you agree to this?"

"You're brother's like *totally* charming," Karen said as she shrugged her shoulders.

"He's *six*," Amira incredulously retorted.

"I *know*. How cool is that? He's the bomb! He's like going be to such the lady's man," Karen replied.

"Not if he doesn't survive to reach his seventh birthday. What was he thinking stuffing all that...*stuff* in my backpack?!"

"That doesn't sound like him," Karen said while shaking her head.

"Again, he's *six*. I swear he barely sounds *human* sometimes, and acts like one even less."

Meredith then appeared at the school door, "No dice Amira! I can't find him!"

"Ahh man," Amira mumbled to herself. "Thanks for trying!" she yelled back.

"Well, I guess we're walking," Amira said to Karen. "If that's cool with you?"

"Yeah, just carry my backpack and I'll grab my bike and walk it to your house with you."

***

Amira and Karen arrived home and sat on the back porch swing. The swing was old; white paint chips fell daily exposing more of the tan, wood underneath. Although Amira often complained about the lack of...well, everything that Plaintown *lacked*, she did love to sit on the porch swing, look out at the horizon since there was nothing to obstruct her view, and dream about the wonders that surely existed beyond. She could sit on the swing for hours watching thunderstorms approach, or talking about boys with Karen, or listening to Meredith strum her guitar, or playing card games with Carlos. She modified her earlier thought: all Texas needed was Kyle, her friends, herself, and her porch swing.

The porch floor actually still looked pretty good since Amira was asked (eh-hem, *forced* she would say) to repaint it a couple of months ago. There was a layer of dust on the floorboards, but that was expected in this climate.

"So when can you eat again?" Karen asked sitting on the opposite end of the swing. Their legs were spread out on the swing touching in parallel, but opposite directions.

"Soon. The sun's supposed to set in about 45 minutes."

A few minutes later, Amira and Karen heard the sound of a station wagon pull into the driveway. "He's dead," Amira said hopping up off the couch to run around to the front of the house. Karen followed close behind. Nara and Hashim had already hopped out of the maroon, dust covered wagon, and Hashim with his arms spread fully out to each side ran into the barn making airplane sounds the entire time.

"Hello Karen," Nara said as Amira and Karen sprinted past her.

42

"Hi, Ms. Talib!" Karen said looking back over her shoulder.

Nara called to Amira, "Amira, I need to go back to school for a few hours. Will you watch after-"

"I'll take care of it mom. Just give me a second!" she yelled while keeping her eyes squarely on the entrance to the barn. There were actually two barns on the property, both painted red, both worn; one worn due to years of use; the other worn due to years of no use. Amira and Karen entered the latter and once inside, Amira called, "Hashim!"

"What?" said the boy poking his head out from the loft where he was playing.

"Come down here!" Amira said while stomping her foot for emphasis.

"Okay, okay, geesh, hold your horses," he said while climbing down the ladder. He hopped down and said, "What?"

"Why on earth did you pack my backpack full of underwear, and grandma's cloth, and my *diary* and your stupid toys?" Amira said staring intensely into his eyes.

Hashim looked puzzled and shoved his hands deep into his pockets as he turned his gaze toward the ground. "Is this a test?" he asked.

"What?!" Amira yelled.

"You told me not to-

"Ahhh! Snake!" Karen yelled pointing just a few feet away where, sure enough, rattled a gigantic rattlesnake.

"Run!" Amira yelled as she turned to the barn's front door. Amira and Karen sprinted out and continued to run for another 30 feet or so. Amira turned around to grab Hashim in order to continue their conversation, but Hashim was nowhere in sight.

"Hashim!" Amira yelled between puffs of air while hunched over with her hands on her knees. "Where is he?"

"Oh my god, did he escape with us?" Karen gasped while lying on her back taking in quick sips of air.

"Oh. No. Hashim!" Amira yelled as she tore back to the barn. She sprinted inside and saw Hashim standing in the middle of the barn, frozen, his eyes completely transfixed on the snake that slowly approached. Amira inched forward and calmly whispered, "Hashim, you need to step back towards me...very slowly." However, Hashim could not hear her. "*Hashim, please,*" she pleaded. His mouth moved tentatively, but no sound escaped his lips.

"*Hashim,*" Amira begged but to no avail.

Both Amira and the snake moved closer to Hashim. Amira slowly angled herself a bit behind and to the side of her brother and then quietly made a hissing sound. She wanted to try and draw the snake toward her. However, Amira knew she must delicately try to draw the snake's attention, for if she were too assertive it's possible the snake would first lunge at Hashim and *then* turn its attention towards Amira.

"Tsssss" Amira hissed again, but the snake ignored her as it slithered toward Hashim.

Amira inched forward as well and as she did so quickly glanced around for something she could use as a weapon against the reptile, but nothing appeared in her periphery. Amira's heart ached as she noticed that Hashim's fingers were spread wide as if expecting his sister to take hold of his hand and lead him away from this cold-blooded nightmare. The snake gently rattled its tail and slightly moved its head back. Something about its movement made Amira's pupils instantly dilate.

Suddenly, the snake sprang right for Hashim's face. Hashim and the snakes' eyes met. The snake opened up its mouth wide displaying its sharp, long fangs. Hashim closed his eyes bracing for the bite, but the bite never came. He opened his eyes and saw the snake staring at him just inches from his face, but the snake was not moving towards him, for it was being held firmly in his sister's hand. Amira had caught the snake right before it could sink its fangs into Hashim.

With lightening quick speed she then tossed the snake hard against the barn wall. The snake *thumped* against the wood, fell to the ground, and then hissed at the siblings, the younger of whom was now hiding behind the older one. The snake then hissed and again slithered out of the barn. Amira grabbed Hashim's hand and cautiously led him out into the open. They could see the snake slither further and further away until it was out of sight. She then turned to her brother.

"Hashim what were you thinking?"

"I don't know."

"Well, try. You could have been hurt...and then mom would have been mad at *me*!"

"I'm sorry."

She hugged him tightly as her arms shook from the adrenaline, which still coursed through her body.

"Okay, okay, no hugging *Amira*. We have rules!" he said as he feigned pushing her away. In truth, he was happy his sister hugged him even if she was crazy for asking him to start packing for her and then acting like she had no idea that she asked him to do that.

Amira released him from the hug, but held him by the shoulders and stared at him. "Hashim, what is wrong with you? Why are you acting so weird? Why-

Karen interrupted their conversation a second time, this time with one word: "Kyle."

"What?" Amira asked turning toward her.

"Kyle. I think he's riding to your house," she said as she pointed about 500 yards down the road, which led to and passed by Amira's house. And sure enough, a boy with shaggy brown hair grew in the distance as he got closer and closer, and even more so when he pulled into Amira's driveway. He rode to within a few feet of Amira and hopped off his bike. Thus, there stood Kyle with gorgeous deep blue eyes, eyes that always seemed magically illuminated. There he stood, wearing blue jeans and sneakers and a blue t-shirt to match his blue, blue eyes that he currently used to stare at Amira.

"Hey," he said.

Amira said nothing, not because she had nothing to say, but rather because she forgot how to control the muscle known as her tongue.

"Can we talk for a minute?" he asked while smiling his perfect, perfect smile.

Amira turned towards Karen.

"Umm, come on Hashim, let's go see what your mother's up to?" Karen said, grabbing him by the hand.

Amira turned back to Kyle and smoothly tried to nod her head up and down a couple of times to signify, *Yes*. An outside observer probably would not have described her head nod as smooth; an observer likely would have gone with "seizure-like," but let's forgive her this once since she made up for that

46

awkward head bob by confidently walking past him so they could talk in private behind the barn, away from prying eyes and ears...yes, she confidently strode about four feet before tripping on a rock and falling to the ground.

"Oh wow, you okay? Here let me help you up?" he said while bending over to lend a hand.

She rebuked the offer though and said, "I'm fine. I'm fine." (Hey, her tongue works! Kudos, Amira.) She hopped up quickly and held out her hands, palms facing Kyle, and said, "See? Fine." She turned and walked ahead of him and closed her eyes as she silently admonished herself for her clumsiness. When they were behind the barn, she turned to him and said, "So what's up?"

"Yeah, so..." he began while putting his hands in his back pockets and rocking back and forth on his feet, "so the whole pool thing was kinda crazy today." Amira just stared at him, so he continued, "Yeah, so I wanted to see if you're okay. Amber felt horrible about it...I *think*...and I'm sure she didn't mean to hit you with the ball, and you know the Jeffries brothers. They're always goofing around being idiots." He raised his eyebrows and grinned as he finished the sentence.

A loud "CRAW!" could be heard somewhere close by, but Amira ignored the sound. Maybe it was due to the embarrassment from earlier in the day or the surge of energy she was dealing with from the snake incident, but suddenly Amira's mind grew clear. And she was clearly *pissed*, and she felt Kyle should know that she was mad. She took a deep breath and seemed to grow three inches as she stood up straight and coldly said, "Was that an apology? Because if it was, it was lame. What happened at the pool was *crazy*? Really? Gee, I wonder why?" she fumed, not even realizing that Hashim had come around the barn's corner. She continued undaunted, "Do you really think your sister didn't *mean* to throw the ball at me? Do you-

Hashim interrupted, "Umm, Amira?"

Amira continued to stare at Kyle who looked more and more ill at ease. "Not now Hashim." To Kyle she said, "Don't you know your sister hates me and is always mean to me?"

"But Amira," Hashim tried again.

"NOT. NOW. And Kyle, don't say that the Jeffries were acting like idiots when you helped them! And-

"Amira, it's important," Hashim whispered.

"What Hashim?!" she said finally taking her gaze off of Kyle long enough to size up her brother. "What do you want?"

"It's Moha. He's escaped," Hashim said meekly.

"What?! How? Hashim if you-

"I didn't open the gate!" he protested. "He just hopped over the fence."

"That's impossible," she claimed as she ran around the barn in order to see where the ostriches were enclosed. As impossible as it was, she did see the closed gate and that Moha was running into the distance, into a hilly section of the vastness.

"Ahhhh," Amira steamed. "Hashim, go inside and tell mom I'm going after Moha and that Karen will look after you until I get back. And Kyle," she said turning toward him. "Kyle...just go *home*."

"Hey maybe I could help you-" Kyle began before Amira interrupted.

"Go. HOME. Kyle. I don't want to talk to you," she said, and amazingly, she did not want to talk to him. She just sprinted off toward the hills as Kyle and Hashim looked on.

***

Whom should I punch first? she thought to herself. Granted, Amira actually wasn't a violent person, and probably wouldn't punch anyone, but a girl can dream, can't she? *Moha? Hashim? Kyle? So many choices*, she thought. She climbed up the first hill to get a better view of where that crazy ostrich could be. "Moha!" she called but the out-of-sight ostrich chose not to respond. *Where is that stupid bird* she pondered as she climbed down the other side of the hill and continued to walk along. Her stomach started to growl, and the sun was about to set, which meant that if she were home she could eat. *Ugh, but I'm not home. I'm out here chasing after a bird! Can my day get any worse?* she thought. Glad you asked: the answer it turned out was yes...actually it could get quite worse...just give it a moment.

Amira continued walking twenty more minutes into nothingness and still no sign of the bird. Her stomach audibly growled again, so she placed her hand over it hoping that by putting her hand on her stomach that would somehow trick the organ into believing it had food to digest. Then, she heard a much louder growl. She quickly looked down at her stomach hoping that it made the noise, but deep down she knew the noise came from behind her. She slowly turned around to see a rather large- *Gosh that looks more like a wolf than a coyote*, she thought. And there stood a coyote (or wolf) about 60 feet above her on a sandy/dirty hill, and it stared right at her and growled again.

49

Okay, she thought, *coyotes are more afraid of humans than we are of them, so just stay calm and walk slowly backwards and it will take off in the opposite direction.* She took a step back while keeping her eyes fixed on the coyote/wolf above her, the coyote/wolf with huge paws and strong shoulders and a thick neck and a salivating mouth full of gigantic teeth and-*okay, okay, best not to think about the coyote...just keep backing up,* she reasoned to herself. She took another step back and then another, and then a large growl made its way to her ears, and this time the sound came from behind her. So she slowly turned around and saw a second coyote/wolf staring at her from above a different hill. Granted having two coyotes staring at you is not good in any situation that doesn't involve you being separated from them by a very large fence, but that's nothing compared to having 3 or 4 coyotes staring at you. Unfortunately for Amira, *eight* sets of eyes stared daggers into her. As she stood in this valley-like area realizing that coyotes slowly approached her from every direction, she suddenly felt very cold. Her feet began to feel numb and all the hair on her body stood at attention. The coyotes/wolves moved forward almost in unison, with their heads hunched low and mouths beginning to salivate at the tasty little girl that would soon be their meal for the day. They moved slowly but purposefully and soon they were 80 yards from her....now 70. Granted, this was the girl who took on a dozen ostriches at once, but even she knew that coyotes/wolves were a much different situation, and she was no match. She couldn't breathe. Tears formed around her eyes. She wanted to yell for her mom, but no words formed on her lips.

When the coyotes/wolves were 50 yards away, they stopped, howled one long blood-curdling howl, making their intentions known to the world, and then they all sprinted towards her at full tilt. Surrounded, all Amira could do was close her eyes as death approached.

Well, that's it I guess. We should probably give her some privacy for her last few moments on earth. I might actually miss the girl. She seemed somewhat tolerable at moments. So, anyway, thanks for reading with me. I know our time together was short, but dear reader I appreciate your attention, and maybe we'll meet again some day, and I'll-

"CRAWWWW!" pierced the sky and suddenly a rather large bird popped over a hill and joined in on the race towards Amira. "CRAWWW!" it bellowed again gaining speed and more importantly gaining ground on the coyotes/wolves that were after Amira. Amira, then opened her eyes and saw a rather angry and motivated Moha trying with all its might to catch up to the beasts. The coyotes/wolves were now 15 yards away and Moha was twice as far away, but he then kicked his speed up a notch. Moha locked his eyes with Amira's, and he crowed again and ran faster still. Moha and the wolves were now mere feet from Amira, converging on her from all sides all at once. Amira realized her only hope of survival was by jumping onto the back of this increasingly swift bird that zoomed toward her. The coyotes/wolves howled in anger and leapt at Amira just as she grabbed onto the bird's long neck and hopped on its back. The coyotes were too late. Moha, with Amira on its back, rocketed into the air, jumping at least fifteen feet high, which caused the coyotes to crash into one another as their target surged above their jumps. Amira and Moha landed about 40 feet away. Once Moha's feet retouched the surface of the earth, he instantly sprinted at an even faster pace away from the confused, bloodthirsty animals that now howled in anger, knowing their prey had gotten away.

***

About a half mile away, a man with a scar that began at his left wrist and continued all the way up his arm and ended somewhere that was covered by his shirt watched the whole event transpire through high-powered binoculars. Keeping the binoculars to his eyes with his left hand, he reached into his pocket with his right hand and pulled out a cellular phone. He pressed a button, put the phone to his ear, and let the phone ring. When someone answered the phone on the other end, he dryly stated, "Yes. The wolves that were sent failed." (Oh, well that's settles it! Wolves, *not coyotes*, almost killed Amira. Well, I don't know about you reader, but I feel better now. I enjoy knowledge). He paused for a second, smiled, and said, "But I believe we found the third princess." He then hung up the phone and continued to stare through the binoculars watching a girl riding an ostrich grow smaller and smaller in the distance.

Huh, I wonder what he meant by *third princess*? Where are the other two? Is there a fourth? Or fifth? All good questions...and that dear reader is why *I'm* your humble, and clever, some would say dashing, narrator.

*C*hapter 2: *The Long Trot Home*

People don't realize the skills it takes to properly pick bananas to buy at a market. Most buyers just look at the color of the bananas to decipher the level of ripeness in a batch. This shows a complete lack of strategy and foresight. Really, what good is buying a batch of 6-8 bananas that are all at the same stages of ripeness? Do you plan to eat them all within the two-day window you'll likely have to enjoy them during the peak edibleness period?

The key is really to buy two smaller batches of varying levels of ripeness thereby extending the number of days you can enjoy eating bananas before being forced to go back to the market to buy more. Why people don't use this- what? You want to get back to the story? Seriously? You prefer hearing about an accident-prone twelve year-old girl with quick reflexes to learning about how to maintain proper potassium levels in your diet? Well, who am I to stand in your preferring a perpetuation of your ignorance? So let's see, where were we? Amira was about to be eaten by wolves, blah blah blah, a flurry of feathers flew in to save the girl from being fodder and so on...okay, okay....

Amira had never paid attention to the cadence of an ostrich's gait before, likely because on the importance scale of a seventh-grade girl, ostrich gaits fall somewhere below boy band ballads and above ummm....fish baiting techniques. However, with Amira's eyes closed super tight it wasn't hard for her to concentrate on the rhythm she felt as the bird's back would separate slightly from her chest with each step it took. It wasn't hard for her to hear the dull tap it's claws would make in the hardened dirt, and so soon the rhythm of Moha's steps melodically tapped within her orchestrating the slowing of her heartbeat, calming her breathing from a shallow staccato to deep, healthy breaths.

Wherever Moha was taking Amira, it wasn't directly home. Moha zigzagged, ran up and down hills, jumped over muddied streams, and then would just jog in a straight line for long spells. The once blue skies darkened into a navy and then soon Midnight blue (even though it was only around 8:30). Really, it was a gorgeous night. Stars began to pop out as there was no moon in sight. Had Amira not been so self-involved and melancholy and opened her eyes for a second, I truly believe she would have seen the beauty that surrounded her, and- Hmm? What's that dear reader? You think I'm being too hard on Amira since she just narrowly escaped being mauled to death by a pack of wolves? Fine. I'll acquiesce this time, but I really do think we need to toughen this girl up. I mean if you can't crack a smile after being but a few feathers from a vicious, painful death, well then when *can* you crack a smile?

Moha suddenly slowed down, threw his head up and let out a soft chirp. Amira hesitantly opened her eyes and noticed Moha had stopped in a tiny valley Amira had never been to before. The valley wasn't "flush" necessarily with foliage but there was definitely more growth in this location than one would expect from land unkempt by human hands. Moha gently bent his legs and lowered his neck so that Amira could easily slide off his back and onto ground. Unfortunately, Amira didn't take the "demount" hint and continued to cling to Moha, and so Moha rolled his eyes and not quite gently jerked his body to the left, thereby *caringly* tossing Amira to the ground.

"Hey!" she yelled as she caringly thumped to the hardened mixture of dirt and sand. Shaking some dirt out of her hair, Amira looked at the landscape around her (the "falling" obviously shook her from her wolf shock). "Where are we? Moha, I just want to go home."

The ostrich stared at her for a second and then squawked and flapped its wings and bobbed its head up and down as if egging Amira on. Amira stared at Moha but Moha met her gaze and then calmly turned his head. Suddenly, Amira realized how stiff she felt. Her muscles had been fully tensed as she clenched Moha's back during the ride and now the pain of that tension made its way to her conscious. She put her arms behind her back until her hands met and then she stretched her arms back as far as she could while simultaneously stretching up, all the way up on her toes, her neck and back as straight as can be, her hair blowing behind her, her eyes closed concentrating on the tension that was seeping away from her body. In that moment, under the starlight, a person staring at her profile while she was in full stretch could see the woman she would become, her regal frame and stature, the beauty that would someday blossom. But, unfortunately no one was around to witness this, except for a rather impatient, tall bird who had no time for such thoughts, so

Moha took his beak and poked her in the stomach while she was still in full stretch, and so Amira *regally* crumpled to the ground.

"What is your PROBLEM?!" (Umm, well apparently *Amira's* problem is short-term memory loss regarding the memory that Moha just saved her from being a wolf version of Kibble 'N' Bits not too long ago). "What do YOU WANT FROM-" Amira didn't finish her question. A slight twinkle caught her eye. A lone flower in full bloom stood at one end of the valley and its petals sparkled, not glistened but sparkled. Amira then noticed the ground was only dirt and sand for a few more feet before a rather lush area of grass began. Amira slowly stepped on the grass and moved toward the flower trying to figure out why the flower seemed so familiar. As she walked towards the flower other foliage started to come into her peripheral vision; she noticed an Egyptian Rubber tree, a small pond with an Egyptian water lily in it. Amira realized that she had been to a place like this before, but not in Texas, rather in Egypt. Amira quickly turned around and stared at Moha in complete awe! "Oh. My. God. Did you transport us to Egypt?!"

Moha tilted his head to the left and dropped his head a few feet and gave her a look, which silently said, "Are you serious? Are you really the dumbest girl in the world?" Well, okay maybe I added that last part, but it was obvious that by Moha's expression that they were still in Texas. Moha then squawked and threw his head back telling Amira that it was time to go.

Dazed, confused, bewildered, befuddled, Amira climbed back on Moha's back, and almost instantly Moha took off with amazing speed and yet utter gracefulness as if the bird almost floated in a state between running and flying. Now, Amira kept

56

her eyes open for this part of the trip. The stars above shone brightly; she breathed in the cool, dry night air deeply while feeling the warmth of Moha's body passing through her. They glided over the terrain at an incredible speed, and minutes later, Amira could see a speck of light in the distance. And soon that light grew into several lit windows, and soon Amira could make out the shape of her house. Suddenly Moha slowed down and stopped and reared his head back and chirped.

"What?" Amira asked. "Umm, we're still like over a mile from the house." (Um, try half a mile lazy Amira). "Let's go. I'm tired."

Moha stood still and shook his head no.

"Come on Moha!" And as Amira was about to give Moha a slight love tap via her foot, once again Moha slightly, but quickly jerked his body to the left thereby tossing Amira from his back. But, this time Amira was prepared for such a movement and as she flew toward the ground she extended both arms with palms open, landed on her hands and quickly did a flip landing gracefully on her feet.

"Aha!" she exclaimed. "Nice try Moha, but it looks like this little girl is ready for your tricks," she said through a smile. "Hey, if you don't carry me all the way home, that's fine." She began to jog and continued, "I'm more than capable of getting home with my own two feet-" she stated matter of factly right before she tripped over a rock and went face first into the ground. Moha just rolled his eyes and shook his head as he began to walk in the direction of home. Amira got up as gracefully as she could under the circumstances that occurred tonight and followed a few paces behind.

***

When Amira and Moha were about 30 yards from the house, Moha took off and quickly jumped over the fence back into the enclosed ostrich area. As Amira walked to the side door, Karen opened it and came running out.

"There you are! Are you okay? You look dirty. What happened? Good timing; your mom is going to be home any minute and my parents are already on their way to pick me up, and I was trying to figure out whether I needed to call the police or not. What took so long?" Karen rifled off. I swear readers: I didn't see her take in one breath.

Amira looked at her friend. She wanted to tell her, but at this moment, she was too tired. "Well," Amira began, but then two headlights from a silver Honda Accord bounced towards them as the car pulled from the street into Amira's driveway. Karen's mother had just arrived. "Tell your mother I said hello. I'm gonna go shower. Can we talk about it tomorrow?"

"Yeah, totally," Karen said. She thought about giving Amira a hug but Amira was way too dirty, so she decided to jog towards her mother's car as Amira waved to the shape through the windshield and walked to the side door.

Amira walked into the home and saw Hashim in his Dallas Cowboys pajamas peering at Amira through the banister while sitting on the stairs.

"I got ready for bed Amira and even brushed my teeth, twice!" Hashim said coyly.

"Thank you Hashim."

"Amira?"

"I'm sorry Moha escaped."

"It wasn't your fault Hashim. You didn't leave the gate open," she said as she walked toward him.

"Wow, you are really dirty. Did you crawl home and get hungry and eat dirt sandwiches because you were hungry from your fast?"

"No little brother. Come on, let's get you to bed."

"But, mom's going to be home soon."

"I know, and you know she likes you to be in bed when she gets home from teaching her evening class," she said patiently while stroking his hair.

"But, I thought I could sit with you guys while you ate dinner since it's dark out."

Amira then realized how absolutely starved she was and her mouth began to salivate like a wolf who has just seen an exposed sheep and- okay, fine, she probably wouldn't prefer me to use an analogy like that under the circumstances. "Hashim, I need to shower, so how about this: you put yourself to bed while I clean up, and if you are still awake when mom gets home, you can come down and sit with us while we eat, okay?"

"Fine," he said, "but I'm not tired." (He was sound asleep 3 minutes later).

Amira stripped off her dirty clothes, thought about putting them in her hamper but realized they were too dirty for her dirty clothing and thus left them in the hallway as she walked into the bathroom. She turned on the shower, stepped in, and let the mildly hot water wash over her. While in the shower, Amira decided not to tell her mother about the night's events. Amira never lied to her mother and didn't like keeping things from her, but how could she describe tonight's events without her mother smiling, giving her a hug, and then reaching for the phone to find out the number of the nearest insane asylum. After her shower Amira dried off (except for her hair which she wrapped in another towel and silently prayed would be dry by next Tuesday), put on her pajamas, took her dirty laundry and dirtier clothing from early in the night and put them in the washer located in the basement as she heard her mother's car pull into the driveway. As Amira walked up the basement stairs, her mother was already setting out food on the table. When Ms. Talib saw Amira enter the kitchen, she smiled at Amira and said, "How is my beautiful daughter?"

Amira smiled back and then immediately began to bawl as she ran to her mother hugged her as tightly as she could.

"Amira, what is it?" her mother asked concerned. "Are you okay?"

Yes, Amira nodded while gulping for air between cries.

"Do you want to talk about it?" her mother asked while wrapping her arms around her petite daughter and holding her tightly as she sat down on the kitchen chair and picked her up and put her on her lap.

Amira still couldn't speak but she shook her head "no" in a way that "said" that she didn't want to talk about it. She was able to smile for a second, long enough to let her mother know that she would be okay, that she just needed to be held, and so her mother held her until eventually Amira's tears subsided and she fell asleep in her mother's embrace. Ms. Talib carried her daughter up the stairs and placed her in bed. She caressed Amira's hair and whispered to her sleeping daughter that she would wake her before sunrise so that she could eat breakfast so that she would have energy for her big day tomorrow. For you see dear readers, the events of today will be nothing compared to what she will be forced to endure tomorrow. Of course I'm talking about the first day of school, the first day of junior high, which in Plaintown, Texas was 7th and 8th grade.

***

Amira slept like the dead she almost was. Her mother entered her room 30 minutes before sunrise. Ms. Talib turned on a desk lamp, which was placed on a desk next to the window, which looked out on the front yard and beyond. Nara then turned towards Amira's bed and looked at what she suspected was her daughter for all she saw were blankets which moved ever so slightly up and down and a mane (or perhaps an avalanche) of hair which completely covered Amira's face as she slept on her side. Nara walked over to Amira catching up to her shadow, which quickly moved over Amira's feet and then legs and body and then past her head. Nara gently brushed Amira's hair behind Amira's ear until she saw Amira's cheek and nose, her lips slightly parted.

"Amira" she whispered. "Amira, it's time to wake up."

Amira didn't budge.

"Amira my banoota," Nara said while caressing Amira's cheek, "I've made omelets and blueberry pancakes. You need to get up and eat my beautiful girl." Again, Amira did not move. So, her mother shook her gently...and then not so gently, and when Amira only moved by closing her mouth completely, Nara shook her again. Still nothing, so Nara gently and with love pinched Amira's nose shut thereby preventing air from reaching Amira's lungs. Amira suddenly groaned, and coughed and then opened her eyes and blinked drowsily several times.

"Mom, what do you want?" She mumbled with her eyes partially closed.

"You need to get up and eat, so you'll have energy for school."

"But, it's summer."

"No little one. School begins today."

After 2 or 3 seconds, the words her mother spoke passed through Amira's hair, into her ear canal and finally were processed by her brain. Amira's eyes opened wide, and she said, "I have school today!" She snapped up, well tried to anyway; some of her hair was caught in the headboard, so when she snapped up she quickly snapped back banging her head on the board.

"Ow, stupid hair."

"Come on Amira; let's go eat."

Amira yawned and stretched her arms out wide, pulled the blankets to the side and hopped onto the wooden floor and quickly placed her feet in her Ninja Turtle slippers, Michelangelo on her left foot and Leonardo on her right. Amira bounced down the stairs probably slightly louder than she had to.

"Amira, hush, you'll wake Hashim," her mother snapped.

"Oh yeah, I forgot he's sleeping" she said looking back over her shoulder at her mother and winking.

"You two. You should be nice to your brother Amira. Some day he'll be a lot bigger than you."

"Yeah, right. He's a pipsqueak Mom," she said while making her way into the kitchen and plopping down at the kitchen table. Amira realized how parched she was and drank all of her apple juice as quickly as a sailor chugs his first shot of rum after being at sea for five months.

"Amira!" her mother said with shock.

"What? I'm thirsty," she said while already half way through her omelet.

"Well, just try not to choke before your first day of school."

"I won't. You know, you don't have to fast with me."

"What? Have my daughter experience her first fast alone? I think not Amira."

"But you already fasted this year. It's not your fault I got mono right before Ramadan."

"Fault has nothing to do with it my daughter. This is something I want to do *with* you, and so I shall," Nara smiled as she placed her hand on Amira's non-fork hand. "Sunrise is in 3 minutes Amira. Finish eating and then go wash up and get ready for school."

"Ohkway" she said while stuffing the rest of the pancakes into her mouth as she stepped away from the table to head back up the stairs.

"Amira?"

"Hmm?"

"If you want to talk later, you know you can tell me anything."

Amira paused halfway up the staircase. She looked down at her feet while the emotions which flowed within played out their war inside her mind. For a second, she thought she'd break down right there and try to explain to her mother what happened, but she took a deep breath, closed her eyes, and said, "Thank you mom, but I just want to keep it to myself for now, okay?"

"Of course my beautiful daughter."

Amira took a step, but then stopped again as her mother said, "Amira?"

"Yes mom?"

"I love you with all my heart. My love is as deep as the Nile. My love is as timeless as the pyramids. My love is-"

"-as pure as a lotus flower" Amira finished. Ms. Talib would say this to Amira every night before she went to bed for years, until Amira felt that she was "too old" for her mother to say it to her each night. But, this morning, the words felt truer and gave her more comfort than they had before. Emotion was about to get the best of her, so she quickly smiled at her mother and then ran up the stairs as tears started to escape her eyes, tears that would soon be hidden underneath the shower.

***

Amira was dressed and ready for school with over an hour to spare since she awakened so early in order to eat. So, Amira took the opportunity to walk outside in the cool morning air. As she was putting on her shoes, Hashim appeared in the kitchen, still in his pajamas and his tiny hands balled up into fists as he rubbed his eyes.

"Amira where (yawn) are you goin'?"

Amira finished putting on her shoes and hopped up and quickly walked over to Hashim, picking up her little brother and swinging him around as she turned 360 degrees.

"Amira, don'! I'm tired" Hashim, still half-asleep, complained,.

"But I'm helping you wake up Hashim!" Amira grinned still spinning him around.

"Mmmmmrrrrrgggg" Hashim eloquently retorted.

Amira stopped spinning him, gave him a hug and held it for 3 or 4 seconds longer than she normally did. She then let go, and Hashim groggily and now unbalanced (his body leaning greatly to the left) staggered into the kitchen to eat breakfast.

Her work done, Amira opened up the screen door and walked outside to see how her feathery friends were doing.

Most of the ostriches were still sleeping, but Moha stood at the far end of the enclosed pen and stood looking out in the direction of the valley, or at least that was the direction Amira thought the valley was in. In truth she couldn't really remember, but she really didn't care all that much this morning.

Amira walked along the fence and slowly, nonchalantly made her way to Moha.

"So," Amira said while staring at Moha through the fence. "How are ya?"

Moha did not respond...(most likely because he's a BIRD Amira...just saying).

"Umm, nothing? Don't you think we should talk about last night?"

Moha just stared off into the distance while chewing on a piece of grass or whatever it is that ostriches like to chew on.

Amira put her tiny hands on the wooden fence and pleaded, "Please, look at me."

Moha inhaled deeply, flapped his wings and trudged over to the fence and stretched out his neck until his head was mere inches from Amira's.

Amira gently traced her fingers around his purple feathers, then rested her hand atop his head and whispered, "Thank you."
***

Although still early in the morning, Amira was ready for school, so she decided she might as well pack up, put on her helmet which tried but failed to tame her hair each and every time, and get on her bike and ride into the horizon.....errr, until she realized that her bike was still at school. Amira thought about asking her Mom for a ride, but she knew that would just lead to more questions, so she quietly walked up to her room to grab the bike lock combination that she had written down on a separate piece of paper, and began her trek via foot to school. She decided to take advantage of the journey and memorize the lock the combination.

Though she set out on foot, Amira still arrived earlier than any other student or teacher. She saw her bike, parked where she had left it, mocking her. She went to the lock and unlocked-it, then locked it, unlocked it, and then locked it again for good measure, and then made her way into the school building. The walls were painted a lime green, painted just pale enough so as not to incite the emotions of the pre-teens/teens that would grace the hallways. Amira walked by a bulletin board which told the students to get excited for Cultural Diversity Appreciation Month that the 7th Grade would be sponsoring this month (amazingly, the Cultural Diversity Appreciation Month always seemed to be sponsored by whatever class Amira and the rest of the MOP squad happened to be in...thus, last year the 6th grade sponsored the month, before that the 5th grade, etc.). Amira made her way through the hallway, her sneakers squeaking slightly on the newly cleaned linoleum floor and found her homeroom. In her pocket was a piece of paper that had been mailed to her mother (and to the parents of all the school children) a week before stating the room number for her homeroom. Finding Room 5F, Amira opened the door and found beige tiled flooring, a green chalkboard, and dull sets of dull-yellow colored metal chairs and desks. Amira, noticed, something unusual though: each desk had a piece of paper on it listing a student's name, and to her horror, right in front of the teacher's desk was a student's desk with the name "Amira Masri" written on it.

"Awwww, this sucks!" Amira said rather loudly.

"What *sucks* Ms. Masri, "said a frumpy woman in her late 40's, wearing an all-black pant suit, who held an even blacker bag which she held with very, very, *very* pale hands who stood at the door and continued, "is a little, whiny girl who lacks the vocabulary to express herself in any meaningful way."

When Amira turned around to see her new history/homeroom teacher she would have thought she had lost her ability to see color since the woman standing at the door was completely devoid of color, save for her overly rouged cheeks. Amira opened her mouth to say something but was interrupted by Mrs. Brown (yes, who was white).

"No, Ms. Masri, I think that foul mouth of yours has said more than enough during this pre-school hour, so do something smart for once in your life, close those lips and go wait outside the school building until ten minutes before class begins."

"But-"

"When I speak Ms. Masri, the only time I should hear the word "But" is if we are having a discussion regarding conjunctions, and since I'm your history teacher, not English teacher, that conversation is unlikely to happen," she snarled. "Students are NOT allowed to roam the school before ten minutes before the school day begins. Please exit my classroom *immediately.*"

Amira, slightly dumbfounded, put her hands in her pocket lowered her head and kept her gaze directed towards the floor ahead of her and exited the classroom.

***

Amira sat out on the curb, actually about 5 feet from the spot she sat yesterday while trying to figure out the best way for a damp, 12 year-old girl who had just been become the laughingstock of the entire school, to get home.

"Well, well, well, I didn't realize recycling was supposed to be put out on the curve on Tuesdays," said a beautiful girl with auburn hair.

Great, Amira thought, just what she needed: A Tuesday morning greeting from Amber and her sheep.

Amber and her minions (Sara, the beautiful blonde and Tina the beautiful Brunette...it was like Amber picked the alpha females from each "race" of hair color) stared at Amira, Amira with jet-black hair that curled and sprang and shot out in all directions. Amber and her friends' shadows cast most of Amira's body into darkness though their reach felt like it extended much farther.

"Oh Look," Amber continued, "my brother's stalker is trying to ignore us." Tina and Sara, holding identical, new folders in front of their chests laughed and laughed.

"To ignore the ignorant is not a challenge, merely a pleasure" Meredith responded from behind.

Amira looked up and smiled so happy that her friend who always knew what to say and always appeared at the perfect time.

"Oh Meredith, I just don't get why you choose to dorkify yourself by hanging out with Dumb-ira here."

"Oh Amber, you realize being the top sheep still makes you a sheep right?"

"Yeah," Carlos, newly arrived on the scene started, "and A-lame-ee might be lame, but at least...ummm."

"Ugh, let's go girls" Amber said and with a perfect hair toss and hip twirl, the three were off.

"Carlos, I enjoy your enthusiasm," Meredith started, "but sometimes your excitement is faster than your brain."

"What do you mean?"

"Quick wit isn't your thing."

"Quick *what*?"

"Exactly."

"Ahh," turning towards Amira, Carlos said, "you know I don't think you're lame."

"Thanks Carlos," Amira said while standing up.

"I just think you could work on your coolness a bit, that's all."

"Thanks" she said through gritted teeth.

"I mean especially after the whole pool incident/love crazy girl thing you pulled yesterday."

Amira just tightened her helmet strap a bit and continued walking.

"And maybe buy a new helmet."

***

Amira, Meredith, and Carlos entered homeroom in that order. Karen already sitting in the back corner waved to them. Meredith and Carlos took seats right next to Karen, and then it dawned on Amira that she was stuck sitting in the first row, stuck sitting right in front of mean Ms. Brown, sitting right in front of Amber, sitting---WAIT! what did she just realize? Oh that's right, sitting directly behind Amira happened to be Amber of Auburn hair and her Pantene-model type bff's.

You've got to be KIDDING me! Amira thought. She walked over to the desk, stared at Amber for a second, sat down and unstrapped her bike helmet as the giggling started directly behind her.

"Quiet!" shouted the black, white, and rouged woman who just entered the classroom. (*Finally*, dear reader a woman who makes sense) "I do not allow careless banter in my classroom," she said while taking tiny step after tiny step toward the center of the room. "This room is a place of learning and you shall respect it as such. When you enter the room, you shall cease to talk. Now, if you please, everyone stand up."

All obliged.

"We will now go to your lockers. As you know 7th graders must share a locker with a fellow student due to space..."

This, Amira was excited about because she and Karen had already discussed sharing the locker together this summer and had prepared the pictures of teen heartthrobs they'd tape inside. So at least there was one thing that was going right for the clumsy little girl today, at least there's- hmm, dear reader? Ms. Brown wasn't finished talking you say? My apologies...let's continue...

"Now it is tradition that the students get to pick their locker partners, but to me," Ms. Brown continued, "stupid traditions are like stupid children, I have no use for them. Thus, lockers will be assigned in an orderly basis by one's first name."

Oh, well that's too bad for Amira and Karen's plan, but what's the worst that can happen under this-

"Amira and Amber, you will be sharing locker 142."

Oh, riiiiiiight. That's gotta hurt...not wolf gnawing on your leg type of hurt, but hurt still.

Amber and Amira glared at each other as the realization that they would be "sharing" anything together dawned on them.

70

Amber grabbed the combination from Ms. Brown and walked over to the locker with her eyes locked on Amira's during the entire stride.

Amber arrived at the dull, orange locker first, put her perfectly tanned hand with fingernails painted perfectly with sparkles and a lavender color on the dial and quickly opened the locker and shoved the combination in her pocket.

Amira walked over to the locker and leaned against the wall as she watched Amber unload some belongings into the locker. "I'm going to need to see the combination-"

"ONE!" Amber interrupted, "we don't need to talk to each other in order to share the locker. Two, *I'm* going to take the top shelf."

"Wait," Amira interrupted, "there's no top shelf; there's only *one shelf*."

"Not true, you can have the floor of the locker for your belongings. Now, three, I actually care about my stuff, so I don't need you bringing your freaky toys in here or drawing Egyptian hieroglyphics inside or bringing some weird herbs or whatever it is you eat for lunch."

"*I'm* not even eating lunch right now."

"Exactly, you are a freak." (Amira, did walk into that one reader.)

"Look, Amber we can at least be civil about-"

"No Amira we really can't. Look, I'll make a copy of the combo in class and give it to you after next period. *After* that, I expect never to see you at the locker when I'm at the locker, and *maybe* then I'll be able to survive the year without getting your freak germs. Deal?"

"You know what Amber? *Fine,*" Amira said through gritted teeth. "If you want to act like a child, I don't care. I'm better than that."

"Amira, you. Will. *Never* be better than me." Amber retorted.

"Amber, will you just leave please."

"Fine!" Amber said.

"Fine!" Amira repeated.

And with that, Amber slammed the locker shut and strode off in one direction. Amira thought that was a great idea and strode off in the opposite direction...well, that was the plan anyway. Unfortunately, part of her hair was stuck inside the locker door and so rather than stride away with her dignity, fate forced Amira to accept slightly less dignity as her head snapped back and slammed into the locker due to her hair being stuck. Ms. Brown continued to pair up students while Amira, head atilt, just stood with her head leaning on the locker door trying to act like she wasn't stuck, but was rather just "chilling" in a comfortable, nonchalant manner. So, Amira "coolly" crossed her arms across her chest.

"Amira!" Carlos whispered a bit loudly.

"What?" Amira asked.

"We're like only 4 lockers from each other, cool right!?"

"Yeah. Cool. Carlos?"

"Yeah," Carlos said while thrusting random items into his locker.

"Do you have scissors?"

"Yeah. Why?"

"Would you bring them to me?"

"Why?"

"Because" Amira said while narrowing her eyes in order to convey she was serious, but due to the semi-funny angle of her head, her narrowed-eyed look looked more like a confused look than a "Carlos-stop-being-difficult" look.

"Because...I'm...awesome?" Carlos said tilting his head in a way to mimic Amira while he walked toward her.

"Because I never told anyone about the time you slept over and we watched Nightmare On Elm Street and you were so scared you-"

"And suddenly the scissors appear out of nowhere for you Amira" he said quickly grabbing them from deep in his backpack. "You know that was years ago. And you promised that you'd never tell- hey, doesn't your neck hurt holding your head like that?"

"I'm stuck," she mumbled so only Carlos could hear.

"You're duck?" Carlos responded. (Or maybe she mumbled it in a way that *no one* could hear).

"My hair...is *stuck* in the locker."

"Why would you close your locker on your hair?"

"Maybe it wasn't something that was planned," she gritted. "Now will you please take the scissors, drag them along the surface of the locker and cut only the strands that are stuck please?"

"Why didn't you just say so A.M?" Carlos slid the scissors along the locker and cut Amira free.

"Thanks. How's my hair look?"

"Huh?"

"My hair, does it look weird?"

"Weird like it always looks weird or "new" weird?"

"Nevermind. Carlos?"

"Yeah?"

"We need to have a MOP meeting at lunch, okay?"

"Yeah, whatever."

"Carlos, if I told you something strange, you'd believe me right?"

"Umm, yeah, I guess so. You don't lie Amira. It's cool."

"So even if I told you something really amazing, you'd believe me?"

"Well, yeah, you're my friend" Carlos said while scratching his head and feeling a bit uncomfortable with the amount of emotion Amira's eyes were showing.

"And you wouldn't think I'm crazy?"

"Amira, you're like 10 times saner than Meredith or Karen, so of course I wouldn't think you were crazy."

"Thanks Carlos," Amira said, so happy to have such amazing friends.

***

"OH MY GOD, you're CRAZY!" Carlos whispered-screamed as his eyes almost burst out of his sockets while sitting at a faux-wooden table with a burnt-orange painted table top that the MOP Squad sat at, all of whom were completely riveted by the tale Amira just spun.

"*Carlos!*" Amira said out of partial anger and partial pleading.

"Oh, right. Sorry Amira. You're not crazy; it's just your story is completely insane," he said diplomatically he thought.

"I remember I once had a dream," Meredith began, "where I swore I-"

"*This WASN'T a dream* Meredith. You guys, you *have* to believe me."

The MOP Squad stared at her blankly, not knowing what to say.

"*Karen?*" Amira meekly asked.

"Amira, you are awesome, and I believe you," Karen started to which Amira's mouth began to form a smile, "*believe* last night was real, and yesterday was a really crappy day for you, so there's probably some scientific reason why-"

"Guys! I didn't make this up. I didn't dream this up. I didn't hallucinate it or anything like that. It happened, and I need you guys to believe me!" Amira said as she pounded her fists on the tabletop. Sadly, Carlos' cupcake happened to be in Amira's right fist path as she slammed her fists down, which caused the cupcake to explode with much icing landing on Amira's shirt and Carlos' t-shirt.

"Aw *man*, I really wanted that cupcake," Carlos whined.

There was a four second silence and then they all just started laughing hysterically. Tears started flowing from Amira's eyes. So much energy still had been pent up from her near-death experience that the idea of sitting in a lunchroom with her three best friends trying to explain about a pack of roving wolves, a super fast ostrich, an Egyptian oasis in the middle of Texas, and all topped off with vanilla frosting; the absurdity came bursting forth in the form of tears. Other students sitting at far more normal tables stared for a few seconds at the Moppers laughing but soon went back to their own conversations about things that normal junior high school kids from Texas talk about...you know, things like guns, Republicans, football and armadillos.

As the laughter died down, Amira sighed and said, "Will you guys at least come over tonight after my swim practice and see for yourself? Moha is *not* normal."

"Of course," Meredith said while putting her hand on top of Amira's. "We'll always be there for you."

"When you get released from the asylum, we'll be there," Karen said.

"When you run out of tinfoil for your alien repellant helmet," Carlos began,

"We'll be there," Meredith finished.

Before Amira could respond, Carlos asked, "Amira, lunch is almost over, aren't you going to eat?"

"She can't dummy. She's fasting," Karen replied.

"Oh, right. (pause) Why?"

"Because, she had mono during Ramadan so couldn't fast then, so now she's fasting to "catch up,"" Karen said.

"She has to fast because she's considered a woman now," Meredith added.

"Oh," Carlos said as the wheels began turning in his head, "do you have to take a test for that?"

"Carlos, you are so dense," Karen stated.

"What do you mean?"

"There's no test," Meredith said while rolling her eyes.

"Okay, well what then? Do you have to do like a certain number of pushups?"

"No" the girls responded.

"Need a certain bra size? Ow!" Carlos said. "Don't kick me Karen, not cool! Just tell me then!"

"It's personal," Amira said.

"But, we're friends here."

"Yeah, but-,"

"Okay, I know I'm the guy of the group here, but I don't like to be left out."

"It's a girl thing," Karen stated matter-of-factly while gathering up her lunch remnants.

"A girl thing like being annoying and passing stupid notes to one another."

"No, dummy, Amira got her *PERIOD*, all right? Satisfied?" Karen stated exasperatedly. Though somewhat stunned, Carlos was satisfied...as were the three closest tables who happened to be within earshot.

"Karen," Amira whined while dropping her head onto the table so as not to make eye contact with any of their fellow student diners.

"Amira?" Meredith said.

"Yeah" a muffled Amira replied.

"Some of your hair is totally in the cupcake crumbs and other locks are in Carlos' soup."

***

The rest of the afternoon was a bit of a haze for Amira. She went to Algebra, and Spanish, and Home Economics but didn't really pay attention to anything that happened around her. All she could think about was last night: the slobber that flew from the fangs of the wolves and their bloodshot eyes, how her heart sank so far down into her gut when she was sure she about to be mauled to death, the shock of seeing Moha burst onto the scene, and how her fingers dug into Moha's neck and how tight she clenched her forearms and biceps (well, "biceps" might be pushing it) as she hurled herself onto Moha just inches out of the reach of the wolves. And now: she thought about how no one really believed her and *how* she had no idea how to convince her friends. She also swore she could smell the scent of a chicken nearby...likely the scent of a bird came from her mind as she thought about Moha...*or*, maybe it was from the hair that was dipped in chicken noodle soup...probably the latter come to think of it. Amira was so consumed with what happened the previous night that she had completely forgotten about the traumatic swim practice of yesterday and the likely ramifications of said trauma that would ensue in less than an hour when she went back to swim practice.

Oh god, KYLE! And the whole underwear/diary debacle, Amira thought to herself. (I feel as though in a small way I'm responsible for her remembering...it's too bad, too bad your narrator enjoyed bringing it up). Amira glanced outside the window with a slight glimmer of hope that perhaps, *perhaps* Moha would be sprinting up to the school to once again save Amira, though she felt that whatever's Moha's backstory, it likely had little to do with him interfering with junior high drama. So with that Amira took to paying attention to the omnipresent clock with a black hand for the hour, a slightly skinnier/slightly longer black hand for the minutes and a burnt-orange second hand, the school clock which stalked students from New York to Los Angeles, from Katmandu to Kazakhstan, from Olympus to Atlantis, from, well okay Atlantis uses waterproof clocks powered by electric eels, but whatever, you get the idea: you can picture the clock perfectly in your mind, unless you've been home schooled, in which case Amira's entire experience will likely be foreign to you, and you might be better off just reading this book in a foreign language to make *your* experience complete.

As the second hand made its continuous, tedious progression around the circumference of the clock, Amira thought about swim practice and how it would be fine really. As long as she kept her head underwater as much as possible, it wouldn't matter if the boys and girls laughed at her. Amira kept her eyes glued on the clock. She didn't look up once to find out about the evils of split participles and hanging conjunctions, nor did she notice the car parked outside across the parking lot and street where a man sat with his horribly scarred arm resting on the window sill, nor did Amira notice the boy who tied her shoes laces together, nor did Amira notice her fellow students pack up and leave. Basically, Amira was in a waking coma.

"Amira?" Karen whispered. "Amira," she said more loudly. She tried the pinch-talk approach. "Amira," she said while pinching Amira's triceps muscle.

"Ow. What?" Amira asked.

"The bell rang like 20 minutes ago," stated Karen.

"Oh," Amira said turning her attention back to the clock.

"Don't you need to get to practice?" Karen asked.

"Huh? Yeah I guess so," Amira stated neutrally as she began to stand up...

***

The scarred-arm man sat in the car stoically. His sunglasses were fit with lenses, which allowed him to zoom in to assess the situation whenever he wanted, but in truth he saw enough, even from a distance. He saw a girl frozen, a girl likely scared and confused. He saw a girl who sat calmly while schoolchildren jittered about her, while a war played out in her head. He saw her classmates leave while she continued to rest her chin on her hand. He saw another girl approach her. He saw Amira snap out of her coma. He saw Amira stand up. He saw Amira suddenly disappear from his view! He grabbed his satchel next to him wondering if he had somehow been spotted, wondering what his next move should- and then she popped up again. His muscles relaxed and he let go of his satchel. A smile crept across his face as he thought, *She has no idea about her legacy. If she did, she would have told someone about yesterday.* The scarred-arm man noticed the teachers exit the school building and walk over to their respective used cars. He then looked back at Amira and smiled, knowing that his plan had already been set in motion. He turned on the ignition and slowly drove away.

***

"Ouch, that looked like it hurt."

"Who the hell tied my shoes together?" Amira asked while picking herself up off the floor.

"Yeah, and why didn't he wait to watch his handiwork?" Karen wondered aloud.

"Yeah, that's a shame" Amira sarcastically grumbled while hopping up on the desk and curling her knees up to her chest so she could reach her shoelace bound feet. She untied her pink and silver Sketchers and out of habit began retying them.

"Amira, why are you tying your shoes back together?"

"What?" she said and then noticing her own handiwork she began untying again, "Karen what is wrong with *me*?"

"Maybe you should skip swimming today and just go home. I can grab Meredith and Carlos and we can go hang out at your place."

"Yeah, right. My mother would have a conniption that I would skip swimming practice."

"Have you thought about telling your mom about last night?"

"No," Amira began while hopping off the desk and collecting her books, "you guys don't even believe me, so why make her worry that her daughter is going insane because that's what she'll think, right?"

"*Amira*," Karen pleaded, "it's not that we don't believe, it's just...?"

"What?" Amira asked. Karen didn't know what to say. "I have to get to practice she said," while brushing past Karen as her hair covered her face.

Karen wanted to say something comforting to Amira, but she just watched Amira exit.

***

By the time Amira arrived at the locker room everyone else had already left for the pool. During the school year, practices were an hour and a half long, but staggered so that the boys and girls teams only had to share the pool for forty five minutes. This week, the girls' team practice began right after school at 3:15 and the boys would begin at 4 p.m. Amira perked up a bit realizing that returning to the scene of her embarrassment wouldn't be so bad since she would be in the water well before the boys- *Oh crap!*, she realized that the practice on the first day of school was always a joint meeting between the boys and girls team, and she was running late.

Once in her suit, Amira took a breath and realized she had to get out there, so she thought like a bandage she might as well get it over with as quickly as possible (Wait!, That isn't the saying at all Amira), so she walked out into the pool area quickly with her head held high.

When Amira reached the door, she closed her eyes, said a prayer, and then walked out ready (as she could be) for the barrage of comments, stares, and laughter that would come her way.

Amira opened the door, took a step out AND!...I wrote, "AND!"...and nothing. Wait a second, that can't be right. Amira took another step and then another, not even a glance from the boys who were standing by the pool's edge. *Wait*, she thought, *am I so toxic that I'm such a freak and loser that they won't even talk to me from now on?* Answers to all of Amira's questions appeared, or should I say *surfaced*, moments later. As with all pool scenes where a beautiful woman exits the water, this scene took place in slow motion. First, just a magnificently perfect, perfectly tanned hand appeared, followed by an even more attractive arm, and then a stunning back, and then a callipygous backside that caused many of the puberty ridden boys to have thoughts (concerns) like, *I better jump in the pool right now before something embarrassing happens*, or, *I think I need to lie on my stomach for 15 minutes,* or *I better go examine the crack in that wall over there away from everyone really closely for the next hour,* or...well, you get the idea. When she fully emerged from the water, it wasn't as if she was dripping as much as it seemed like the water was crying because it had to leave her body. The woman, the *young* woman in her early 20's with flawless skin, slightly darker than Amira's, who wore a red, one-piece bathing suit that looked tailor-made for her body, a woman who when she pulled off her swim cap let down straight, thick shoulder-length raven hair, a woman with a perfect smile and intoxicatingly gray eyes, suddenly spotted Amira and started to walk towards her.

Amira was frozen in her spot. The boys on the other hand acted more like sunflowers following the sun since their heads, in perfect sync, slowly turned 180 degrees as they followed the woman's orbit past them.

This woman stopped a few feet in front of Amira, and said, "You must be Amira."

"Yeah," Amira offered helpfully.

"We missed you at the meeting."

"Yeah," Amira agreed.

"Not much of a talker huh?"

"I talk," Amira said, though her tone made it sound more wishful than true.

"Okay," she smiled, "let me introduce myself, "I'm Maria Olave," your new swim coach."

"What happened to Mrs. Underwood?" Amira asked. Mrs. Underwood was and up until now had been Amira and all of the other girls' swim coach for years.

"She had a family emergency she had to attend to in California. Anyway a friend of Mrs. Underwood's who knew me, knew that I was taking graduate school classes in Dallas and that I was a collegiate swimmer, so they asked if I'd be willing to fill in."

"For how long?"

"I don't know. As long as it is necessary, I guess. But don't worry, I'll be fair to everyone. Even though you missed the meeting, I'll still let you try out on Monday."

"Tryout for what?"

"For the swim team silly. You're a swimmer right?"

"Yeah," Amira replied. (seriously Amira. We're back to "Yeah" answers again?)

"Well I like to judge talent first hand, so I'm going to hold tryouts, and I'm expecting a lot from you Amira because I've heard great things." Maria put her hand on Amira's shoulder and squeezed gently, caringly.

"Yeah," Amira said, obviously still stunned by Maria's beauty.

Just then Kyle appeared from the other side of the gym. Amira tried to make eye contact with him, but his attention like every other boy was solely focused on Maria Olave, right up until the point when Kyle unintentionally bumped into two smaller boys who were also transfixed by Maria and sent them flying into the pool.

The ensuing splash seemed to break Maria Olave's enchantment since everyone started laughing about what just happened.

Maria winked at Amira and said, "Well, I told the girls they could go home to rest up for the big day tomorrow, so you should go home and rest up too. It was nice meeting you Amira," she said as she walked into the coach's locker room.

"Yeah," Amira replied. (Note, dear reader that the above exchange likely will NOT make it into the Conversation Hall Of Fame.)

***

The Mop Squad stood outside the pen where the ostriches stood milling about. Carlos had his hands in his back pockets and swayed back and forth. Meredith put her hands on her hips and spent an inordinate amount of energy smiling and looking at Amira as if her energy could encourage something (*anything*) to happen. Karen sat down cross-legged and put her elbow on her knee and her chin on her hand in a half-decent impersonation of the 6th patriarch of Zen Buddhism...what? That reference doesn't put an image in your mind? Well, go look it up.

Meredith reached out and grabbed Amira's hand and squeezed ever so gently. Karen turned her attention to a twig that sat near her while Carlos' swaying became more and more violent until it looked like he would either throw himself forward or backward onto the ground any second.

Finally breaking the silence Carlos said, "Yeah, I don't see it Amira." Carlos finally stopped his swaying to add gravitas to his words. "I mean we're just staring at lazy birds.

"Just wait," Amira said.

"How long we gotta wait for?" Carlos asked.

Meredith kicked Carlos in the side of the shin.

"Hey! I'm just keeping it real here. I mean I got *stuff* to do."

Looking up from her seated meditation, Karen asked, "What stuff?"

"I don't *know*. You *know*. *Things*. Like Stuff."

Amira rolled her eyes, huffed and called, "Moha! Moha, come here!"

"Which one's Moha again?" Meredith asked expectantly.

"The one with the purple feathers on his head."

"Oh. Which one has the purple feathers?" Meredith asked, stepping on her tiptoes trying to see through the throng of birds searching for the one that supposedly was Moha.

"I'll grab him," Amira said as she broke away from the MOP squad and hopped over the fence to go round up Moha. Almost instantly, Moha began making his way towards the fence in the area that Amira just hopped into. The way Moha moved toward Amira did not go unnoticed by the MOP squad. Karen hopped up, and the three of them ran over to the fence to get a better look. Amira's eyes brightened as Moha approached. *Finally*, she thought. Finally her friends would believe her. Finally this girl with crazy curly hair who had a propensity to get

85

in fights with gravity and lose, finally this girl who had been carrying on about wolves and who still thought the jury was out on whether the Easter Bunny exists, was about to offer the proof needed to win her case of sanity before her peers. Okay, I may have made up the whole Easter Bunny thing, but you get the idea...

With each step that Moha made toward Amira, the anticipation that something amazing was about to happen grew with each Mopper. Moha picked up his pace and Amira spread her arms out in a welcoming manner and smiled as the bird obligingly approached. However, as Moha came running toward Amira and then past Amira, the MOP squad's excitement dwindled. Moha then stopped near where Meredith, Karen, and Carlos stood due to a flower it seemed that Moha spotted and wanted to examine.

"How 'lon do 'e 'ave to do dis" Carlos asked Meredith while trying to not to move his lips.

"As ong as it 'akes." Meredith said with an equally frozen mouth. "She's are fren, so we 'ave to hel' her."

Amira stared at her friends for a second seeing through their false smiles to their truthful stares of concern. She had to show them she realized. She had to show them how she rode on Moha.

"Here, watch," she said. Amira took a deep breath, walked to within about 25 feet of where Moha stood examining the ground, and with the laser sharp concentration of a gymnast running down the lane during a vaulting portion of the competition, Amira took off, sprinting toward her feathery steed. Meredith, Carlos, and Karen watched in amazement.

"Wow, Amira's really fast" Carlos uttered under his breath.

"Yeah," Karen agreed.

Amira zoomed by her friends and was now 10 feet, 8 feet, 5 five feet from Moha, and then she jumped, ready to impress her friends by landing on Moha's back to show he was ready and willing to take her anywhere, and as she flew through the air her confidence grew...and grew...right up to the point where she slammed into the side of Moha and fell to the ground.

"Oooh" the non-Egyptian members of the MOP Squad said in unison.

Muttering Arabic and more localized Egyptian swear words under her breath, Amira slowly picked herself up and smacked the dirt off of her pants. She turned to her friends and said, "I just screwed up my jump, that's all."

Hashim, holding a football, suddenly appeared behind the non-ostrich jumping friends. "Hey, what's going on here?"

Not taking his eyes off of Amira who was now trying to mount Moha by climbing/clawing on him from behind, Carlos said, "We're watching your sister go crazy." Meredith and Karen both kicked him in the shins.

"HEY! OKAY! New rule: no kicking Carlos! I'm not as tough as I look, okay?"

"You don't look tough at all," Meredith responded.

"Which proves how much I don't like being kicked."

"Why's Amira going crazy?"

Hopping down from the fence and turning toward Hashim, Carlos said, "It's not her fault. *All* girls go crazy eventually."

"Is it because she likes boys now?"

"Yeah my man, that could be part of it."

"Carlos? Do you want to throw the football around?"

Turning in time to see Amira fail again to mount Moha, Carlos said, "Sure little man. Ladies, H and I will be back.

Okay, Amira thought, *maybe if I just*...Amira tried a standing jump but that failed. So, she grabbed some pumpkin seeds from her pocket and convinced Moha to drop his neck at which point Amira stealthily tried to climb on Moha's neck. She flung her arms around Moha's neck and then hopped up at which point Moha jerked his neck slightly to the right which caused Amira to flip right over his neck and back onto the ground on the other side.

"You're getting closer Amira, keep it up!" Karen yelled.

The failing continued for a few more minutes until Moha became distracted by the wind or something equally as interesting and ended up just hopping away leaving Amira on her butt, covered in dirt with her hair adorned by several feathers. Meredith and Karen hopped the fence to help Amira up.

"Maybe it depends on the situation," Meredith offered while offering her hand to Amira.

"Obviously," Amira said as Karen plucked feathers from her hair.

"We can try again tomorrow if you want," Karen added.

"No. I'll just...I don't know. Look, I know you two are worried about me and think- I don't know what you must think."

Meredith and Karen stood on each side of Amira and both wrapped an arm around her as they walked back to the house.

Meredith said, "We *think* whatever happened to you, that's it's going to be okay. And we think you should tell us about a certain *boy* visiting your house yesterday! I can't believe you didn't tell me. Karen told me after school today!"

"It just didn't seem important after-" Amira stopped herself realizing there was no point discussing the "after" at this moment.

Meredith rested her head on Amira's shoulder for a second and then lifted it and said, "Amira, I don't care if an asteroid is headed for earth. Next time Kyle talks to you, you call me, *immediately*."

Perking up slightly, "Do you really think there will be a next time?"

"Boys are like Canadian geese: they may go away but they always come back."

Amira and Karen stared at her not understanding the reference.

Meredith rolled her eyes and said, "Watch: HEY Carlos, Hashim come here!" she yelled seeing Hashim running in a circle around Carlos obviously exasperated that Carlos wasn't throwing him the ball.

"What do you want?" Carlos asked.

"Just come here." she reiterated. Then, Carlos and Hashim started jogging over.

"See?" Meredith said smiling at Karen and Amira. All three girls started cracking up as Carlos and Hashim arrived.

"What? What's funny?" Carlos asked. The girls just continued to laugh. Turning to Hashim, Carlos said, "See my man, *crazy*."

"Yeah, crazy" Hashim said while scratching his head and staring at Amira, not realizing he might know more than anyone standing around him about what was going on.

***

Amira sat on the porch watching the sun slowly set over the horizon. Meredith, Karen, and Carlos had all left an hour earlier. Normally they would stay for dinner, but since Amira was fasting, the idea of waiting for the sun to set to eat did not inspire them to stick around. So, Amira sat on the porch swing as Hashim played with his Legos, reenacting a siege on a Lego Castle with a Lego spaceship while an almost empty bowl of macaroni and cheese sat idly by. Amira rocked back a forth, slowly, deliberately staring out at the horizon wondering what her father and the rest of her family were doing in Egypt right now (umm, try *sleeping* Amira...it's called time zones). She wondered how her favorite cousin Aini would react if she told her the story. Would she believe her or would she too give Amira that "look," that look that said, *I care about you but I should probably slowly take the butter knife you're holding away from you just in case.*

After the spaceship successfully averted the arrows of the Lego Knights and crashed into one tower, Hashim said, "Amira, I'm still hungry."

"There's more macaroni and cheese in the kitchen. Go get some more if you want."

"But I want to eat with you and Mom."

"Then you should wait to have your second bowl."

"Could I eat half a bowl now and then the rest later?"

"Hashim, who *cares*? Sure."

"Cool," he said dropping the spaceship onto the skyscraper, which neighbored the castle. "Don't touch anything," he said while waiving his hands over the era-confused Lego setting as he hopped up, grabbed his bowl and fork and started heading for the kitchen.

Touch YOUR stuff, she thought. She still hadn't dealt with him for *causing* her embarrassing moment the other day. *What the heck was he doing packing all of that personal stuff in my bag?* She thought about pinning him down, kneeling on his shoulders and forcing him to explain himself, but she wasn't sure her nerves could handle the confrontation right now. So, she just sat there swinging her legs gently and concentrated on the horizon, which swayed up and down, in sync with the motion of the porch swing.

Dinner came and went without much to report. Hashim complained that he was full and was miffed at Amira for letting him eat too much before Amira and their Mom could eat. After dinner, Amira volunteered to do the dishes, which allowed her to stare out the kitchen window, which was above the sink and overlooked the ostrich pen. She couldn't really see much due to the lack of light, but she imagined Moha in there milling about with a smug ostrich smile on his lipless face laughing at how goofy he made Amira look in front of her friends today.

After the dishes were done, Amira sat with her mother at the kitchen table as her mother prepared for her class the next day while Amira worked on her homework. They sat in silence, save for the occasional yawn that Amira emitted from time to time.

"Why don't you go to bed my sweet banoota?" said Ms. Talib peering at Amira above the coke-bottle glasses she wore when reading.

"Yeah, I guess I will. I'm finished with my homework anyway."

"Are you sleeping okay?"

"I think so, but I've been tired lately."

91

Hashim came hopping down the stairs. "Mom, I'm tired, can I go bed?"

"Of course my child."

"Can Amira read me a story?"

"Aren't you getting a little old for having me read you stories?" Amira groaned.

"Hush," her mother said to Amira. "Go brush your teeth and Amira will be right up."

"Cool!" Hashim said bounding back up the steps.

"He looks up to you Amira and likes spending time with you. Appreciate his love and read him a story."

"All *right*. All right." Amira said while closing up her Algebra book.

"Thank you. Now come give your mother a hug, so I can inspect my beautiful daughter."

"*Mom*," Amira sighed. "I'm not beautiful."

"You *are* my child. Come here," she said as she extended her arms out. Amira walked over and hugged her mother. "Amira" her mother asked while they embraced.

"Yes?"

"Why are there feathers in your hair?"

"Aww, *man*. I thought I got them all."

"What have you been up to?" her mother asked, releasing the embrace enough for her to look at her daughter in the eyes.

"I was trying to teach Karen, Meredith, and Carlos a bit about ostriches today, but I don't think I'm a very good teacher yet because I guess I don't know as much about them as I thought I did."

"Well, lesson one should be, how *not* to get feathers in your hair, okay?"

"Yeah, yeah. Hey, I didn't ask for this hair. You and Baba gave it to me."

"Well, someday you'll thank us for it...although probably not until you learn how to control it a bit," she said while pulling a feather out. "I swear Amira, your hair has more adventures it seems than most explorers have in a lifetime."

"I know, I know. I'll tame it someday," she said while smiling at her mom.

"I suppose you will. Now go upstairs, read your brother a story, brush out those feathers and then get to bed yourself."

"Aye, aye, Captain Mother" Amira said while giving a salute. As Amira skipped up the stairs, her mother just shook her head and smiled at her children, her beautiful and smart children, her *bizarre and nutty* children. (Okay, I may have added that last one.)

When Amira arrived in Hashim's room, he was already under the covers with a book sitting next to him on his bed and only the desk lamp on in his room.

"What am I reading tonight?" Amira asked.

"Well, don't read the whole book because that would take weeks, but maybe just a few pages of *The Prince And His Three Fates.*"

"Sure," she said plopping down on his bed next to him, so that he could rest his head against her arm.

"Amira?"

"Yes Hashim?"

"Carlos said you were going crazy?"

"He did?"

"Well, he said only because you're a girl."

"Well, girls only go crazy because boys drive us *nuts*," she said while tickling his side for a second.

"*Don't.* Amira?"

"Hmm?"

"Does sleepwalking mean a person is crazy?"

"No, Hashim, I don't think so."

"Oh. Amira?"

"Hashim, if you keep asking questions, I won't be able to read to you at all."

"Just one more question," he said while closing his eyes and repositioning his head on her arm.

"Okay, what?"

"If you *do* go crazy, will you let me visit you at the insane asylum?"

"Yes," she said grumpily.

"Will you let me eat your Jell-O?"

"*Hashim.*"

"Sorry," he mumbled while putting his hand on her hip as he curled up beneath the blankets.

Amira began to read the story, but before she reached the end of the first page, Hashim's snoring began to drown out her voice, so she gently put his head down on the pillow as she stealthily extracted herself from his bed. When she reached the door, she looked back at her little brother and thought, *Why are you so weird sometimes Hashim?*

***

Hashim slept peacefully for the first four hours that night. His body did not move as he slept deeply, dreaming about playing football with his father. Hashim probably would not have moved at all that night had not his sister awakened him as

94

she had done several times before over the past few weeks. Amira stood a few feet inside Hashim's room and stared absently out his window.

"*Amira*, what do you *want?*" he asked not even bothering to raise his head from his pillow.

"Hashim, I need your help," she said neutrally.

"But you said that before and then got mad at me."

Amira ignored him and walked over to the window. Hashim had already decided yesterday that Amira *must* be sleepwalking which is why she acted so strangely. He wanted to tell his Mom about it or talk to Amira about it, but each time Amira made him promise not to tell anyone about their conversation or even to talk about it to Amira. Since all she seemed to do was come into his room, make the same request, and then go back to bed, her "craziness" seemed harmless to him so he thought it best to keep his promise to her, even if his promise was to a "sleeping" her.

"Hashim," Amira said while staring absently outside the window, "I need to help them."

"Who?" Hashim asked (again).

"I don't know. There are two girls, maybe three. They look-"...and then she'd trail off for a few seconds. "Hashim, I need you to pack a bag for me."

"But you got so mad at me for doing it *before*."

"Hashim, you have to do it because *HE'S* watching me. But, he won't be watching you. You need to pack..." and she would list several random items that Hashim would have to pack for her, and then she would begin to drift off and make Hashim promise not to say anything, to anyone, *even* Amira. He realized if he agreed quickly, he could go back to bed. And then, Amira would turn and walk out of his room. The first two times Amira did this Hashim followed her, but each time she just walked back into her bedroom and stretched out on her bed like nothing had happened. Thus, Hashim watched her leave his room and closed his eyes, so he could dream more about playing football.

*C*hapter 3: *Crazy Like A Fox*

Dear reader, your humble, kind, generous narrator does NOT promote violence of any kind. *However*, if I were to promote violence, let me share with you my thoughts on where violence should be promoted, if in fact that is what I am doing, which of course it is not. I hate, HATE, *hate* people who walk three to four abreast on New York City sidewalks while staring up at buildings, thereby forcing others to walk at a snails pace behind them. To be so inconsiderate that you're willing to take up the entire sidewalk while you stare like an idiot upward instead of looking where you're going is fascism PURE and simple. I think the punishment for such an act is that we law-abiding and considerate citizens should be deputized on the spot and be allowed to kick these sidewalk-hoarders in the back of the knee, stunning them and inhibiting their balance for just long enough that we can step over and/or pass around them and go about our day in a normally paced fashion. Again, I'm not advocating violence, but if you aim your kick to the upper part of the back of the knee even the strongest perpetrator will crumble without even putting up a fight. Why am I bringing up New York sidewalks during a story that revolves around an adorable Texas tween? Well, for that dear readers, all I can say is: have some faith...and patience.

Like the morning before, Amira was rousted from sleep by her mother thirty minutes before sunrise.

"What's going on?" asked a groggy Amira.

"Your brother decided to make us breakfast," her mother whispered to Amira.

"What's he making us?" Amira asked.

"Scrambled eggs and toast," her mother asked peering deeply into Amira's eyes obviously searching for the answer.

"Why is he making us breakfast?" Amira asked.

"I think he feels left out by not fasting with us."

"He's not missing much," Amira replied.

"Well, hurry and get up. I need to go supervise his generous endeavor."

"Okay, I will. I'm up. I'm up."

"And be sure to be very thankful for breakfast. This means a lot to him. He made me promise to wake him up early in the morning, so he could do this for us," Nara said gently squeezing Amira's shoulder.

"I will, of course," Amira said rolling her eyes.

A few minutes later, Amira appeared downstairs to find the kitchen abuzz with activity.

"MOM! I think it's ready!" Hashim said from the stool. He then hopped down and left the stove unattended obviously confident that his mother would take care of it from here on out. "Amira, good morning! I made breakfast."

"I see that Hashim," she said bending down to give him a hug. "You didn't have to do that."

"Well, sometimes you help out when I mess up, so you know. I'm glad you're my sister."

"And I'm glad you're my brother," she said messing up his already messed up hair on his head.

"Okay, let's eat Amira," Nara said carrying over two plates of eggs and toast and setting them down on the kitchen table.

"I even already added salt and pepper, so you could just start eating."

"You are so wonderful Hashim," Nara said kissing him on the head.

"You're not eating with us Hashim?" Amira asked.

"I was hungry when I woke up, so mom made cereal for me first. You need strength to cook."

Amira took a bite, and truth be told, the brat did a good job. It actually tasted quite good. She smiled, "Hashim this tastes *amazing*. Thank you. It really hits the spot."

"Great!" Hashim said obviously pleased.

Amira felt a slight tingling in her mouth...from a spice of some kind. "Hashim what did you add to the eggs?"

Hashim scrunched up his face, "Umm, just salt and pepper I think."

Nara had an expression similar to Amira's on her face. Nara looked over the at the counter and noticed a salt shaker and thin glass container with a label that read, "Ground Habanero Peppers." "Hashim, did you put Habanero Peppers in the eggs?" Nara asked smiling as tears slowly began to form in her eyes.

"Umm, maybe. It's okay right?!" he asked.

"Hashim, you making breakfast is *amazing!*" Amira said not quite answering his question.

"Hashim," Nara began, "would you mind going upstairs and grabbing the Lego spaceship you built? I bet Amira would really like to see it."

"Sure. Oh, I think I took part of it off," Hashim said with a disappointed look on his face.

"Well, how long would it take you put back together?" Amira asked as pools formed in her eyes.

"I don't know. Maybe seven minutes?"

"Perfect!" Nara said picking him up from his chair and setting him on the ground.

"Thanks Hashim! That would mean a lot to me," Amira said.

So excited that his sister finally took more of an interest in his LEGO building, Hashim exclaimed "OKAY!" as he ran out of the room and ran/stumbled up the stairs.

Nara and Amira began laughing and crying at the same time.

"Mom, my mouth is on *fire!* What did he *do?*"

"Shush child," Nara said through tears. "He must have grabbed the habanero pepper when I wasn't looking. It's the hottest pepper in the pepper family."

"Mom, I'm in pain here," Amira said.

Nara was on it though. "We only have a couple of minutes. Pour two glasses of milk, I'm going to cut up a lemon."

"What will that do?"

"I think the acid from the lemon cuts through the spice, and the milk coats your mouth."

"Will that *work?*"

"Let's hope so," she said through amazingly clear sinuses.

***

Amira, mouth no longer burning, sat outside the school building tapping her feet in an attempt to achieve rhythm (an attempt that continuously *failed* mind you) as a way to kill the 15 minutes she had until she could go inside. Suddenly a newspaper smacked the pavement right next to her.

"*Amira!* You might not be crazy!" Karen exclaimed while plopping down next to Amira and giving her a bear hug.

"Huh?" Amira asked confused (but "sanely").

"Look at the paper! I wanted to call you last night, but I thought it was too late!"

Amira glanced at the newspaper, which was open to page 8 (always hard-hitting news on page 8 of course, like human interest stories about pancakes or how a hound dog was issued a jaywalking ticket by an overzealous policeman, etc.). Amira read the headline aloud,

PLAINTOWN PRESS • *September 2, 1999*

UNKNOWN "AVENGER" SAVES TEENAGE GIRLS
Last night, three girls were attacked in Central Park by a gang of Neo-Nazis wanted for questioning regarding the murder of a high school prep star last week in Brooklyn. The attack on the girls, however, was thwarted by..."

"*No*, not *that* article! That one!

EGYPTIAN ARTIFACT VANDALIZED?
Last night, for reasons unknown, an ancient Egyptian desk on loan to the Natural Historry Museum from the Abdul-Muhaimin Foundation was moved by unknown assailants...."

"*Ugh!*, No, THAT ONE," Karen nearly squealed pointing to the article right below the one Amira had been reading.

> THREE SIGHTINGS OF RAVENOUS WOLFPACK
> Last night, the Plaintown, Texas police responded to several reports of wolves roaming the countryside about 40 miles northwest of Dallas. Mr. Richter, Sergeant, of the Plaintown Police force, claims that wolves do not exist in Texas, and that people likely mistook a few coyotes for wolves. When asked how each person could have mistakenly claimed that the wolves all had grey hair, Mr. Richter stated that the sunset often causes people to mistakenly think the color they see of someone or something is accurate when in fact it is not. Although several ranchers complained of missing livestock, the police are not actively searching for any pack...

"Amira, isn't this great?! You didn't dream it up after all. You *did* almost die! Awesome right?!"

"You two are *so* weird" Amber piped in while walking by them without even a glance in their direction.

"Karen, I think I need to find that place that Moha took me," Amira said while taking off her helmet and putting it over her knees, so she could rest her chin on it while she hugged her legs close to her body.

"Why?" Karen asked sitting down next to her friend.

"Something strange is going on."

"That's an understatement," Karen replied.

"I think," she then paused, "I think I'm supposed to-Karen there's got to be some kind of *meaning* behind all this, right?"

"Maybe. I guess."

"Do you think the MOP squad would want to go for a hike on Saturday?"

"Hmm, let me think about that. We could (A) go for a hike searching for adventure with our possibly *least* sane member leading the way into a potentially dangerous area with bloodthirsty wolves on the loose...*or* (B) we could listen to Carlos complain about how you, Meredith, and I aren't paying attention to some British soccer match he's forcing us to watch on TV where we don't even get to hear the players sexy British accents because they're too busy running around. Well option (B) is a lot safer, *but...*"

"We're going for a hike?" Amira asked smiling.

"Yeah, it's not really a choice, is it?" Karen said.

"I LOVE YOU!" Amira said hugging/tackling Karen next to her as Amira's helmet clunked to the ground.

"What happened? What's going on?" Carlos asked while pulling up on his bike.

"We're going on an adventure on Saturday," Karen gleamed.

"What?"

"It's going to be a lot of fun," Amira said.

"Where?"

"Just show up at Amira's house Saturday morning. It's going to be a surprise," Karen said.

"Oh, well, can we go after the Chelsea match? It's going to be awesome. They're playing-"

"What time does the match start," Karen interrupted.

"11 a.m."

"Ahhh, shoot, that's when we're going. *Darn.* I hate it when life does that: starts two awesome things at the same time," Karen quipped while standing up and heading towards the school door.

"You could at least *attempt* to try to lie to me," Carlos stated. "I mean I think that's the polite thing to do."

"We're sorry Carlos," Amira said putting her arm through his arm, so they could walk side by side. "You deserve better actresses as friends."

"*Whatever*," Karen began, "Come on Carlos. What's it matter? Wouldn't you rather hang out with three beautiful girls on a Saturday than watch a bunch of foreigners run around for no apparent reason."

"Heck ya!" Carlos said. "What hot girls are you guys inviting on Saturday?"

Karen tilted her head and gave him a cold stare.

"Oh, you mean you two? And probably Meredith, right?" Giving a thumbs up, he continued, "That's sounds *greaaat*."

They walked out of the sun and into the unnatural lighting used in all schools. Amira almost skipped down the hall with her arm linked through Carlos' arm because she was so excited that her friends were beginning to believe her, and she couldn't wait to show them the valley she discovered. She was so excited she almost forgot that she shared a locker with the devil. Karen and Meredith's locker was one of the first ones, so Karen stopped at her own locker letting Carlos and Amira continue down the hallway. As Amira and Carlos continued along the 7th grade lockers, Amira's "half-skips" became regular steps, and when she saw that Amber was talking to her minions, Sara and Tina; a few feet from their shared locker, her gait slowed even more. However, she noticed that Amber had left the locker open and was enthralled with whatever gossip she and her friends were gabbing about, so she could easily get into her locker likely without even a glance from Amber.

Amira snaked along the lockers as stealthily as possible. Amber and her friends paid zero attention to Amira as she approached. Amira smiled slightly realizing that she obviously had made too much of the situation, and that everything would be fine. She reached to grab her history book, and Amber, without looking, kicked her leg back quickly slamming the locker shut and coming within millimeters of slamming the locker on Amira's fingertips.

"Hey!" Amira yelled whipping her hand back instinctively (though I'm not sure why that's so instinctive. Seriously, what's the point of jumping back *after* the danger has passed? People are stupid.) "I needed to grab a book and you *nearly* took off my fingers."

Amber flipped her hair over her shoulder with her hand thereby sending some amazing fragrance, like vanilla, cinnamon and perhaps a hint of cherry, into the air, thereby momentarily incapacitating all around her as the intoxicating aroma made its way through their nasal passages. Amber then turned slowly toward Amira.

"We had a deal A-moan-i or is it A-whine-i? You are not to use the locker while I'm using the locker." Amber glared at Amira without blinking.

"One: you weren't *using* the locker. And *TWO*, I never agreed to your stupid deal," Amira said while glaring back at Amber. (Ooh, this is fun, I haven't seen a glare-off in at least two weeks!)

"Amira. I'm just trying to make the best of a horrible, awful, disgusting situation. I'm trying to create a peaceful solution. Is that a foreign idea to an Arab?" Amber said with what can only be described as an *aggressive* smile.

"That statement was ignorant and bigoted. But, I'm willing to play to your stereotype just this once to wipe that smile off of your face," Amira said while stepping forward to within a foot of Amber.

"Ladies, *ladies*, maybe we should all take a breath," Carlos said trying to separate the two."

Amber continued to stare at Amira, but said, "I'll tell you what Carlos. Once you're tall enough to look me in the eye, *then* you can talk to me. Until then, butt out."

Carlos took a step back and said, "Amira, (pause) go for the kidney. No one likes to be hit in the kidney."

Then, the bell rang, letting students know that classes begin in two minutes.

"Saved by the bell, Amira. See you in class," she said as she turned on her heel and walked briskly away.

"She's just so...so...AWFUL," Amira said clenching her fists so hard that blood stopped circulating to her fingers.

"Yeah, tell me about it," Carlos said. "But, still really, *really* hot."

"What?!," Amira said turning her full attention to Carlos. "She's disgusting."

"Internally, yeah. But, come on Amira: she's *H-O-T*."

"Ugh, I was wrong. She's *not* disgusting. *Boys* are disgusting," she said turning toward her locker.

"Yeah, but we're also kinda awesome," Carlos said as he put her arm on her shoulder.

Amira stared at the locker for a second. "AHHH *MAN!*" she said while softly resting her forehead on the locker and then tapping her head gently against the cheap steal several times.

"What?" Carlos asked concerned.

Turning toward him but still keeping her head in contact with the locker, "I totally forgot the locker combination."

"Don't you have combination written down?"

"Yeah," she whined.

"So what's the problem?"

"It's at home."

"Well, that's not helpful at all, huh?" Carlos said with a poor attempt at a cowboy-western, "Howdy partna" type accent. Snapping out of it, "Come on. We don't want to be late to Ms. Brown's class. I heard she gives detention for that without even one warning."

"Doesn't she also give detention if you don't have your book?" Amira asked.

"Oh yeah! So you're screwed either way. So I guess just grin and bear it. High five?" he asked raising his palm.

"High five," she said tapping his palm with hers.

"Nope, you have to mean it," he said with his palm still in the air."

"High five!" she said more loudly and hit his hand with more force.

"Now we're talking!" he said as he turned to walk with her to class. "So where are we going on Saturday?"

Shuffling along next to him and absently counting the tiles from her locker to the class door, "Oh, don't worry Carlos. You'll like it."

***

"Guys are you sure we should be doing this?" Carlos asked sheepishly as he stood on Amira's porch.

"We owe it to her Carlos," Karen said while unzipping her Hello Kitty backpack in order to make sure she had everything she needed (sun tan lotion, water, snacks, a sense of reason...woops, I think she forgot to pack that last one). "Whatever happened to her has really been bothering her, so we need to help her."

"Okay, that's great, but let's say everything she told us was true. Doesn't that just mean we're literally walking into a lion's den?...umm, that's full of wolves."

Meredith was sitting on the porch swing, strumming her guitar almost silently, something she often did while pondering questions such as the meaning of life, the meaning of boys, the meaning of the Uniform Commercial Code and its impact on trade among NAFTA countries (granted some thoughts were more prevalent than others). Finally, she said, "I think Karen's right. We need to help her. And besides, it's sunny out today and warm; the wolves are probably laying low until the evening even if they are out there, so as long as we head back before it gets too late, we'll be fine."

"Fine. Fine. But if she wants our help she should at least be ready on time."

"She just has to pee. She'll be right out."

"Didn't she just pee?"

"She woke up early and hydrated," Karen replied.

"*Why?*" Carlos asked.

"Because she's fasting dummy, just like she was doing yesterday, and just like she will be doing tomorrow, and yes, just like she's doing today."

"But, we're still going to order pizza tonight right?" Carlos asked seemingly with more concern than he displayed over the threat of wolves.

"Hey guys!" Hashim said while running through the front hall.

"Hashim, my love, how are you?" Meredith said smiling broadly.

"Meredith, what are you gonna teach me today?" Hashim asked while hopping onto Meredith's lap and positioning himself so his left hand rested next to hers on the neck on the guitar.

"Hmm, how about a C chord?" Meredith said. She really only ever taught him the C, A-minor, and E chords because his hands were tiny, but he never seemed to mind the repetitive lessons.

Amira then walked to the door and came out on the porch. "So are we ready?"

"Ready for what?" Hashim asked not looking up from the guitar.

"We're going for a little hike Hashim."

"Can I come?"

Amira rubbed his head and said, "Not this time."

"But-"

Amira cut him off quickly, not wanting to waste any time arguing with her little brother. "Look, Hashim. I'll make a deal with you. Mer, Carlos, and Karen are going to stay over tonight, and I promise you can hang out with us this evening, okay? And we'll probably watch a movie or something, so if you're nice to mom today, she'll probably let you watch the movie with us, cool?"

"Can I sit with Meredith during the movie?"

"Well ask her?"

Hashim bent his neck back so he could see Meredith.

"Well of course. Why wouldn't I want to sit next to my future boyfriend" Meredith winked.

"Cool!" Hashim said.

"Good. For a second I was worried that maybe you met some new girl at school," Meredith said while putting her hand over his on the guitar.

"Nah, they're not as cool as you."

Meredith smiled. "Okay, now remember, you're my prom date, right?"

"Yup."

"Did you order your penguin suit?"

"Not yet" Hashim replied. "How much time do I have again?"

"About five years," Meredith said.

"Okay, well, I probably won't order it just yet then."

"That's fine."

"I'm going to be a football player for Halloween this year." Hashim stated, obviously thinking a penguin suit, really was a "penguin suit." That, or he's planning to live a life full of non-sequiturs.

"Okay, well, we're gonna go. Will you put my guitar inside in the case?" she asked.

"Yup." Hashim said while grabbing the guitar and running inside and then banging it against the doorframe causing a loud thump/twang to resonate.

"Sorry!" he yelled not looking back but still running down the hall.

"It's okay sweetie!" Meredith said while slightly cringing. "Shall we?" Meredith said looking at her fellow MOP squad-ers.
***

The first hour of walking they were in good spirits making fun each other, laughing, the girls singing boy band ballads until Carlos threatened to become a meth addict if they didn't stop. They then had a ten-minute discussion about whether any of them knew what being a meth addict actually meant, but this topic seemed to stump them all.

***

"NO WAY!" Karen exclaimed while throwing her hands above her head in exasperation.

"Why do you doubt me?" Carlos asked.

"Because of you. I doubt you because it's *you* we're talking about," Karen said placing her hands on her hips.

"Meredith?" Carlos beckoned.

"I think I'm gonna have to agree with Karen, Carlos. I don't think you can pull it off" while giving Carlos a light hip-check."

"But I'd have twelve months. A lot can happen in twelve months. Amira?"

Amira pushed out her lips, squished them together and moved them from side to side as she pondered. "You know what? I think he *can* get two girls to kiss him in the next year. Carlos is talented like that."

Carlos gave a fist pump and then ran up to Amira to get a high-five.

"Ahhhhhh yeahhhhh ladies, Carlos is here. Forget about tomorrow, let the kisses follow as the moment moves you!"

"Ugh, Amira why do you egg him on?" Karen wailed while rolling her eyes, head, and neck.

"Because, she's a sophisticated, beautiful woman, that's why," Carlos said while putting his arm around Amira's shoulder.

"Yeah, you know, I'm not going to kiss you, right?" Amira said quietly.

"That wouldn't count anyway. Friends don't count," he whispered back giving her a wink. Then more loudly, "I appreciate the OFFER Amira, but no need to kiss me just to prove a point to the little girls trailing behind us that I'm kissable. They're just jealous anyway."

Meredith started coughing and then *hacking* as she fell to her knees. Carlos, Karen, and Amira rushed to her.

"Mer, what's wrong?" Carlos asked.

Meredith still hacking grabbed Carlos' shirt and said, "I (hack) can't (hack) breathe. (hack-hack) There's a gas (hack, hack) bag in front of me (hack-hack) who's (now in a normal voice) using up all the air," she finished now winking at Carlos.

"Are you sure you don't need CPR?" Carlos asked closing his eyes and puckering his lips as he leaned in toward her.

Laughing Meredith shoved his shoulders pushing him to the ground. "I would rather suffocate."

"The more you deny it Meredith, the more likely the universe is gonna end up having you kiss me," Carlos said as he hopped up.

Karen scowled throughout Meredith and Carlos' flirt-, well, I can't even call it that...let's say their *attempt* at flirting because honestly, they could both use a lot of practice with the subject. So, Karen did what any jealous person would do, and as Carlos stood up she yelled, "Dead leg!" and kneed Carlos in the calf causing him to fall back to the ground.

Various names were then thrown about among Meredith, Carlos, and Karen, but Amira could not hear them, for the previous conversation led to a series of unsettling daydreams for Amira. A setting sun, a field full of lilies as Kyle stared deeply into Amira's eyes before tilting his head to his right as he slowly moved closer to Amira, closing his eyes as his lips traversed the air to her lips. A full moon, a beach full of pure white sand, waves crashing on the surf, Kyle wearing white pants and a white shirt (let's hope it's not past Labor Day Amira...that would be tacky), the stars shining bright as Kyle leans in to...now, they're in Egypt, in front of pyramids, minutes before sunrise as the sky in the East is beginning to turn a lighter shade of blue; they had been up talking all night, pouring out their hearts to each other, sharing their hopes and dreams, and now after their minds had become one, Kyle leaned in to kiss Amira as a warm breeze floated by but suddenly there's a gust of wind which blows Amira's hair in front of her face, so instead of their lips locking, Kyle begins to choke on Amira's hair and he doubles over as he coughs.

Oh no!, Amira thought. *What if my hair gets in the way? What if Kyle tries to kiss me and my stupid hair gets in the way?* (Once again, Amira's rational thinking shines brightly.)
***

The Scarred Arm Silver Eyed Man found their tracks within 30 minutes. He wasn't sure what they were up to; it was possible that they were just going on a "fun walk," but he followed at a comfortable distance just to be sure. Even if they were going to the oasis, he doubted he'd be able to gain anything from it since it was unlikely he'd even be able to see it without...without certain items, but still he tracked. For, any additional information he could gain would be useful for the days to come.

***

"Come on Carlos, *pleaaaaaase,*" Meredith begged, clasping her hands in front of her.

"*Guys*, I do it for my grandmother."

"We know," Amira said. "We think it's sweet, and we want to support you."

"No, you guys want to know the date of the recital, so you can come and laugh at me."

"What if we promise not to laugh?" Karen said skipping merrily a few paces behind.

"I'm being real. You will laugh. You haven't seen the pants my grandmother made me. They're really *tight*."

Quickly all three girls began their teenage girl adolescent cackles (i.e. high-pitched laughter) that likely caused several lemmings to jump off a cliff somewhere in the world. Seriously, is there anything worse than 12-13 year-old girls laughing?

***

"So Amira, do you have any idea where this place is?" Carlos asked at the midpoint of hour number two and half way up a hill.

"Not exactly," Amira admitted. "I'm kinda hoping something stirs my memory."

"Well, can we stop to eat at least?" Carlos asked while plopping down on a rock and unlacing his shoes to set free a number of pebbles his shoes had accumulated.

"*Carlos*, Amira can't eat!" Karen said as Carlos opened up his backpack and pulled out a peanut butter and jelly sandwich.

"It's okay," Amira said. "I don't mind."

"Then can I have some Carlos?" Karen asked.

"Oh, I see. First I'm being rude, and now I'm supposed to share with you?"

"It's those twists of fate that make life worth living," Karen smiled while bumping him to move over, so they could share the rock.

Meredith stood a few feet away from them staring down the hill and humming.

"What are you humming?" Amira asked as Karen and Carlos laughed as they faux-fought over the sandwich.

"Barenaked Ladies. They're Canadian, you know," Meredith said while smiling at Amira. "Sometimes I find that if I've forgotten where something is or a fact that I should know for a quiz, I hum and it comes to me. Do you want to try?"

"I don't know any Barenaked Ladies songs," Amira said while putting her hands in her pockets and staring at an ant that was walking by in the dirt. Amira often felt uncomfortable when one of her friends mentioned some pop culture reference that she felt she *should* have known but often didn't."

"It doesn't have to be Barenaked Ladies Amira. We're looking for an Egyptian Oasis, right?"

Amira nodded.

"Well, then maybe you should hum some Egyptian song," Meredith said.

"Yeah, in *theory* I could do that, but most of the Egyptian songs I know sound less like singing and more like a shrieking war call that frightens most small animals. Not exactly something you can hum," Amira winked.

"We're gonna find it you know."

"How can you be so sure?" Amira asked.

"Sometimes you just know," Meredith shrugged. "Want to try humming?"

"Well, I do know one song that I could hum, but I don't really have a singing voice.

"I won't judge you Amira."

"I know," Amira said. She glanced at Meredith, smiled, took a deep breath, began to hum, "LA-de-nooo-"

BAM! A gunshot pierced the sky. Amira and Meredith gave each other a frightened, hurried look. Amira looked back to make sure Carlos and Karen were okay, but could really only see Carlos since he was lying on top of Karen covering/protecting her.

"You two okay?!" Amira whisper-screamed.

"Yhhh" Karen mumbled into Carlos' chest.

"Yeah," Carlos chimed in from atop Karen. "Where'd the shot come from?"

"From over the hill?" Meredith said while ducking down and slowly, stealthily making her way to the top of hill.

"Mer, wait! Maybe we shouldn't-" Amira pleaded before Meredith cut her off with a swing of her arm in an obvious "be quiet" movement.

"Crhos, I cmph brth" Karen mumbled.

"Oh, *sorry!*" Carlos said shifting so that Karen could breathe but still staying on top of her.

"Quiet guys," Amira hissed before turning to Meredith. "What's going on?" Amira asked Meredith who was crouch down at the top of the hill obviously staring intently at something.

With a deep sigh but without breaking her gaze Meredith said, "Trouble and stupidity. A bad combination."

"What are you talking about?" Amira asked when she reached the top of the hill, but Meredith didn't need to answer her question since the answer was obvious to her once Amira reached the top and crouched next to Meredith. Amira had little tolerance for ignorant, dim-witted kids. She had even less tolerance for ignorant, dim-witted kids with guns. Her heart sank when she looked down and saw the Jeffries twins, the human Rubik's cubes (minus the complexity) at the bottom of a small valley both carrying rifles with scopes and aiming them at various objects that neither Amira nor Meredith could make out.

"Great, the Tweedle Dumb twins have guns," Amira said as her fingernails dug into the dirt in disgust. "What are they doing out here?"

"Maybe they read about the wolves," Meredith began but then Amira gave her a side look, which communicated the fact that it seemed highly unlikely the Jeffries ever read anything. "Or more likely they heard about it. I think their dad is friend's with the sheriff, isn't he?"

"Yuck. Is it even legal for them to have guns?"

"It's Texas." Meredith shrugged. "In Canada they wouldn't be allowed to, but here? It's probably considered healthy."

"Should we try to sneak around them?" Amira wandered aloud.

"I wouldn't want them mistaking us from a distance and shooting at us."

"Right," Amira agreed.

"So I think we should wait. Hopefully, they'll get bored and go home ASAP."

"Yeah, maybe," Amira said while turning over to lie on her back and look up at the blue sky above. Amira then lifted up her upper body onto her elbows so she could look down at Karen and Carlos approaching. "What were you two fighting about?"

"Nothing" Carlos said through gritted teeth.

"We just won't be able to pretend for much longer that Carlos isn't a boy," Karen said.

"What do you mean? You pretend I'm *not* a boy?"

"Umm guys?" Meredith interjected.

"Nothing. Just that we're all growing up. Certain things begin to change, like you getting a bit excited down th-"

"Hey, I wasn't excited. I-"

"*Guys.* Amira, look," Meredith said pointing toward the horizon.

At first Amira scanned the openness (some would say the *emptiness*) and saw nothing, but then...

"Is that-" Meredith began.

"Moha" Amira finished as all the color drained from her face. She saw Moha running towards the MOP Squad's general direction, but Amira realized that also meant Moha was running toward the Rubik's Cube-headed delinquents carrying guns. Amira knew Moha was fast but was sure that he could not outrun a bullet. Amira's heart beat faster and faster as Moha ever so slowly (from her perspective) inched his way farther from the horizon and closer to Amira and her "enemies."

"Maybe they won't-" Meredith started before she and the rest of the MOP Squad saw one of the Jeffries' brothers grab the other by the shoulder and point in Moha's general direction. One of the twins put the scope to his eye for a second and then brought it back down just as quickly and shook his head up and down as they high-fived each other.

"Oh, wow," Carlos added not very helpfully.

"I've got to stop them," Amira said in a panicked voice. "I-, I, I" Amira said obviously preferring to highlight the fact she prefers speaking in the first person when horrified. Amira scanned the ground around her, circling and circling for something.

"Amira, what are you doing?" Karen asked concerned.

"I need to find a rock! Something I can throw at them!" Amira said desperately.

The non-Arab members of MOP stared at Amira for a few seconds as she scanned the ground.

"Are you going to throw a rock at them?" Carlos asked hesitantly.

"Do you have a better idea?" Amira asked.

"Yeah," he said as he stood at the top of the hill and started yelling toward the Jeffries' brothers. "Guys, wait! Don't shoot!"

The Jeffries turned their attention (and guns) toward the top of the hill as Carlos hit the deck. "Well, don't shoot me either! (now, to the MOP squad) Who points a gun at someone without looking first?" he said through gritted teeth. "These guys are morons."

"Who's up there?" Jeffries-1 asked.

"It's Carlos!" Carlos said waiving his arm above the ridge but keeping the rest of his body hidden.

"Well shut the hell up. We're hunting here," Jeffries-2 yelled back.

"Don't shoot at the bird! It's not wild, it's domestic!"

"If it's out here, it's fair game! 'Nuff said!"

While Carlos and the Jeffries were having a useless exchange, Amira finally found a rock worth throwing. It was a beautiful rock, a rock with substance and panache, a rock with-well, okay, really it was just a rock: uneven, dirty, and dark that was about twice the size of a golf ball. Moha was getting closer and closer; likely within seconds he'd be in range of the Jeffries' brothers' rifles.

"Are you seriously going to throw a rock at them," Karen asked sheepishly.

"I'll aim for their feet. I just need to distract them long enough to figure out a way to get Moha safely away from them."

"Amira haven't you heard the saying, never bring a rock to a gunfight?" Carlos asked.

"That's not the saying," Amira said.

As Amira stood at the top of the hill aiming her rock and hoping for a modern-day, Muslim version of an old Jewish story (not exactly a standard blueprint for success in Hollywood or in Texas by any means) about a boy named David, her fellow MOP Squadders slowly (but supportively) inched down (away) the other side of the hill, so that they could still see Moha if looking to their left but could no longer see the Jeffries twins on the other side of the hill. Amira instinctively knew that Moha would be in range any second, so she had to act quickly. She stood at the top of the hill, pulled her arm back while grasping the rock with her right hand, felt the flow of the adrenaline pulsing through her body, adjusted for the wind that blasted around her, squeezed the rock slightly harder as her eyes narrowed and then was struck in her lower back by the butt of the rifle of the youngest Jeffries brother, Brad. The strike sent her spinning uncontrollably down the hill, doing un-volunteered somersault after un-volunteered summersault, her hair looking like a black tidal wave that continuously crashed against the rocks every few feet at the crest of each interval. Amira tumbled and toppled down; turned and turned; tiny pebbles cutting up her forearms, knees and really any skin that happened to be exposed. She finally was able to partially turn out of her somersault-spin and roll length-wise which helped her use her arms and legs more as breaks to slow her tumble down. As she slowed, she began to scream, not out of pain, but of fear. "STOP!" she screamed over and over as she tumbled towards the Jeffries twins. "Please stop!" Finally her unasked for descent ended about 30 feet from the Jeffries twins with both Brandon and Brendan holding the scopes of their respective rifles to their eyes as they put Moha in their sights.

The twins ignored Amira, as Brandon (or maybe it was Brendan) yelled, "Ready. Aim, Fi-yaaaaa!"

And so they did. The snap/bang filled the valley, swarmed the hill and seemed to flood the entire area within the horizon. Amira's eyes quickly sped from the Jeffries to Moha who was still quite a distance off. However, Amira, the rest of the MOP squad, and the Jeffries clan could all clearly see Moha collapse and fall to his side almost instantly after the gunshots.

***

Gunshots, thought the Silver-Eyed Man. As far as he knew he was the only operative out here, and no one would dare hurt her, not *yet* anyway. They still needed her. But there was always the possibility another "entity" could be after her. There were always rumblings, unsubstantiated rumors. *Well, if she dies, there are other ways*, he told himself. He continued forward on a higher alert level.

***

Amira wanted to scream, but this time no sound sprang forth from her throat. The best she could do was mouth the word, "No," once and then twice, and then three times. It's hard to tell how long this repetition would have continued, for it was interrupted by the Jeffries boys sprinting towards their kill. Her face blank, Amira stood up and as if on autopilot and sprinted towards the downed animal, determined to get there before them. Amira didn't know what spurred her on; she was pretty sure she had no healing type of powers and was sure that she could do the nothing to the bullet holes that had blasted through her new found avian friend. Tears formed quickly, blurring her vision as she sprinted toward the animal.   The Jeffries twins while laughing, likely deciding where they would mount the bird's head.   Thirty feet behind Amira, the MOP Squad and Brad Jeffries ran toward the downed bird as well, yelling (the Mop Squad in concern, Brad in derision) out Amira's name. However, the world was silent to Amira. Her footsteps left no sound in her mind, and with each step, more and more of her numbed. She no longer could smell anything, or feel anything; it was as if her body was shutting down, like grief had taken on the form of a gel-filled bubble, which prevented her from experiencing the world around her. Without realizing it, Amira quickly past the Jeffries twins who were a bit surprised that they were being outrun by a girl.

When she reached the chick-filet (what? Too soon?), Amira dropped to her knees, threw her arms around the bird's neck, and buried her face into the soft, silky feathers.

"Woo-weeee" Brendan yelled, panting heavily with his hands on his quadriceps, exhausted from his own sprint. After all, it takes a lot of energy carrying around a rock hard, heavy square noggin'.

"That was awesome!" Brendan continued.

"Yeah, I can't believe I nailed it in one shot," Brandon said mimicking his brother's breathing pattern.

"*You* shot it? No way, I totally nailed that thing."

"What? That's *bull*!"

Amira's tiny fists clenched slightly over a handful of feathers as she took a deep breath to collect herself before attacking the two yahoos arguing about who murdered her friend. Amira didn't care what her mother would think or the authorities; she was going to hurt them. Amira didn't care that the dim-watted (yes watted, not witted, as their "light bulbs" only glow *dim*) males behind her were armed and obviously dangerous. Regardless of what the world would think, regardless of the consequences, regardless of the fact that Moha's chest was moving up and down ever so slightly, regardless of the potential for jail, regardless- wait, go back: what was that about Moha's chest moving? Amira's eyes widened. She slowly turned her gaze to Moha's eyes, which happened to be meeting her gaze. Then, Moha winked and closed his eyes.

"Hey Lame-a-nee, what's the name of your stupid bird? We want to make sure we spell it correctly on the plaque we're going to place under the mounting," Brandon laughed.

"Yeah, Amira, where do you think we should put your friend here? The garage or bathroom?" Brendan laughed.

Amira had a sneer on her face, hidden from the Jeffries by the fact that she was turned away from them. Amira's eyes narrowed. Her sneer twisted and contorted into a half-puckered, skewed-to-the-right look as she calmly got up from her knees. Amira wiped her eyes with the back of her hands and turned toward the buffoon aggressors.

"I think you should leave," she said with her hands on her hips.

"Ooooh, the little girl *thinks*. Wow, Amira I'm so scared air-head Amira told me to do something," Brendan said while resting his rifle on his shoulder as his younger brother Brad arrived on the scene, so he could high five his brother Brandon.

Wiping the tears from her eyes, Amira with a look of anger on her face slowly circled around the twins+1 placing them between her and the ostrich. The Mop Squad then arrived by her side with a chorus of "Amira! Are you okay? Amira!" but with a quick raise of her hand toward the sky, Amira silenced her friends while keeping her stare locked on the Brothers Dim the entire time, not even bothering to blink.

"I am giving you one last chance to leave or-"

"OR *WHAT!*" Brendan asked mockingly. "What are *you* going to do?"

Good question one would think. However, the better question for Brendan to ask at that moment likely would have been, "What is the giant bird that just silently stood up behind me going to do?" Though, if he had the knowledge to ask that question, his life in general probably would have been much richer.

The Mop Squad's eyes widened in awe, but the Jeffries just assumed that they were showing their fright toward the Jeffries clan.

Brandon chimed in, "Yeah, Dumb-mani, what are you gonna do, sick some camels on us? Are you gonna-" Hmm, as brilliantly insightful and culturally enlightened as Brandon's query was going to be, he unfortunately did not get to finish because by the time he reached the word "camels" Moha had stood fully upright, his wings stretched as wide as possible, his neck stretched as high as possible, and his beak open as wide as possible and then let out a sound that seemed part squawk, part bark: a "*squark*" if you will.

"SQUARRRRRRRRRRRRK" screeched Moha. He then snapped his beak downward with lightning speed, snatching Brandon's gun before any of the Jeffries could react. The "squark" caused all the Jeffries to flinch/cower, and in those brief moments of shock and fear, Amira was upon them. She grabbed Brendan's gun away from him, did a 360 degree turn and swung the gun down behind Brendan's legs sweeping him off his feet, causing him and his cubed head to hit the ground with a loud thud. Amira then elbowed Brad in the ear, which caused him to drop his gun, allowing Amira then to deftly pick it up as well.

"RUN!" she screamed at the Jeffries, which I guess was her way of mildly suggesting that they leave their current longitudinal location as quickly as possible. Inspired by some mixture of Amira's words and the bird's resurrection, the Jeffries brothers followed Amira's "request" and ran as far away as quickly as possible.

"Holy sh-(beeeeeeeeeeeeep)" Carlos stated with a lack of eloquence. "Amira, you *kicked* a-(beeeeeeeeeeeeep). Wow. I mean. Like, holy-"

"I think what Carlos is trying to say," Meredith said while glancing to her side to give Carlos a "look," "is: are you and Moha all right?"

Amira delicately placed the guns on the ground. "I'm fine," she said. "I think Moha is too. Are you?" she asked the bird (yes, she asked the bird). Amira walked over to Moha to examine him. Moha first balked at Amira's attempt, but he quickly calmed down as Amira gently placed her hand on his neck as she slowly examined him. She first checked his right side and then his left side. She was about to turn back to her friends to say that she didn't see anything when she noticed a streak of featherless skin. One bullet had obviously missed Moha by a matter of millimeters (yes, I too am culturally sensitive since all Egyptians use the metric system rather than the English system because they're all communists).

"Oh my god. One of the bullets *just* missed him. LOOK!" Amira said pointing to the streak as the MOP squad gathered around.

"Wow," Karen said while putting her hand on the newly bare bird skin. "That's amazing. Do you think he *knew* to dodge the bullet?"

"I have no idea. Does it matter?" Amira asked. (I don't think so, but then again, I'm not the one who chose to be buddy-buddy with a bird. I prefer more sophisticated conversations with you know: *words* in them that are spoken by things like *people*, but I guess that's just the elitist in me.)

"Do you think we should head home?" Meredith asked sheepishly.

Amira shook her head no and said, "Maybe Moha can lead us to the oasis that I told you about."

"I don't know Amira. Maybe the Jeffries were a sign that we shouldn't go on," Karen said.

"What should we do about the guns?" Carlos asked.

"I don't really want to carry them around. We should dispose of them. Carlos can you take out the bullets?"

"Yeah. Sure, let me just put my Rifle Camp training to use," he said while rolling his eyes.

"No need to be snotty about it. Meredith?" Karen asked.

"Yeah, we don't even lock our doors in Canada. And learning to shoot was never high on my priority list when we moved here."

"Gosh, Mop Squad, can't we at least be a bit more stereotypical Texans? I think that might help our cactus cred," Karen said shaking her head.

Amira closed her eyes and silently sighed to herself. She already felt different enough, even from her MOP squad friends that she hoped to never have to say the following sentence, "I know how to unload the guns."

"You know how to shoot?" Carlos said not hiding his surprise.

"Yeah, I have relatives in the military. My great uncle took me out to a range in Egypt a couple of years ago." And so Amira unloaded the rifles and said, "Let's carry them a bit, maybe there's a river we can dump them into. I don't really want to explain why we're coming home with three rifles to my mother." (Oooh, dumping weapons into a river? How metropolitan of you Amira.)

"So Moha, which way do we go?" Amira asked with a big smile on her face and her hands held up high in a display of excitement I'm guessing, the kind of childish, girlish display of excitement that screams, *Yay, I'm naïve and immature and secretly still believe the Lochness Monster is a distinct possibility, hooray! I do cartwheels when I'm nervous and believe that [enter teenage heartthrob's name here] will marry me eventually when we run into each other at the airport as I'm on my way to spend a year studying 16th Century art in Paris where I'll get to hang out in cafes and speak fluent French and study ballet but impress the class with my unique hip-hop skills that I picked up solely from watching music videos on MTV and blah blah blah...* hmm, that was a lot of detail, but anyway, back to the story.

Moha just stared at Amira.

"Maybe you need a password," Carlos offered while taking duct tape out of his bag, so he could tape the rifles together.

"A password? Really Carlos?" Karen said while kneeling down to retie her shoes.

"Do you have a better idea," he said while giving her the old stink-eye.

"Noooo, but I know that when I don't have an idea to keep quiet."

"When have you *ever* kept quiet? You have a mouth like a 7-11: it's always open."

Meredith not wanting to hear them bicker thought that maybe the password wasn't a bad idea, but rather than saying a password, she thought maybe singing would inspire the ostrich, so she sang the only bird song she knew, a song that was popular in Canada, but hadn't made its way to the United States just yet. She straightened her back, put her hand on her stomach, looked at Moha, hummed for a second to find her key and sang, "*I'm like a bird, I only fly away-ay. I don't know where my soul is. I don't know where my home is. All I need you to know is. Your faith brings me to tea-ear-ee-ers. And it pains me to tell. That you don't know me so we-ll-el-el. And though my love is rare. Though my love is true...*"

Amira, Carlos, and Karen watched silently. It wasn't the first time that Meredith just burst out in song in front of them, but it was the first time Meredith sang in such a heartfelt manner to a bird, a bird who just kept turning it's head from leaning to the right to leaning to the left, as if it thought it could understand what was going on if it looked from a slightly different angle, but every angle failed to offer forth the needed information.

"*Ohhhhh, I'M LIKE A BIR-HERD! I only fly away-ay. I don't know where my-*"

And suddenly Moha took off in a northwesterly direction.

"Yes! What do you think *aboot* that? Who's drinking Tim Horton's coffee now, huh?" Meredith said, attempting to talk smack in her own Canadian way.

"I can't believe-" Carlos began.

"That worked," Karen finished.

"My voice inspires. What can I say?" Meredith winked. Well, dear deader I know *I can* say that there's a fine line between inspiration and desperation, as in a desperate attempt by a bird to escape, like say escaping from the voice of a twelve year-old Canadian girl, but let's let her live in ignorance and give her this victory because well, Canadians deserve that every once in awhile.

Moha didn't run so fast that they couldn't keep up, but rather he kept a distance of about forty yards ahead of the Mop squad, likely so that he wouldn't have to "chat" with the tweeners, especially that crooning Canadian. Also, Canadians and ostriches have had a long history of mutual distrust and angst. What? You don't believe me dear reader? Don't say I didn't warn you next time you find yourself in a fistfight in Peterborough, Ontario due to the ostrich tat on your arm.

The Mop Squad had a newly discovered excitement and hop in their step, most likely from the leftover adrenaline in their system due to the gunshots, though I'm willing to accept the possibility of cocaine. I mean the Mop Squad has always seemed a bit crafty to me, what with their ability to pull off pastels and all. Note, the previous sentence of course excludes the Canadian among the group; Meredith is pretty and would become a beautiful woman, but Earthy tones definitely suited her best.

Anyway after another hour, after three failed attempts by Carlos to ignite a conversation centered around soccer, after two acoustic/acapella renditions of Barenaked Ladies songs, after six near fall-on-your-face trips by Amira, after multiple arm bruises left on Carlos by Karen objecting to something he said, Moha broke from the pack and took off up a hill and disappeared over the top. Then, the four lemmings (Mop Squad) took off after him.

Halfway up the hill, Carlos belted out between breaths, "Amira? How much (pant) longer are we gonna follow this (pant) bird? You realize he's a bird right? (pant) Are we sure he has a decent sense of direction? Is that a survival skill an ostrich needs?" he finished while resting his arms on top of his head and trying to breathe deeply to calm his heart rate.

"I don't know Carlos. I think we just need to trust him."

"Sure because when have birds ever led us astray?"

"*Exactly*," Amira smiled, obviously oblivious to the sarcasm that dripped from his statement.

Though this anti-conversation could have continued for a long time, the topic became moot when they reached the top of the hill and saw the valley of "Egypt" sprawled below them.

"What the-" Carlos began to say, but lush green valley below him interrupted his thought process.

The non-Egyptians looked with wonder at the scene in front of their eyes. Meredith, Karen, and Carlos all staggered a few steps down the hill.

"This doesn't seem possible, eh? I want to *doot* my own eyes, but I can't," Meredith said, her Canadian accent becoming more pronounced as the sentence went on, as if her brain wasn't sure where her body was located in the world presently and thus resorted to the default setting.

"I smell...*life!*" Karen exclaimed as she realized the land before her was not barren like then land behind her.

"Did we just enter a Miracle-Gro commercial?" Carlos asked.

"Nope. This is Egypt, Carlos...well, this is *like* Egypt...but in Texas," Amira replied.

"And you've been here before?" Carlos asked.

"Definitely."

"And you're not confusing your memories...like maybe you were brought here as a child but you just mistakenly remember it as being in Egypt?"

"Believe it or not, I know when I'm in Egypt and when I'm in Texas.

"Wow, Amira. I'm sorry," Carlos said neutrally as he bent down to feel the deep green grass around him.

Smiling broadly as she looked down on a field, a field from her younger years, and a field that was absolutely in her present as well, in a valley that belonged a third of the way across the world, she asked, "For what?"

"I *still* thought you were going crazy and that this place was a figment of your imagination. I was sure you were delusional."

"Thanks," Amira said narrowing her eyes and trying to send him angry "vision daggers" through her periphery.

"I can't believe I lost twenty dollars to Meredith for this."

"Yup," Meredith said standing next to Carlos.

"Wait, you two *bet* on my *sanity?!*"

"Hey," Meredith said defensively with a look of hurt on her face, "I bet you *were* sane. That took a lot of faith considering the circumstances."

"She has a point Amira," Karen said wrapping her arm around Amira's waist.

"Thanks guys. Way to humor your friend with this trip," Amira said, her spirit slightly dampened by her knowledge of what her friends had still thought of her up to this moment.

"Hmm," Carlos said. "Do you hear that?"

"Hear what?" Amira said, suddenly alert.

Smiling coyly Meredith said, "Yeah, I think I *do* hear it Carlos. Karen?"

Karen looked up for a second and said, "it's like a mixture of honey and a buffalo stampede."

"Oh, guys," Amira said slowly backing away.

"Too late Amira," Meredith said shrugging your shoulders. "It's a HUG-ALANCHE!" she yelled as the three "forced hugged" Amira causing all to fall to the ground.

"Haven't Arabs been persecuted enough in this country? I thought we agreed that we out*grew* this stupid game," she said while stuck in a friend-created cocoon, struggling underneath their weight.

"Hug-alanche only speaks forgiveness-ese Amira," Carlos said.

"Never!" Amira said. "You can take my freedom, but you can't force me to forgive." A pause, then, "Fine. Fine. I forgive you all for thinking I was crazy."

"*Mean* it," Karen laughed.

"I mean it! Guys I can't breathe!" Amira said through exasperated laughter.

Meanwhile, Moha could only look on and shake his head, obviously quite disturbed that the fate of the world likely was in the hands of a girl who was "busy" dealing with a hug-alanche. Now on principle, Moha was against all stereotypes and despised perpetuating falsehoods, but seeing the "Princess" wrestling on the ground with her friends, completely oblivious to the stakes at hand, if the opportunity had arisen, Moha would have gladly foregone all of his beliefs and buried his head deep into the sand.

***

The tracks began to blur as if the wind had picked up solely in the path before him. He had seen this happen before, but he continued undeterred. The Scarred-Arm Man knew that neither victory nor defeat would occur today, but any information he could gather would help him. *Patience* had been ingrained in him. After years of pursuing of searching, he could feel his goal approaching, perhaps not as quickly as he would have liked, but approaching nonetheless.

***

After Amira dug herself out of the hug-alanche, the Mop squad moseyed on down the hill to check out this hidden valley (sans ranch).

"This seems out of place," said Karen.

"You think?" Carlos said derisively.

"Like when Carlos tries to act like a man," she continued seamlessly.

"It is out of place," Amira said as she re-examined the lily flower and other valley objects now in the light of day. Amira bent down to the flower again and stared into its white lily-ness. "I used to go here every summer at least once."

Meredith sat down cross-legged next to Amira and asked, "I thought you said you were only here once before, after you were attacked by the wolves."

"That's true too. I know this is crazy-"

"I think you've earned the right not to say that Amira," Carlos said leaning his knees gently on Meredith's back.

"This place exists in Egypt, like *exactly* in Egypt," Amira said still staring at the flower.

"What do you mean?" Meredith asked.

Amira took a breath, moved from kneeling to sitting on her tush and looked at Meredith and Carlos. "I mean the number of trees and flowers, the location of each tree and flower, the color of the grass, and even the valley part of it: it *all* exists in Egypt too, like looks exactly like this place. I used to go here...*there* with my cousin and grandmother. We'd always-"

"Amira, what's this?" Karen yelled across the valley.

Obviously enthralled with Amira's story, Meredith and Carlos sprang up like their lives depended on it and ran over to Karen as Amira finished the memory in her own head. She and her cousin, Aini, would play a game where one would have to close her eyes and skip while the other directed the sightless cousin to prevent her from running into a tree or bush, but part of the fun to them was failing or thinking they were failing, so there would be countless giggles and screams as the girls played. Their grandmother would often shake her head but smile watching them. Their grandmother then would spread out a blanket under a certain tree and-

"Amira, come on!" yelled Karen

Underneath a bush almost completely covered in leaves and twigs was a slab of rock embedded into the earth. The surface was in parts pinkish, other parts bluish and shimmered as if some nineteen year-old club girl with too much body glitter had been grinding on top of it all night. However, as interesting and pretty as the rock surface was, what was etched, painted, and carved on it was even more fascinating. Hieroglyphics, Chinese characters, Sanskrit, Latin and Greek letters all adorned the surface.

"That's so strange," Karen said.

"It's like someone vomited culture onto the rock," Carlos astutely put it.

"Was this in Egypt too, Amira?...Amira?" Meredith asked.

The world started to spin for Amira, not in the "I'm six and spinning is so much fun to do in the summertime" kind of way but rather in the "the world is spinning, I can't stop it, and I think I might be ill" kind of way. Amira was about to lose her balance completely and fall on her face, but Meredith caught her before she did and steadied Amira.

"What is it?" Meredith whispered to Amira while propping Amira up by her elbow. "Have you seen this before too?"

Amira just nodded her head first, like she was trying to reenact a conversation with Kyle, but then mustered the words, "Yeah, but not in Egypt. I think it's on a cloth that's been in my

family for a long time. I don't know why I feel so dizzy though. I feel so light," she said while looking at Meredith, as if asking Mer to confirm that she was in fact "light."

"You have *that* on a family heirloom," Karen asked quizzically.

"Yeah," she replied, shaking herself free from Meredith after convincing Meredith and herself that she could stand on her own.

"That's…weird," Karen said.

"Is it?" Carlos said while walking around the stone, hoping that a different angle would offer up an understanding of the current events. "I mean after Amira was attacked by *wolves*, after she was saved by an *ostrich* (Moha sniffed or maybe huffed loudly as Carlos pointed at him), after a valley that exists in Egypt, can we really say that this stone combined with Amira's family heirloom is *weird*? Maybe this is just normal for Amira," he decided while throwing his arms up to the heavens.

"I can't tell if that was an insult or not," Amira said.

"*Babe*," Carlos began (every once in awhile he tried out his "suave" persona…the attempts were all failures) "I mean I love you, but you have to admit: you're weird."

"Like you should talk!" Karen said pushing him.

"Well, obviously I'm weird too since I'm friends with the girl, but maybe I'm not *as weird* as Amira. That's all I'm saying."

"Believe me. You're plenty weird," Karen said.

"Guys, come on!" Meredith started. "We're the Mop Squad. We don't turn on each other. We're ALL weird, equally. Sad, but true. Granted, we have moments where one of us is stranger than the others, but that's fleeting. We're weird, and I love that about us. That's right, I. Love. Us."

Amira, Karen, and Carlos simultaneously rolled their respective eyes and turned and walked away from the rock.

"What?! It's *true*," Meredith said standing pat, but smiling.

"No I was wrong," said Carlos. "*You* Meredith are the strange one."

"Yeah definitely Meredith," Amira nodded.

"Totally," Karen said.

Meredith skipped joyfully up and wrapped her arm through Carlos' arm. "Well, fine. If that's what you need to think in order to sleep at night, I'll accept that. I'm *that* good of a friend."

"*God*, Meredith, are there just forests and forests of Maple trees in Canada? Because you are *SAPPY!*" Carlos said.

"That joke was sappy," Meredith replied.

"Your mother's sappy," Carlos retorted.

"Let's head back to my house," Amira said. I need to digest this over pizza and cookie dough, and it will probably be dark by the time we're back."

"Mmm, yummy in my tummy!" Carlos glowed.

As they followed Moha out of the valley and back into the desert, Amira realized that in all the "happenings" of today, she hadn't thought of Kyle once in hours. Not once did she think of his gorgeous jaw line, not once did she imagine putting her fingers through his hair, not once did she imagine what it might be like to kiss him, to touch his soft kissable lips, not once did she dream about what it would feel like to hold his hand while walking down the hallway in school, not once did she- (oh my god Amira! Stop, you're killing me! *Me*, your loyal narrator, the teller of your tale, and you're injuring me. If I've said it once, I've said it a thousand times: there's nothing worse in life than being able to peer into the mind of a pre-teen girl. *Nothing*.)

***

As they blindly followed Moha, for some reason convinced, he would lead them home, Amira saw what looked like a tiny stream off in the distance.

"Cool, guys let's dump the guns over there!" she said.

"Are these guns valuable," asked Carlos while staring at the guns that were hanging out of Karen's backpack.

"I never actually bothered to look," Amira said as she grabbed one of the unloaded guns. She double-checked the rifle to make sure it was empty and then pumped it and quickly wheeled around and aimed at some imaginary target in the distance as she peered through the scope and concentrated on the weight distribution of the rifle.

"Umm, these definitely weren't cheap, so I bet they get in trouble for losing them she smiled satisfactorily. "But, really who cares?" We need to dump them.

***

The man with scarred arm had slowly, methodically been catching up to the Mop Squad, but for much of it, he had been too far behind for them to be within his view, even with his binoculars. But, now finally, he had them in his sight, he had them right where he- *What the hell?!* he thought as Amira whipped around with a rifle pointed eerily in his direction. He dived behind the hill. He had not been expecting Amira to be armed. This he found *peculiar*. He smiled; if she put up a fight, he might prefer that. Injuring a helpless girl always seemed a bit unseemly to him, but if the girl wanted to fight back when the time came, then putting her down might be more satisfying. He stealthily glanced over the hill to make sure he wasn't "made." The man with the long, jagged scar on his left arm saw the Mop Squad again on the move, heading in the direction of Amira's home.

***

After the MOP Squad had found a few medium size (10 pound) rocks along the stream's edge to tape to the guns, and after they threw the weapons into the middle of the river, they continued home, discussing important issues in a tweeners' life like what toppings they should get on their pizzas. From what I could gather when I wasn't busy considering the various methods of suicide, it seemed that Amira and Carlos were pineapple fans whereas Karen and Meredith seemed to prefer a more carnivorous set of toppings. Again, what's the fate of the world matter when you have such a fractured and diverse set of pizza topping opinions? Oh, the horrors.

***

The Mop Squad arrived back at Amira's house a few minutes before the sun completely set over the horizon. Amira's mother greeted them at the door.

"Where have you all been today," she asked smiling and giving each child a hug.

"We were exploring *all* day Ms. Talib," Carlos said, "and we're *starving*."

"Carlos! We're guests here. Act like one," Karen admonished.

"Part of being a guest is being honest. Right Ms. T?" Carlos winked.

139

"Yes child. What would everyone like for dinner?"
***

The television with the aid of a VCR blared images and music from some teen oriented romantic comedy. Carlos and Karen sprawled on the carpeted floor with their heads pointed towards the television and partially empty bowls of chocolate chip ice cream in front of them. Meredith sat on the couch with Hashim holding a Nerf football on her lap. Amira sat below them resting her back on the bottom part of the couch staring at the TV, but really staring *beyond* the TV trying to make sense of the day, but coming up with nothing. She'd have to ask her mother about the cloth, but she was too tired to do so tonight. She knew her mother would be busy prepping for her classes tomorrow, so Amira decided she'd ask her mother after swim tryouts were over on Monday. *Swim Tryouts!* she thought. Now, she wished she hadn't spent so much time and energy walking around today. She decided she better just relax on Sunday, so that she would kick Amber's butt on Monday. Although there were plenty of crazy things going on in Amira's life, the idea of diving into a pool and exerting her body to its physical limits calmed her. At least one thing made sense to her, and sometimes that's enough.
***

Amira, and Hashim in tow, entered the pool area about thirty minutes before she was due to be there.

"Why do I have to be here?" Hashim asked annoyed.

"Because Mom's at school, and she wanted me to take you with me."

"Oh yeah. Can I play with Transformers or do I have to read?" he asked.

"Whatever you want. Just go sit in the stands and not bother anyone, okay?" she said pointing to the stands to her left.

"I won't. I'm not *four* you know."

"I know," Amira smiled.

Walking up a couple of the bleachers, Hashim turned and asked, "Amira are you going to win?"

"Hmm," Amira said tapping her forefinger to her cheek. "Do you want me to?"

"Yeah! You're my sister!" he said holding his hands above his head.

"Fine, then I will," she winked. "Now, go play okay?"

"Don't have-ta ask me twice," he said stumbling up two more bleachers as Amira continued on her way.

The boys' team coach, Mr. Johnson, decided to follow Maria Olave's lead and hold tryouts as well. By the time Amira had entered the room, Kyle had already won three races and was about to begin his fourth. As he stood on the podium, their eyes met and Kyle smiled and waved quickly before turning his attention back to the race. Amira's heart began its own race as it quickened its beating almost instantly. Her smile was wide and so light that it could have carried her entire body to the ceiling. She raised her hand to waive back, but as she did so she stepped into a donut shaped, red lifesaver that was at the bottom of a huge netted bag that contained various buoys, paddle boards and other devices all swim teams use. Still distracted by Kyle she was already halfway through her second step before she realized what she doing. She quickly tripped and became entirely tangled up in the netting, twisting around for good measure leaving her in a fishnet type cocoon. *Fudge*, Amira thought to herself, but thankfully Kyle had not seen her recent suave move since his focus, and in fact everyone's focus in the gym, was on the race. It took Amira a couple of minutes to detangle, but she did so in a decent amount of time and thankfully with little fanfare.

The smell of chlorine never felt "normal" to Amira. It smelled so clean, so pure, so evilly *toxic*. Amira could imagine all the germs and organisms it could kill and it always unsettled her that she was then expected to swim in bacterial cemetery. Letting go of the thought, Amira opened her swim bag and took out her swim cap.

"Amira?" Amber said sweetly.

Amira felt like closing her eyes and taking a deep breath but didn't want to give Amber the satisfaction. Amira wished she could easily finish fitting her hair under her swim cap to show Amber and all around how graceful she was, but she was honest with herself and knew that it was about a 37-step process that took at least 10 minutes. So with several ringlets fighting for air and succeeding at various points around her, Amira accepted that she must respond to Amber's calling in her disheveled state and said, "What?"

Amber smiled derisively, yet beautifully. Her hair perfectly fell around her shoulders as if the strands were excited that they could bond with her flawless skin. Amber stood as if she were on the catwalk and ready to turn 180 degrees and walk back down the stage, so she could change into some equally fascinating designer gear. Her head was slightly atilt, her arm bent and resting confidently on her hip, with one leg straight and the other angled at about 15 degrees. Amber took her time with this moment, knowing, *knowing* how pretty she looked and how, ummm, how should I put this gently: how *unkempt, unruly,* and potentially insane Amira looked at the moment. Yes, I think that description captured the moment correctly, delicately, and with much needed sensitivity.

Amber flashed her perfect smile so that everyone not within three feet would think that Amber was just wishing Amira good luck, and through her teeth said, "When I crush you during today's race, I hope you'll realize that we don't *need* you, a freak, on the team and maybe you'll do the right thing and go swim back into whatever hole you and your family came from and maybe move back to that country, saving us from getting whatever freaky shots we'll need to counteract any foreign diseases run through your body." And then more loudly, "Good luck!" as she turned on a dime and walked down the "catwalk" away from Amira with her hips swaying in a way that should only be done by a female who could at least vote in the general election for a candidate of her choosing.

Amira wished she had some witty retort ready for this moment, but she did not. Rather, she chose a more straightforward and silent route and just raised her hand up, palm turned toward her own face and dropped four fingers, choosing to drop four that would lead many to believe that perhaps she was *not* a lady.

"I hope that you're solely trying to stretch out each finger individually Ms. Masri, and it was just my misfortune to have caught you at this singular moment," the definitive adult female voice said from behind Amira. Again, Amira wished she had already finishing stuffing her hair under her cap as she turned to face Coach Maria Olave who had both a whistle and stopwatch hanging from a "rope" around her neck. Ms. Olave wore a white, collared short sleeve shirt and khaki form fitting shorts, as if she had just finished filming a commercial for some San Fran clothing line like The Gap or maybe some newly created line like, "Prep Preferred, Putting the Pep back in Prep since 1964." Amira imagined what the commercial would look like in her head, probably with tons of males running into each other and other inanimate objects due to being too busy watching Maria walk down the street. In truth, Amira created a pretty cool commercial (I'd buy the product), but unfortunately in doing so, she forgot to respond to Ms. Olave's statement/question and thus just stood there looking less than sane with her hair-spouting-randomness and distant-look-in-her-eyes aura.

After about fifteen seconds of silence, Coach Olave realized that Amira had no response coming and so continued, "I understand that competition can sometimes lead to anger and behavior slightly more vulgar than is accepted, but try to funnel that anger into your performance, okay?"

Amira stared blankly for a few more seconds as the commercial ended, and then realizing that her hand was still frozen in place with one finger sticking up prominently, she turned off the television in her mind and dropped her hand, and said, "Oh right. Sorry. Yeah, of course. Right."

Maria Olave smiled, put her hand on Amira's shoulder, and whispered, "That's okay, I once ordered twelve different wakeup calls spread throughout the night to my biggest rival's hotel room the night before a race, so who am I to judge? Good luck Amira. I'm sure you'll make me proud." She then winked and walked away, leaving Amira alone to deal with her hair and what seemed like an ever-shrinking swim cap.

As Amira continued fitting her hair improbably under the cap, the MOP Squad approached from behind her.

"You ready to kick Amber's butt?" asked Karen.

"Nothing would make me smile more," Amira replied as she stretched her left arm across her chest and then her right arm so as to stretch out her triceps muscles. "I'm glad you're here, but you guys didn't have to come."

"Eh, it's small town Texas, not exactly like we have tons of options, anyway," said Carlos truthfully.

"Well, thanks again."

"You're going to win, Amira," Meredith said giving her a hug, so it's all good."

As the Mop squad took their seats next to Hashim who was all too happy to have company, Amira realized it was time to prepare for the race. She would need every instant to prep for this. Yes, not a moment to spare before the race. Yes sir ree, not one second to spend on anything but the race. Amira cherished these moments, and guarded them, protected them from- OH WAIT, here comes Kyle!

"Hey," Kyle said.

"Hey," Amira said while trying to imitate Amber's model stance so as to look as sultry as possible.

"Do you have a leg cramp?" He asked raising an eyebrow.

"What? No. Why?" she asked.

"You keep stretching out your leg over and over like you have a calf cramp."

It seemed Amira's imitation needed some work. Kyle was right. Amira kept stretching out her right leg hoping to recreate that perfect 15 degree angle Amber used when standing, but Amira kept "missing" the mark and thus created a 60 degree angle then 5 degree angle and then bounced up to 40 degrees and back to 5, etc.

"Oh! Yeah, that cramp! I forgot to eat enough potassium today."

"Oh," Kyle said nodding his head in understanding. "I've got a banana in my bag would you like some."

"Oh, no thank you," she said shaking her a head a bit too aggressively.

"You're cramping though. You should have some banana. It works great," he said opening up his bag to pull out the banana.

"No! I mean thank you, but I can't," she said, her mood dropping exponentially because she'd have to point out that she's "different" (a.k.a. "a freak") to this Adonis in front of her. "I'm fasting," she said quietly.

"Really? Oh. Why?"

"Umm, God?" she said.

"Okay. Umm, so are you going to the dance this Friday?" he asked.

"Umm, there's a dance?"

"Yeah, I'll probably go," Kyle replied.

Amira still trying to play it cool said, "Yeah, that's cool. Sounds like fun."

"So you're going to go?" Kyle asked while sporting a confused expression.

"Yeah, I mean whatever. Yeah." (Are we *sure* Amira's fluent in English?)

"Awesome, so maybe I'll see you there. Well, good luck in the race!" he said throwing his bag back over his shoulder as he walked by Amira.

"Thanks," she said meekly.

Leaning in toward her, he whispered, "Don't tell anyone, but Amber's been acting like a huge brat the past couple of days because I think she's worried about losing to you." He winked, smiled and then walked past her, and with just that statement, Amira's mood suddenly improved immensely. *Kyle is soooooo amazing. He always knows EXACTLY what to say,* Amira thought to herself. Really Amira? Really? What are you basing that statement on? I'm rolling my eyes, dear reader.

***

Amira stood on the block that seemed to float a few feet above her lane of water. She pulled down her goggles and scrunched her nose as the unpleasant and uncomfortable goggles suctioned around her eyes. Once her goggles were on, her view of the world turned myopic both literally and figuratively. Suddenly, the universe became much smaller, her breathing much bigger. She felt her abdominal muscles expand and contract with each cycle of breath. She then proceeded to do a maintenance check. She began with her toes, flexing them up and down. Then, she concentrated on her calves and then quads and hamstrings, and then hip-flexors and lower back muscles. Whenever she felt a constriction, she would breathe "into" the area and soon enough her muscle tissue would listen to her and release any tightness. She then bent over and placed her palms on the platform with her legs straight. After, she placed her hands behind her legs and pulled bringing her head to her knees. She then crouched down and popped up quickly beginning to waive her arms around, imagining her arms drawing arcs along the horizon in all directions, imagining her arms stretched up touching the sky. With a quick whistle, Coach Olave, commanded Amira and the rest of the swimmers to take their place. Amira crouched down in preparation for the 200-meter race. Be it a twist of fate, a statistical anomaly, or the dullness of Plaintown's community (I choose to think the latter...or is it latter-ist?), the 200-meter freestyle was the premier event due to a series of girls going on to win state championships in that event. It was even more personal to Amira because it was the event her father swam in the Olympics for Egypt many years ago. The photos from the Opening Ceremonies of the Moscow Olympics always fascinated her. She could stare at them for hours: the photos of her father walking with the other Olympic competitors from Egypt, his now dated track suit, what it must have been like.

Amira couldn't spend much time thinking about her father though since the race was about to begin. Amira's mind emptied as her focus narrowed its scope to two things: the silence she created around her and the impending instant when the sound of the whistle would flood her mind. This brief solitude, the few moments before a race, were always the most peaceful Amira would feel. Not boys, bratty girls, mean teachers, pesky brothers, nor ostriches could penetrate her thoughts during these pre-race moments.

Then the moment arrived, the whistle pierced the air and suddenly all of Amira's senses exploded as she surged into the water. She heard the splash of her and her competitors, tasted the chlorinated water, felt the coolness of the water, and watched tiles pop in and out of her vision with the stroke of each arm. Amira approached the far pool end one second faster than she had ever done before (though she did not know it at the time), but coming out of the turn, that certain swimmer who had been swimming immediately to her left and after the turn, now to her right, was still half a length ahead of her. Amira could "sense" that the swimmer was Amber. A new source of energy seemed to grow in Amira's core and her strokes became even faster, but try as she might the second 50 meters (the length of the pool) went the same as the first 50 meters with Amber in the lead, but as Amira made her second turn, something else, something deep within her rushed to the surface, more of a "force" than an "energy" that propelled Amira forward. With each stroke, Amira moved slightly closer to, then past Amber. One hundred twenty-five meters into the race, Amira (to Amber's horror as she too was aware of being Amira's "lane neighbor" in the race) suddenly was ahead by more than a body length. However, any sense of triumph Amira might have felt in that instant was lost completely due to the flashes. *For a tenth of a second an image of a girl, pretty but ill, flashed in her mind. Then the next image was that of a man who's face was completely shadowed, chasing her. The next was that of a rock the size of a tennis ball. The rock was a dark blue, heavy and warm. Then, she was running down a damp, cramped, dark hallway or perhaps it was just an underground passage. She was running fast, but the heavy footsteps coming from behind were hitting the ground faster than her footsteps and the noises behind her were growing louder, and then she turned a corner and saw*-oooh right, Amira was actually in a pool at the moment, a race more precisely, and she snapped back to reality just in time to realize that she had *no* time to complete a much needed turn since she was about to hit the concrete side of the pool.

Amira lunged downward pulling her right shoulder in as tight as she could hoping to somehow flip her body around so that her legs and more importantly her feet could take the brunt of the force of the wall, but it was not be. Amira did twist her shoulder 180 degrees, but that was the last thing she did before impact. The back side of her shoulder was the first thing to hit the concrete, but like a roller going over dough much more surface area of the roller (her body) was to follow. Immediately after her shoulder, the top center of her back hit, then her lower back, then her buttocks and the back of her head. On the plus side her legs were saved from a similar fate because they missed the wall all together and came flailing/bursting out of the water like a synchronized swim routine that had gone horribly, horribly awry (and lacked a synced partner) with the routine ending with her heels nailing the concrete that surrounded the pool. Had Amira's feet contained ears she would have been able to hear the loud and synchronized "OOOOHHHHHHH!" that emanated from the crowd. But alas (or thankfully), the only ears on Amira's body originated (and ended) on the side of her head, so all she heard was the water-muted scream that shot forth from her mouth while still underwater and still upside down. The scream was not based in pain, but rather anger. Amira could not believe that *that* wretch of a human being, Amber, was going to win the race. But almost instantly that anger was replaced with fear. The images Amira saw scared her, and for a few more moments she forgot that she was still upside down and under water.

Chapter 4: Rhythm Of Life

Really, there are few universal truths in life (like never loan money to twenty-somethings who wear backpacks decorated in campaign and other slogan buttons) and granted some are more important than others, but although a small universal truth, I still think females of the world should hear this one and heed it. If you're not playing football, there's never a need to wear shoulder pads. Some will say that fashion is cyclical and that we're all just slaves to whatever time we grow up in, and sure enough some Rock Star will come along and wear huge shoulder pads and pundits will call her edgy or that she's making a statement of some kind, and then the female masses will follow suit. The truth, however, is that if you choose to wear shoulder pads, the only statement you're making is: "I've made some mistakes in my life and let others influence me into making those decisions." Now, you don't have to accept this universal truth, but know this at least: feeling slightly edgy will not outweigh the loss you'll feel when realizing four years worth of photos and memories will be beyond salvageable due to your shoulder pads. Just trust me: no man has ever thought, "Yeah, I thought she was pretty, but she wasn't wearing shoulder pads, so

I just walked on by..." I should talk about bangs as well, but Amira's probably been underwater long enough, so perhaps later...

The view of the world for an adolescent teenager under water, upside down, through bluish tinted goggles is murky at best. Amira's view worsened moments later after the sound of a far away "swoosh" (that wasn't far away at all) created bubbles and swirling water all around Amira. After a second, she made out a nice pair of female legs to her left and a nice pair of male legs to right. However, she didn't have much time to gaze at their comely calves and perfected proportions since she almost immediately felt several arms on her back and the back of her head and neck lifting her up to the surface. As she moved from underwater to above water, the sound suddenly became quite crisp.

"Amira? Did you hit your head? Can you move your arms?"

Slightly dazed, Amira replied by waiving her arms and giving a thumbs-up.

"I didn't hit my head...much, really just my shoulder and back," she said to Maria Olave who was three quarters immersed in water.

Amira then turned to look the other way and realized Kyle was the other person holding her. To Amira's amazement, he too(!) had jumped in to help. "Oh, hey Kyle. What's up?" she asked trying to sound cool and calm, though she was pretty sure she was blushing due to the excitement she felt over being "held" (partially) by Kyle.

"That looked painful, Amira. You sure you're all right?"

Attempting to act nonchalant Amira replied, "This? Please. I do this all the time."

"Really? You run into the side of swimming pools all the time?" Kyle asked with a raised eyebrow.

"Let's gently lift her onto the stretcher," Maria Olave interrupted.

"Stretcher? Oh, I don't need a stretcher," Amira said tearing her eyes away from Kyle to look at Maria.

"It's just a precaution, Amira," Maria smiled back. "We want to make sure you didn't hurt your neck or spine."

Just a precaution! Amira thought. *WHO cares about my neck or spine? What about the hurt this will do to my social life. The "freak" strapped down on a stretcher is not a good look for me*, she screamed silently to herself as they lifted her out of the water and onto the stretcher that was now beside the pool, brought poolside by Mr. Johnson and the school's athletic trainer.

"I swear I'm fine," she protested again as they placed her on the burnt orange, slightly cushioned stretcher.

They then began to strap down her legs. Amira wanted to say, "I'm going to look like a crazy person strapped into this thing," but in truth she didn't look half bad...well, half bad when compared to the neck brace/halo they were about to put on her.

"Wait, I still have 2 races left!" Amira said as Maria Olave and Coach Johnson lifted up the stretcher.

"Sorry Amira, but you're done for today. Don't worry though. You can still practice with the team, and I'll hold tryouts again in a couple of weeks," Maria Olave said as her shirt and shorts dripped continuous chlorinated droplets onto the ground leaving a trail behind her, so all would know exactly where the girl on the stretcher went. "I think it's important to make everyone compete for spots on a regular basis, so there will be other chances," she finished. Maria thought this would comfort Amira, but two weeks of Amber taunts that were sure to follow sounded like an eternity to Amira.

"Two weeks?" Amira repeated with a look of horror/anger mixed on her face. "Ahh, mannnnnn."

"Let's just worry about your health today, okay?" Maria said as they reached the trainer's room and put the stretcher on a trainer's table.

"Wait," Amira said. She tried to look around, but the neck halo prevented her from doing anything but dart her eyes back and forth. "My brother's in the pool hall. Will you-"

Suddenly a tiny hand darted above her.

"I'm right here Amira. You okay?"

"Yeah, I'm fine Hashim." She felt his hand wrap around a couple of her fingers.

"Amira, Mr. Johnson and I are going to call the hospital and your mother, okay?" Maria Olave said.

"You really don't need to," Amira pleaded.

"It will be okay Amira," and with that Maria and Mr. Johnson left the room.

There was a ten second silence and then, "I think you should have turned faster," Hashim said.

She sighed and said, "I think you're right."

"When you hit the side, it slowed you down," he said.

Amira smiled because although she could not see his face, she knew his exact "serious" facial expression that accompanied each sentence he spoke. "Yeah, not one of my better moves."

"Did it hurt?"

"Not so much. I'm just embarrassed."

"Why are you embarrassed?" Hashim queried while trying to hop up on the table but not really succeeding because of the contraption that had Amira tied down. He tried different angles, different sides, and different spots, but all his attempts failed.

Trying to describe the emotional grenades that surround all pre-teen girls to a 6 year old boy was beyond Amira's communicative skills, so when he returned to her side, she squeezed his hand back and closed her eyes.

After a minute or so, she heard footsteps and without opening her eyes, she knew the MOP Squad had arrived.

"Oh no, Amira are you okay?!" Karen yelled rushing to her side."

"My shoulder's sore. That's it! I swear! I feel like a moron trapped like this." Only Amira's hands could move, so the conversation was full of Amira utilizing "jazz hands" and nothing else.

"You're sure you are okay?" Carlos asked looking at Amira.

Amira stared back and said, "Yeah. I'm just gonna have a bad bruise."

"You're 100 percent positive?" he said looking down on her halo enclosed face.

"Yes! I'm fine! What do you want me to say?!"

Carlos smiled and said, "Nothing. I just want to thank you from the bottom of my heart. Thank you."

"What? Why?" Amira asked completely confused.

"Because I got to see your coach step out of the pool in a wet shirt that umm, changed it's color and it's ability to cover, ummm...Thank you. Thank you. Thank you!"

"Not now Carlos!" Meredith said pushing him out of Amira's limited view. Now whispering to Amira, "Did you see who jumped in the pool after you? He LIKES you!"

"I actually *talked* to him before the race" Amira said, her smile beaming through the halo.

"Oh my god! What did he say?!" Meredith asked leaning down so that her face was almost in the halo with Amira's.

"He asked me if I was going to the dance?" Amira said opening up her mouth in a "Can you believe it?" expression.

"Yay!" Meredith whispered, and then Meredith and Amira giggled and jumped up and down in excitement (well, Meredith jumped while Amira was still confined to using ultra-energetic "jazz hands").

"What's so great about Kyle?" Carlos asked while rolling his eyes.

"Shhh!" condemned Karen. "Why not tell the whole world?!"

"Okay," Carlos said shrugging his shoulders.

Karen then tried to kick Carlos in the shin, but he expected it and deftly blocked the kick. "Hah! Nice try there Kickin' Karen, but it seems I'm too quick for your-ahhh!" he said falling down as Meredith strongly nudged him in the back of the knee without even looking in his direction.

"Not cool guys. Not cool," he said. "But still totally worth seeing Amira's coach like that," he continued popping up.

"Like what?" Maria Olave asked standing a couple of feet behind Carlos. She had entered the room moments before.

Surprised, Carlos flinched and jumped around. Staring at a still dampened Maria Olave, all Carlos could get out was a soft, quiet, "Awesome." And, then he walked out of the room without another word.

Maria Olave walked over to Amira. "A Dr. Sedgwick, from Mercy Hospital is going to be here in a minute just to make sure you're okay. I also called your mother, and she'll be here soon." Maria saw the fear spread over Amira's face, so she continued, "I told her that you can move your feet and hands, and that you likely just bruised your shoulder, so she knows that you're okay."

"Amira, can we play when we get home?" Hashim asked grabbing her arm.

Maria looked down at the little boy with curly hair who was holding his sister's arm while he looked at the floor kicking his shoes. "And who might you be?" Maria asked while picking him up.

Not one to shy away from attention, Hashim beamed and said, "I am Hashim. I'm Amira's brother, and I play football a *lot*."

"You do huh?" Maria said raising an eyebrow. "Do you also protect your sister and keep her out of trouble?"

Hashim scrunched his lips and scratched his head, pondering the question as seriously as a six-year-old could. "I try, but sometimes I can't."

Maria laughed and said, "You *try*? What's that mean?"

Hashim just shrugged his shoulders and smiled.

Soon thereafter, Dr. Sedgwick arrived. He first had Amira move her left toes and then her right toes. Then she moved her fingers. He then opened/detached the halo and released her straps. Amira sat up, and he checked her spine, her neck, and the gash on her shoulder. He then had her count backward from

100 by subtracting seven at a time. Though she got stuck at 65 for one second, that pause was due more to boredom than any neurological problem. Following the countdown, the doctor bandaged her shoulder, told her to rest for a few days since she probably suffered a deep contusion around her shoulder joint, and reminded her to pay better attention in the water next time.

Nara Talib arrived as Dr. Sedgwick was leaving. However, his departure was delayed as she questioned him thoroughly outside of the training room for five minutes about Amira's conditions. When Ms. Talib finally entered the training room, Amira was sitting up on the trainer's table with her back leaning against the wall. She had put on sweats and a t-shirt since sitting in a damp bathing suit was not all that comfortable after awhile. Hashim sat between Amira's legs with his head resting on her stomach. He used her legs as hills as he "drove" his Hot Wheels toy cars over her right leg, onto his right leg, then down on the table, and then back up his left leg, then onto her left leg, etc. When the Mop Squad heard Ms. Talib's voice, they departed the training room by the back door knowing that Ms. Talib would want to have a pow-wow with her children.

"Momma!" Hashim beamed with his arms stretched out waiting to be picked up.

"Mmm, hello my baby," Ms. Talib said picking him up and holding him. She smiled at Amira, and shifted Hashim to her left arm and hip. "How are you my beautiful daughter?" she asked while leaning down to hug Amira with her free arm. This also allowed Nara to check out Amira's bandage without her daughter "shooing" her away.

"I'm fine. I just- I don't know Mom. I screwed up. That's all."

Ms. Talib ran her fingers through Amira's hair. Did your father ever tell you about his first national race when he was 15?" Amira shook her head no. "He came out of a turn at too steep of an angle and the next thing he knew he was kicking the swimmer in the lane next to him. He and the other swimmer were both so surprised that they both stopped racing for a second. Next thing you know your father was finishing last. So, there will be plenty more opportunities for you to shine brightly in the water. Do you want go home?"

Amira shook her head "yes." Hashim gently "shook" his mother's head yes as his way of saying he too was ready.

"Hey mom, Amira's going to a dance this week!"

"She is?" Ms. Talib inquired while looking down at her daughter from the corner of her eye while still holding Hashim in her arms.

Hashim leaned in a whispered (loudly), "I think she likes a boy."

"Hashim!" Amira doth protested too much.

***

After 5 minutes of arguing with her mother about not needing a ride to school, Amira peddled along, smelling the slight morning dew and trying not to concentrate on the pain the bouncing of her backpack caused her shoulder and back. Of course, trying *not* to concentrate on it, just made her concentrate more on the pain, a mixture of a deep throbbing, as if the bruise itself had grown a heart, and sharp pain as her new skin kept slightly tearing due to the friction of the bouncing pack. She thought if she slowed down a bit the bouncing of the backpack would decrease, and she was right. So, she thought that if she decreased her speed even more the bouncing would decrease further. And again she was right. However, she decreased her speed so much that she lost her balance, jerked her arms to the left which caused the front wheel to jerk left, which then caused her to tip over and wipe out onto the slightly softer dirt-sand mixture which outlined the road.

Thankfully Amira fell to her left, so she landed on her left, non-bruised side, which would now of course be bruised as well. Through picking bits of gravel out of her knee and again showing off her skills with the Arabic language by spewing certain "words and phrases" that she would never say in front of family members, Amira failed to realize that perhaps this fall was for the best since now she had the potential for her bruises to be more symmetric. Oh well, some people are just myopic I guess.

Another plus of the "gentle" crash was that Amira became angry, and her anger over being abnormal, of being "different" of being forced to the sideline instead of leading the swim team in races, of being confused about what was going on in her life and what the images meant, propelled her forward pain free for the rest of the bike ride.

Amira arrived at school and locked up her bike at least knowing that she had her bike lock combination memorized. She then sat down in her normal spot and opened up her textbook to pull out her history book since in all the fuss about just missing breaking her neck in the pool the day before, she forgot to finish her homework and study for a quiz she had today.

However, trying to concentrate on a shallow version of the intricacies of the Texas Revolution during the Mexican Civil War seemed like a futile endeavor (especially since there weren't any pictures on these specific pages). Instead of nodding along to the facts regarding General Santa Anna's strategic goals, she found herself reading the same sentence over and over again as the images she saw in the pool floated in and out of her mind. With a loud sigh, her eyes wandered away from the Times New York font and toward the faculty parking lot, where she saw her least favorite teacher, Ms. Brown (who was white) talking to a man whose arm looked slightly disfigured, likely due to a scar, but from Amira's distance she could not tell for sure. The man was tall and strong. His hair was thick and black, but cropped short. His skin was tanned, and Amira couldn't tell his ethnicity. He wore large, jet black sunglasses on his face, and for the most part his facial expression was neutral as he spoke to Ms. Brown (still white).

Their conversation was short. Ms. Brown grabbed a bag from her car and abruptly turned away from the man and walked toward the school. The man then turned toward Amira's direction, and although he wore sunglasses, Amira felt him staring at her. A horrible chill spread throughout her spine as she quivered and quickly looked away. After a few seconds, something compelled her to look at him again, but when she looked up, he was gone. She stood up to see if she could spot him but to no avail. She then glanced at her Hello Kitty watch and realized it was time to go inside. She pulled off her bike helmet and was about to place her textbook back in her backpack when she noticed a pair of quite stylish shoes standing before her. *Amber!* she thought, not even needing to look up to confirm her suspicion.

"Maybe you should keep the helmet on at all times *Amir-dumb*. After all, there are walls *everywhere*! I wouldn't want you to injure yourself." Amber said as her minions cackled.

"What scares you Amber? The fact that I'm faster than you in the pool and you only won because I made a mistake *or* the fact that I'm better than you *period*, in *or* out of the pool?"

The confidence in Amira's voice visibly shook Amber's own confidence for a split second. However, she recovered quickly, took a step forward, and glared at Amira even though the two were already uncomfortably close. She inhaled a deep breath, and declared, "Not. On. Your. Best. Day."

Maybe it was the being nearly eaten by wolves or almost drowning in four feet of water, but Amira felt no need to cower before Amber, so she replied, "Maybe you should check with your brother about that."

Blood started to move away from Amber's face. A snarl then appeared; she opened her mouth, but then seemed to change her mind. Instead she smiled and said, "Even if my brother somehow liked you, he would see through you within a day. You're pathetic Amira. Nothing can change that. You're a waste of space and resources, and I don't understand how someone like you ever got into this country." With that, she turned around, flipped her hair and began to walk away.

However, as the vanilla/cherry/spiced scent of Amber's hair floated toward Amira, rather than placating Amira's anger, the scent stirred it. You know how when you're angry you imagine doing something nasty to the other person? For instance, Amira imagined just *yanking* on Amber's perfect hair, but like all of those dreams you know you'd never act on them, and so, oh wait. Never mind. Amira *did* choose to act on the impulse.

162

Amira's arm reached out, her hand clenched around Amber's hair, and she yanked it not with ferocious strength, but just enough to shock Amber completely and make her yelp and turn around.

Before Amira or Amber could act or counteract or react, Ms. Brown stepped outside having seen what had just transpired.

"Ms. Masri! You take your hands off Ms. Anders this second. Maybe where you come from simple battery is tolerated, but it is *not* tolerated at this school," she finished as she marched towards Amira and grabbed her by the elbow (which, in truth, would technically be a simple battery as well).

"But-" Amira protested.

"But *nothing*. You will come with me and sit inside the classroom until class begins, and after school you will sit in my classroom for detention."

"But I have practice after school."

"NOT today you don't."

***

The rest of the morning involved Amber and her friends staring at the back of Amira's head while Ms. Brown stared at the front of her head, followed by math and science, and then a lunch time conversation with the MOP Squad that centered around Amira's bruises and what Amira was going to do next about the Egyptian oasis. Really Amira could have used a "break" from her life and talked about the dance, but the dance was still 4 days a way, a lifetime in a 7th Graders' mind...okay, obviously beginning that evening all talk would likely shift to the dance, but this lunch was really the first opportunity the non Arab MOP Squadders had to quiz Amira about her mental and physical health.

Thus, Amira tried to stay positive. She said her bruise didn't hurt "that" much, but she hoped it healed by the time of the dance (a good attempt to switch subjects, but a failed one). They asked about the oasis and what she thought it all meant. Amira could have enhanced the conversation by talking about the visions she had in the pool, but she was tired and angry about what transpired yesterday and this morning and what would transpire after school in detention, so instead she just ended up venting about Amber. She had meant it to last just one sentence. Amira didn't like speaking bad of someone after all, but today she was willing to make an exception, and so what began as a simple, "I'm just soooo annoyed with Amber turned into a twenty minute diatribe about all the ways Amber had wronged Amira over the years, and Meredith and Carol just nodded and told Amira that Amber wasn't worth the effort, and even Carlos was silent and not once felt the need to mention how externally beautiful Amber was.

After classes ended, Amira marched slowly back to Ms. Brown's class. When she arrived at the door, part of her wanted to rebel, to keep on walking down the hall, change into her bathing suit and go to practice. What could Ms. Brown do really? Were they going to throw her out of school for skipping detention? Give her more detention? What if she skipped those as well but always turned in her homework and aced all her classes? Were they going to kick her out of school? Would that even be legal? Of course, it's always easy to be brave and rebellious in one's own head, but the fear of being kicked out of school and her mother's assured disappointment in Amira if she did act in the above way was enough of a deterrence for Amira to open the door and walk in to face her captor.

When she opened the door, she found Ms. Brown standing in the room with a knife in her hand. Ms. Brown stared at Amira, or perhaps due to the force of her look, maybe she stared *through* Amira. Amira was suddenly afraid; now, she wanted to run not out of rebellion, but survival, but before Amira could decide what to do Ms. Brown slashed her knife-wielding hand downward and sliced in half an apple that lay on her desk.

"Sit down," Ms. Brown said coldly as she broke her stare and turned her attention to quartering the apple.

Amira curled her shoulders forward, let her arms go limp and dragged her backpack along the floor as she made her way to her desk. Amira then pulled out a textbook to begin on some homework.

"I don't think so Ms. Masri. Detention is meant as a punishment, not as a study hall where you can complete your homework and then rot your brain in front of the television when you get home. Now put that book away."

Amira rolled her eyes and complied.

Not looking up from whatever work Ms. Brown was doing she stated, "Once you're done rolling your eyes, go to the back of the room, and there you will find a book on manners. Take the book back to your desk, pull out a pad of paper and a pencil and copy verbatim Chapter One."

Amira's eyes widened. "Seriously?" she asked.

"Ms. Masri, if I wanted to have a conversation believe me, I would have chosen detention for someone far more interesting than you."

Amira was too exhausted mentally to care at this point, so she got up from her desk and grabbed the book. Only when she got back to her desk did she realize that Chapter One of the book was sixty pages long.

"Chapter One is sixty pages long!" Amira said (umm, I think someone already mentioned that fact).

"Then I suggest you get started."

"But it could take me hours to finish."

"The first good point you've made. I'll have the principal's secretary call your parents and tell them to expect that you're going to be late due to your *detention*." And with that, Ms. Brown got up from her desk and left the room to walk down to the principal's office leaving Amira with her book on manners that likely lacked a chapter on how to politely utter Arabic profanity under one's breath. Oh well, to be fair, I guess Amira had not read Chapter One *yet*.

After an hour, Amira still wasn't halfway through copying Chapter One; she put down her pencil in order to rub her palm and stretch her hand/wrist.

"Where are your parents from Ms. Masri?"

It took a few seconds for Amira to realize that Ms. Brown was talking to her. The silence that had taken place over the past hour had basically made Amira turn off her ears.

"Do you not know the answer to the question?"

Amira wanted to ask why it was any of her business, but even though she cared little for Ms. Brown's company, anything at that moment was better than writing about proper elbow placement during dinner hours (although she did look ahead and was slightly excited to get to the section on sock-hop etiquette if only so she could imagine Kyle in 1950's "proper" adolescent boy attire while asking her to waltz (Amira's images of 1950's America were not wholly accurate) and then going out for

French fries and a milkshake, which they would share by using two straws.

"Ms. Masri!"

Amira snapped out of her daydream. "Oh, um Egypt. My family's from Egypt."

"Why did you move to Texas?" Ms. Brown then asked although her interest seemed to wane since she was back to working on....well, whatever it was she was working on as she asked Amira the question.

Good question, Amira thought, but she figured that wasn't the response Ms. Masri was looking for.

"I don't know. I never asked them," Amira replied. She wasn't sure why she said that. She asked that question often, whenever she was upset about something that happened at school or whenever they'd return to Texas after a summer of fun in Egypt when she'd already begin to miss her grandmother and cousins. However, her parents never quite gave a satisfactory answer, always something along the lines of, "We think it's best for you and Hashim, blah blah blah."

"A lack of curiosity will lead to a boring existence."

"I'll keep that in mind," Amira said thinking that copying down manners might not be that bad after all.

"Responding to adults in a sarcastic tone *also* won't serve you well if you expect to be a useful member of society."

Another thirty minutes passed, and then again Ms. Brown interrupted Amira's copying. "How many more pages do you have left Ms. Masri?"

"Twenty-two."

"Then you can finish the rest tomorrow in detention."

"*Tomorrow?!*" Amira said slightly too loud.

Ms. Brown pulled her eyes away from her notes and again glared at Amira. "I realized you were a miscreant but I didn't realize you were a *slow* miscreant. Ms. Masri I don't have time to wait here all night for you to finish your assignment. I have a life."

Amira soooo wanted to question her on that statement, but instead kept silent.

"You will report here after classes end tomorrow, and we will continue teaching you manners since obviously social etiquette did not emigrate with you."

Amira wanted to point out that *she* herself did not emigrate, but leaving the room was far more satisfying than any retort she could have offered, so to get her revenge she "mistakenly" placed the book on the wrong shelf.

***

The bike ride home was surprisingly pleasant. Dusk actually filled the landscape with beautiful colors that did not have to fight for space or attention with things like foliage or flowers. The pain she felt in the morning had dissipated because she ingeniously (ingenious in her own mind; from my point of view ingenious would have been accurate had she thought of this prior to her morning ride) put a towel on her back for cushioning and then tightened her backpack so it would not bounce around. And so she rode home taking in the Texas atmosphere with what seemed like an actual smile on her face.

***

When Amira pulled into the driveway, she noticed a red Volkswagen that she had never seen before. She parked her bike next to the side door which led into the kitchen and found her mother and *Ms. Olave* sitting at the kitchen table. Ms. Olave

168

was sipping coffee and laughing with her mother as Hashim sat underneath the table playing with a Lego set. As she opened the screen door, Hashim looked up and smiled and said, "Amira, why do you always get into trouble at school when you could be playing with me instead?"

Amira smiled. "I'm sorry Hashim. Hello Ms. Olave. Mom, is everything okay?" she then asked, not quite sure why her swim coach was in her kitchen.

"You tell me my daughter," her mother said with a smile that conveyed that whatever it was, Amira wasn't in *too* much trouble. "Are you going to continue to get detention?"

"No, mom. I'm sorry. I screwed up, but I do have to go back to detention tomorrow," Amira said dropping her book bag next to a cabinet and sitting on the floor so that Hashim would come over and sit next to her. She knew Hashim liked company when he was playing on the floor. Hashim scurried over and sat next to her so that their hips touched on the floor and he could bat his head into her arm as he worked on building his Lego pirate ship (he liked to multitask). "And I'm sorry Ms. Olave that I missed practice today, and I guess for missing practice tomorrow."

"Don't worry about it Amira. You're supposed to be taking it easy for a couple of days anyway. And, I'm not here because you missed practice. I'm actually in your mother's finance class at UT-Arlington," Maria Olave beamed. "Small world!, huh?"

"Your coach is a great student, Amira, *and* I've never had to give her detention," she winked.

Laughing, Maria went on, "Oh please, your mom's a great teacher. That's the reason the class has gone so well for me."

"It turns out Ms. Olave knows an old friend of the family," Nara said.

Surprised, Amira asked, "Who?" as she put down her backpack.

Nara smiled, but her eyes exhibited a hint of sadness, "Asad Khalid. You probably don't remember him Amira. You were still quite young the last time you saw him."

"How do you know him Ms. Olave?"

"Oh, well-" Maria stumbled to answer, but Nara finished for her.

"Asad is a bit of world traveler, Amira, which is why our family hasn't seen him in a long time."

"I met him in Barcelona a few years ago," Maria said. She took a sip of her coffee, and then changed the subject, "Mmm, so, how's your shoulder doing?"

Amira stretched out her right arm and moved it around without thinking as one normally does when another asks about an injury. She then said, "Actually pretty good. It's a bit sore, but it's already feeling a lot better." She moved it around a bit more and then wrapped it around Hashim's shoulder pulling him closer and thereby making him laugh.

"Ms. Olave is going to join us for dinner. Amira go wash your hands and mix a salad please. I already prepped all the vegetables, so you just need to mix it together. Hashim, go put your toys away, okay?"

Popping up off the floor, "Okay. Ms. Olave do you want to see my football collection?"

Maria hunched forward in her chair, "Hashim, I would *love* to."

With a huge smile and while putting his Lego people in his pockets as he cradled the ship, "Great! Come on, it's all up in my room." He then reached out his hand, which Maria accepted, and then he pulled her down the hall and up the stairs.

"So you pulled the hair of another student?" Nara asked once Maria and Hashim were out of earshot.

"She said some really mean, bigoted things, and I lost my temper," Amira said as she dried her hands and opened the fridge.

Her mother tended to the lamb that was cooking in the oven. "Amira, if someone is narrow minded, do you really think a successful strategy to broaden her mind is to resort to violence?"

"No, but-"

"No, Amira. No caveat is necessary because any caveat would be meaningless. Look, coming to America, your father and I knew that we would be subjecting you to certain people who would not appreciate aspects of our family. And, your father and I have not been deaf to hearing hurtful statements either, but you must rise above it."

"I know. It's just hard," Amira said as she opened up the Ziploc bags of vegetables pre-cut by her mother.

"Amira, people in this world are often scared. But, you're future is so bright that at times it brings me to tears. And because I know the world will open up to you (like a wolf opens its mouth to embrace its prey...what? Oh, that's not where she's going with this sentence?), you must, *must* bring people up with you rather than try to stoop to their level. Do you understand?" her mother asked as she kissed Amira on the top of her head.

"Yes," Amira sighed as she mixed the vegetables with orange, plastic tongs she grabbed from a vase near the kitchen sink.

"I'm not sure you do yet," Nara said to her daughter as she rested her chin on Amira's head, "but in time you will. Now, grab the oil and vinegar and go to the spice rack and pick out two to three spices that don't have Habanero pepper in them. The sun sets in about ten minutes."

The dinner went well. Amira enjoyed the addition of Maria Olave at the dinner table. Maria entertained Hashim and made Nara laugh. She asked tons of questions about Amira's family and their lives here and in Egypt. After dinner ended, Amira felt slightly embarrassed that her family hadn't asked many questions about Maria's life. Maria, however, didn't seem to mind, and after they all helped clean up (even Hashim seemed happy to help, obviously trying to leave a good impression with Maria), Maria thanked Nara profusely, told Amira not to stress too much about missing practice the next day and that she hoped her shoulder healed quickly, and finally got on her knees so she could teach Hashim a "cool" handshake/fist bump. Then she was off, and Amira, her mother, and brother watched the lights from Maria's VW grow fainter and fainter. It was such a fun dinner that Amira actually forgot about her troubles. The oasis, the ostrich, the scary images, her mean teacher, they all floated around her mind somewhere, but tonight she felt completely relaxed due to Maria's presence, and due to how her mother seemed so relaxed in Maria's presence. Amira realized she hadn't seen her mother laugh that much and seem so at ease in a long time.

Hashim then yawned and looked up at his mother.

"Want to go to bed my child?" she asked, yawning herself.

Hashim nodded quickly and then slowly, droopily, made his way up the stairs, so he could prepare for bed.

Nara continued, "After you brush your teeth, I will come up and read you a story." She watched him make his way up the stairs, and then she turned to Amira. "Are you going to bed as well?"

"I'll be up in a minute. I have a bit of homework to do."

"Okay, well don't stay up too late. After detention tomorrow, come straight home, I have a surprise for you."

"What's the surprise?" Amira asked obviously not fully understanding the meaning of every word in her mother's sentence.

"*MOM! I THINK I USED TOO MUCH TOOTHPASTE!*" came a young boy's voice from upstairs.

Without answering Amira, Nara kissed her daughter's forehead, and walked up the stairs to get ready for bed herself.
***

"No Mom, I don't need a dress," Amira said with her head leaning against the car window. When Amira arrived home from school the next day, she found her mother with her car keys in hand and Hashim sitting on the kitchen holding a Nerf football and wearing a Superhero-type eye-mask. Her surprise was that Nara was taking Amira dress shopping for the dance whereas Amira was rooting for a surprise in the form of an ice cream cake or ear piercing, but a dress was actually not on Amira's wish list since the "girls these days" generally wore their coolest pair of jeans and blouse, etc. Dresses were so old fashioned for a junior high dance, and Amira wanted no part of anything that reminded her classmates that she was different.

"But every girl needs a dress for her first dance," Ms. Talib said to her daughter who was fidgeting with her hair as she looked out the passenger seat window of their station wagon.

"Yeah, like maybe fifty *years* ago!" Amira said rolling her eyes.

"Amira, I wasn't even born fifty years ago," Ms. Talib said out of the corner of her eye, but still keeping the "non-corner" portions of her eyes on the road (safety first).

"And *I* wasn't even born seven years ago," Hashim chimed in from the backseat as he bobbed his head up and down and side to side obviously to some unknown rave that was going on in his head.

"Why do you care so much Mom?" Amira asked as she continued to stare out the window.

Ms. Talib smiled and put her hand on Amira's shoulder (Umm, what happened to two hands on the wheel Ms. T?!), "Because you are my princess and you should wear a gown to your first ball. It will help you stand out."

"It's a dance not a ball mom, AND I don't WANT to stand out. Believe me, I already stand out. I'm the girl who arrives at school with ostrich feathers stuck in her hair, the girl who can't eat lunch because of fasting, the girl who never had a Christmas tree and who never heard of the tooth fairy or Easter bunny, the girl who has a non-white skin tone but doesn't speak Spanish. Trust me, I don't need a dress to stand out," she finished looking back out the window at all the nothingness they were passing.

"Some day you will relish your uniqueness Amira. You will smile proudly at your wonderful culturally mixed and worldly life."

"Yeah, well mixed cultures and global experiences aren't exactly celebrated in small town Texas."

"Why are you even going to the dance Amira? Are the kids going to play games or something?" Hashim asked, now bobbing his head as he looked out the window as he swung his legs back and forth hitting his heals on the bottom of his seat.

"Umm, no dummy. It's a *dance*, so kids *dance* at a dance. There are no games there." (Oh, there will be plenty of mental games going on Amira, but you know the old saying: "if you can't spot the rube at the dance, that means the rube at the dance is you. Maybe I should just call her Amira McRube for the rest of this part of the story.) However, as Amira overly-chastised her younger brother in a way that only twelve year-old girls can do, her words began to sink in. *Wait, everyone will be <u>dancing</u> at the dance,* she thought. *Do I even know how to dance? Karen, Meredith, and I sometimes dance as we sing boy band ballads, but-* (Let's take a pause from her thoughts for a second, shall we? What Amira calls "dancing and singing to boy band ballads" would better be described as she and her female friends, Karen and Meredith, jumping up and down on their beds and screaming every third word that they remember of the boy "bland" ballad as they laugh uncontrollably. The Joffrey Ballet they were *not*. St. Olaf's choir, they were *not*.)

Although her anxiety was still at a heightened level, other thoughts began to form, *As long as I dance like however Karen and Meredith dance, no one will be able to make fun of me.* (Umm, I'm not quite sure I follow that logic Amira, but please continue) *Wait, will there be slow dancing? Will Kyle ask me to slow dance?! How do I slow dance? Should I raise one arm out to the side when he asks or will he think I'm a dork and am attempting to do* I'm-a-little-teapot? *Or do I just throw my arms forward? Or, will he then think I'm some kind of Egyptian mummy freak with my arms outstretched straight ahead? Stupid mummy stereotypes. I better call Karen when I get home to discuss-*

"Child? Amira? *Amira!*" her mother said in a raised voice that was slightly muted by the window that now separated them. Hashim and Ms. Talib were now standing outside the car since Nara had pulled into the store's parking lot and exited the car with Hashim in tow while Amira continued to daydream. "Are you coming into the store or do you want Hashim here to pick out your dress?"

"Maybe they have one with dinosaurs on it!" Hashim said earnestly looking up at his mom.

That statement was sufficient to snap Amira out of her daydreaming. "Sorry," she said as she pressed the button to release her seatbelt. The seatbelt unexpectedly snapped back quite quickly, the metal buckle becoming entangled with Amira's hair thereby dragging Amira's hair up to the corner of the car, which was enough to drag Amira's forehead to the glass. A muted thud made its way to Ms. Talib's ears as she watched her daughter smack her head against the glass.

"Honestly, child, you are going to get a concussion if you keep this up."

A muted "Ow," then passed through the glass barrier as Amira rubbed her forehead and detangled her hair from the seatbelt.

***

Amira came out of the dressing room in a red-and-white polka dot dress.

"Hey, you look like Minnie Mouse!," Hashim yelled happily.

Without uttering a word, Amira went back into the dressing room to try on another dress. A minute later, she came out wearing a rather burnt orange dress.

"You look like Cheetara from the Thundercats!," Hashim beamed.

"Okay, Hashim stop comparing me to cartoons!" Amira hissed. "And besides, she doesn't wear a dress on the cartoon."

"Oh yeah," Hashim admitted. "Are we almost done Mom?" he asked grabbing onto his mother's leg.

"Seriously, Mom can we go?" Amira added.

Nara smiled at her moody daughter and said, "Just a couple more." However, Nara was wrong. Amira only needed to try on one more, a purple dress. When she came out of the dressing room, Nara just smiled, and despite not wanting to wear a dress, Amira couldn't help but feel a bit excited about it.

"Your grandmother would be beside herself if she were here right now, my daughter."

"It is kinda cool, isn't it?" Amira admitted.

"You look like Barn-"

"Don't!" Amira said quickly cutting him off before he could finish his thought.

***

The next morning, Nara awakened her daughter before 5 a.m. Nara sat on Amira's bed and lightly rubbed Amira's arm as she said, "Amira, my beautiful daughter, you need to wake up."

"Huh?" Amira asked groggily.

"Come downstairs, I've made breakfast, and we need to talk."

177

"What time is it?" Amira asked through narrowed eyes since her mother just turned on the lamp next to Amira's bed.

Nara kissed Amira on the forehead and just repeated, "Come downstairs."

With that Nara left the room leaving Amira to stretch her arms well above her head. Amira then rubbed her eyes and attempted as she always did to pat down her hair, which as it did every night seemingly tried to escape from her head in every direction possible. Amira next pulled the cover to the sides, and placed her bare feet on the cold wood floor. Now standing she more fully stretched her body and in doing so emitted a soft, but high-pitched "Eeeek!" The young teen wearing "Little Mermaid" inspired pink-and-green pajamas slipped her feet into her pair of Ninja Turtles slippers and walked downstairs, obviously not concerned about the cartoon/cultural clashing her current wardrobe created.

Amira walked into the kitchen and sat down next to her mother at the kitchen table. She took a deep sip of ginger tea her mother offered her before asking, "What's up?"

Nara paused for a second as she gathered her thoughts. Nara placed her hands in front of her, frowned, and said, "My sister is ill."

Suddenly concerned, Amira asked, "Mom, what's wrong with her?"

"The doctors are not sure," Nara replied honestly.

"Are we gonna go to Egypt to visit her then?" Amira asked.

Nara was silent for a long time. Amira could tell that whatever Nara was going to tell her, Amira was *not* going to like it.

"That's what I wanted to talk to you about."

"Mom?" Amira said now in a raised voice. "What?"

"Hashim and I are going to Egypt, but..." her mother trailed off as her eyes watered slightly.

"But what? But, I'm *not* going?!" Amira asked now upset.

"Amira, you would miss too much school and you have swimming, and-"

"And those are all *lame* reasons, Mom. Why can't I go?" Amira asked as she slammed her mug of tea down on the table more forcibly than she meant to. "Sorry," she said in a softened tone.

"Your father and I have made the decision Amira, and it's final."

"But-" Amira began to protest, but her mother silenced her by placing her hand on Amira's hand.

"Amira, this wasn't an easy decision, but I need you to trust me."

"But, it's not *fair,* Mom!" Amira protested.

"It isn't fair Amira, but I *need* you to accept this decision. It was not made lightly."

Amira stared at the table and more quietly said, "I hate it here. I miss Egypt. I miss my cousins and my grandmother. I don't belong here Mom. We don't *belong* here."

"Amira, we *do* belong here. There are moments when it may not seem that way, but...but we are blessed. We are blessed that we can call two countries home. And, I know you're angry, but I do not believe that you hate it here. I think you do not believe that either."

Amira remained silent, putting her elbows on the table and her hands over her face. She did not cry, but she felt she had to hold her head in order to keep her composure, to keep her emotions in check. She was partly furious, partly sad but could tell from the tone of Nara's voice that nothing she said would change her mother's mind. Nara sat silently next to her daughter allowing her daughter to work through her emotions. Moments later, Amira and Nara heard muted footsteps, then feet shuffled along the floor foretelling Hashim's entrance into the kitchen. Hashim looked like he existed in a state between sleep and waking life.

Hashim plopped into a chair next to Amira and let out a huge yawn. He then said, "Can't we make a rule that there's *no* fighting before 10 a.m.?" Hashim waited for a response from either his mother or sister but none came, so he continued, "I'm just saying it would be helpful to everyone in the world, that's all." He let out another loud yawn as he stretched his body in every direction. He then yawned again.

Amira opened her eyes so she could roll them at her brother. "Come on Hashim. It's not *that* early. Stop yawning. "

Any type of attention from his sister generally made Hashim smile. However, at this moment he did not smile. He narrowed his eyes and stared at Amira as penetratingly as someone his age could do. He looked almost accusingly at Amira. What his stare was accusing Amira of was unclear.

"What?" Amira finally asked raising her hands above her head in an over-exaggerated expression.

Rather than reply, Hashim turned his attention to his mother. "Mom, may I have cereal and some hot chocolate?

"Yes, Hashim you *may*," Nara said, obviously happy her lessons in "may v. can" were paying off.

"I'll get it," Amira said in part because she needed to move and in part because she couldn't remember what she did to make Hashim give her that look, so she felt slightly guilty.

"When are you leaving?"

"Tomorrow."

Amira poured more water into the kettle that her mother had used to boil water for the tea and turned the stove back on. She then opened a cupboard and pulled out a puffed rice cereal with a cartoon picture of happy looking elves who may or may not enjoy what many in Texas would call an "alternative" lifestyle. She then opened another cupboard and then a drawer to grab a bowl and spoon respectively. Amira then took out goat milk from the fridge, and as she poured the milk into the cereal, she asked, "What am I supposed to do while you both are gone?" She knew her mother would never allow her to stay by herself in the house.

"I've asked Maria Olave to stay with you," Nara said as she stared at her drowsy son who kept nodding off for fractions of a second.

"Ms. Olave?" Amira did not hide her shock. She placed the cereal in front of Hashim. "Why her?" Amira assumed she'd have to stay with Karen or Meredith, and she was going to hint that perhaps Meredith's family would be a better fit since Karen's family seemed overly intense at times.

"Because I knew she would. She's a friend of Asad's, so she's a friend of our family."

"Oooohkay. Wait, when did you talk to her?" she asked as she poured the cocoa mix into a mug in preparation for the hot water.

"I called her right before I awakened you. Now sit with your brother. I need to go make some arrangements, and then Hashim, I need to talk to you after you're done with your breakfast, okay?" Nara said.

Hashim just nodded his head up and down and stared at his cereal bowl. He still looked overly tired and disheveled, like the world's youngest commodities trader. The kettle whistled, so Amira grabbed the kettle and poured the water into the mug. She then took the mug to Hashim and sat back down, trying to process all that was going on in her life.

"Thanks Amira," Hashim said still staring at his cereal.

Amira just sat silently next to him staring at the ceiling. Amira wasn't sure how long she remained fixated on nothing until Hashim broke the silence.

"If you needed to hide something, where would you hide it?"

Amira kept her attention on the blankness of the ceiling. "You are sooooo random."

"I think I'd hide it in a castle," he said matter-of-factly. As he sipped his hot chocolate, his energy level perked up slightly.

"You are like Randy the Random Dinosaur, Hashim," she said finally taking her eyes off the ceiling.

"Who is Randy the Random Dinosaur?"

"You. You are."

"No, I'm not," he said assuredly.

"Ugh, I'm *teasing* you Hashim!" Amira sighed pushing her hair forward to cover her face.

"Oh," Hashim replied with a wry smile on his face that Amira failed to see through her ringlets. "Why were you and Mom fighting?"

Amira breathed in and out deeply and then slumped down in her chair. "I'll let Mom explain."

"Why can't you explain?" he asked as he slurped down more of his hot chocolate.

"Because," she said through rolled eyes.

"Mom says '*because*' isn't a sentence," he retorted in a slightly annoyed voice.

"Whatever." (Nice comeback Amira. You just got schooled figuratively and *literally* by someone half your age. Be proud.)

"Amira, are you going to stay mad for awhile?"

"*UGH!* Hashim. I *don't* know. Are you going to bug me?" She pushed her hair to the side, so he could see her eyes staring at him.

"Well, probably," he answered truthfully. "Can we play later?"

Amira realized there was no use fighting with a six year old at 6 a.m. "Sure."

"Great! Can I have a couple of marshmallows?"

"*Hashim*, it's too early for marshmallows?"

"Says who?" he asked.

Amira was fairly certain he got that reply from listening to her. "Says people who make marshmallows."

"Why would marshmallow people not want kids to have marshmallows?"

Whether moved by his argument or just unwilling to continue this line of questioning, Amira walked over to the cupboard nearest the fridge, grabbed a bag from the top shelf and grabbed a few marshmallows, which she then put in his mug.

Hashim laughed and said, "Thanks!"

"Hashim, sometimes you are *too* much."

"Yeah, I get that a lot."

"From whom?"

"Marshmallow people."

Amira laughed which made Hashim laugh and snort hot chocolate out of nostrils. This amused Hashim even more, and he gave a "fist pump" in celebration. After their laughter died down, Hashim reached over and grabbed Amira's hand.

"It's gonna be okay Amira," he said earnestly.

"How do you know?"

"Because," he said through a huge, Cheshire Cat smile.

***

The school day was a blur to Amira. She had vague recollections of being called on in class, of Carlos cracking jokes at lunch, of Amber sneering at her at one point, of walking by Kyle in the hallway possibly without saying hello to him, but basically her entire day was spent daydreaming of Egypt. Her emotions bounced from anger to homesickness to sadness to confusion; it was as if she experienced what it would be like to have multiple personality disorder without the nasty side effect of having multiple personality disorder. When the school day ended, Amira returned home without stopping by swimming practice, so she could see her mother and brother off to the airport.

"Come here Amira," Nara said from the master bedroom.

Amira entered the room and sat next to her mother on the bed. "Don't you and Hashim need to leave for the airport?"

"In a little while. But first we have work to do," Nara said with a smile.

Amira was not really in the "Yay, let's do chores!" mood, if such a mood even exists, so she sat silently next to her mother and narrowed her eyes at Nara.

"I'm sorry I can't take you to the dance and pick you up. But, what I can do is teach you a few more tricks on how to deal with this beautiful gift you often ignore: your *hair*. So grab the corner chair and sit in it in front of the mirror."

Amira did as she was told and silently sat in the chair resigned to the fact that she was going to be stuck in Texas while her mother and brother spent time in Egypt.

As Nara effortlessly (magically) worked through Amira's hair while still over emphasizing her movements so Amira could see what she was doing, Nara said, "I promise when I get back from Egypt, we shall talk Amira. Just know that everything I do, I do out of love for you, for your brother, for your father."

"I know Mom. I just wish I could go with you."

Nara hugged her daughter as they looked at each other through the mirror. "So are you going dance with this boy you've chosen not to tell me about."

Amira could not help but smile. "Maybe...I hope so."

Nara beamed, "No need to hope Amira. You will because you are going to look so *beautiful* at the dance."

"*Mom*," Amira said rolling her eyes.

"Just remember, you got your good looks from me, no matter what your father's mother says," Nara winked.

Ten minutes later and Amira's hair looked better probably than it had ever looked. Then Nara asked Amira to help her brother bring the luggage out to the car as Nara went through her "travel checklist" making sure she had their passports, etc. After loading the car, Amira stood outside with her brother waiting for her mother to appear momentarily. Amira had been silent as she put the luggage in the back of the station wagon and her brother sensed that Amira didn't feel like talking, so he remained silent. After another moment, Nara came outside.

"Ms. Olave will be here later tonight. She said she had a few things to take care of first, so please do your homework in the meantime, okay?"

"Yes, Mom."

"I left you some dinner in the fridge. You just need to heat it up, okay?"

"I will."

Nara smiled. "Now give me a hug."

Amira did as she was told and hugged her mother and remained hugging her much longer than she normally did. Then she picked up her brother and hugged him as she carried him to the other side of the car.

"Ahh, Amira you'll see me soon," Hashim said.

"I know. Now, don't get into any trouble okay? You know I think it's more fun when we get into trouble together, right?"

Hashim just laughed and nodded his head as Amira put him in the child's seat and closed the car door.

Amira then walked back to the driver's side, and Nara hugged her daughter one more time before getting in the car. A few moments later and Amira was left watching her family drive away.

Amira wasn't quite ready yet to hit the books, so she walked over to the ostrich pen to see what the birds were up to. As it turns out, not much was happening. She sought out Moha, but he seemed to choose staring at the horizon over paying attention to Amira's ramblings, so after several non-starters, Amira gave up talking to Moha and walked back to her house. She grabbed a schoolbook and sat out on the front porch swing where she then set the textbook down and just swayed lightly back and forth as she stared blankly out over the terrain.

When the sun set, Maria still had not arrived, so Amira decided to heat up dinner without her since Amira was starving, and she was sure Maria would not mind. Since she didn't have her mother or Hashim to talk to, she ate silently and quickly, and then she was ready to do her homework. Well that's what she told herself, but after staring at her assigned math problems for an hour without picking up a pencil to even begin, she then decided she needed some more water. Then, she realized maybe it was a "location thing" that was causing her to procrastinate. Amira didn't feel like doing her homework at the kitchen table since her mom wasn't going to be there to sit next to her she thought, so Amira grabbed her backpack and walked into the living room, turned on a lamp, and nestled into a comfy navy colored chair that sat near the corner bookshelf that contained books ranging from dictionaries to financial and mathematical textbooks to children's books for Hashim to a small book with a torn cover that looked to have Chinese characters peering out from the tear. That's interesting. Oh well, too bad Amira's such a dedicated student that she would never look up to take in the contents of the library since procrastinating was so outside her nature and- oh never mind; after forty-seven seconds of studying, Amira sighed, put down her textbook, and turned her head to stare at the full bookshelf. She noted the book almost immediately. Amira pulled the book down from the shelf and realized it felt quite light (yes "small" and "light," just the type of book Amira would be attracted to). She then peeled off the tattered cover that barely covered anything because it had so many holes in it.

Imprinted on the binding itself there were Chinese characters that looked similar to the characters she saw inscribed on the rock in the hidden oasis as well as the characters embroidered on the cloth her family had held onto for all these years. She pulled down the book and re-nestled into the chair in order to peruse the book's pages. She turned to the first page, which was in Chinese as was the second page. She began quickly flipping through (looking for pictures I guess), but she quickly stopped after a few more pages because the characters changed to Sanskrit. After several more pages Sanskrit became Russian, which then became Latin, and then Italian, and about halfway through: English.

It read, *Be you male or female, from north or south of the Equator, whether you are from the far East or far West, for your sake, I hope this book has fallen purposely into your hands, for the dangers that you now face are quite real, and by opening this book, know you have likely hastened your own death.* (Well, isn't this book cheery? I assume this author was *not* formerly employed by Hallmark. Seriously, can you imagine if this author was in charge of "Get Well" cards? It would read something like, "You have cancer. Whether you are strong or weak, brave or scared, young or old, currently a malignant tumor whose only goal is to kill you grows inside your body, nourishing itself by eating you. For your sake I hope all trusts and wills have been recorded on your behalf." Geez, what a downer, huh? Okay, back to the book...)

Hopefully, you have made it to your 18th birthday without too many dangerous situations befalling you. (Umm, yeah, about that...) *However now that you enter adulthood, your responsibility to protecting the Qistone takes precedence over personal safety. Depending on your proximity to the stone during your formative years, you've probably felt its "pull." Yes, the stone will connect you to the energy that surrounds all of us; it will connect you in profound ways with patience and practice. Always be mindful of the energy flow you will soon embrace, for it can help you in ways far more important than with just speed and strength. Regardless, I'm sure you've realized to lean on your guards and guardians during any difficult moments.* (Guards and Guardians? Umm, does Moha count?). *This book is not meant to give you all the answers, for the risk is too great. This book is meant to point you in the right direction and to act as part of the key you need in order to enter the Qistone's cave. An heirloom from your family that has been kept secret and known only to you and your inner circle acts as the other half key to the protected "area" where the stone is kept. What is being asked of you, the dangers you are being asked to assume is not fair by any means. There will be dark times ahead. That is certain. However, during this journey you will find strength you didn't know you had, endurance you did not think possible, and love more powerful than you can imagine. Part of this will come from the Qistone, but part will come from within. Know that others have preceded you, and God willing, others will follow you. Your connection to others in this predicament exists, always. Never forget that. No matter how bleak the outlook, no matter the odds, no matter how little time is left, know there is always hope, there is always a chance, and know that you are not alone.*

Though we will not meet, I love you for who you are and for what you will do. Trust yourself. Trust your instincts. Trust those who love you, and even if all seems lost, fight. The world needs you.

May each of your steps be blessed. And remember to relax. (Ahh yes, even though every time you turn a corner someone may be waiting to kill you, you should consider investing in a hammock.)

Amira's spine tingled as she read the passage. The hair on her head felt like it stood on end as if she were touching one of those "static balls" at a children's science museum, and in spite of herself tears formed in her eyes. She felt tired, weak, but also light and prideful. She felt saddened not to know her "predecessors," but she also somehow felt joyful for whatever it was they did. Amira re-read the passage and tried to think of the family heirloom that acted as the key. She stared around the room, but nothing jumped out at her. She then flipped through the book again, and it became so obvious, she couldn't believe it wasn't her first thought: the multi-cultural cloth. What else could it be? It's not like any other family heirloom felt like its purpose was to protect..."whatever." She read the passage several more times until she had committed it to memory. She thought about reading it one more time, but then through the window, she saw headlights on the road that then turned into the driveway. Maria was about to arrive. Amira thought Maria was cool and all, but didn't really want to discuss this book she had just found with her swim coach, even if she was a friend of a family friend, so she threw the book into her backpack and pulled out her history book so that Maria would think Amira "studious."

Amira heard the engine shut off and the car door being closed followed a few moments later by the kitchen door creaking open.

"Amira?" Maria asked.

"I'm in the living room Ms. Olave!" Amira yelled back.

Maria entered the living room. "Ah, there you are. Sorry for arriving so late. Life is tricky sometimes, you know?" Maria smiled showing off her perfect teeth.

"Totally," Amira answered. "No problem though. I've just been studying."

"Oh good," Maria replied as she looked at Amira and then above Amira for a few seconds. "Anyway, how are you doing? Everything okay?"

"Yeah, everything's fine. I did eat dinner though. I'm sorry I didn't wait but-"

Maria waived her off as she sat down on the coach, "Please, no need to apologize. It was my fault for being so late. I would have felt *horrible* had you waited for me. I know you're fasting. Oh, I wanted to tell you that I'll give you a ride to the dance tomorrow. Your mother said that afterward the kids are going to some burger joint and that your friend Karen's mom is going to pick you guys up and take you home. Does that sound cool?"

"Yeah, that sounds great."

"So are you excited for the dance?"

"I think so. I'm a bit nervous I guess," Amira replied honestly.

"Ahh, don't be nervous. You will have plenty of dances in your life, so if this one doesn't live up to your expectations, so what, right?" Maria said.

"Yeah, you're probably right," Amira said. Then she yawned. She realized she was quite tired since she had awakened so early in the morning. "I actually think I'm going to go bed. I got up really early this morning. Do you need me to show you where anything is?"

"I'm all set. I spoke to your mother on and off throughout the day. I think she told me where to find *everything*," Maria said with a wink.

"My Mom would do that. Well goodnight then," Amira said as she grabbed her backpack and got up from her "study" chair where she accomplished zero in the way of studying.

"I'll see you in the morning, Amira. Sleep well," Maria said.

Amira went upstairs to get ready for bed as well as examine the cloth she had placed in the drawer on her nightstand table. She somehow had the patience to first wash her face and brush her teeth as if she knew that once in her room, she wouldn't want to leave until the morning. After she put on her pajamas, she opened the drawer and pulled out the cloth to examine it further. She thought after the book she stumbled upon that perhaps the cloth would have more meaning for her, but as she held it, she didn't feel anything, no sense of peace or meaning. So she turned off the lights and placed it on her nightstand and stared at it as she rested her head on her pillow.

***

Amira couldn't wait for the lunch period at school so she could discuss the book she found with Mer, Karen, and Carlos. So, after Algebra, she jetted to the cafeteria and took her place at the normal MOP table. When the MOP Squad arrived she explained to them about the book she found and her plan to go back to the oasis this weekend.

"What do you think the book was talking about?" Meredith asked.

"I have no idea," Amira admitted.

"It all sounds so vague. Why was the author being so obtuse?" Carlos asked.

The three females paused to stare at Carlos.

"My mom just bought me PSAT flashcards," Carlos said rolling his eyes while shaking his head. "I'm supposed to learn ten words a week, so that when we get to high school, I can try to increase my chances of being a social outcast. Of course my mom thinks her strategy will help with "my future." But, seriously why was the author of your weirdo book not passing out the details? It's almost like he wasn't *exactly* sure what he was talking about."

"I'm sure he or *she* knew exactly what they were doing," Karen retorted while staring at her brownie and trying to decide whether to take the time to pick out the walnuts from the chocolaty treat.

"Well, it's all I've got to go on for now, so come on, let's try and act excited over what I found," Amira said through a somewhat exasperated smile. She didn't quite understand her friends' hesitation into believing in her plan...maybe because of all the warnings of death and danger, or perhaps her friends just prefer the writings of more established authors that actually make a living writing due to their talent and such, writers who sit at a desk with a glass of whiskey and a view of a forest, a person who concentrates solely on the writing rather than some hack sitting on a couch in torn jeans with music and/or the TV blaring who writes intermittent sentences when he's not busy being distracted by beer commercials while watching football or by the need to belt out lyrics to pop songs that become annoying after the 25th time listening to them, but that then somehow become fun again after the 225th listen.

"Do you want us to come with you?" Meredith asked with a look of concern. She bit her lower lip and stared at you intently when worried.

"If you guys wouldn't mind? I know we've already done this trip once, but-"

"Amira of course we're gonna rock the ole hick to the oasis with ya," Carlos said while popping the walnuts Karen had picked out of her brownie into his mouth.

Usually I would say yes, but I'm gonna try to convince Moha to take me. It's the only way I can get there, look around, and then get back before Maria comes home. But, if I find anything, I promise to take you guys back there this weekend."

"Yeah, for sure we're going! Do you think Maria will mind us going?"

"I doubt it. But, we should leave early in the day on Saturday to make sure we get back not *too* late in the afternoon."

"Define early?" Carlos replied.

"God forbid someone interrupt your beauty sleep," Karen said rolling her eyes.

"Hey, some of us plan on dancing the night before," he began as he busted out "The Robot" followed by a shoulder-shimmy.

"You are such a *dork*," Karen said.

Laughing Meredith said, "It's aboot time we saw your moves!"

"That's right ladies. The Carlos is dancing dream for all the lovely disco queens out there!"

And with that the conversation turned away from the oasis and toward the impending dance.

***

Thursday and Friday went by in a blur. Amira saw Maria in the morning, at practice, and then usually late in the evening since Maria said she had some things she needed to get done, so really they didn't see much of each other. The Mop Squad talked about the dance at lunch each day, and every once in awhile would discuss the mysterious cave Amira was supposed to find, but mainly, the dance took precedence. Amira worried that she'd be way overdressed for the dance, so Karen told her to wear shorts underneath the dress, and pack a top in her purse, so if she really felt out of place she could just change quickly. Amira thought this to be a brilliant idea.

There was no practice this Friday because Maria wisely realized that the girls' focus would be lacking severely so rather than waste everyone's time, she let the girls go home after school to prepare for the dance.

This was great for Amira because she would definitely need time to work on her hair. Amira stared at the mirror in her room and tried to remember exactly what her mother had done just a few days prior. After several maneuvers, a twist here, pulling some ringlets through a loop there, and Amira dropped her hands and realized she had somehow created a cross between a beehive and slouching capital letter "L" on her head.

Maria then knocked at her open bedroom door, "I thought you might like some help getting ready for the dance." Maria stared at the "nest" atop Amira's head.

Amira nodded her head quickly up and down. "Please!"

"No problem. I have several cousins who have hair similar to your hair, so I think I can help."

Amira went on to explain what she thought her mother had done and how her hair had been pulled "back" but then her ringlets were allowed to fall down and around her shoulders, and after several minutes, Maria almost recreated what her mother had done.

"Oh my god, that's amazing!" Amira said. "Thank you so much," she said hugging Maria.

"No problem. You have such beautiful hair. It was fun working with it."

"It's beautiful when other people do it. Usually when I try to tame it, it wins."

"Don't worry. You'll figure it out. It just takes a couple years unfortunately. Now go put this dress on that your mother told me about, and then I'll do your makeup."

Amira's mouth dropped open.

"I cleared the makeup with your mother. She said I could put a bit on if you'd like."

"I like!" Amira yelled in a high-pitched voice. She was so excited at how "mature" she was going to look, she hopped all the way to her closet and then bathroom to change into her dress. Yes, dear readers, I could describe the makeup session in great detail, but I figure you'd prefer I finish the story rather than attempt to hold my breath long enough in order to fall into a self-induced coma, so we're just gonna skip that, okay? Thanks for your understanding.

Once all ready, Amira walked down the stairs.

"You look truly beautiful Amira," Maria said. "Let me take a picture for your mother, okay?"

You didn't need to ask Amira twice as she unconsciously went into a pose as Maria pulled out a camera. Maria snapped the photo and smiled. "So are you ready to go?" Maria asked.

"Yup!" Amira said as she hopped up and down.

They walked outside, when Amira realized she forgot her purse.

"I forgot my purse. I'll be right back," Amira said as she skipped back toward the house."

"Okay, I'll turn the air conditioning on the car while you get it. Amira opened the door and ran up the stairs and only tripped twice. She grabbed her purse, which was empty save for a pack a gum and a few dollars, from her room, and was ready to leave when something compelled her to grab the family heirloom cloth and the mysterious book she had found. She placed both in her purse and then hopped all the way out of the house and to Maria's car.

***

Like magic, the school's gymnasium transformed into a ballroom befitting the swankiest event in New York City. Well, okay, sure you could still see the basketball rims, and the boundary lines outlining the basketball court, and the three point line, and you could see the girl's volleyball net wrapped in one corner, and of course the bleachers, though pushed back, were forever present. Okay, fine the room still looked like a gymnasium basically with just a smattering of streamers, a few balloons, some all purpose tables that were transformed from parent-teacher conference tables into an immaculate "punch and treats" (rice krispie treats, brownies, etc...because obviously the thing kids entering and currently in puberty need is more sugar) table; further, the parent-teacher conference tables were magically transformed for the evening by the festive Arbor Day (there was a sale) tablecloth made out of paper.

However, to the 7th-8th Graders at Davy Crocket Junior High School the sight of the randomly placed decorations as music blared could not have looked any more majestic. The energy in the room, fueled by dormant crushes, dreams of what the night could bring, nerves, and hormones, seemed to infuse everyone and everything in the gym, errrr ballroom with a magic gooey substance that could only be described as...as...laminated lame.

As various degrees of station wagons and minivans appeared at the curbside dropping off one to five kids, the gymnasium slowly filled. However, even if the boys and girls had shared a ride together due to living in the same neighborhoods, once inside the boys and girls almost instinctively chose *not* to share the same airspace. The boys seemed to be hanging out in one group, highfiving each other, pseudo-wrestling, jumping up and down, and doing all the other types of things boys this age do in order decrease their attractiveness in the eyes of just about everyone.

The girls on the other hand had their own obnoxious rituals of excitedly hugging one another, flashing their hands with their fingers fully extended and spread apart to show off their manicures and nail polish, the incessant giggling and whispering that grew louder and louder as more of them arrived. After talking about themselves and then the girls around them, they'd turn their attention to the boys and what they were wearing and whether they thought "so and so" would dance with them or whether Boy A could dance blah blah blah chorus, blah blah blah coda.

Most of the girls wore jeans or skirts and their like totally most favorite awesome blouses and often were successful at matching their earrings with their belts or necklaces or mini purses that contained mints in case a boy wanted to kiss them.

Thankfully, Amira's Egyptian background would make her unaware of the above frivolous rituals, so once she walks into the room your long suffering narrator can focus on describing more pleasant things.   Right before Amira entered the gymnasium, she took a breath, determined finally, *finally* to enter a room with grace, poise, and in a distinguished manner. Focusing on her abdomen, she took a deep breath in, pulled her shoulders back as she raised her neck and head up high, and as she exhaled she took a step forward, and then another step. Each step was confident, and her demeanor and posture screamed out calmness. Okay, "scream" was probably a poor choice of words, but you know what I mean: whatever "it" was, she had it. True, maybe it was the poor lighting or perhaps it was the mild haze caused by the overuse of perfume and cologne, but as Amira stepped inside she looked radiant.   Having listened to her mother's hair tips and with Maria's help, for possibly the first time in her life and her hair's existence, each midnight-on-a-starless-night black ringlet seemed to have a purpose behind its location atop and around Amira's head. The very slight amount of makeup Maria put on her highlighted her natural beauty, and the light purple-tinted blush and deep purple dress somehow transformed Amira from an awkward and unsure girl into....*AWWWW MANNNNNNN! Seriously! Crap.* The second Amira saw her friends, Meredith and Karen ran up to her, and instantly they all began jumping up and down, giggling for little or no reason, and pointed excitedly at each other's shoes as if they had existed on a barefoot continent for their entire lives. So I guess this proved once and for all: young teen girls are pointless regardless of location, ethnicity, or culture. Okay, well, let's just skip to the end of the dance shall we? Hmm? You're not cool with that? But, dear reader, surely you feel my pain and are concerned about my well-being, right? Okay, fine. That's cool. Just don't expect me to get you anything on your birthday.

"Amira, you look *Gorgeous!*" Meredith beamed.

"The dress is the bomb!" Karen exclaimed!

"You guys..." Amira replied, slightly blushing but definitely enjoying her moment in the sun...well maybe not the sun, more accurately her moment in the ten year-old mildly reflective disco ball, but you get my drift. "You don't think the dress is too much?" Amira asked semi-sheepishly. Again, I think taking an acting lesson or two would help her. Just saying.

"Are you kidding?! Kyle is going to *die* when he sees you," Meredith remarked as your narrator wondered if her choice of words were somewhat dangerous on a night like tonight, but we'll get to that later...later because you asked for the dance.

"No Amira, he *totally* will flip when he sees you," Karen agreed.

"Thanks!" Amira glowed. "You guys look beautiful too. Meredith you look hot in that top. You could totally pass for 16." Meredith had on jeans and a black top that was form fitting and plunged slightly at the neckline.

"Really?" Meredith asked as her smile seemed to threaten to envelop her face.

"YES!" (no)

"Great! Well, Karen here couldn't look hotter in her pink skirt and matching top!" Meredith said.

Karen's top had no plunging neckline, almost the opposite in fact, and her skirt dropped almost to her ankles. "Thanks. You two don't think it's too much pink? I don't look like a Pepto-Bismol bottle?" (well, now that you mention it...)

"Totally not! You look really pretty in that color" Meredith and Amira said earnestly.

"Thanks," Karen said relieved. I had to wear this outfit tonight because I think my parents were worried that if I showed any "knee" tonight I'd come home seven months pregnant without shoes on and with a new habit of chewing straw."

Meredith and Amira looked perplexedly at Karen.

"My parents are nervous like that. You know that," Karen said while rolling her eyes in an upward pointing arc.

"Hey purple grape, where's your fruit basket, nerd?!" Brendan asked Amira as he and his brothers walked by on their way to the "boy" contingency.

"I'm not even sure that makes *sense*," Amira said through rolling eyes.

"Hey guys," Karen said to the brothers.

The three brothers turned their heads simultaneously and stared angrily at her. Karen then smiled and then turned her hands into "guns" and started "dance-shooting" and hopping around to the music that was playing. She then turned her "guns" into one rifle, made one final shooting motion, winked at them, and then turned and danced with her back to them in order to return her attention to Meredith and Amira who were now both laughing.

The brothers each took a step forward, but then just narrowed their eyes for a second and turned away, obviously not ready to reengage Amira with so many people around and slightly unsure whether or not they would win after their last encounter ended in defeat. Granted, Amira was aided by a bird, a *big* bird, a non "Sesame Street-Let's All Learn How To Count Together" *big* bird, but still, that would be hard to explain to their peers, and that experience also made them wonder what else she had up her sleeve.

"I can't believe you just did that," Meredith laughed trying not to tear up because she didn't want to screw up her eye shadow and liner.

Karen just shrugged her shoulders. "You know what they say, 'You mess with the MOP, you get the broom.'"

The girls laughed even louder.

"I don't think anyone would say that," Amira cackled.

"Well, maybe *we* should. I feel like the MOP Squad needs t-shirts or something. So, I think we should start thinking up mottos," Karen smiled back and jokingly stuck out her tongue.

"Speaking of the MOP Squad, where's Carlos," Amira asked as she glanced around the gym.

"Oh, he's here, but he's hanging out with the *guys*" Meredith replied, dropping her voice an octave on the word, "guys."

"Really?" Amira asked.

"Yeah," Karen continued, "I guess even he feels pressure to appear as macho as possible tonight, so he's over there flexing with the other boy yahoos." Karen then looked over her shoulder at the now quite large contingent of boys and sure enough among the throng was Carlos, laughing and hitting guys on their triceps muscle.

"Oh," Amira frowned. Though they would never admit it, all three suddenly felt slightly *slighted* and missed his company, as if they just realized that the MOP Squad would not be able to share every experience together, or at least not in the same way.

"Soooo, now what are we supposed to do?" Amira asked Meredith and Karen. Both Karen and Meredith just shrugged their shoulders. Obviously all knew step 1 was to go to the dance and step 3 was to dance with boys, but they forgot to discuss that precious step that connected step 1 with step 3, the ominous "step 2" that had derailed courtship attempts throughout history. They weren't alone; no one seemed to be taking the lead at this initial moment. So they just did what nervous kids tend to do and released their energy by joking with their friends at an even higher volume level.

As Amira laughed with her friends, her eyes couldn't help but float towards the group of boys on the opposite side of the room secretly hoping to find a certain someone's eyes. She was about to give up hope when suddenly through the darkness and murkiness, she found that oasis of blue she was searching for as her eyes found Kyle's. They only locked on each other for a split second and then both instinctively glanced away hoping the other didn't notice they were looking. To prove their point, each laughed harder and engaged more deeply into the conversations of their respective friends, but every few seconds each would glance in the other's direction, sometimes looking when the other one was, sometimes not, basically playing just a really, *really* dumb game of cat-and-mouse with the only result being each pretending to be more animated with their own friends.

Dear reader, I know you can't see me, but just imagine a brick wall and then imagine my head slamming into it...repeatedly. This "game," and I use that term loosely and wish I could put a sticker on it stating, "For Ages 2 and up" because complexity was obviously not part of it, could have gone on all night.

But the deejay, some college or post college kid, possibly a PhD student, who by his/her very definition made some very, *very* poor life decisions during his/her existence to arrive at this point, this "point" being a point*less* degree and spinning records to kids half his age, finally piped in, "All right, all right, all RIGHT!" (Yeah, seriously: all right) What is the haps my amigos and amigas?! I'm about to kick the music up a bit, and I *want* to see some *dancing!*"

The deejay had on baggy jeans, a *Morrissey* t-shirt, "cool" (but not really) shades, and a funky baseball cap flipped to the side, basically a getup that would get him killed in many a bar in Dallas, but here, at this dance, that occurrence, though not out of the realm of possibility, seemed remote.

Regardless of this guy's lack of "street cred," or for that matter: *any* cred, the kids seemed to listen to him as the two groups slowly made their way onto the dance floor. Hesitantly, groups of girls started dancing in a circle as some boy-band that thought they (or more likely their songwriters) were the first to cleverly realize "love" could be rhymed with "above" (if looking for love's location) or "dove" (if going for a metaphor of love's beauty) or "glove" (if love is cold) or "truv" (if the songwriter is lazy and wicked retahded; what's up Woostah?) sang some wretched song via the loud speakers. And so too the boys "jokingly" started doing dance moves in a large group as well, and like two spiraling galaxies making their way across the universe for their inevitable clash, the single sex dance circles slowly merged into unisex dance circles where no one was dancing with a partner but neither was anyone dancing alone.

Not everyone was dancing, however. Amira, Meredith, and Karen made (bounced) their way over to the punch and treat table where they met up with Carlos since it became "okay" to speak to him once the sexes began to mix on the dance floor. Carlos, had actually slicked his hair to the side and wore jeans and a sky-blue Oxford shirt with its collar flipped up (hopefully for an ironic reason...that or maybe he was going for a Vampire-Smurf look).

"Wow Amira, you look," Carlos began "umm, like a *girl*."

Not blown away by the compliment, Amira tilted her head forward slightly and said, "Thanks Carlos."

"No, I mean it suits you," Carlos continued. "It's like...it's like I can see how you can become like really hot when you're older."

"Carlos, you're not really helping yourself here," Amira said rolling her eyes but also unsure whether to be offended (for her *present* supposed lack of hotness) or greatly flattered (for her *future* hotness).

"Hey even your bruise matches your dress," Carlos astutely pointed out. Sure enough, Amira, Meredith, and Karen all looked at the bruise/scrape that still existed on the back of Amira's shoulder blade and it *did* seem to match for the most part.

Yawn, the MOP's "banter" continued for a spell with Meredith and Karen telling Carlos the type of accessories he *should* have worn tonight and Carlos telling them where they could stick those accessories. The girls of course also struck

Stephen McNamee ● The Ostrich

several modeling poses as Carlos just shook his head, which of course made them want to strike more poses. As this went, so did the dance, with poppy pop song after poppy pop song being played, and slowly the sexes seemed almost fully intermixed.

Then, the deejay came on and said, "Cool, cool, *cool!*" (not cool) "So y'all havin' a good time or what?" (WHAT!!!!) The kids however seemed to cheer. "So you cool cats seem to be heating up (wait, *what?!*), so I think it's time to get a bit mellooooow. How about a slow song?" (No, I'm good thanks...oh) And so he threw on some soft ballad, and slowly the kids began to pair off.

"Come on, you're going to dance with me," Karen said as she pulled Carlos out on the dance floor by the wrist as Carlos gave a perplexed look to Amira and Meredith.

Amira quickly scanned the dance floor hoping to lock eyes with Kyle again, but when she saw Kyle, her heart sank as he was already dancing with Amber's brunette friend, Tina.

"I wouldn't worry about it," Meredith said as she looked where Amira was looking.

"What?" Amira asked trying to play dumb.

"What, whatever. Don't play dumb. It's just one dance. I'm sure Tina probably took a claw and grabbed him before he could make his way over here."

Mark, a tall, thin blonde who wore his basketball jacket to the dance and who Amira had probably talked to once in her entire life walked over to where Amira and Meredith were standing.

"Hey Marnie. Meredith, 'Sup?" ('Sup *indeed*)

Marnie? Amira fumed to herself as she smiled up at him, "Hey."

"Hey, Mark, how's basketball going?" Meredith asked.

"Uhh, our first game is a couple of months away, just practice right now."

"Ahh, you guys going to beat Stephen Austin Prep this year?" Meredith asked as Amira looked on in wonder. Meredith could talk to anyone, but what was always shocking was that Meredith could talk to anyone *genuinely*. She always knew facts about other people and could earnestly engage them in discussions. This continually fascinated Amira, and also made Amira a bit jealous.

"Yeah, totally, especially after last year."

"Right." Meredith replied.

Yeah, last year, Amira thought to herself. *What the hell happened last year?* Obviously, Amira's attention rarely focused in on the round ball action.

"The buzzer beater was so lame," Meredith continued.

What the hell is a buzzer beater, Amira wondered. *Who did the beating? Was the buzzer beaten physically?* Every once in awhile there'd be a bit of Americana/lingo that Amira hadn't heard before. Because she grew up in Texas, her family quickly learned about football, and Amira actually knew enough about the game to feel like a "normal" Texan, and she actually knew a bit about hockey because of Meredith, but basketball she hadn't gotten to yet.

"So Meredith, you want to dance?" Mark asked to Meredith's knees.

"Oh, umm, well Amira and I were actually in the middle of a conversation, so I can't right now, but promise to ask me later and I'll say yes, okay?"

Confused, Mark nodded slowly.

"Promise?" Meredith smiled.

Her smile seemed to put him at ease, "Yeah, later's cool. I promise. Peace," he finished as he walked away.

"You didn't have to turn him down for me," Amira said while secretly thrilled, *THRILLED* that Meredith didn't leave her alone like a loser.

"I don't mind Amira. Like I said about Kyle: it's just one dance. There will be others," Meredith winked back. "Hey check out the lovebirds (Karen and Carlos). She's totally *not* letting him lead."

Amira looked and laughed because Meredith was correct. Carlos and Karen were slow dancing but the space between them was wide enough for a moped to drive through. Carlos had his hands above Karen's hips and she had hers draped around his shoulders in what would seem like a calm, non-aggressive formation, but the war was fought on the ground. Every time Carlos tried to take a step he would inevitably hit one of Karen's feet, which would cause her to shake her head. At first she looked angry, but quickly she started to smile and laugh, and then Amira and Meredith could see her mouthing the words like, "Left...Left, right, left, right..." and on and on. When Karen turned towards Amira and Meredith, Mer and Amira made faux "kissy faces" which led Karen to tilt her head and stick out her tongue at them as she laughed. The laugh was short lived as another Carlos step landed squarely on her left foot.

As the song volume quieted signifying the end of the song, Karen dragged Carlos back to Amira and Meredith.

"He's not *hopeless*, but we should start training him now," Karen said.

With a grimace on his face, he said, "How do you know that *I'm* the one who needs to work on dancing Maybe you were *causing* me to step on your feet."

"How do you figure?" Karen asked.

"Well, maybe as a *girl* you should have *anticipated* where my feet were going," he said obviously surprised by how sound his reasoning appeared.

"Yeah, I don't think so Carlos, but I'll dance with you next to find out," Meredith said. "Unless you want to dance with him again Ms. Karen?"

"No, I need to let the top of my feet heal for a minute," she laughed back. "He's all yours."

Meredith smiled and took Carlos by the hand and held it with her arm extended out. She then placed his other hand on her hip and her hand on his shoulder, so they could waltz onto the dance floor as the next slow song came on. Karen and Amira watched them waltz off, and then Karen quickly turned toward Amira.

"So has Kyle seen you yet?"

"I think so," Amira whispered.

"Why are you whispering?" Karen asked.

"I don't know," Amira replied honestly. Amira then scanned the dance floor but with a sinking of her shoulders she couldn't even see Kyle anymore. She looked at her purple flats that had sparkles around the toes and thought that perhaps she had just been another foolish girl thinking that her dream world had anything to do with reality. Then, she looked up at Karen and noticed that Karen was trying but failing to contain a smile.

"What?" Amira asked.

But Karen didn't answer, and really she didn't have to since Amira tracked Karen's eyes by turning 180 degrees and saw what Karen saw: Kyle approaching. Amira quickly struck what she thought of as a "sultry" pose but from my perspective looked more like she was just suffering from another calf cramp with just a sprinkling of muscle tremor.

"Hey," Kyle said.

"Hey you," Amira said and then wondered where the "you" in "Hey you" had come from.

"You look...great," Kyle said as he ran his fingers through his hair.

Amira got lost for a second, lost following his fingers thinking they were five clipper ships sailing through an ocean of gold. (thankfully, I haven't eaten in a few hours) After coming back to reality she said, "Thanks."

"Would you like to dance," he asked through a small smile.

Amira told herself to wait three seconds so as not to seem too excited. She failed to consider though that what an excited, young teen girl thinks is three seconds is actually about .3 seconds, so she almost instantly said, "Yes!" in a slightly too loud voice.

"Cool," Kyle nodded as he reached for her hand to lead her to the dance floor.

Amira gently took his hand and prayed to Allah. She felt she didn't ask Allah for much, but now she *begged* him to protect her from fainting or from tripping or from embarrassing herself, from being attacked by wolves....okay, maybe I added the "wolves" part. Holding Kyle's hand seemed to impair her vision for all she could see was him and therefore, thankfully, couldn't see the numerous sneers she got (especially from

210

Amber and her minions) as they made their way into the outer throng of slow dancers. After what seemed like an infinitely long walk, Kyle stopped and turned to Amira. He went to let go of her hand, but she held on for about a second too long, so he slightly had to jerk it free. He then put her arms around his neck and his hands on her lower back. Amira's heartbeat quickened. Kyle gently pulled her closer, and Amira went to place her chin on his shoulder when suddenly the deejay broke through the music.

The deejay said, "Sweet, SWEET, *sweet!*" (not sweet) "We don't need this slow stuff right now! Let's kick it back up a notch, yeah!"

Amira and Kyle had slow danced for all of about ten seconds, but Kyle let go of Amira and stepped back and shrugged. With that, he began to dance surprisingly deftly even as the beats pumped out faster and faster. For a split second, Amira was inwardly dismayed about missing out on a slow dance with Kyle, but then she realized that she was still *DANCING with Kyle(!)*, so after listening to the music for a couple of seconds to figure out the tempo, she too began to dance.

Dear reader, I'm not quite sure I have the literary skills or necessary vocabulary to describe what next occurred. I did not think it possible for four limbs to dance to four separate, independent rhythms simultaneously, but somehow Amira accomplished that feat. Aside from the multiple rhythms, she interspersed her movements with what can only be described as epileptic jerks of her body. At first Amira and Kyle were smiling at each other, but with each passing beat, the smile on Kyle's face faded. Others around the pair also began to watch in disbelief at what was occurring before their eyes. Amira danced obliviously onward as if in a trance, and yet, she continued to add new wrinkles to her movement like having her wrists seem to work independently from her forearms which in turn worked autonomously from her shoulders. I would liken her performance to a train wreck dear reader, but I'm not sure that would be fair....be fair to train wrecks because (1) I'm not sure a train wreck ever threatened so many lives at one time, and (2) a train wrecks' movements were far less chaotic. Thank god Amira was saved from further embarrassment due to the wolves that crashed the party.

Chapter 5: Friend Or Foe

I think Arbor Day gets short shrift when it comes to holidays. I mean let's be honest: trees do a lot for us. They give us air to breathe; they give fruits and nuts a place to grow. They shade us and let us know when its windy due to their swaying. They allow us to use hammocks and build tire swings and tree-houses. And, all they really ask in return is a day to celebrate their wonder. But when is the last time you ever heard someone ask, "Hey man, what'd ya do for Arbor Day?" So I say spend some time in the realm of an elm. Give some time to pine. Tell a cherry blossom it's awesome. Put a hood on that wood...well, maybe skip the last one for double entendre reasons...well, *actually*, in that case do NOT skip that one. Safety first people. But yes, the next time Arbor Day comes around, do the right thing. You'll feel better about yourself. Anyway...

It took a few seconds for all to grasp the situation. In truth many eyes went from Amira to the wolves *back* to Amira and her "dancing" and *then* back to the wolves as their brains finally caught up to all they were seeing. The first few wolves arrived like silent assassins, sulking in the shadows and establishing a perimeter. They didn't howl or growl; they just prowled the outer boundaries of the gym. It's likely that the students and chaperones at first assumed someone let in a stray dog and then another stray dog, and then they probably picked up on the size of the animals.

Surprisingly at first no one screamed. Everyone, human and animal alike just stared quietly taking each other in. The deejay didn't see the animals but knew something was up when the dancing stopped and everyone froze, so he quickly turned the music off (what? no, "Who Let The Dogs Out?! to solidify your lameness Mr. Deejay?). When the music died down, Amira mercifully stopped her dance of (social) death (seriously people, I think she set back Middle Eastern dancers by twenty years). The motionlessness of the situation lasted several more moments. Amira first scanned the crowd but didn't see anything wrong. She then looked at Kyle because in Amira's mind, who wouldn't want to look at Kyle? His face however lacked its usual wry smile and mischievous eyes and was replaced with some cross between wonder and fear. Amira followed his gaze which she realized (disappointingly) was focused *not* on her but rather several feet behind her. When she turned around, she saw two dark circles; in the center of the circles were two irises that glowed red due to the light reflected from the disco ball, and around those eyes was a whole lotta fur.

This is not happening, Amira thought to herself. She weighed her options, but none seemed good.

Normally, she would be worried for her friends, but she was fairly certain that the wolves were here for her and her alone. Silence pervaded the room. All that really could be heard were the quickened breaths of several students and the soothing hum of the air conditioning unit which acted as if nothing out of the

214

ordinary was occurring. Finally, a wolf jumped through a window and roared. The animal's intrusion onto the kids dance floor shattered the silence and lack of motion and seemed to act as a spark which unleashed the frenetic energy that had been building all at once.

Screams bellowed from tiny frames, sneakers squeaked severely, breaking up the yelling in a staccato fashion. Kids and adults were running every which way. During the chaos of bodies flying in every direction, the wolves lost track of Amira. Thus, Amira decided it was time to run, so she ran. She darted toward the refreshment tables looking for any kind of barrier.

Finally, one of the wolves spotted Amira and charged after her. Amira saw the wolf out of the corner of her eye and quickly weighed her options. Realizing she had no options and with a form that a Major League Baseball player would find inspired, Amira slid under the table just as the wolf dove for her. Amira knew she wasn't dead when she heard a loud clank. Underneath the table she stared at her very own Egyptian killer. The only things that separated her from death were the metal leg poles that formed an "X" on each side. The wolf had entangled itself in the X with its neck caught in the "upper quadrant." Amira and the wolf stared at each other. The wolf snarled and then snapped its jaw shut just millimeters from Amira's face. With that, Amira started to "speed scooch" backward along the floor as the wolf pulled the table forward after her. Thankfully the table legs rested on the floor with rubber "booties"; this caused a ton of friction as the table moved, so the animal failed to close the distance between them. Finally, the table hit a wall, which caused the wolf to get even more stuck in the X as the metal dug into its skin. However, now it could reach Amira with its jaw, so it snapped at her again, but Amira was too fast. Amira rolled out from under the table keeping her body as low as possible, and by doing so her ankles and feet escaped underneath the wolf. Amira hopped up and ran toward the nearest door, which wasn't an exit but rather just led to the hallway which led to more of the school.

The MOP Squad knew Amira was in trouble, but they looked at each other helplessly, not knowing what they could do. However, as Amira passed another refreshments table on her way out of the gym, Carlos took action.

"Amira! Here!" Carlos yelled as he threw a huge silver tray full of brownies at Amira. Several brownies nailed Amira in the face, in her hair and on her dress. For a moment she just stared at Carlos and gave him the "WHAT THE HELL ARE YOU DOING- WHY ARE YOU THROWING BROWNIES AT ME WHILE I'M BEING CHASED BY WOLVES?!" look that Carlos had seen more than once in his life.

"The *chocolate*. No one in the canine family can digest chocolate. It's like puppy poison!" he said smiling and then shrugging his shoulders as if to say, "What did you expect?"

Amira remained completely still, mouth agape, not knowing how to respond. Thankfully, she didn't have to say anything since suddenly another wolf made a beeline right for her. Almost instinctively Amira grabbed the silver tray and swung it at the wide-open mouth full of sharp teeth that was headed in her direction. Her swing connected with the full force of her strength, which was surprisingly a lot for a girl weighing in under 100 pounds. The force stunned the wolf. It fell to the ground, whining and staring at its paws. It kept wiping its face as if it could somehow wipe away the pain. Amira then took a bite from one of the brownies she caught, but she decided to share it with a wolf that had a scar along the left side of its face that was heading right for her. Her aim was perfect; she threw it precisely into the wolf's mouth. The wolf swallowed without really thinking about it, but unfortunately the puppy poison did not seem to work instantaneously.

So, Amira made a dash for the hallway and darted out into the hall. The fluorescent lighting now seemed alien to her coming from the darkened gymnasium. Everything in the school from the lockers to the flooring to the classroom doors seemed too yellow, like tooth decay, and yet everything also sparkled like a really depressing "vacancy" sign of a desolate motel. Amira wished she had a weapon right now. She considered popping into various classrooms and trying to break into various teachers' locked desks because she assumed at least one teacher illegally carried and stashed a firearm on school property, but if she entered a room and was wrong, she might just succeed in trapping herself. *Okay, think Amira. You can do this. What have I learned that could help right now?* At that moment, the stark truth crystallized in her mind: her formal education clearly lacked wolf survival skill techniques. Find yourself on fire? Stop, drop, and roll. Tornadoes or Nuclear attacks? Hide under your desk. Homeroom under attack by wild animals? Hopefully you remembered to update your emergency contact number because "you be dead." From television she knew that to best a shark you punched it in it's snout or eye, to outrun an alligator you ran in a zigzag fashion, but when being hunted by a pack of wolves...nothing, absolutely nothing came to mind. Not only school, but also society as a whole failed her in this instance.

Amira felt Moha was her best chance at escape, but she had no idea how to contact him. She hoped she had a psychic connection with him since he did, after all, save her once from the murderous pack. She closed her eyes, scrunched her face, and tightened all her muscles as she called out to him in her mind, but nothing, other than making herself look horribly constipated, occurred. However, when her eyes were closed, she was able to hear a very deep growl. She peaked out with one eye, and less than thirty yards away was another wolf.

The wolf charged at Amira. Amira realized if she ran she was *meat*, so if running away meant death, she thought therefore that logically running toward the wolf must mean the opposite death. (That's actually an interesting theory...that will likely lead to death, being mauled horribly, Kyle losing all attraction for you when he sees your gored corpse in the hallway and hall, but definitely an interesting theory...well, a *theory* anyway...okay more of a hypothesis, but *Good Luck!*) Amira put her hand on a locker to steady her nerves, and then with a scream, she charged at the wolf. Although there were no witnesses to this dear reader, I swear to you that Amira's tactic stunned the wolf, for it lost its snarl for a split second and tilted its head to the side in a "You know I'm wolf, right?" expression. You know what also stunned the wolf? The classroom door Amira flung open at the last second as they were about to meet.

A loud crunch occurred as Amira braced herself on the opposite side of the door so that the animal would take the full brunt of the force of running into a heavy door. Amira didn't bother checking on her handiwork. She bolted down the hall, turned a corner, and stopped. About a hundred yards away she saw an exit to the parking lot and a staircase leading to the second floor of the school building. *Freedom*, she thought. Well, maybe not freedom since I'm fairly certain that wolves can survive for quite sometime *outside* of school buildings, but outside probably did seem like a safer bet under the circumstances. However, again, it's quite possible more wolves were outside. Amira heard more growling and now howling down the hall, so she figured no time like the present to go for the door.

She sprinted down the hall, her purple sneakers making high-pitched squeaks as she suddenly became thankful she didn't wear heels because she didn't know how to walk in them. Within fifty yards from the door, her squeaks were replaced by barking from two wolves closing in on her from behind. Within thirty-five yards from the door, she swore she saw a man cloaked in shadow (but for his purple eyes) standing outside the door, but when she blinked the image was gone. Within twenty-five yards of the door, the wolves had halved the distance between Amira and them. After ten more yards, Amira could hear the panting of the dogs' breath. Hopelessly outnumbered in the sharp teeth and claws department and knowing full well that she at less than one hundred pounds could not compete with the wolves' strength, Amira decided to use the one thing she had to her advantage: traction. The staircase and more importantly the staircase siding ascended next to her. The second she felt the animals' hot breath on her back, she planted her right foot and jumped to her left. As Amira jumped so too did the animals but the slippery linoleum flooring prevented them from launching themselves fully. Amira's hands grabbed onto the side of the staircase, and one of the wolves latched onto the hem of Amira's dress. With a loud tearing sound, six inches of Amira's dress tore away, but the tearing was not enough to stop the wolf's forward momentum, so as Amira hung to side, the wolves landed and then went sprawling/sliding/flailing forward all the way to the door. Amira then planted her feet on the side and kicked out and up as she held on to the top, which allowed her to flip over the side and onto the staircase. This gave her precious seconds to ascend the stairs and flee from her attackers before they regrouped.

Amira ran up the stairs and had two choices, go left or right. Seeing as neither choice to led to a magical hang glider, Amira took off to the left. The first classroom door she tried to open was locked. So, she ran to the next one and that too was locked.

"Amira!" someone yelled further down the hall.

Although the person was covered in shadow the fact the mystery person could speak (rather than howl) was enough for her to trust him over the wolves. As Amira drew closer she realized it was *Kyle!*

"Come on! In here!" he said as he moved his arm in a circling motion emphasizing he meant for her to join him in the classroom. When she reached the room, he closed the door and deftly planted a chair underneath the handle and then quickly moved some more desks towards the door.

"You okay?" he asked. "You took off so quickly, I figured you must have been more afraid than anyone."

Amira wanted to tell him she was afraid *FOR GOOD REASON*, but trying to explain to Kyle that the wolves in fact *were* bigoted toward Arab-Texans would have sounded less than believable. "Was anyone hurt?"

"I don't think so," Kyle said. The wolves growled and tore apart some tables and streamers, but they mostly just sniffed around like they were searching for something. "Maybe a family of rabbits or something somehow snuck into the school."

Or something, Amira thought. She then realized that *she* was endangering Kyle. She didn't know what she would do if he somehow got hurt, and on a superficial level, she'd be *REALLY PISSED* if his immaculate face was scarred or shredded by a wolf.

She then heard howling from down the hall. Obviously, a wolf or two had now made it up the stairs.

"Look, Kyle, I appreciate you worrying about me, but I think you should go," she said as calmly as she could, like the voice she'd use to an elderly person when explaining how to use a computer.

"Well, yeah, I think we should go together."

Suddenly, something scraped at the door, followed by a deep growl.

"Oh god," Amira said looking at the door.

"I'm sure we're fine," Kyle said in a relaxed tone. "The wolf smells us, but once it realizes it can't get at us, it will move on because humans aren't really part of a wolf's diet anyway."

A second of silence followed, and then a *CRASH* against the door that was powerful enough to make the desks on the humans' side of the door bounce around.

"Hey, did I tell you how pretty you looked tonight?"

Amira's attention quickly turned from the door to Kyle. "Oh, thank you," she said coyly.

"I'm serious. Purple is a great color on you."

CRASH!

"You think?" I was considering going with this green dress, but my mom thought this one fit better and,"

"No. Totally, you made the right decision."

Now beaming, she said, "Well, thank you Kyle. That's very-"

SMASH! A definite crack and indention now appeared in the middle of the door.

Well, that settled it! After Kyle's compliment, there was NO WAY Amira and Kyle were dying tonight.

"Do you like the stars?"

"Like the space kind?" he asked.

"Exactly," she said as she grabbed his hand and walked over to the window. She unlocked the door and was glad that there was a downward sloping four-foot ledge that ended with a gutter that she and Kyle would be able to climb onto.

"Amira, I really don't think that wolf is going to break in here. That is a pretty thick doo-"

Unfortunately Kyle could not complete that sentence due to the door *almost* splitting in two from the wolf's latest assault on the inanimate, wooden object (I'm still talking about the door, *not* movie star Paul Walker...just didn't want to confuse you).

Amira was already outside on the ledge. "Come on," she said as she reached for Kyle's hand. For the second time this evening, Kyle took Amira's hand. They both laid flat against the sloping siding made of a mixture of tar and...well, I'm sure something else, and they planted their feet in the gutter which didn't feel quite that sturdy. They had to go about twelve feet before reaching another area of the roof that would allow them to climb onto more even and sturdy ground.

"Let's just move slowly, so we don't shake the gutter loose," Amira said.

Kyle agreed with her until a wolf's mouth suddenly appeared at the window and snapped at him missing him by less than an inch. So that plan went out the window (What? Not a fan of a play on words? Was that a play on words?), and suddenly Amira and Kyle were shimmying as quickly as they could. Thankfully the wolf was not suicidal, so it just growled at them for a few seconds, and then disappeared back inside. They reached a corner of the building where two different sections of the building (the gym and the rest of the school) converged. However, the gym roof was higher than the school's, so this led to the creation of a crevice that Amira could stick her foot in and use as leverage to climb up about seven feet so that she could reach the top of the school's roof. Kyle followed suit and soon enough they were standing on top of the roof, and truth be told, the stars actually were quite pretty that night.

"So now what?" Kyle said.

"Well, there's a fire escape you can use to get back down to street level," Amira said wishing that she had the courage to really say what was on her mind, *Now what? Now you kiss me. Kiss me Kyle. Kiss me until you realize your love for me is strong. And hold me as you kiss me, and-*

Her *Gone With The Wind*-esque dream was interrupted by Kyle with a less romantic grammar question.

"You mean there's a ladder that *we* can go down," Kyle said.

"Yes," Amira said, and by yes she meant *no*. (Girls) Amira knew that her presence next to him endangered his life, so it was time that they separate. It was time that they separate...I wrote that it was time for them to separate...(pause)...like right *now*. Amira just stood staring at Kyle *so* wishing they could kiss, with their adrenaline flowing from fleeing, with the stars shining brightly due to a new moon, with the song of police sirens playing in the distance (obviously love affects how certain things are interpreted by the brain).

As if reading her mind, Kyle said, "Amira, I..."

They looked at each other for a few seconds. Without either's knowledge, they were slowly inching toward each other. Their movements were minute, but ever so slowly their lips were closing the distance between them. Kyle closed his eyes as he leaned in, and Amira was about to do the same when suddenly she saw a head with a beak pop up momentarily over the side of the school. She thought she was imagining things, but then a half-second later Moha's unmistakable head popped into view again.

Amira hopped up and waived her hand at Moha trying to shoo the bird away during this most amazing of moments, but in doing so her shoulder elevated as Kyle's chin was descending. Thus an unpleasant collision ensued, unpleasant for Kyle because it felt like he got hit in the chin, and unpleasant for Amira because she just decked the love of her life. right before a kiss attempt.

"Ahhh, Kyle yelped. He held his left hand over his mouth checking for blood. His eyes were opened as wide as possible, and he stared at Amira in shock.

"Oh my god! Kyle are you okay?! I'm so sorry! I'm not very good at this thing, and I umm, I think I missed," she said frantically as she put her hand on his arm and stared at his mouth hoping she didn't just ruin his smile.

"Come on, let's get you down the fire escape," she said leading him by placing her hand and arm on his. "Again, I'm *so* sorry."

"It's cool," he said. "I probably shouldn't have, well...yeah."

No! No! You TOTALLY should have! Amira thought to herself, but instead, she said something a bit more subtle and quite a bit more awkward under the circumstances.

"Kyle, I had a really good time climbing around with you tonight," she said with a sincere smile on her face. (Yeah, good time, what with the wolves terrorizing everyone and Amira's shoulder becoming intimate with Kyle's chin, I'd say fun was had by all!)

He stared at her for a second and added, "Yeahhhh."

Yeah, me too?! Amira hoped, but nothing followed his equivocal "yeah." Kyle began descending down the fire escape.

"Oh, wait Kyle. You go ahead. I...umm...forgot something in the room, so I'm going to go get it."

"What? Amira, just come down and you can walk in the building *normally* and grab it."

"Yeah, I see your point, but I'm totally cool. See ya in a bit!" she said through a smile and took off across the roof.

Kyle stood there for a second, pondered going after her, felt his sore chin, and figured that comprehending girls was *beyond* him and so continued down in a confused and possibly concussed state.

Although the roof was flat on this part of the building the side opposite where Amira dropped Kyle off began to slope a bit where it met the gym's roof area, which had more of an upside down "U" shape to it. Moha was still jumping up and down (and obviously this bird had some "hops" because that's quite the jump in terms of height). Amira reached the edge and looked down.

"Okay, I *see* you, you stupid bird. Couldn't you have waited like *two* more minutes before screwing up my life?" Moha just looked up at her, snapped his beak open and shut, and kept jerking his neck to the side seeming to beckon her to jump down.

If Amira slid down the sloping side and then "dropped" the rest of the way, it would basically be a twenty-foot freefall. Obviously, that was out of the question*nnnholy sh--*, Amira took three steps back, closed her eyes, opened them, took a deep breath, and then slid down the side for a few feet before her body separated from the building due to something the intellectuals like to call, *physics.*

Moha's eyes *widened* dramatically as if to say, *"WHAT THE HELL ARE YOU DOING?! I MEANT FOR YOU TO HURRY DOWN. I DIDN'T MEAN FOR YOU TO JUMP!"* (Well, perhaps next time, if there is a next time, Amira and Moha will be better able to understand each other...sort of like the old saying, "If you jump off a building and don't die, there are likely lessons to be learned." Granted, it's a not well-known saying, possibly because of the high success rate gravity has at defeating a person's life force when mixed with concrete sidewalks.

As Amira fell, she wondered what happened to the wolves. She continued to wonder that right up until the point a wolf burst out an open window and tried to snatch Amira out of thin air. The good news was that the wolf missed Amira; the *bad* news was that it did succeed in grabbing Amira's dress. So, Amira hung about twelve feet above Moha with her dress partially above her head (turns out wearing shorts underneath was a *good* decision).

"Ugh! Stop damaging my *dress!* I LOVE this dress! (translation: *Kyle* loves this dress). And right that instant, Amira decided to find out how applicable Shark Week on the Discovery Channel was to her every day life. When the wolf yanked at the dress in order to "pull" Amira up, Amira didn't fight but rather embraced the upward momentum, clenched her fist, and unleashed a potent punch right on the wolf's nose.

Completely confused and in a decent amount of pain, the wolf released Amira's dress. As Amira fell toward Moha, she expressed her displeasure with the wolf's action in a way that could be understood by both the hearing and hearing impaired communities of the United States.

Amira landed butt first on Moha, but the landing still jarred her. She landed facing the opposite direction from Moha, which gave her a nice view of four more wolves that were locked onto Amira and Moha. Amira failed to gain her balance since landing on Moha, so she began to tilt. Moha jerked his body underneath Amira as she leaned precipitously to the left. However, this allowed the wolves to catch up to the dynamic duo...well, not quite dynamic...maybe the "dynamically *decent* duo." The first wolf lunged for Amira, but Moha kicked back and up with his leg and nailed the wolf right in the face, which stunned the wolf as it fell to the ground. Two more wolves came up to Amira and Moha and chose a new strategy. They each ran along side of Moha, one on each side, and then the one on the right threw its body into Moha's with all his strength. This caused Moha to bounce uncontrollably to the left thereby making Amira fall to the right. Thankfully, Amira fell feet first and used the wolf's back as a mobile step which she used to bounce back onto Moha before the wolf could realize what just happened. However, as she did so the other wolf crashed into Moha. This time Amira felt herself falling backward so she over compensated by throwing her body forward, but her lunge was too much, so she smashed into Moha's neck and tried to cling to it to regain her balance, she twirled 180 degrees and her grip slipped. The next thing Amira knew she was viewing the world upside-down with her legs rapped around a shocked Moha. Moha stared down at her as Amira tucked her chin to her chest, so she could look up at Moha. Amira gave a quick half smile, her attempt at an apology. Moha pressed onward since stopping would lead to certain death.

This new riding position though had the disadvantage of slowing Moha down as Amira offered a more literal version of hanging an albatross around Moha's neck. A wolf with a scar on its face made its way up toward Amira. Amira swore the animal's breathing sounded slightly labored, and she remembered that she had fed the untamed dog a brownie. *Huh, maybe Carlos was on to something*, Amira thought to herself. In about two seconds the wolf would be running parallel with Amira, so she cocked her arm back, and screamed, "STOP!" Moha tried to stop and skidded forward. The wolf tried to as well, but wasn't as quick at stopping. As the wolf skidded past, Amira punched the wolf as hard in the stomach as possible, which led to the wolf moaning on the ground. Amira then released her scissor grip on Moha and fell to the hard dirt ground. She quickly got up and hopped back on her feathery transportation for the evening. Amira smacked Moha on his hide telling him to get a move on as Amira prepared herself to take on more wolves if they caught up to them. They heard the howls from behind for a while, but soon the howling faded and Moha's planned randomness in terms of route seemed too much for the wolves to follow. Soon as more and more stars filled the sky, Amira relaxed. She took in the world around her: the sights, the smells, the sensation of the cool night air on her skin. She missed her family already and wished she had talked to her mother about the book, but she felt that could wait. Whatever was going on, could wait. She breathed deeply, and a calm settled over her. Of course, it's always quietest before the storm.

Moha didn't take Amira home but rather took her back to the oasis. Amira hopped off Moha.

"Okay, now what?" Amira said staring at the feathered beast. "You know, I bet if you offered up a clue this could move along faster." Believe me Amira: I couldn't agree more.

Amira decided to go back to the rock that had all the various drawings/writings on it since that "randomness" seemed to be a theme among the book, cloth, and rock. As she crouched down to look at the boulder, no sudden heavenly insight appeared to Amira. She placed her hand over the rock hoping to *feel* some invisible opening or handle, but nothing. Then, she tried to move the rock, at first pushing it as her sparkly purple flats dug into the dirt/sand creating tiny dunes as her efforts failed. Then she tried pulling the rock and then tried rocking it side to side, but it did not budge.

Making sure Moha wasn't looking, Amira sighed deeply, shocked at what she was about to do: the most stereotypical thing she could think of. She summoned the spirit of Ali Baba and said, "Open Sesame!" Nothing. She then turned and saw Moha shaking his head in obvious disgust.

Wait, she thought. *Maybe I'm the key. Maybe I need to say my own name to let it know it's okay to open up.* She stared at the rock for a good ten seconds, and then said, "My name is Amira Masri." Nothing happened so she continued, "My name is Amira bint Mahdi bin Qudamah Al Masri, and umm I am hear to protect the ke-, umm, the che-, umm" (she didn't know how to pronounce "Qistone." FYI: it's 'chee-stone').

She paused for a second. Then, with all the courage she could muster said, "I'm here to protect the Q-I-stone, so by the power of...of...the *ostrich*, I have...the POWER!" Nothing, though I think she just confused her relationship with this rock to He-Man's relationship with Greyskull. Thus, it seemed Egyptian She-Ra here was stuck. So, Amira sat on the rock and pondered.

"You know you could be more helpful!" she yelled to Moha.

Moha ignored her and continued eating whatever the heck he was eating at the other end of the oasis.

"Ooh, I'm Moha. I have feathers and ignore girls in distress. I'm a big deal on the Masri ranch. All the female ostriches want me. Stupid bird." Amira finished her mini-tantrum and decided to open her hand bag that matched her dress and pull out the book and cloth. She placed the cloth over the book and then held the two items in both hands. She didn't understand it. Every children's story she had ever read, led her to believe that she should succeed at finding the opening to the mysterious cave. That's how the stories work. She never remembered a book ending with something like,

And so the heroine reached the door which separated her mundane world from the magical land of *Flying Chocolate Magic Fun*, but since the door was locked, the girl went back to the library to do her homework never to return. She did however end up going to college and majoring in accounting. Now she's mildly successful and somewhat satisfied with her life, though if she were honest with herself she could probably stand to lose ten pounds if she wasn't so lethargic.

So Amira continued to sit on the rock. Ten minutes went by. Then another ten.

...

...

...

"*[BEEP]!*" she swore as she smashed the book between her legs down onto the rock, which surprisingly caused the rock to disappear.

As the rock slid out from under her, Amira thought to herself, *Hey, it's opening!* And then realizing she was falling backward, she thought, *Ow (thump) ow-ow-ow,* and that thought continued all the way down the stairs.

Amira rubbed her neck and then stood up to stretch out her back, lightly pressed various areas of her body to make sure everything was still in tact, and wiped off the dirt from a dress that was becoming more and more of a lost cause.

"Did you know about the whole rock disappearing thing?!" she called up to the opening where the rock used to be. Moha stuck his head through the opening and just blinked non-committally a few times. "Ugh, now what. It's dark in here." Amira took a step and stubbed her toe on something made of metal or hard plastic. "Ow! Seriously people, invest in lights!" The whiner then bent down and picked up the object she ran into and found to her surprise, a flashlight.

"Oh, umm thanks?" she said, a bit unnerved that her request was answered so quickly. She turned on the flashlight and the cave illuminated quickly. The walls seemed to sparkle almost on their own since there was no way the flashlight could be causing this much light to be reflected. Amira moved the light around and realized she could either go left or right. She chose left because she thought that it maybe was *slightly* brighter than whatever lay to the right, and any extra light was fine with Amira. She continued down the passageway for several minutes until she noticed a slight warming of the air. She continued on and after another minute, she realized the air was most definitely warmer. She turned a corner and then noticed the walls sparkled even brighter. After about another twenty feet, she entered a rather sparse "alcove." The room was empty save for a stone pedestal that seemed to glow at the top, a few books which rested on a stone ledge, and a few rocks scattered about.

Amira was about to go to the pedestal but then noticed a series of books lining a shelf that was placed next to the pedestal. Amira felt compelled to examine the books, so she walked over to where the books were and grabbed the one with the shiniest cover, thereby continuing the discriminatory practices of readers worldwide of going for more attractive looking books. As she opened the book, a letter fell out.

*A*mira,

عيد ميلاد سعيد

Happy Birthday my child. And yet you are no longer a child as you should be reading this letter on what is now your eighteenth birthday. The book you used to enter the cave is the Book of Connectivity. As I write this, the book is in my possession, for I used it to enter this cave as well. However, I have made arrangements for it to arrive in your possession on your eighteenth birthday. The fact you are now reading this letter is proof that the book has reached you alive and well.

I'm certain these past few years have been tough with you unable to return to Egypt. And yet I hope you will forgive your parents, for they were only doing what I asked of them. Amira, it was too dangerous for you to be in Egypt until you turned eighteen, and so your parents promised to keep you away once you reached puberty, for the pull of the Qistone coupled with the group known as the "Society" who want to extract it from you were just too much of a risk. But, I get ahead of myself. There is so much to tell you, yet I write this in haste, so I must decide where to begin.

Centuries upon centuries ago, a light flashed along the sky. Unlike any other light before, it crossed continents and oceans and gleamed brighter the closer it fell to earth. It was difficult to decipher the illuminated object's path, but a few people in rather different parts of the world were witness to this event. Of those that saw the "comet," a few powerful individuals were compelled to send emissaries to follow its path. However, I believe it would be more accurate to state it was the comet that "compelled" those individuals to send those individuals to follow.

Envoys were dispatched. Although some traveled by sea and others by land, although the distances for some were thousands of miles whereas for others it was less than a hundred, these "groups" arrived simultaneously. The object decided that either all could discover its location or none. The groups knew not what they discovered, but they knew the object was powerful.

The object was not found whole. Originally it was made up of seven connected orbs, which came to be called Qistones. However, only five Qistones were found.

Although the groups represented different cultures, different masters, different religions, one trait they all, or rather, they almost all had in common was wisdom. For, they knew that no one group should possess all of the Qistones. For over a year, negotiations took place among the groups, and at the end of the countless discussions, it was decided that the Qistones should be divided among them. However, one group went along with the negotiations in bad faith, planning all the time to take the Qistones for themselves. The night after the agreement, this renegade group, now known as the "Society," attempted to seize all the orbs, but their attempt was thwarted, barely, and although defeated, they escaped with their own orb. I will tell you more about them later, but first let me discuss the men and women who originally protected the Qistones from the Society, the men and women known as The Continuum.

The Continuum decided to lie upon return to their homes, for kings and rulers were too often ambitious and power-hungry and thus could not be trusted with the knowledge of these orbs' existence. The Continuum even thought it best to hide from one another where precisely they would hide their individual orbs so as to further protect the Qistones from those not wise enough to handle them. However, they kept a hidden channel of communication open with one another to make sure each group's Qistone was safe.

It's no accident the cave you're in and the area outside the cave will look exactly like the Qistone's location in Egypt. The Continuum all agreed to hide the orbs, but how to hide them was never discussed. And yet, each group had visions of where the Qistones should "rest," and thus the caves were built. As for the plant growth outside the caves, the energy of the Qistones must be behind that phenomenon.

I'm sure you want to know what a Qistone "is." All things are energy. Therefore we are all connected. As energy flows around and through us, these Qistones are focal points, nodes that concentrate this energy and align our connectivity. People and animals react differently to the orbs, but for some the effect is far greater than for others. You, Amira, are one who reacts most strongly to the orbs. Thus the Universe will open to you. You will connect. You may even experience visions of different times or different places, of people you may or may not have met yet. But be patient, for your understanding of the Qistone and your ability to control your interactions with it will take time.

For century upon century, it has been those that are most affected by/most connected to the Qistones that have been asked/compelled to protect the orbs. And, because of this connection, you must protect the Qistones. But fear not, for the protection is not one-sided. The Qistones are intelligent and aware, and they protect themselves and those connected to them

235

in various ways. Whether by sending you a guardian or by sending you information to steer you in the right direction, the orb works with you.

For countless generations, your extended family has played a part in the Egyptian Qistone's journey, and its secret has been guarded carefully. Only those who needed to know were told. You see it was never known exactly who of the new generation would most connect to the orb, so until called upon, your family members lived their lives normally.

Before you were born they decided to move to the United States in order to study. However, your mother became pregnant with you. Your mother thought it best to stay near her family, and your father agreed. But, I had a vision Amira that you would play an important role in the Qistone's destiny but that you would be in grave danger if you grew up in Egypt.

After long, impassioned discussions, your parents agreed to move to the United States immediately. However, we also agreed that the family should come back in the summer times in order for you to spend time with your extended family and to be near the Qistone's hiding place at least for short periods of time in order to keep the "connection" alive.

Another part of the agreement though was that once you reached puberty, you would not return to Egypt until your 18th birthday. The most dangerous time for someone, a "princess" as someone in your position is called, is between puberty and adulthood, for the Qistone starts to "call" for you, but you are not physically, nor mentally fully developed yet, and thus your handling of the orb could prove dangerous.

So your parents moved to Texas, far away from the Qistone's resting place, far enough away where I thought you safe. What a shock it was to me then to discover today one of the missing orb's located within a day's walk from where your parents settled!

You and your parents left for Egypt this morning. I was to spend a few days resting at your parents' home alone while your family was away, for my travels have made me weary. However, I received an urgent message, a message containing dire news that requires my immediate attention. And yet, something this morning compelled me to take a walk into the countryside, and I found this location containing one of the lost Qistones. By attempting to protect you from the Qistone, I had your family move to a location that housed *ANOTHER OF THE STONES!*

Amira, after the news I received, I'm not sure if I can have any more contact with your family, at least not until I figure out a way to do so safely. So, I sit here writing to you. Know that although I may not be able to speak to you or your parents anytime soon, I still fight for you and the Qistone, and I will do everything in my power to keep you safe Amira.

These are dark days Amira. Within The Continuum, a secret society of warriors, Protectors, was established to protect the orbs, and I rank among their number. For generation upon countless generation, we have served the Qistone and those connected to it loyally. However, years ago one among us breached his loyalty.

Before your birth, rumors of Protectors disappearing surfaced. Protectors are spread throughout the world in order to keep tabs on those that want the Qistones for their own nefarious reasons and also to connect with other Protectors of the other orbs. Protectors are ready to be called upon at a moment's notice, but so many among my brethren are now gone Amira.

We, believed ourselves to be strong, to be nearly invincible; one or two of us might fall, but that would just strengthen the rest among our ranks and quickly the other side would realize their attempt to gain the Qistones would be futile. Perhaps, that was the Society's plan all along, allowing us to believe too deeply in our strength so that when they did launch their most recent assault, we would be caught off guard.

When I set out on a journey to warn the Protectors of our Qistone and the Protectors of the other orbs, I never expected to discover what I did; the carnage was beyond a scale I thought possible. Time and time again, I tracked my brethren down only to discover they suffered some "accidental" or mysterious death. I hurried my efforts, thinking that I could catch up to whomever was decimating our ranks but to no avail.

For now, Amira, you are safe. Your connection to the Qistone and your current location are known only to me. However, my first goal as I leave here will be to find someone I can send to you to protect you during the years between puberty and when you reach 18. There are a few Protectors the Society most certainly has not reached, and one in particular, I think will serve you well. Your parents will know whom she is when she arrives, for I will give her a personal artifact of mine that your parents will recognize. I wish I could do more at the moment, but there are other pressing matters, I must tend to.

I take solace from the fact the Society does not know where you are, but there's also one more thing the Society does not know, and in these dark times that lack of knowledge may prove essential to our side. Over the centuries, the Society has made several attempts to gain control of the Qistones. It became apparent that in order to protect the orbs, a redundancy of protection was needed. Thus, centuries ago, it was decided that a second set of Protectors would be created and stay fully isolated from us.

Only the head Protector of each Qistone knew about this group's formation and that knowledge has been passed down over time. Originally, the four head Protectors sent three of their own brethren to create and expand this second unit of Protectors. The sole task of these twelve chosen men was to prepare for a time when they might be called upon. They were to remain dormant as long as a doomsday situation, a situation like the first set of Protectors being destroyed, did not occur. Thus, they set off to a secret location that not even the four head Protectors knew about. At this secret location, they trained hoping never to be called upon. Knowing that it could be centuries before being summoned, they also trained others to take their place, to expand their ranks and to carry on the tradition of waiting and training.

There is only one way this isolated unit of Protectors may be summoned. In each of the caves built by The Continuum, there is a mixture of ink and "dust" from the Qistone, the same mixture used on the cover of the Book of Connectivity that allowed you access to this location. The isolated Protectors took some of this mixture with them and were told to use it to paint certain symbols and words on a wall where they settled. The phrase you will find is, "Rise my brethren and light you shall bring." These same words can be found written on the wall of the cave, which houses the Qistone in Egypt. When two Qistones are brought together and a Princess places her hand on the writing on the wall, the connection between the Princess and the dormant Protectors will be strong enough to "light" their wall, and they will know it is their time to rise up, and they will come Amira.

I tell you this because there may come a time when you must call upon them and if things are as bleak as I fear, you may be the only one capable of summoning them since you will have access to the Qistone in Egypt and now this Qistone in Texas. I have seen too much to believe that you having access to two Qistones is a just a coincidence.

The power the orbs contain rises exponentially when two or more of the Qistones are brought together. An orb, alone, will give you strength, but two will give you so much more and will connect you even more profoundly to your surroundings. However, attempting to connect two orbs is extremely dangerous because it means one Qistone must be brought out into the open, and while in transit, the Society will have an opportunity to seize it, and if they succeed...well, the consequences send shivers up my spine.

The Society's destruction of the Protectors has been systematic and precise. This realization coupled with new information I've discovered forces me to take a new tact. I must go on the offensive. My goal is not to win; that's not possible. My goal is to do enough damage that I can protect you and others like you until you're ready to take up the cause.

The Society is patient Amira. Their goal is to take over the world, but their steps to achieving that end are well thought out and never done in haste. As long as they are moving forward, they are content. They believe time is on their side. They won't strike unless they believe success is certain. They are also wise enough to understand that their objectives are best achieved silently until their power base is fully secured. Therefore, they won't overwhelm you with numbers, at least not yet, because that would draw too much unwanted attention to their ideals and identities.

Amira know that optimism brews beneath what I tell you, for I believe in you Amira and believe in who you are and who you will become. Trust your instincts. Although I've only met a quite young version of you, the little girl I met was highly intelligent and strategic beyond her years. I'm sure I'd be even more impressed with how you've grown since. So, all is not lost. Perhaps, we can turn the tide back in our favor.

There's so much more to tell you, but already I have spent too much time in this cave, and I must go now Amira. Allah willing, we will meet again in better times when you are grown, healthy, and happy.

With Loyalty and Love,

Asad

And there the messaged ended. Amira folded up the letter and put it in a tiny pocket in her purse. She then walked over to the pedestal and looked down and saw this amazingly bright orb. She realized in terms of shape and size it was the same size of the ball in the pendant her grandmother had given her, but obviously her pendant did not glow like this. She then frowned remembering she had somehow lost her grandmother's pendant. She hesitantly reached out with her index finger and when she was sure she wouldn't be burned, she touched it and it felt like a glass marble would feel. She ran her fingers along the edges of the ball and realized that it was sitting in the pedestal, but that

Amira could press down the circle which surrounded it, and sure enough the glowing orb popped up.

Amira held it in the palm of her hand, mesmerized by the swirls she saw within it that seemed to chase one another in an endless game. The pedestal then made a noise as a slab of stone moved over the depression which had held the orb. Amira gently put the orb in her purse for safekeeping. She realized she wouldn't be able to carry the books with her, but no matter, she could grab them tomorrow, so with the Qistone secure on her person, Amira exited the room. Amira practically ran down the hallway so excited that she finally understood (well kinda) what was going on! And now, she realized who Maria was and why her mother trusted her, so much.

What an amazing night! Amira thought. Sure there was that minor hiccup of wolves threatening the lives of all the students at the dance, but I think we should applaud Amira for her upbeat attitude since she'll have plenty of teen years ahead of her to brood.

Amira ran up the stairs and as she entered the topsoil of the oasis, the stone slid back into place closing the cave entrance behind her. Amira then jumped back on Moha and commanded, "Okay boy, let's go home!" and then Amira leaned forward in order to be in sync with Moha as he sprinted forward, but Moha didn't budge.

Amira sighed for a second and then feebly added, "Please?" which then caused Moha to take flight, and by flight I mean run really fast along the ground.

When Amira reached her house, she hopped off Moha and turned to the bird.

"Well, thanks again for saving me, and..." Amira began before realizing that Moha was staring out in the distance. "Are you listening to me?"

Moha, rather than making eye contact to show how "interested" he was in her blubbering let out a tiny squawk and then took off into the night.

"Okay, that was a bit rude!" Amira yelled after him, "But thanks again!"

Amira ran to the door which led to the kitchen. She opened it up and found Maria sitting at the kitchen table with a look of worry on her face. "Maria!" she exclaimed and gave her a big hug.

"*Amira*, are you okay? I heard about what happened at the dance. I was getting worried."

Pulling out of the hug, "I'm fine! More than fine! I think I understand what's going on!"

"You do?" Maria asked with a look of confusion.

"Umm, totally, I think, maybe, sorta, a little, but do you mind if I just jump in the shower quickly and then we can talk? I've got dirt all *over* me."

Maria's expression softened. "Of course, take your time."

"Thanks!" Amira said as she quickly left the kitchen and ran up the stairs.

***

The shower had felt wonderful to Amira. Now in jeans, sneakers, and a t-shirt, she felt even better than she had just twenty minutes earlier. She was about to go downstairs to talk to Maria, but then she realized, she should call her mom. She had been angry with her mom over so many things when all her mother was doing was trying to protect her. She also wanted to ask why she found that book in the first place since Asad's writings made it sound like she should have received when she was eighteen not twelve...not that she was complaining, but still a bit weird. She also wanted to call and talk to her mother about all that had been going on with her. She felt like a fool for not sharing with/confiding in mother before, but now she would make up for it. Amira walked into her parent's bedroom and grabbed the phone, but when she picked it up, she couldn't get a dial tone.

Stupid Texas phone service. Well, maybe Maria had one of those cell phones that were becoming popular nowadays, and they could call the phone company and have someone out first thing in the morning, so she could call her mother then. She'd rather talk to her mother now, but it could wait.

Amira practically hopped down the stairs and found Maria sitting in the living room looking out the window.

Maria smiled her Oscar-worthy smile, "Feel better?"

"*So* much better," Amira said plopping down into a comfy chair across from Maria. "So, Asad sent you here to protect me, huh?"

Maria was taken aback for a second, but she quickly recovered, "In a way you could say that. How do you know about that?"

"Well irregardless, (or regardless if you enjoy English), Asad left me a letter in a cave I found telling me about you and the kee-stone."

Maria's facial expression changed about six times before settling on a look of joyful surprise. "There's a *second* letter?" she asked a bit too forcefully and then more gently, "Oh, and it's actually pronounced "chee-stone."

244

"Yeah, there's a second letter. Did you only know about the one he left for me in the book?"

"Yes, I only knew about the book."

Amira couldn't wait to tell her she actually found the Qistone (*chee*-stone), but she wanted to build the suspense just a bit.

"Do you have the letter?" Maria asked with a smile.

"Sure! I have it with the Qistone I found. Let me grab it."

A look of surprise once again flashed across Maria's face, but this time the "joyful" element seemed lacking. "Amira, did you find the Qistone?"

Amira smiled brightly, "I did."

"That's fantastic news," Maria said. "Now, Amira I need you to take me to it and give it to me along with the book that Asad left for you because it's really important that I take it to a safe place as soon as possible since it's not safe for it or for us to keep around here."

"But I thought in Asad's letter he warned me not to let it leave my possession?" Amira said.

"He may have Amira, but the world's changed a bit since whenever Asad wrote that."

"Oh, okay, well I don't have to take you to it. I brought the Qistone here." Amira hopped up from the chair and began to walk out into the Hall to where she had placed her purse, but as she reached the purse a thought occurred to her, *Why did Maria say "second letter"? How did Maria know about the book Asad had left? That book wasn't supposed to get here until I was eighteen and Asad said it would be sent to me directly.*

"Hey Maria, what two items did Asad give to you to give to my mother?" Amira asked from the hallway as she quietly unzipped her purse and put the Qistone into her pocket.

"What?" Maria asked from the living room.

Amira realized that the book didn't appear until after the night Maria had first visited with her mother and that the book arriving when Amira was eighteen was only mentioned in the letter Amira found in the cave. Amira slowly stepped backward toward the kitchen, "In Asad's letter that I found tonight, he talked about you giving my mother two items to prove that you were here on behalf of Asad."

"Oh, *right*. It was a tiny Egyptian statue and a watch with an engraving from Asad on it," Maria said stepping out into the hall with a look of concern on her face.

Liar, Amira thought to herself as her heartbeat quickened. "Very cool," Amira said with a smile on her face. "So when I said, I had it here, I meant I had it *near* here, like I hid it in the barn, so just hang on a second, I'm gonna go get it" Amira said as brightly as possible. Amira prayed that Moha was back from wherever he went because she had a sinking feeling that she needed to get away as quickly as possible. "Be right back," she said and turned toward the kitchen door, but standing at the door was the Silver-Eyed Scarred Arm Man.

"Hello Amira," he said in an eerily neutral and deep voice. "I think you have something that belongs to us."

Amira was cornered. She realized that now. In front of her stood Maria, the traitor. Behind her stood the scarred-arm man. They out-weighed her, they out aged her, they outnumbered her, and they obviously out-witted her, for she felt quite trapped. Really the only thing that could even the odds was if she could summon an ally, an ally who could even the numbers, who could make she and her ally outweigh her enemies, an ally who could stand above them all, an ally with feathers. Amira didn't scream out loud, but rather she concentrated on the bird with all her might, beckoning him to rescue her. The bird had already saved her from wolves on two separate occasions, so why not ask him to save her from two different kinds of wolves that were no less dangerous. *Come on Moha, I need you!* she yelled silently to herself, and surprisingly, Moha heard her.

***

Moha was miles away, studying various escape routes, but he and Amira shared a connection, and he quickly sensed she was in trouble. Moha instantly took off in the direction of the Amira's home. You might think that flightless birds would be jealous of their airborne cousins, and generally you'd be correct, but not in Moha's case. Where was the sport in just flying *out* of danger? What could be more fun than outrunning your prey, seeing your prey with its tongue sagging out of its mouth because it was overheating due to the exertion? Sure it was fun for Moha to jump *over* things now and then and maybe there were times that soaring above it all would be useful (like when trying to escape from a certain teen and her friend), but those moments were few and far between. No, for Moha, the ground was where it was at, so he ran. However, "ran" would be an understatement. His "feet" barely graced the ground as he traversed more and more land. His legs moved so quickly had anyone been around to see, they may have thought they were seeing a floating torso attached to a long neck and head zooming four feet off the ground.

***

The next several minutes were like a blur. Amira turned to run but she was trapped between Maria and the Scarred-Arm Man, who was lightning quick and grabbed her almost immediately. She remembered screaming, but she didn't remember any sound from the scream. She remembered watching Maria go into her purse and pull out Asad's book. Amira then felt the man's strong, frightening arms shake her and pat her down, until he found the Qistone in her pocket. She remembered staring at his face, and the feel of despair as the man greedily stared at the stone that turned his silver eyes golden sporadically for seconds at a time.

***

Moha came across a river and leapt over it effortlessly, as if he just felt like creating a perfect semi-circle shaped arc if one were tracing his path. Although Amira was in trouble, Moha was coming.

***

The next thing Amira knew, she was lying on the floor in Hashim's bedroom, her arms and legs bound.

"I am sorry," Maria said to Amira standing above her. "But know your sacrifice in the grand scheme of things will be worth it. You, unfortunately, were just caught up in something far bigger than yourself. Some men, many, many years ago made a mistake and took items that didn't belong to them, and now you must pay for their misdeeds. I know that's not fair."

"What was the name of the woman you killed?" Amira asked.

"What?" Maria replied.

"Asad's friend. His *real* friend. The woman who was supposed to protect me. What was her name?"

The question caught Maria off-guard Amira noticed since Maria's coloring definitely dropped a shade. However, Maria did not answer.

To say Amira was *pissed* would be an understatement. "How do you expect to get away with this? People will know you killed me. My friends will know. They will hunt you down!" Amira said.

"Why would they think anyone killed you Amira?" the Scarred Arm Man said after he entered the room. "You are going to be just a poor victim of a horrible electrical fire that spread amazingly quickly while Maria, a *devastated* Maria, had gone out to deal with a family emergency."

Amira just gulped in horror, the thought of being burned alive was not a pleasant one.

The Scarred Arm Man saw her expression, and added, "Amira, I am *not* a monster. The smoke will kill you well before the fire gets to you. You'll be long gone before the fire burns your body and all evidence of foul play. So don't worry about the pain. You'll be okay," he finished and then winked at her. "Oh, and feel free to scream. You're at the back of the house, so even in the off chance that someone drove by they wouldn't hear you screaming."

***

Moha zoomed faster and faster along the endless mixture of dirt and nothingness that encompassed much of this area of Texas. Moha cruised along fiercely, yet stealthily. Soon, a tiny decently lit house appeared on the horizon, which only caused an increase in Moha's speed. Though currently trapped, Amira was just minutes away from rescue, from safety. The bird was on a direct collision course with the Egyptian-Texan homestead.

Moha was perfectly aligned with the house as he ran. Like a laser, Moha-The-Brave flew directly towards- oh hold on: Moha-The-Brave ever so slightly adjusted his course. Moha-the-Magnificent zoomed directly to the right of the house, which I guess makes sense since he'd probably want Amira to sneak out of the house and hop on his back due to his size, which would make an indoor rescue attempt more difficult. So yes, Moha-the -Mover whizzed toward the left of the house and then whizzed to even, um, left-*er* of the house. Okay, obviously he wants to take a wider arcing path toward the house, maybe for stealth reasons. And now Moha-the-Fearless adjusted his course even more to the left, and then more...and then more...and then even....okay, well now Moha you're just running in the opposite direction. Yes, Moha, Amira's rescuer and guardian, performed a brave, perfect, wide arching U-turn and sprinted as fast as he could away from the house. Oh well, maybe next time Amira.

***

Most of us like to think of ourselves as "good people," but are we? It takes very little for us to think ill of or wish illness upon someone else. For instance, don't you find yourself illogically angry at a friend or co-worker who coincidentally wears the same shirt as you do one day? The conversation is always the same:

Jane: "Hey, Chris! No *way*! You own this shirt *too*! How funny?

Chris: "Totally funny. Well, I guess great minds think alike!"

Jane: "Lookin' *gooood* today Chris."

Chris: "You too Jim/Jane!"

What a cute exchange, right? But internally you know Jane is wishing Chris would burn at the stake for embarrassing her and creating potentially awkward situations. And you know Chris is hoping Jane gets impaled by one of those beach umbrellas with the pointy end that you drive into the sand, *anything* to ruin Jane's shirt by causing it to be torn, or blood stained. Now if Chris is more pious, perhaps she just stews all day long in her office hoping Jane spills various condiments on the shirt or that the shirt gets caught in the elevator thereby ripping it off.

And then the two spend the rest of the day hiding out in their respective offices hoping that will be enough to prevent the cliché-Pavlovian type statements like, "Hey, you're wearing the same shirt as _____ today!" to which you'd likely want to reply with something like, "One more overly obvious comment like that and I swear to you I'll eat your first born."

Then an awkward silence ensues.

So yes, dear reader, as you sleep tonight, cuddle up with those morals, those "do-gooder" impulses, those "how can I make the world a better place," type thoughts. That's fine, but I'll be cuddling up with a pair of scissors just in case I mistakenly interrupt you while you're in the middle of counting money or jellybeans.

Anyway maybe this is obvious, but Amira's situation weighed heavily on her. Sure, there was the whole being bound by some plastic type strings/handcuffs that cut into her wrists. Sure, there was the whole "they just set my house on fire and I'll likely die a horrible death" angle as well. However, in a moment of clarity/gravity, Amira felt like a failure. Amira *failed.* She failed herself. She failed her friends. She failed her family, and she failed the world (these are her thoughts, not mine. I generally make a point not to pile on tween girls who are about to be murdered. That's where I draw the line. Sure, it may not be a pretty line, or a thick line, but it is a straight line...well, if I happened to use a ruler that is...otherwise it's actually rather curved and jagged. I'm just saying don't shoot the messenger...unless I, the messenger, was about to be burned alive. Then, feel free to shoot the messenger. Seriously. Who wants to be burned to death?).

Amira didn't know what the world would be like if this group, if this organization, controlled all the stones, but the idea that her brother, her younger brother, who made her smile, who made her laugh, who only wanted to make others smile, would have to live in that world sickened her...and then angered her. Amira channeled that anger into strength. She told herself, *I'm not going out like this.* Okay, well that statement sounds more like something someone named Vinny from Brooklyn would say. Okay dear reader, *fine,* I spaced out for a second and was only half listening to her, so I paraphrased her thought, but you get the idea.

She concentrated on the plastic "ropes" that bound her feet and hands, and with laser like focus, she began her attempt to pull her arms and feet away from each other. She took a deep breath in, and as she exhaled she used all her strength in her tiny body, all the adrenaline that she ever had, and she broke through the plastic with the power of the Incredible Hulk! Just kidding, her attempt to escape failed fully. Come on people: the girl weighs like 85 pounds. She's not going to break free from plastic cuffs by shear force. That didn't stop her from trying the same thing seven more times, but eventually she realized this strategy was a big ole' loser.

Amira rolled from side to side scanning the room for anything she could use to "saw" her way free, but since her arms were bound behind her and her handcuffs were connected to her "feet cuffs" by another piece of plastic, her mobility was limited and her "saw" options seemed non-existent.

Amira now exhaled in defeat as she lay on her side. Realizing the end was likely in sight, Amira now looked around the room differently. Toys were strewn about everywhere. Amira couldn't believe these items would be the last thing she'd see in this world: not Kyle's face, or the MOP Squad, or her father, or beautiful mother, or Hashim, but only Hashim's toys. There were his G.I. Joe action figures and instruments of war (toy planes) scattered throughout. He had Star Wars figures chilling with Transformers. Underneath his bed were several Lego structures: a spaceship, a boat, a faintly glowing castle, a train, a city and- *Wait a second!* Amira's eyes *widened* in awe and shock. *There's no way. It couldn't be, could it?* she thought to herself. And then, for the first time in a long time, she smiled as she stared at Hashim's toy collection a bit more carefully.

Chapter 6: Hashim's Big Night Out

The interruptions had slowed considerably over the last week, so much so that Hashim closed his eyes without even wondering what shenanigans a sleepwalking Amira would talk to him about tonight. Hashim pulled the covers up tight around his chin and turned on his side to drift into sleep, so he could dream about football and brownies and cartoons or whatever it is six year-olds dream about. His consciousness began to fade right up until the point he heard the slight creaking of wood, which alerted him that someone was opening his door.

Hashim slowly opened his eyes and saw a gentle shadow moving across his wall. "Amira, can we do this tomorrow night. I'm *tired*."

A sleeping Amira sat on his bed and said, "It's time Hashim."

That statement was new. Hashim struggled with the covers, so he could sit up and look at his sister. "Time for what?"

"They're watching me Hashim, but they won't watch you. You need to get the stone."

Perplexed, Hashim squished his lips together and stared at his sister. "Get what stone?"

"The Qistone," she said neutrally. "Moha will take you there. Grab your flashlight. And take these items," she finished handing him an amber colored, opal shaped amulet, which their grandmother had given Amira, a small book, and the cloth, which contained various writings and images.

"You want me to take Grandma's necklace? Why?"

"Because when you take the stone, you'll need to replace it with this."

"Amira, are you being serious?"

"Also, take this backpack and hide it behind the barn."

"But I've done that before Amira and you got so mad at me."

"It will be okay Hashim. We may get separated for a few days, but it's going to be okay."

"Amira, I think I'm too old for this," he said using an expression he had heard his mother use recently.

"I can feel the book Hashim. The Book Of Connectivity is in this house. You need to take it along with this cloth," she said as she held out the family heirloom. "When you return, place the cloth back in my room, and replace the book where you find it."

"How will I know where to find it?" he asked.

There was a pause. Several seconds went by and Amira remained silent. For a moment, Hashim thought that perhaps this would be the end of their conversation, but then she replied, "It's in the living room. Climb on the navy chair and you'll see the book next to your books on the bookshelf. Now hurry Hashim. You need to return as quickly as possible." Amira then walked over to his desk, grabbed his flashlight and put it on his bed before leaving the room.

Hashim considered going back to bed, but he was worried that Amira would bother him again if he did, so keeping his pajamas on, he put on his sneakers and sweatshirt, grabbed the backpack and flashlight and quietly walked down the stairs. He entered the living room, climbed on the navy chair, and much to his surprise, found the book Amira was talking about. He yawned and then walked out the kitchen door. His plan was to walk outside, find Moha, ask "Do you have anywhere you need to be?," watch Moha stare blankly back at him, turn around, walk up the stairs, and go to bed, so at least he "tried" to help his sister. But, if she disturbed him again after tonight, that would be *it*. He'd tell his mom, and they'd bring Amira to the doctors and either she'd get well or they'd tie her to her bed at night. Either way, Hashim would get to rest peacefully.

Hashim put his backpack on, went out through the kitchen door and absently walked over to the ostriches. He slipped through the fence and under the light provided by countless stars, he searched for the line of purple feathers on top of an ostrich's head that would designate Moha. It only took about thirty seconds to spot him. Moha stood apart from the other birds in a corner of the closed-in area.

"Hey Moha, so-" he began but failed to finish because with lightning speed, Moha snapped his head down, nipped at the backpack handle and easily tossed the backpack and therefore Hashim onto his back. Then he hopped over the fence and took off into the night.

The exchange shocked Hashim for several seconds, but then the joy of flying through the desert replaced his initial reaction. He wrapped his arms around the bottom of Moha's neck, and let out a, "YEAH!" into the night air as they raced away from his home and from his crazed sister.

When they arrived at the oasis, Hashim slid off Moha and walked around scratching his head. The oasis *felt* familiar to him, but he didn't know why. However, the smell reminded him of summer, of being in Egypt with his extended family, of he and Amira forgetting that the secret code (Arabic) they used when discussing someone right in front of them in Texas was quite easy for others to break when in Egypt. Hashim spotted the tattooed rock rather quickly and walked over. The stars offered some light, so he could see the various writings on it, but he couldn't make out any of it. So, he placed his hand on the rock at the top left side and gently moved his hand over the surface of the rock moving from the top to the bottom and back up to the top in a Zamboni like fashion, and yes dear reader, I did just make a hockey reference in a story about an Egyptian family in Texas; if Hashim can create Lego landscapes combining over a millennia of history within an area of less than two feet, I feel like I at *least* should be able to mix temperature zone-challenged cultural references .

During Hashim's third "trip" down the rock, his index finger came across a subtle indentation, probably less than a tenth of a millimeter in depth. He continued to trace his finger along the indent, and he soon noticed its path created the parameters of a rectangle. Hashim then stared more closely at the rectangle that he just *barely* could make out and noticed it was about the same size as the dimensions of the book Amira gave him. So, he decided to test out his hypothesis and pulled out the book which was wrapped in the family heirloom of a cloth. Hashim placed the book on the rock's rectangular location and felt pretty pleased when his guess was right. However, his victory was short lived as the rock dissipated and gave way to a staircase leading down into an underground cavern.

Somehow this unexpected event didn't faze Hashim, possibly because next to his deranged sleep-walking sister, hidden passages didn't seem that odd. However, his "un-fazed-ness" more likely stemmed from the fact that Hashim had absolute faith in his sister and was certain she wouldn't send him on an errand that would lead to his death, even if her sanity was not at an optimal level currently. Hashim turned back and saw that Moha seemed quite calm, so Hashim turned back to the opening and walked down into the unknown muttering something about how Amira *definitely would be playing football with him whenever he wanted after tonight.*

Halfway down the steps, Hashim reached into the backpack and grabbed the flashlight. He turned on the light and almost instantly the cavern illuminated, thanks to the mysterious reflective material mixed into the wall surfaces. At the bottom of the steps, Hashim had a choice: go right or go left. Hashim chose left because he always went left when working on one of the mazes in his activity book that his sister or mother would pull out for him during long flights to and from Egypt. Now, granted, this strategy failed often, and Hashim was known, at times, when he'd reach a dead end, to "hop" over the two dimensional barrier with his three dimensional pencil and continue on his journey through the maze; some would call that cheating or that it defeated the entire purpose of working through a maze. However, to Hashim it just seemed practical.

Hashim kept himself company by making airplane noises with his arms stretched out like wings, and then he'd switch into being a swordsman using the flashlight as his sword (yet still making airplane noises), and then he'd quickly change fantasies again and this time use the flashlight as a gun as he'd yell out "Bop-bop-bop" in short bursts.

Hashim continued his walk for another minute or two until he noticed a slight warming of the air. He turned a corner and then noticed the walls sparkled even brighter. After about another twenty feet, Hashim entered a rather Spartan "alcove." The room was empty save for a stone pedestal that seemed to glow at the top, a few books which rested on a stone ledge, and a few rocks scattered about. Hashim had no desire to read at this time of night, so he walked over to the pedestal. He wasn't tall enough to see the top of the pedestal, so he rolled over a heavy rock that he could stand on. Even standing on top of the rock, he still had to stand on his tip-toes in order to see what was causing the top of the pedestal to glow. He looked down and saw a golden jewel that was not only glowing but also giving off warmth. The jewel was embedded in the pedestal; surrounding it was writing that circled the jewel and spiraled outward. Hashim recognized the words in English and some of the Sanskrit, but most of the writing made no sense to him, so he ignored it. Hashim figured this must be what Amira was talking about when she said he'd need to replace "it" with their grandmother's necklace. Too young to worry about whether grabbing a warm and glowing orb could have dire consequences, Hashim absently reached down and squeezed his fingers around the jewel to get enough of a grip that he could pull it out. His hand instantly felt warm and powerful as he grabbed the golden orb. His hand tingled, similar to the sensation one would feel when one's hand is asleep, except that the tingling was pleasantly calming. Most people when experiencing a new, magical, powerful sensation, would choose to relish in the moment; however, Hashim just wanted to get back to bed, so he tossed (yes *tossed!*) the golden rock into the backpack and pulled out his grandmother's/sister's necklace which contained a medallion with a amber colored opal in the center. Hashim thought about just dropping the necklace on top of the pedestal, but he noticed that his grandmother's opal and the glowing, warm orb in his backpack looked to be the same size. Thus, Hashim looked more closely at the medallion in his hand and noticed that two circular "bumps" on the medallion could actually be buttons. He pressed them down and sure enough heard a "click" and the amber jewel released. Hashim put the replacement orb into the pedestal's "hole." Hashim then turned around, began to hum, and hopped along out of the stone room. He realized that even though the orb was in his backpack, it still seemed to emit light and the walls sparkled stronger than ever. So Hashim hastily (i.e. without stopping or turning around) dropped his flashlight into an outer open pocket of his backpack, so that he could have both hands free to...to...do I really have to describe it?...Oh, all right, so he could have both hands free to clap, snap, shoot fake guns, high five imaginary football teammates and whatever else his mind could come up with during his walk out of the cave.

***

When Hashim exited the cave, the hole that was now behind him quickly closed as the marked up rock reformed (not that Hashim noticed). Moha instinctively knew instantly that

Hashim had the flowing (yes, I think flowing is a good adjective here, as I'll explain later) orb, so as Hashim approached, Moha gave his most regal bow. Hashim, however, mistook the act as Moha just bending over to let Hashim on, so Hashim clumsily (as in mistakenly stepping on Moha's closed eyelid) climbed onto Moha as he bowed. Although Moha didn't say much or anything at all, I'd like to think he wished he could take back his act of deference.

***

Hashim and Moha reached home about forty minutes later. Their ride home was quite serene actually, so no point in rehashing it. As they approached the barn, Hashim took the Qistone out of the pack and then unceremoniously dumped the backpack behind the barn, per Amira's instructions. Moha then dropped Hashim off just outside the kitchen door, and Hashim quietly snuck back into the house. He noticed the clock in the kitchen read, "3:58 a.m." Hashim shook his head at his sister, and as stealthily as possible, he climbed the stairs knowing he was just moments away from much deserved sleep.

***

Not even halfway through his first REM cycle, a sisterly yell awakened Hashim. This time, however, his sister's voice did not originate from his bedside, but rather, from downstairs. Although the sound jarred Hashim from his dream state, he was willing to let it go and fall back asleep, but as oft to happen when expecting silence: your body becomes quickly in tune with whatever is *breaking* that silence. Thus, instead of sleeping, Hashim's consciousness focused in on the sounds he heard from downstairs and quickly made out that he was hearing two voices: one voice from his Sister-who-taketh-away-sleep and his

261

Mother-who-tucks-him-in-and-kisses-him-on-the-forehead-as-she-wishes-him-a-restful-night-of-beautiful-dreams (who do you think Hashim would be siding with this morning?).

Reluctantly, Hashim *dragged* his tired body out of bed and decided he might as well milk this uninvited disturbance (is that a bit redundant?) and get some hot chocolate out of it. So, Hashim *un*-gingerly walked down the stairs, thereby regally announcing his arrival to his family members currently residing in the state of Texas.

Hashim royally arrived moments later and sat down next to his sister because despite her subconscious animosity towards his beauty sleep, he loved hanging out with her.

"Can't we make a rule that there's *no* fighting before 10 a.m.?" Hashim asked. He waited for a response, but his sister and mother *mistakenly* (in his mind) remained silent like they forgot how great he was. So he continued, "I'm just saying it would be helpful to everyone in the world, that's all." Still nothing. *Okay, time to pull out all the stops,* he thought to himself (it's possible I'm paraphrasing again). Hashim took a deep, but quiet breath in, and then let out a loud yawn that he emphasized by opening his mouth as wide as possible and stretching his body as far as he could. *Still nothing,* so he let out a more meager yawn, now feeling somewhat defeated. I mean, what's a kid gotta do around here to get a cup a Joe, er "Cho" as in chocolate.

Amira opened her eyes so she could roll them at her brother. "Come on Hashim. It's not *that* early. Why are you so tired?"

Seriously, did that JUST happen? (I'm paraphrasing his thoughts again) *Did my sister just roll her eyes at her brother, her totally awesome brother who gave up, NAY SACRIFICED, a good night's sleep, so he could run an errand for the more-messed-up-than-she-realizes-and-ungrateful sister?* (Thankfully, Hashim was not in charge of naming his family members: long names just wreak havoc on standardized test forms.) Thus, Hashim did something he rarely ever did and gave her the "look."

"What?" Amira finally asked raising her hands above her head in an over-exaggerated expression.

Ugh, it's chocolate time! Hashim thought to himself, so he turned his attention away from his sister and directed it toward his mother. "Mom, may I have cereal and some hot chocolate?" He knew using "may" instead of "can" combined with a mother's guilt about waking up her young son would *totally* seal the deal on his request being granted.

"Yes, Hashim you *may*," Nara smiled.

"I'll get it," Amira said.

Hashim watched his sister grumpily walk to the cupboards. Normally, he'd ask her what she was sad about, but this morning he was content to let her stew, for he had his *own* problems, like how was he supposed to play He-Man, football, *and color* before his afternoon allotted nap time without falling asleep?! He felt like there was something else he was supposed to do, but he couldn't quite remember. So, Hashim just watched as his sister poured the water, that would soon be combined with the chocolate powder creating a wonderful concoction of delicious, into the kettle to heat up.

"When are you leaving?" Amira asked as she worked (*slowly* from Hashim's point of view) towards accomplishing getting breakfast for Hashim.

What *was* Hashim forgetting he had to do? He went through his mental checklist of play activities.

"Tomorrow," Nara said in answer to Amira's question.

Play football, check.

"I've asked Maria Olave to stay with you," Nara said.

Watch cartoons, check.

"Ms Olave?" Amira placed the cereal in front of Hashim. "What?"

Eat my cereal and then ask for more, check.

"Because I knew she would. She's a friend of Asad's, so she's a friend of our family."

Mmm-mmmmm, cereal you are so awe-some! You make my tongue dance and my stomach go "Grrr-grrrr-yummy-yummy-grrr-grrr!", Hashim hummed internally, obviously now sidetracked from his task at hand.

"Oooohkay. Wait when did you talk to her?"

Cereal, you are my BEST friend! You give me energy to play football and score touchdowns as you go "Crunch-crunch-crunch" in my mouth! (My god, it's called "rhyme-scheme" Hashim. Try it sometime. Maybe pull yourself away from Care Bears or whatever cartoon you watch and try to improve yourself.)

"I called her right before I awakened you. Now sit with your brother, I need to go make some arrangements, and then Hashim, I need to talk to you after you're done with your breakfast, okay?"

Amira then placed hot chocolate in front of Hashim and sat down next to him.

Hot chocolate! Yes! Hot chocolate, you are my favorite drink! "Thanks Amira!" *I drink you up and then put the mug into the sink!* (Hey! A rhyme! There you go!) *But I wish I had some marshmallow-low-lows that I would eat with my elbow-oh-whoas.* (Baby steps) There it was again. That thought that "wasn't" stuck inside Hashim's head but failing to form.

Sing to his Mom as she cleaned up around the house, check. *Play with Legos*, check. *Hide mystery golden ball, so world doesn't end*...that must be it! But where to hide it? Hashim wondered. "If you needed to hide something, where would you hide it?" he asked his sister.

"You are sooooo random," Amira said. Very helpful, Amira. Very helpful.

Hmm, this was going to be tricky. How was Hashim supposed to find time to find a brilliant hiding place when he had *so much* to do today? But then, suddenly, out of nowhere, like a lightning bolt piercing a seemingly clear night sky, it hit him. The answer had been there the entire time. He wouldn't have to lose any precious playtime, after all. He just needed to combine the activities, the activities being (1) playing and (2) protecting the world. "I think I'd hide it in a castle," he reasoned. He then took a satisfied sip of his hot chocolate and filled in the tiny details of his plan.

"You are like Randy the Random Dinosaur, Hashim," Amira said, now looking directly at her brother.

"Who is Randy the Random Dinosaur?"

"You. You are."

Hashim thought about this for a second as he went through a mental checklist of all the Halloween costumes he'd ever worn. It wasn't a long list since he had only gone trick-or-treating once in his life, and there he pretended to be a football player. Halloween, surprisingly (to some), was not a big deal to Hashim,

265

since afterward his mother would go through all the treats to make sure certain ingredients weren't found in the candy, which often took a long time and decreased his overall haul. "No, I'm not," he said assuredly.

"Ugh, I'm *teasing* you Hashim!" Amira sighed pushing her hair forward to cover her face.

"Oh," Hashim replied through a smile. He figured she was teasing him, but he recently learned a cool trick where if he acted like he didn't know she was teasing him, it exasperated her and completely turned the tables. Hashim took another sip of hot chocolate; his sips were bigger now that the liquid had cooled slightly. As the effects of the sugary substance spread throughout his body, Hashim began swinging his feet, which didn't reach the floor when sitting at the kitchen table, back and forth at a faster clip. "Why were you and Mom fighting?"

His sister took a deep breath, which signaled to Hashim that she did not want to talk about it. But like those other signals in life, like signs that read "Do Not Feed The Animals" or "Closed Course. Do Not Attempt At Home," Hashim chose to ignore the signal and press forward.

"I'll let Mom explain."

"Why can't you explain?" he asked as he slurped down more of his hot chocolate.

"Because," she said through rolled eyes.

Hashim was well versed in this response, for he used it often when his mother would question his decision making process at times like:

Hashim, why are your Legos in the fridge?

Hashim, why is their a football underneath my mattress?

Hashim, why is their a pint of ice cream in the dryer? (Hashim had been planning an awesome game where he'd hide prizes all throughout the house and Amira would have to find them, and they'd get to spend all day playing together. He had been planning this for weeks. Of course, he hadn't yet figured out how to get Amira to actually *play* his game, but he was working on it...hence the ice cream in the dryer.)

Hashim, why are you wearing your pajamas underneath your shorts?

"Mom says '*because*' isn't a sentence."

"Whatever."

Hashim began to see the annoyance involved in dealing with one-word answers. "Amira, are you going to stay mad for awhile?"

"*UGH!* Hashim. I *don't* know. Are you going to bug me?" She pushed her hair to the side, so he could see her eyes staring at him.

That question was not hard for Hashim to answer. "Well, probably. Can we play later?"

Amira's frozen demeanor seemed to thaw slightly. "Sure."

Realizing Amira's sour mood had sweetened, Hashim pounced on the opportunity to achieve a more satisfying morning experience. "Great! Can I have a couple of marshmallows?"

Chapter 7: Smooching And Farewells

Hashim! You are brilliant! Amira thought to herself. Well, she *thought* she thought to herself, but really, she was speaking out loud.

"Hashim, I don't know how you...You are the most amazing little brother in the whole world! I can't believe you out witted an entire international organization! I mean you still ask me to help tie the laces to your dress shoes!" Amira began to laugh loudly (maniacally) as she stared at the faintly glowing castle, which was hidden under Hashim's bed. Amira was positive the Qistone was in the castle, so although she might die, at least her killers would destroy the Qistone along with her.

Amira didn't know why, but she began to feel hope. Sure maybe things were burning all around her (well, actually below her at the moment), but Amira's thoughts turned to brighter things. She imagined laughing with her brother and mother over something Hashim said or did. She imagined the MOP squad discussing some "serious" topic while making fun of each other. She imagined Carlos and Karen arguing aimlessly. Her imaginings became so clear, it felt to Amira like she could really hear them.

"I can hear you argue, and I love you guys for it!" Amira laughed out loud. She then imagined what the conversation would sound like,

"You could be more supportive here, Carlos!" Karen hissed.

"You could have more control over your body and smaller feet!" he replied back.

"Guys, come *on*. We can talk about this stuff later," Meredith implored.

"I'm just used to having Karen stick her foot in her own mouth, not *my* mouth."

That's kind of a strange conversation to imagine, Amira thought to herself. "Like a *really* strange conversation!" Amira said aloud.

"Is she *talking* to someone?" Carlos asked.

"I'm not sure," Karen said, "but who could she be talking to?"

"Maybe if you hurry up, we can find out!"

"Then hold still!"

"Okay, it's not like ostriches make for the most stable ladders!"

Wow, Amira has really strange hallucinations.

Totally strange hallucinations, Amira agreed. (Wait, is she now so self absorbed that she's imagining there's a narrator out there to agree with, someone who would have the distinct displeasure of chronicling all of her annoy-ed-ness? Oh, wait...crap.)

***

Maybe She Went To Al & Moe's (Or 10 Minutes Earlier)

"Wha?" Carlos garbled in Karen's direction through a mouthful of fries.

"I can't *believe* you. You never believed we'd find her at Al & Moe's, did you? You were just *hungry*," Karen said shaking her fists to the heavens.

After swallowing he said, "Look, our original plan was to go to Al & Moe's after the dance, so why not check there first?" After taking a long sip of his vanilla-Oreo milkshake, "I'm sorry I don't know where girls go after being chased by wolves. Maybe in the future the MOP squad should think of a meeting place in case one of us is in danger of being mauled. Lesson *learned*, okay?"

"Well, you didn't have to order once you saw she wasn't there!" Karen hissed back.

"I was hungry, and we were there! They have good advertising, okay? The whole 'Remember the Al & Moe's famous Pizza tacos!' commercials are really catchy. Besides, Amira would *want* her friends to be well fed when searching for her, right Meredith?"

"Don't bring me in to this," Meredith said looking straight ahead.

"I think your order of fries *brought* you into this," Carlos stated.

"At least I didn't order *seconds*, Carlos!"

"Yeah, well you might want to wipe the mustard from your lip before passing judgment."

Meredith sighed, wiped the mustard from the side of her lip. Carlos and Meredith began to bicker again, but Meredith silenced them with one word, "Bird."

"What?" Karen asked.

"I think there's a large bird coming toward us," Meredith said pointing down the deserted road. Although this road lacked streetlights, through the darkness seemed to be a creature with wings flapping slightly in and out as the creature ran down the street.

"Is that an ostrich?" Carlos asked.

"Not just any ostrich," Karen interjected. "It's-"

"Moha," Meredith finished.

"But where's Amira?" Carlos wondered with a hint of fear in his voice.

Moha slowed to a jog about twenty feet from the MOP Squad members until he came to a complete stop a few feet in front of them. Moha looked at each one of them with his large dark eyes and then jerked his head violently and let out a loud, "Squawk!"

"I think he's trying to tell us something. What is it boy? Is Amira in trouble!?" Karen responded!

" '*What is it boy?*' Did you just watch an episode of *Lassie* or something?" Carlos asked.

"Oh, *I'm sorry* Carlos. Are *you* proficient in speaking Ostrich?" Karen glared back.

"Guys! Not *now*. Amira needs us," Meredith said as she put her hands on each of their arms. Meredith then walked up to the bird and slowly, gently put her hand on the ostrich's long neck.

Moha ducked his head down so that now their eyes were inches (sorry, *centimeters*) apart. Moha then lowered his body as low as he could and seemingly gestured for Meredith, et al to hop on.

Meredith gingerly climbed onto Moha's back. "I think this is our best bet at finding Amira. So let's go."

Karen and Carlos looked sideways at each other quickly making sure the other had agreed to follow the Canadian and the bird's plan of action. Carlos nodded slightly, and Karen hopped on behind Meredith, and Carlos hopped on behind Karen.

With that the Mop Squad Reuniting Express took off into the dark Texas night. Meredith leaned forward and securely wrapped her arms around the base of Moha's neck as Karen leaned forward and wrapped her arms around Meredith as Carlos leaned forward and wrapped his arms around Karen.

"Carlos?" Karen queried.

"Hmm?"

"Would you mind *lowering* your arms about six inches?"

"Oh! Carlos said. "Sorry about that."

"No problem," Karen replied.

With his arms secure around Karen's waist, he asked, "Do you guys think Amira is okay?"

The question was met with seconds of silence, finally broken by Meredith's response, "No, but she will be. She has us."

I must admit dear readers. I kinda like Canadians. Any culture that feels like the best way to resolve differences is through fisticuffs fought on a sheet of ice is okay by me, so maybe we should accept Meredith's optimism.

***

"GUYS! Are you really there?!" Amira shouted! (this time meaning to speak aloud).

"Amira!" Karen yelled back. "We'll be right there!"

Amira rolled 180 degrees away from facing the area below Hashim's bed and toward the window where she *strangely* saw Karen standing at her window. I use the adverb "strangely" to describe it, for Amira and Hashim's bedrooms were on the second floor, and it would be a stretch, or at least Karen would have to *stretch*, for Karen to reach a height of five feet. But sure as shamrocks, there stood Karen. Of course, from the outside, you could see that she wasn't standing on the ground but rather Carlos' shoulders. Carlos' face was smashed against the side of Amira's house as was the rest of his body, but he too was not standing on the ground, for if you followed his shoulders to his torso down to his feet you'd see that his left foot stood atop the head of an ostrich and ditto for his right foot (but a different ostrich).

Karen pulled open the window and hopped in using Carlos' head for leverage one last time.

"Oh my god Amira! Are you okay?"

Tears formed in Amira's eyes and she smiled brightly. "Everything's great," she said and actually meant.

Karen stared at her for a second, "Yeahhh, that's *one* way to look at it." Karen ran over to Amira's desk and opened the top drawer. "Amira where does Hashim keep his scissors?!"

"Left side, middle drawer."

Karen quickly grabbed what she realized were "safety scissors" and plopped down next to her tied up friend. Karen attempted to cut the plastic that bound her friend, but the lack of sharpness made it more difficult. "My god, can you even cut *paper* with these things?!" Nearly stabbing Amira as Karen used all her strength to cut through the plastic, she cursed at the safety features which surprisingly backfired in situations like these. Finally though, Amira was free.

"Thanks!" Amira said as she instinctively rubbed her wrists and then caressed her ankles, gently running her fingers over the lacerated sections of her skin.

Karen grew concerned as she looked at her dazed friend. "Amira, we kinda need to leave...like right now."

"What's going on in there guys?!" came a voice through the windows. "The fire's spreading, and I think the side of the house is beginning to feel warm!"

"Yeah, I'm *handling* it Carlos! Pipe down!"

"Your face pipes down!" yelled the angry, disembodied voice.

"Amira, Carlos is right. We need to go now."

Amira looked up at her worried friend, "I know. Just one second," and with that she reached underneath her bed and pulled out the Lego-made castle. "I'm ready."

Karen paused for a second. "I thought maybe you'd snag a picture of Kyle or something."

Amira ignored the comment, moved her fingers past the moat and pulled down the drawbridge. She reached inside the castle's entrance and let the slight warmth guide her fingers toward a round object, but she couldn't quite grab it. "Shoot," Amira said as she tried again. Then, she remembered she was dealing with a castle made of plastic squares, not concrete, so she just pulled off the castle from its Lego land and grabbed the glowing golden orb and piece of folded paper that sat next to it. Amira opened up the piece of paper and read the following,

"Amira, I threw your bag behind the barn. Please stop waking me up. Love, Hashim, your brother." Amira felt the energy of the orb pulse through her...or at least she thought she did, for the sensation lasted only a few seconds.

"Whoa! What's that?" Karen asked pointing at the orb and momentarily forgetting that the upstairs could explode in a ring of fire any second.

"This..." Amira began.

"Okay, guys, *seriously!* I think Moha's threatening me. I mean I know he's a bird and all and doesn't speak, but those eyes are *fierce!*" Carlos yelled from outside.

"This...is beautiful," Amira finished, not knowing what else to say. "Let's go!"

Karen gingerly climbed out the window onto Carlos' shoulders and then climbed down him part of the way before hopping down to the ground from the side. Amira, next climbed out the window onto Carlos's shoulders. As she scooted down Carlos, she placed her feet on the ostriches and hugged Carlos quickly.

"Thank you Carlos," she whispered.

"Yeah, you'd do the same for me. I mean I would never get myself into a situation like this, but yeah, no problem."

Amira hopped down and would have hugged Meredith had Meredith not bear-hugged Amira first.

"Amira! Thank god! Are you okay? We called the police. But, what's going on?" Meredith said all in one breath.

"We need to get out of here," Amira said, her sense of joy about being alive now being replaced partly with the cold reality of the danger she and her friends faced.

"We should wait for the police, right?"

"No. We can't. I'll explain as much as I can, but we have to go *now*," Amira said walking off into the barren land outside of the Masri property.

"Amira, the road is the other way," Karen stated reasonably.

Had Amira been a fan of Frost, perhaps she would have said something witty (for her) like, "It's time we travel down the road less taken." Sadly, Amira's literary repertoire consisted mostly of girls forming clubs concerning babysitting or "Choose Your Adventure Books." Thus, Amira just replied, "I know" and continued walking into the wilderness, or maybe it's the *non-wilderness*. Or, if I were to translate what Amira said into terms she might understand I might write, "If Amira says, 'I know where the road is,' turn to page 47. If Amira says, 'Pavement is like lame-ment,' turn to page 103. If Amira replies, 'I like chocolate.' turn to page *Get A Life* because that's obviously what you need if you're reading this right now.'" But alas, let's move on.

***

Amira first took them behind the barn as she fell to her knees to search the ground.

"So Amir-cat, whatcha doin' over there?" Carlos asked, but Amira did not have to answer as she quickly pulled out, or rather *yanked* out a backpack that looked well...*packed* and was hidden underneath some leaves and branches.

"Amira?" Meredith asked, now completely baffled.

Amira didn't hear the question. She was too fixated on the backpack. She quickly unzipped several pockets to see the contents. She had seen most of these contents before when she had fallen into the pool only to discover her brother had packed several of Amira's things in Ziploc bags. Amira saw her diary,

276

clothing, money, a Ziploc bag containing the small bottle of ground Habanero pepper, her passports (both US and Egyptian), really all she would need to runaway, and runaway is what Amira intended to do.

Finally as a plan formed in her head, Amira looked up at her friends, "Guys, I'm gonna need your help."
***
"So you want us to lie to the police?" Carlos asked.

"Yes," Amira said.

"So you can ride your bird to New York?"

"Yup."

"And then hop on a flight to Egypt?"

"You listen well Carlos-san," Amira replied, adding the "san" as an attempt to alleviate some of the tension in her friends' faces through the use of Karate Kid inspired humor. The attempt, much like Cobra Kai's goal of winning the All Valley Karate Championship, failed, but at least she tried...I guess.

"*Why* again?" Carlos asked.

"These *people* who tried to kill me are after this stone," she said holding up the Qistone. "They believe the stone is very powerful, and as you guys witnessed, they believed it enough to try and kill me."

"Okay, I'm with you so far," Carlos replied hesitantly.

"These guys are powerful, and my only chance to protect myself is if I get myself and this stone to Egypt because there are people there who can help me. I don't have time to explain that right now, but trust me, I need to get to Egypt. I need you to lie to the police because right now, I'm not sure who I can trust. These people or this group or whatever is really good at infiltrating *places*. If the police know that I'm in the United States, then the people trying to kill me will know too and they might be able to track me.

"My mother and brother had to leave for Egypt on short notice, so the only people who know they're gone are you three, me, Ms. Olave and whoever she works for. So if you guys tell the police that my brother, my mother, *and me* ALL had to go to Egypt due to a family member's illness, they won't try to find me, and I have a feeling Ms. Olave and her friends will only use the police if someone else alerts them of my disappearance. I don't think they would want the attention it would bring if Maria Olave told them I was missing, right after my house burned down.

"The police will try to contact my family in Egypt to tell them about the house, but my guess is that it will take *days* for them to figure out how to get a hold of my mother, and by then, I should be in the air on a flight to Egypt. Plus, Maria and her *friend* set up the fire to make it look like an accident, so the fire although tragic, won't be classified as arson, so it *won't* be a police priority. I'm sure they don't care all that much about an Egyptian family. They may even just wait until my family gets back into town, and maybe they'll just contact the insurance company in the mean time or something."

Silence followed for the next several seconds as the MOP Squad silently communicated with each other by staring at one another and using various facial expressions involving raised eyebrows, furrowed eyebrows, and scrunched up mouths.

"Okay, I think you're right about the police, but why New York? Wouldn't it be easier just to hop on a flight in Dallas?" Karen asked.

Amira stared at Karen for a few moments. "I thought about that, but I'm pretty sure that any minute now Maria and company are going to realize the stone they have is a fake, and my guess is they're in a position right now where they can see the fire trucks and when they see that no body is dragged out of the house, they're going to know something is up. There's no direct flight from Dallas to Cairo, so, if I hop on a plane in Dallas, I'd have to change planes in D.C. or New York, but while I'm in-flight between Dallas and the East Coast, they may be able to track me, and they could stop me from making my connecting flight, but if I just disappear for a few days during my trip to New York, then maybe I can sneak by them before they realize it."

Another silence followed and then Meredith asked, "Okay, let's say you get to New York and get on a plane to Cairo. If they are this powerful wouldn't they be able to track you once you're on the plane and catch you in Cairo?"

"Maybe. But, I think they separated me from my family for a reason. I think whatever they want or need to do, they need to do it here. If I can get into Egypt, I feel like at least I'll have a shot at...at figuring out what to do next. Again, by disappearing for a few days, maybe they'll stop looking for me, or maybe they'll look for me in the wrong places or something. I think my only advantage is that they try to stay as secret as possible, so if I hide from them, they only can find me and stay in hiding by doing only so many things. Plus, I'm pretty sure they won't be expecting this."

"No. This they will *not* be expecting," Carlos confirmed.

"And you think a brown skinned girl riding an ostrich won't draw attention?" Karen asked.

"We'll only travel at night and we'll stick to remote areas. I think Moha's pretty talented at keeping us hidden."

The four of them then turned to look at Moha who was standing about fifteen yards away staring up at the stars it seemed.

"Okay, if we go along with this plan Amira, you *must* keep us informed," Meredith said with hands on hips.

"Guys, I can't promise I'll be able to call everyday."

"Yes you can," Carlos responded seriously. "Maple Leaf is right, you need to let us know you're okay."

"But they might tap your phone. Calling you could put you in danger. They could be able to trace the call."

"Then we'll use that to our advantage," Karen stated. "Look, we'll keep the calls short, so there's no chance they'll be able to trace it...and...*and* we'll always start each call the same. One of us will ask, *'Where are you?'* and you always reply, "I can't tell you. It's too dangerous."

"*That's* the spy code we're going to use? I feel like it's lacking something...what could that be...oh *yeah*: imagination," Carlos said through rolling eyes.

"The point is that it's so simple, if they are listening in on our conversations, they'll believe it because it's so simple."

"Karen's right. It will protect us because if they think we don't know anything, then they won't come after us, and it won't give them any information on Amira. But, we'll at least know you're safe," Meredith finished walking over to Amira and placing her hand on Amira's arm to emphasize her concern.

Amira tapped her foot on the ground as she thought about their request. Hearing a familiar voice each day might not be a bad thing, and Karen was right: a simple code could protect them just in case these killers thought about going after the MOP squad searching for answers. "Okay. I'll let you guys know where I'm *not*," she smiled. "And, once I reach New York, I'll let you know by saying something, um something like..."

"Like, 'Boy I sure could use an apple right now, a big apple to eat,'" Carlos blurted out.

"And you were making fun of *my* creativity a minute ago, and *you* come up with eating a 'big apple' as your code for, 'I'm in New York'" Karen said as she stared daggers at him.

"*Hey!* I'm not *trained* in spy techniques. *Sorry*," he finished but didn't mean.

"Hmm, how about you say-" Meredith began and then actually finished her sentence, but what's the point in listening to this dribble-drabble right now? Deciding on a code to let them know she's in New York obviously is a complicated endeavor and of primary importance when the fate of the world is at stake. I mean it's right up there with deciding which flavor of chap stick to buy (I prefer vanilla over cherry), which boy band ballad you'd want to commit suicide to (I think "Bye Bye Bye" by N Sync is the clear frontrunner), whether Snuffalopagus is imaginary or not, the likelihood of coming across Rosario Dawson's phone number, or oh wait, that Rosario Dawson thing actually *is* important. Seriously, would you want to live in a world, dear reader, without Rosario's phone number? I didn't think so. And okay, perhaps I'm guilty of projecting, but at the very least, we didn't have to listen to the MOP Squad for a few minutes, and surely that is a good thing.

"So when are you leaving?" Carlos asked after their previous conversation had mercifully ended.

"No time like the present, right?" Amira said giving a meek fist-pump.

"You are going to get through this," Meredith said confidently.

"Yeah, it turns out you're surprisingly *hard* to kill," Carlos winked.

***

Amira hopped on Moha, and looked down at her friends who obviously were *not* yet sold on her plan.

"It's going to be okay guys," Amira said trying to smile.

"Amira people tried to burn you *alive* tonight," Meredith countered.

"Obviously things could have gone *better*," Amira admitted. "*But*, Maria and her friend underestimated how amazing you three are. So here I am, crisp-skin free!"

"Amira, if on your journey, anything happens, *anything* that makes you think you need to abort this mission, you call us," Karen demanded, "and we'll figure out some way to get to you."

Now Amira did smile, "I will. I promise."

Moha appeared restless. He stomped his feet and jerked his head up.

Amira looked at him and rubbed his neck, "Okay, okay." She turned toward her friends, "Well..."

"Wait," Carlos said.

"What?" Amira asked.

"I think you need a catchphrase."

"What?"

"You know, like how the Lone Ranger would always say, "Hi-O Silver Away!" before he'd take off. I think you need something like that."

What a stupid thing to say. Lives are at stake. The fate of an ancient power could fall into dangerous hands at any moment. Amira had no time for this obviously, so she kicked her heels into Moha and...and I wrote, "so she kicked her heels into Moha and"...oh *come on!*

Amira sat there pondering. "What could be my catchphrase?"

"Hmmm, maybe 'Big Bird Be*gone!*'" Carlos offered with a bit too much zest and Moha swung around and dropped his head just inches in front of Carlos' so that Moha could stare at Carlos. It seems Moha preferred not to be compared to an alphabet-loving, easy-going, jaundiced bird with an overactive pituitary gland and a shaggy imaginary friend. Although I must admit, maybe that comparison is fair since Moha's "friend" Amira and Snuffalopagus possibly share the same hairdo.

"That makes it sound like Amira's telling Moha to get away from her," Karen interjected. "What about 'Mops Squad to the Quad!'"

"What does that mean?" Carlos asked.

"I don't know...maybe we should have a secret lair and call it 'The Quad.'"

"Building a secret lair sounds like a lot of work," Carlos said.

"Yeah it does," Karen admitted.

"And then it sounds like we'd be telling our enemies where we were going," Carlos.

"Well, that wouldn't matter if its location was a *secret*."

Meredith shook her head, "How about, 'From Canada to Cairo, from Seoul to Santiago, fear the MOP, the MOP you can't STOP!'"

"That seems like less of a catchphrase and more like an inauguration address," Carlos said.

"I kinda like it," Karen said. "It sounds deep" (like a three-day old puddle maybe).

Amira agreed, "Yeah, it sounds...*worldly*. Let me try it, 'From Canada to Cai-ooooh!'" Moha took off, unfortunately not fully versed in the custom of waiting for the hero to *finish* the catchphrase before leaving.

Amira fell backward, but clenched her legs to stay atop Moha. When she regained her balance she looked back at her friends and waived before turning her attention to the ground around her. She leaned in toward Moha and quietly whispered, "We have to make one quick detour first, okay?"

***

The Scarred-Arm Man stared at the golden glowing stone in his possession. The size of these stones always surprised him. He knew they were small, not much bigger than a child's marble, but the idea of so much power flowing through something so tiny never ceased to amaze him. The stone's power pulsed through his body as he held the stone. He felt stronger, healthier, and more in tune with the world.

Maria handed him the high-powered binoculars as the house burned brighter and brighter.

"You look uncertain," the man said to Maria as he put his eyes up to binoculars in order to stare at the flames.

"No, not uncertain. We did what needed to be done, but I take no joy in taking her life," Maria said while keeping her eyes on the flickering dot in the distance.

The man handed the binoculars back to Maria, obviously more interested in staring at his prize possession.

Maria stared through the binoculars once again. What was a flickering dot quickly took on more and more details. She could see the smoke escaping from the windows on the first floor. Soon the fire would spread to the second floor. The Scarred-Arm Man had told the truth about one thing to Amira: the smoke would kill her before the fire reached her...at least Maria thought it would. She *hoped* it would. Maria liked Amira. She reminded Maria a lot of herself at that age. Perhaps if their lives had been switched, she would be the one facing death and Amira would be sitting on the hood of the Jeep, but such is the luxury of thoughts like these when you *aren't* the one swallowing polluted air that sears the inside of your lungs.

Maria had enough of watching the house burn; she began to pull the binoculars away from her eyes when she thought she saw something, a movement that was more *concrete* than the wafting of smoke or flickering fire. Maria tried to zoom in even more, but even these binoculars had their limits. She wasn't sure if her mind was playing tricks on her or if she actually did see something. There was *zero chance* that Amira broke free from her plastic bindings, but still...

Maria knew they didn't have the luxury of being wrong, even with the Qistone now safely in their possession. "We need to go back," Maria said stoically.

"We stationed our vehicle here for a reason: to avoid suspicion."

"I saw something," Maria said.

The man tore his eyes away from the stone and stared intently, deeply into Maria's eyes. "You are afraid. That is understandable. To go before the Committee even when you are sure you succeeded, is no easy experience. Even the strongest of men have quivered in their presence."

"But what if she escaped?" Maria asked.

"How could she escape when-" but he didn't have a chance to finish his thought because even without looking through the binoculars, he could see a series of tiny dots flashing as they inched towards the house. "That doesn't mean she escaped necessarily. It's possible someone happened to drive by and called the police and fire department." The volume of his words tapered off as he said the sentence. He didn't believe this was a coincidence that the police arrived on the scene so quickly. "Even if she did somehow escape, she can't go far, especially without the stone. The stone is the most important thing. If she escaped, we shall catch up with her before she becomes a threat."

Maria stared into the distance, trying to decipher what happened in the house during the past few minutes. Finally, she said, "I think she's already a threat."

Normally, the man sitting next to Maria would concur with her assessment, but after so many years *searching*, after so many sacrifices willingly given, he finally, *finally* had the object to make all his doubt escape.

"I think we should take it to him. He'll want to see it, before we bring it to the Committee." Maria said.

"No. He had his chance with the other one. We take it to the Committee and *only* the Committee," he replied as he stared at her with his eyes that seemed to shift from silver to grey and then back again depending on the light.

Maria met his gaze. "He's here you know. And he somehow *knew* another stone would be found near her in Texas. He may expect us to bring the stone to him."

"Yes, but he won't disobey the Committee. We were tasked with retrieving the Qistone from the girl and bringing it to the Committee, not to him. If he wants to keep tabs on our progress, that's fine. But we do not report to him." The scarred-arm man placed the orb into a small, but beautifully crafted wooden box that was obviously designed solely to carry the orb he held in his hand, for the glowing ball perfectly fit in a semi-circle shaped depression. "Let's go," he said as he walked around to the side of the Jeep and hopped in. He then placed the box in a cup holder between the front seats and put the keys in the ignition.

Maria hopped off the hood and went around to the passenger side. Once Maria sat in the passenger seat, her companion backed the Jeep up and then turned it around as dirt kicked up all around. He drove quickly, but not too quickly, for he didn't want to draw attention to the off-road vehicle while off the road. He drove without the lights on, but that mattered little since there was enough light from the sky and few obstacles for him to worry about.

Soon they were on the highway at which point the Jeep's headlights came on. They drove in silence, obviously not caring to discuss tonight's victory. In fact, Maria did not look like she was in a celebratory mood.

Out of the corner of his eye, the Scarred-Arm Man focused his attention on her as she stared absently out the passenger window. She was tense, distant, much more so than he would have expected. Now that the effects of success had worn off some, he knew he could not dismiss her feelings. Maria had spent time around Amira and her family. His extensive field experience taught him to hone in on those closest to whatever situation he was dealing with, for whether they knew it or not, their reactions to situations told more than most intel one could gather from a distance. Thus, the fact she was uncomfortable was a red flag. It was not just that Maria had feelings for the girl. Something she noticed about Amira, recognized in Amira made her doubt their own success. He reached over to get her attention, but as his hand passed above the wooden box, he paused. His heartbeat quickened, not due to the effect of the box's content, but rather due to the lack of effect. He felt nothing as his hand remained above the box. He was sure the box shielded the Qistone's power to a degree, but- Suddenly, a thought occurred to him that he did *not* like. He whipped the car over to the shoulder and slammed on the breaks.

"What the hell?" Maria asked glaring at him.

He grabbed the box, and said, "Get out."

"What?" she said.

He had already opened his own door and was circling around the front of the car and walking out into the darkness.

Maria opened the door, hopped out and said, "If she *was* saved, we should put more distance between us and them."

He ignored her and continued walking into the emptiness of the land surrounding the road. He waited for her to reach him, and then slowly opened the wooden box. Inside the orb still glowed but not nearly as much as it had even twenty minutes before. He grabbed the Qistone and held it tightly in his hand as he closed his eyes.

"What is it?" Maria asked as she followed him into the darkness.

"Impossible," he muttered.

"*What*?"

"The pulse is...*weakening*."

"What do you mean?"

He handed her glowing orb but remained silent.

She took the Qistone and stared at it as it rested in her upturned palm. She felt a slight tingling in her hand, but the power of the stone seemed to be fading. "How can this be?" she asked. "I've never heard of stone losing..." Her voice trailed off.

"A Qistone does not lose its power," he said through gritted teeth. Even though there was little light around them, Maria could see the rage that flashed in his silvery eyes.

"But *how*? We took the stone from her. She took the stone from the cave that protected it. The look in her eyes as we took the stone from her."

His voice was now calm when he spoke, "I don't know how she did it, but she somehow...she..."

"She tricked us," Maria finished. "She switched the real Qistone out, and let us take an imposter. How the hell did she do that?" Maria asked more to herself than her companion.

"Now, I am angry," said the man. He turned away from her and walked back towards the Jeep.

"What should we tell the Committee?" Maria asked.

"The truth. We're going to find the Qistone and drive a stake through the girl's heart to ensure she dies. No longer will we worry about making a scene." He stepped back into the car and sat back down into the driver's and waited for Maria to join him. "We were nice to her before. We will not make that mistake again. She will *pay* for this."

"The Committee wanted this done without complications," she said as he turned on the ignition and pulled back out onto the road.

"They *want* the Qistone. In the end, they will forgive us for any mistakes we made."

"How do we find her? She's got at least an hour start on us."

"We find her by figuring out what options we've left her," he said as he sped down the highway.

"We separated her from her family. She has friends in town still, but she must know they can't protect her."

"Correct," he said wanting her to arrive at the same answer without his prodding to make sure his reasoning was accurate. "She has one of the stones. Her family is in Egypt now. Another stone is in Egypt."

"So, the only course of action is...she's going back to Egypt, isn't she?"

"That's what I would do," he replied.

"How does she expect to make it back to Egypt without us catching up to her? She's obviously smarter than even I gave her credit for. But, she's still young. She's scared. She's isolated. She'll make a mistake."

"I agree," he said.

She opened the glove compartment, pulled out a cellular phone and pressed a button. Almost immediately, someone clicked on, and she said, "We need to tap into all train stations, airports, and bus stations within a hundred mile radius. (pause) I don't care to hear about the complications that poses. Do it and keep your methods hooked in for the next forty-eight hours," she said as she hung up the phone. "We'll find her."

"We will," he said. "In the meantime, I think we question some of her classmates."

"That could draw too much attention to us."

"Don't worry. I'll do it non-violently. It will seem innocuous. It's time we bring in the police."

"But, if we do and they find her before us, it's possible she'd cry loudly enough that they'd sequester her from all until they figure out what's going on," Maria said with a surprised expression on her face, surprised because the man sitting next her was *not* one to ask for help.

"I have a different idea on how to use them," he said.
***

Aside from the oasis, there was one other area Amira considered "hallowed ground" in Texas. She had never actually stepped onto the ground but on more than one occasion, she and sometimes she and Meredith and/or Karen would find some excuse to make a detour pass through this heavenly area known to most as the Ander's estate, home to one Kyle Anders. Amira always imagined what it would be like to "enter" onto this mysterious ground. At times, she likely daydreamed about it. However, she knew this heavenly fortress was guarded by a horrible monster, a monster with gorgeous hair and perfect teeth whose words were as piercing as her claws: Amber. Thus, Amira early on accepted that this place was best to view but not to visit. Amazing though how small things like near death experiences can change your perspective on things such as hallowed, yet dangerous grounds. As Amira rode along on top of Moha, she imagined walking up to the Ander's front door, ringing their surely melodic and witty doorbell, and confidently asking to speak with Kyle no matter who answered the door.

Even if Amber answered and attempted to close the door in Amira's face, Amira would elegantly but forcibly stick her foot in front of the door preventing Amber from shutting the oak door, so Amber would know then and there that Amira was *not* joking around and that she wasn't leaving until she spoke to Kyle.

Amira and co. (Moha) approached from the back of the house since the roads weren't the best place for a duo on the run. As they approached his family's quite expansive backyard, Amira gently pulled back on Moha's neck telling him to slow down. Moha came to a complete stop behind a large tree, and Amira hopped off.

"Be right back," she said to Moha with a smile, and walked toward the house. She walked past a row of hedges, saw the lights on in the house, confidently turned 90 degrees, walked several more steps confidently, then turned another 90 degrees, walked bravely back behind the hedges, and decided to sit down and curl up in a fetal like position. So maybe Amira wasn't quite ready to knock on that front door just yet.

Her heart thumped loudly and thudded against her chest as if it were trying to escape in order to run from the potential embarrassment of seeming like a crazy person for trying to talk to Kyle at such a late hour.

"Okay Amira, you can do this. You may not survive this cross-country trek, so you owe it to yourself to find the courage and do this. So get up and go! Don't even think about it, just go. (nothing) Okay, we can't wait here all night." True, so Amira just sat there until Moha ambled over.

"What?" Amira asked the bird. "I'll go in a second, I just need to-" finish that sentence? Perhaps, but Moha had other plans as he used his closed beak to "encourage" Amira.

"Ow! (poke) Hey, stop that!"

Moha poked her again in the side as she twisted and turned in failed attempt after failed attempt to protect herself from his prods.

Amira hopped up. "Okay, *okay*. I'm going. But just know: that was *not* cool," she finished pointing her finger at him in a chastising manner, though Moha seemed unfazed by her anger. He just winked and ambled back behind the tree, allowing Amira some privacy in this moment.

Amira turned toward the home and through a window saw movement inside. She willed her feet forward one step at a time, wishing she had *taken* the time to think of funny, witty things to say to Kyle on the ride over. With each step, she became more certain that her heart would explode and Kyle (or worse Amber) would find her in the a.m. splayed out in the morning dew with some crazy expression of heartbroken anguish on her face.

Amira looked more intently into the window and realized that there was a person at the window. For a second she thought the person saw her, but the person then turned away for a second and then back, and his/her movements didn't seem the frantic movements you would expect of someone who just spied an intruder in the backyard. Another step closer and Amira realized it was Amber at the window. *Crap*, she thought. It took another step to see that Amber was moving her arms furiously up and down. Amira wondered if she was doing some cool new dance move, but then realized she was just washing dishes. Then Kyle(!) came into view. Amber handed him a plate and he dried it! Oh my god, Amira had never seen a plate dried with such perfection, with such loyalty and integrity with (wait, WHAT?! Did that just happen? Did she describe his plate-drying as being loyal and full of integrity? Well, dear reader, I am *not* full of integrity at the moment, but I am full of something, so I guess I'll go relieve myself. Be right back. (pause) (pause)...(pause) and I'm back! Hmm? Oh, don't worry I always wash my hands. Anyway, where were we? *Right*, Amira was describing what a day in hell would be like for me. Amira continued watching in a mesmerized, stalker-esque, fashion. Kyle and Amber seemed to laugh and elbow each other. Seeing Amber like this, doing a domestic chore and acting sisterly confused Amira because it almost made Amber seem...*human*, like she had feelings and possibly cared for others. This line of thought made Amira slightly ill, like when you eat chicken that's been in the fridge for three and a half days when you're starving and you heat it up and dig in and 95% of you is certain that everything's okay, but there's that 5% of you that wonders whether you just signed your death warrant. That's kind of how Amira felt watching this display of normalcy featuring Amber.

After the shock of the family interaction wore out, Amira realized she had a problem. She couldn't wait all night for Kyle, but at the same time having a conversation with Kyle in front of Amber wouldn't do any good either. So she prayed, prayed that Allah would give her this moment and make Amber go to bed. Amazingly, her prayers were answered, for Amber shook her hands to rid them of excess water, grabbed an out-of-sight towel, hugged her brother, and then walked up a set of stairs surely just going to bed. More importantly, Kyle remained behind still drying dishes. This was her chance!

"Kyle," she whispered. Umm, obviously Amira is acoustic deficient when it comes to understanding sound waves, for you can't *will* a whisper through a pain of glass.

"Kyle," she whispered again this time adding a waive to her whisper. Should I mention that waiving lacks effectiveness when shrouded in darkness? Do you think she'll next try to "poke" him from twenty feet away to get his attention?

"*Kyle,*" she whispered again this time stepping forward, not seeing the sprinkler, tripping, and falling on her face.

"Frick! Ow, stupid sprinkler!" (Yes, Amira, blame the inanimate object.)

Although Kyle failed to *hear* his name, perhaps his ears were burning...*or* perhaps he heard a "thump" outside (an Arab ninja, Amira was *not*), for Kyle looked out the window, but failed to see anything. So, he walked to the backdoor and slowly opened it, maybe fearing that if he opened the door quickly, he'd be in a three little pigs-big bad wolf situation, which to be fair, would be a legitimate concern after the whole "wolves crashing the middle school dance" fiasco.

Kyle opened the screen slowly and then partly stepped outside and peered out into the darkness. He failed to see anything, so he began to close the screen door when he thought he heard a "ky'."

"Hello?" Kyle whispered to the darkness.

"*Kyle,*" Amira whispered again.

"Uhh, Amira?" Kyle said scanning the yard but seeing nothing but blackness.

"Down here," Amira said still on the ground.

Kyle ducked down into a crouching position, "Why are you on the ground? Are you hiding from something?"

"No, I just fell."

"You okay?"

"Yeah, can I talk to you for a minute?"

"Yeah, of course." Kyle said. He looked behind back into the house to see if his parents or sister who all had gone to bed were "stirring," but he didn't hear any stirring sounds coming from inside. Thus, he gently closed the backdoor and screen door preventing any sound from being emitted, save for a slight "click" from the screen door.

"What's going on?" he asked as he lightly stepped across the yard.

Amira hopped up in super-quick motion and brushed her hair out of her face as gracefully as possible, as if signaling that her task which required her to lie flat on the ground was successfully completed. "So, what's up?" she asked with a smile.

"Ahhhh, you tell *me*," he said smiling back but obviously confused. "No wolves chasing you?"

"Hmm? Oh that," she began batting her arm in front of her in a *brushing the experience away* type motion, "I think something like being chased by wolves is a once in the lifetime kinda thing" (that happened *twice* to Amira in less than a month).

"That was *crazy, right?!*" Kyle said his mouth now agape in awe of the experience that was replaying in his mind.

Yeah *crazy*. I mean sure, not as crazy as riding an ostrich to New York, not as crazy as having your swim coach attempt to burn you death (is there irony in a *swim* coach trying to *burn* you?), not as crazy as a powerful glowing orb resting in your

296

backpack, and not as crazy as having a secret society after you and your family, but sure: crazy.

"Yeahhh, *totally* crazy," Amira said trying to make it sound like other than the wolves, she was *totally normal* (good luck with that!) and would totally be the type of girl you'd want to take to prom in about five years time.

Kyle's eyes widened, and he grabbed Amira pulling her towards him. For a second, Amira's legs weakened as her heart melted and she smiled dumbly, but then she realized something was up.

"What's wrong?" Amira whispered now worried that Maria and Co. had somehow *already* tracked her down.

"Amira, I think there's something (pause) behind (pause) the hedges. Something that's *not* human. Let's just slowly back up toward the house and go inside for a minute."

The thought of entering Kyle's sanctuary made Amira's eyes glaze over in a drunken-like stupor, but a survival instinct kicked in, and she realized that entering his house would be too dangerous. Her goal in drawing him out was to separate him from his family for a few minutes, so she could explain why he'd need to keep her whereabouts secret, so she knew she'd have to bite the bullet, even if it made her seem like more a freak:

"Oh that? Yeah, that's just Moha," she said. Kyle looked at her quizzically. "My ostrich," she reluctantly finished as she studied her feet with her eyes.

"Your ostrich? Like you take him for walks like a poodle or something?" Fortunately for Kyle, he could not see the glare that was suddenly cast in his direction from the quite large, quite powerful, quite "ready-to-throw-down-at-the-slightest-insult" bird through the hedges.

"Sorta like a poodle...but different. He's kinda my ride too."

"Your *ride*? I thought Egyptians preferred camels for that."

Part of Amira wanted to say that most actually prefer *cars*, but she wasn't here for that type of conversation.

"Yeah, well you know, we try to mix it up sometimes."

"That makes sense."

Amira dragged her toe across the ground, releasing some pent up energy as she tried to figure out what to say next. "So listen, I had a really good time tonight, even with the wolf thing."

"Yeah, me too," Kyle said.

"So, I kinda am leaving tonight for a little while, and I need to ask you a favor," Amira said taking her eyes off her toes and locking eyes with Kyle for a couple of seconds before looking back at the ground.

"Leaving, what do you mean?" Kyle said. During most of the conversation, he had his hands in his back pocket, one leg slightly in front of the other as he rested his weight on the back leg, which made it seem like even when standing, he was almost seemed to be "sitting" he seemed so relaxed. But, for this question, he took the opportunity to take his left hand and push the hair out of his face in an exaggerated way so as to show off his (cough) bicep and make sure his eyes could be fully seen.

"So my family had to go back to Egypt for a little while because my aunt is sick."

"I'm sorry. I hope she gets better. So that's why you're going back?"

"Yes (no), but it's a bit trickier than that. Some people, maybe the police, maybe *might* ask some student some questions because my house kinda burned down tonight.

"*WHAT?!*"

"Well, I mean not the *entire* house, (more to herself) at least I don't think. So anyway, if anyone asks you about me, I need you to say that I left immediately after the wolves showed up at the dance in order to catch a flight at the airport."

"What? Why?"

"It's important that the police think I'm already in Egypt, or at least, with my family so that no one looks for me over the next few days."

Kyle put his hand gently on Amira's shoulder. He stared caringly into her eyes and said, "Amira, did *you* burn down your house?"

"What? NO! *No.* I did *not* try to burn down my house. The people who tried to kill me did though, and they're still after me...well, at least I think they will be after me again, once they figure out I got out of the house...before dying."

"Amira, you're not making *any* sense," Kyle whispered (obviously trying to use gentle tones so as not to "disturb" the disturbed girl in front of him...well, that's my opinion anyway).

"I *know.* I'm not good at this," Amira said now frustrated. Due to her anger, she sped up her speech, "It's just been a really crazy month, and I really like you, and wish I didn't have to go, and I wish people weren't trying to kill me and that wolves didn't try to kill me, and I wish we could spend some more time together because-"

Unfortunately, for the world, Amira never got to finish that (gag) "fascinating" sentence, for Kyle leaned in and kissed her, and wait, what? Did I just write....oooo-kay, well when their lips touch, as long as she doesn't lift one of her legs back in one of those cheesy kissing poses, I won't have to smash my head through a window. Yes, as long as she doesn't lift her leg back, I'll continue to digest my lunch rather than release it back out into the world. The muscles in Amira's left foot and ankle tightened slightly. *Don't do it Amira.* Then she subconsciously clenched her calf muscle. *For the love of god girl, don't you dare-*, AHHHHH *MAN!* Amira lifted her left leg forming a backward "L" shape as their lips remained lightly attached to each other's. Ugh, the scene is so cute that I'd considered slitting my wrists, but rather than bleeding out, I'd fear syrup would pour out instead and just make me want to eat waffles, and that would suck because I prefer chocolate chip pancakes. This *girl*: I mean here I am, chronicling her story, and she just continues to ignore my feelings and how *ill* she makes me. Rude, readers. Rude. Okay, fine, let's give the kissing bandit and co-conspirator a few seconds of privacy, and as I decide whether or not to defenestrate myself, I promise to continue narrating the story. Just give me a second to compose myself. *Ugh*, I'm still disgusted. Well, at least I'm not the only one since Amber, who was watching the scene from her bedroom window with her lights out, seemed equally disturbed. You know readers, I always liked Amber; she seems decent enough. Anyway...

Finally their lips, like Simon & Garfunkel, like Michael Jackson and his nose, like a prom-bound Oklahoman teen and her purity pledge, parted ways. Amira wanted to dance (even though she can't), wanted to sing (trust me: no better), wanted to hop up and down and scream "YES!" because there was no place she'd rather be at this moment than standing in front of Kyle staring into his eyes post-kiss. Actually, that statement wasn't exactly true, for Amira really wanted to be with Karen and Meredith at this moment, so she could rehash every single detail ad nauseum, likely causing me to impale myself with a stress relief ball.

Amira knew the moment couldn't last forever, especially since the fate of the world possibly rested upon her shoulders, so Amira....Amira knew this moment couldn't last forever, so...okay, seriously *move* Amira. Amira knew this moment couldn't last forever, so she...eh-*hem*! Forgive me dear reader, but I have to do this: suddenly a gust of wind appeared out of nowhere hurling a sharp twig in Amira's direction and actually nicking her on the back of the calf.

"Ow!, what was that?" Amira said finally breaking her gaze with Kyle. (Your welcome.)

"You okay?" Kyle asked all concerned and stuff.

Amira shook her head as a way to clear her mind, "Yeah, I'm fine." She didn't meet his gaze because deep down she knew she really did have to go. "So, will you promise not to say anything, even to the police? I know this is weird and I'm asking a lot, but Kyle, I *need* you (now with her head tilted down and slightly to the side and her eyes looking up into his eyes) to trust me," she said quietly. Wow, she's going to be a man-eater when she's older. Clap. Clap. That was impressive.

"Yeah, I promise," Kyle said.

"I have to go," Amira said even more quietly.

"You're going to be okay, right?" Kyle asked her as he lowered his forehead in order to rest it on top of her forehead in a truly touching manner...well, it would have been touching had

Amira not flipped her head up quickly and banged into his forehead in a somewhat less touching manner. That was the second time Amira nailed Kyle in the head tonight...it seems young Miss Masri prefers her boys a bit lumpy and concussed.

"Ahh-oww," they said in unison as each took a step back and angled to the side in an attempt to hide their anguished faces from one another. To add insult to injury the automatic sprinklers turned on spraying Kyle in the midsection making it look like he just wet himself. Amira and Kyle ran behind the hedges to prevent any further soaking.

Well that was enough for Moha who grabbed Amira's backpack with the helmet hooked to it and brought it out to Amira.

"I guess it really is time to go," Kyle said staring at the large bird who he swore was looking at him with a look of intimidation.

"Yeah, we have to cover a lot of ground tonight," Amira said.

Amira and Kyle stared at each other and then feeling it might be awkward to kiss in front of an ostrich, Amira and Kyle hugged.

As they embraced, Kyle whispered, "Take care of yourself. And if you ever need anything..."

Amira just smiled as they broke their hug. She threw on her helmet, not even worried about the various directions her hair went as she smashed it on her head. She put her backpack on, and hopped on Moha. "I'll see you soon," Amira said, and she really, *really* hoped that sentence was true.

*C*hapter 8:

Life Is A Highway, Except When It's Not

The hardest part about the first night's ride was the lack of dialogue Moha offered. However, Moha's inability to communicate with Amira did *not* stop her from talking to him, but still, she would have enjoyed the conversation much more if it weren't so one-sided. But you work with what you got, and Amira had to talk to *someone* about what happened earlier in the evening.

"Moha, did you *see* that?! I can't believe I kissed Kyle! It was like the MOST AMAZING moment ever!" I doubt Moha concurred in that belief, though these current moments in time might be leading the way in the opposite direction.

"Moha, his lips were so *soft*. I mean I was totally scared at first because I worried I'd do something stupid like trip and fall because I was so surprised, but I totally didn't. (Congratulations?) I think I came across like *totally* confident, like I knew what I was doing, you *know*? (I really hope I don't) Do you think that was his first kiss too?! Oh, who am I kidding? This is *Kyle*. I'm sure he's kissed other girls before. Do you think I kissed better though?! He seemed like he liked my kiss too! How's my breath?" She breathed on the back her hand and tried to concentrate on the smell while zipping across the dark, country landscape.

There have been inspirational speeches by great and sometimes not-so-great leaders throughout history, but none of those speeches could have inspired Moha to run faster than Amira's current orations. Seriously, as Amira rehashed, analyzed, embellished, and parsed every moment with Kyle, Moha found a hop in his gait; he found a fourth, fifth, sixth, seventh, and eighth gear if you will. Had Amira not been stuck in such a non-Zen like state, she may have noticed how much ground they were covering. My guess is Moha believed (mistakenly) that if he ran fast enough the sound of the air whizzing by them would be enough to drown out her ramblings.

"...and *when* he ran his fingertips gently, but powerfully through my hair..." (Oh, we're still "there?" Okay, well this might be a good time for us, dear readers, as in you and me, your faithful narrator, to catch up for a minute. So, what's up? What's on your mind? Hmm? Oh don't worry, we'll get back to the story if anything comes up, but trust me, this will take awhile. Have you ever had a carton of milk or something that's been in your fridge so long that not only is it now spoiled, but it's so old you're actually scared to dispose of it because part of you feels like you have to be considerate and dump the liquids before throwing the carton away, but you just have no desire to actually open it? So, it just stays in your fridge indefinitely, which only makes it more likely you'll never take care of it?)

"...*Moha*, it was like a *dream*, but better! But do you want to know what I was *thinking* as we kissed?" (No, I'm actually good. But, thanks. So yeah, how evil do you think a woman has to be before a guy will find her unattractive? For instance, Maria Olave is a *stunner*, jaw dropping gorgeous. She EXISTS to wear bathing suits. I mean sure she recently attempted a malignant heart type murder, but do you think most guys could get past that? I mean, you've been listening to Amira drone on; don't you find her just a *tad* annoying? And Maria seemed *conflicted* about trying to kill Amira. That counts for something, right? Now, I'm not defending Maria's actions, but maybe Maria can be redeemed. Maybe she lost her way and she just needs someone to love her, someone to confidently dissuade her from her homicidal tendencies. It's possible she's worth the risk, right? I mean you'd at least give the relationship four or five dates, wouldn't you? Would it be easier to consider the argument if I described how she fills out a bathing suit again? Look readers, if you can't be honest with yourself, then you might as well just move to New Jersey right now, find a "beautiful" home that you "always wanted," cut out that coupon you found for Applebee's, order that watered-down daiquiri that was made using a corn-syrup and a banana "flavored" pre-packaged mix and tell yourself how fulfilled you are because you're surrounded by friends.)

The Amira-Kyle story continued on indefinitely by one overly eager girl, but let's skip ahead a bit. My guess, dear reader, is you're wondering about this cross-country trip with Amira and Moha and how exactly it's going to work. That's fair. I mean sure we've been together for hundreds of pages now, so I'd hope I would have built up a bit of goodwill, but if not, that's cool too. I appreciate your cynicism; it's like that breeze that comes off the ocean on a hot summer's day while you're resting in a hammock and pretending not to hear that uncomfortable argument your neighbors are having about someone's perverted online activities, in a word: refreshing (but why write one word when you can write fifty?).

Moha ran throughout the night. In the distance Amira could often just make out car lights that appeared less frequently as the night wore on, but otherwise, Amira and Moha had the world to themselves. Moha never seemed to slow or tire. Through the night, he ran. Well, most of the night he ran, but about an hour before sunrise, Moha slowed down when they came across a sleepy town where a diner could be seen in the distance and which was covered in the back by a wooded, deserted area.

Moha trotted into the woods behind the diner, and Amira hopped off.

"Where are we?" Amira asked Moha, still unable to grasp his lack of speaking ability.

"Okay, so you know the plan, right?"

At this Moha, actually winked and then took off.

"I'll see you later then," she said as he quickly disappeared within the trees.

Amira walked into the diner suddenly realizing how hungry and tired she was. Adrenaline had taken her through the night, but now that she had fully calmed down and dissected the night before: her brain was ready to rest, but all in due time. Amira first needed nourishment. Amira spotted a corner booth and gratefully sat down in a cushioned seat. She sat facing the door. Right or wrong, she wasn't too afraid about her assassins finding her just yet. If they were around, they surely would have attacked she and Moha *before* Amira entered a populated area. At least, that's what she hoped.

"Well high hon'," said pleasant, plump waitress who approached the table. The woman wore one of those quaint "waitress" outfits, this one was a yellow-and-brown ensemble, a yellow skirt and top, and frilly brown apron wrapped around in front. She was in her early 30s Amira guessed, hair a bit too blonde to seem natural, but otherwise, the woman just smiled and seemed warm enough.

"So what is someone your age doing here by yourself at this hour?" she asked not in an accusatory way, but more out of curiosity.

"Oh," Amira smiled now quite glad she had actually spent part of the night thinking about answers to questions like this, "my father and I are staying at the motel down the street (yawn) and he told me to go grab something to eat since I guess I was bugging him," Amira said while rolling her eyes dramatically. (Again, I'm just saying acting lessons couldn't hurt.) "And, once I'm done, I'm supposed to bring back a "cup of joe" she added using her fingers to create quotation marks in the air as she said, "cup of joe" in her attempt at a deep, husky voice.

The waitress laughed. "I see. So what can I get for ya?"

"Umm," Amira quickly scanned the menu. "I'll have the blueberry pancakes, two scrambled eggs, toast, and hash browns, please. Oh wait. Cancel the eggs, I'll just have a fruit salad instead." Ordering eggs while fleeing on a bird felt too awkward to Amira. I'm choosing *not* to mention the ingredients that often go into making pancakes, but you know dear reader. You know.

"Well now, someone likes to eat, huh?" the waitress smiled.

"Oh! And orange juice and water please," Amira said.

"Coming right up," the waitress winked, as if bringing out food and doing her job was for some reason just their little secret that required an unbreakable code like a wink. Seriously, I think winking is way overused in society. Admittedly, I'm also cranky in the morning.

Amira figured it might be time to figure out exactly where she was. She looked at the couple of cars in the parking lot and noticed the license plates read, "Tennessee." *Holy cow!*, Amira thought to herself. Moha covered more ground than she realized. At this rate, she and the bird would arrive in New York in a day or two (actually 2.2 days if they continue to cover as much ground). She looked at the front of the menu to see if maybe she could gather any more information. *Manny's Diner*, the menu read, "Serving Munford, Tennessee since 1982!"

Where the hell is Munford, Tennessee, Amira asked herself. Next to the salt and pepper shaker was a folded local "news daily" entitled, "The Munford Minute!" and in smaller text below it read, "Munford, just like Memphis, but smaller and with less stuff!" Amira guessed (rightly) that Munford must be a suburb of Memphis. Amira knew they must have traveled quite a ways, and she was excited that her plan might actually work. Her food came, and she scarfed it down as if it were her last meal. The blueberries mixed with butter and maple syrup tasted divine. The hash browns were crisp on the outside but hot and moist on the inside, and the orange juice tasted like they had a grove out back. As Amira ate, she imagined Hashim sitting across from her, swinging his legs as he'd sing some nonsensical song like,

"Pancakes, earthquakes, you never make my belly ache.
I poor the syrup on you and mix you with melted butter
I don't know why Mom won't buy me Fluffernutter.
Oh Pancakes for my sake,

Mommy can I have another! Second verse Amira!"

"Hashim, I don't know the second verse."

"Well, it has pancakes in it," he'd say as he'd pause to eat more pancakes.

Amira smiled at the memory, but then the gravity of her situation slowly moved across her face, relaxing the muscles that allowed her to smile until her lips and eyes sunk downward.

According to the Munford Minute, sunrise would occur at approximately 6:13 a.m. Amira, looked out the window and noticed the distant sky changing to lighter and lighter shades of blue. Amira was tired, but she had a couple of things to do before she could sleep.

The waitress appeared a few moments later, "Can I get you anything else sweetie?"

"Actually, two things, and both are kinda random," Amira smiled while using her "innocent eyes" look.

The waitress smiled, "What do you need?"

"Where's the library? And do you think I can exchange this ten dollar bill for a roll of quarters?"

"That is a bit random, isn't it? Well, the library is just three blocks north of here, and you absolutely can get a roll of quarters."

"Great thanks!" Amira said. "The meal was terrific. Can I also get the check?"

"Sure hon'. I'll be right back with your check and a roll of quarters."

"Thank you!"

***

Amira walked down the main street, which unsurprisingly was called, "Main Street" and walked north towards a 1970s structure that was beige in color and completely devoid of imagination. Amira guessed that must be the library, and as she approached, sure enough, the Governor Sam Houston Public Library stood before her. *Sam Houston, I thought he was the governor of Texas*, Amira thought to herself. She walked up the white cement steps leading up to the doors and saw it did not open until 7:30 a.m. This did not deter Amira, for she had some business to attend to, and thankfully, right out in front of the library was a payphone. Amira cracked up her roll of quarters, put a few in and dialed Karen. Although early in the morning, Amira knew Karen would answer. The phone rang once...then twice...then three times...then four...although early in the morning, Amira knew Karen would answer... *"Hello you have reached the Yu family. We are unable to answer your call at this time. Please leave a message."*

Seriously, Karen! Amira thought to herself.

"Beep"

In a happy voice, Amira left a message, "Hey Karen, this is Amira calling just to say hi. Everything is fine here with my family. I hope I'm not missing too much at school. Tell the MOPs hello for me. Miss you. If I have time, I'll try calling later."

Amira hung up and took a breath. The next call would be a bit trickier. She picked up the phone again, and dialed zero.

"Hello, operator? I need to make a call to Cairo, Egypt. *How much?* Okay, I'll deposit the quarters." *Well,* Amira thought, *this is going to be a short call, regardless* since her quarters would run out quickly. She told the operator the number and as she waited to hear the ring, she partially hoped her mother would not be there because she didn't want to lie to her mother, and more importantly, she wanted to make sure her mother stayed in Egypt because it would be too dangerous for her to come back to the United States, and the faster Amira got to Egypt and somehow "contacted" the guards/guardians, the better. After a long pause the phone finally rang (Narrator's note: though the conversation takes place in Arabic, I have taken the initiative to have it translated for you reader. Though I could care less about her conversation, I'm guessing you'd like to hear it, so from now when Amira is conversing with an Egyptian just assume it's been translated into English.), and after the second ring, Amira's grandmother answered.

"Hello?! Who's there? Are you sure you have the right number?" an elderly female voice said.

Amira smiled. She'd know that voice anywhere. The voice brought Amira so much joy, so much love, so much warmth.

"Hello grandmother, it's your granddaughter, *Amira*. I'm calling from the United States." Although Amira's grandmother was whip smart, for whatever reason, answering the phone frazzled her. Her grandmother preferred face-to-face interactions or letter writing. The whole phone experience just irked her.

"*My* Amira?"

"Yes, of course *your* Amira. I will *always* be your Amira, Grandmother."

Though the connection was distant and tinny, Amira could feel her Grandmother begin to smile. "Amira! How are you? Wait, *why are calling*? Are you okay? Are you eating enough? Your mother told me you're mad at her. Talk to me my beautiful girl."

"I'm fine Grandmother. I actually don't have much time to talk. I have to get going, but is my mother there?"

"No, she's with your aunt at the moment, so I'm here with Hashim who's catching me up on all of your lives in the United States."

Amira rolled her eyes, unable to imagine Hashim's *version* of their lives.

"Hashim says you like a boy."

Hashim! Amira thought.

"Is he cute?"

"*Grandma!*"

"You deserve a cute boy, Amira."

"Yes, he's *very cute*, Grandmother."

"Good, I would expect nothing less."

"Please, deposit an additional seventy-five cents," a neutral, female voice chimed in.

"What Amira? What's going on? What are you talking about?"

"Oh, shoot, nothing grandmother, just hold on," Amira said fumbling for more quarters.

"Please deposit an additional seventy five cents."

Amira finally got the quarters in. "Sorry, Grandmother, that's...well, that's a just a long explanation that's not necessary. Anyway, I need to get going, but tell my mother *I* will call *her* tomorrow, okay? Got it? I will call *her* because I'm not going to be home much today, so if she called I and probably Maria would not be around to answer. So, will you tell her that?"

"Of course darling. Would you like to talk to Hashim?"

Amira knew that her family's phone may be tapped, so she better get off the phone, *but* she couldn't resist hearing one more familiar voice. "Okay, but I have to go in a second."

There was a slight pause, and then "Hey Amira! I'm hanging out with Grandma in Egypt!"

"Yes, Hashim, I figured that out. Listen, I need to go, but I just wanted to say I love you, and I found your gift, and you are the most AMAZING brother ever!"

"Yeah, I get that a lot."

Amira laughed, "Really? Do you have another sister I don't know about?"

"Nah, I just know you think it," he said while laughing out loud.

Amira became serious for a second, "Listen Hashim, I need you to keep a secret, okay? It's really important."

"Well you *know* I can keep one since you've already asked me to keep so many."

Amira didn't know what he was talking about, but now was not the time to inquire. "Okay, well I have one more. I'm coming to Egypt."

"You are!?"

"Quiet, Hashim."

Whispering, "You are?"

"Yes, I'll be there in a couple of days, but no one can know, okay?"

"Why?"

"Okay, Hashim?"

"Yes, okay. I'm not *five*. I understand."

"Now, Hashim, the only, and I mean *only* way you can tell anyone is if Mother tries to come back to the United States *before* I get there, okay? That's the *only* time you can tell her. Got it?"

"Yep."

"Do you promise?"

"Amira, I promise. I got it, okay? Can I go back to playin' with Grandma *now*?"

"Yes."

"Amira?"

"Yes, Hashim?"

"Can we stop with the secrets for awhile after this?"

"Yes, Hashim. Now, I need to go, but I love you, and you are *amazing*."

"Yeah, yeah. Talk to you later alligator."

"In a while croco-"

"Please deposit an additional seventy five cents."

"Ugh!" Amira felt she had already pushed her luck, so she just hung up and *prayed* that Hashim kept her secret. She knew it was a gamble telling him, but part of her was horrified her mother would find out about the fire and then be unable to contact Amira and therefore hop on a flight just as Amira was hopping on a flight to see her.

Amira still had some time to kill before the library opened. She considered walking around town a bit, but then she felt that would just mean she'd walk by more people, so perhaps remaining stationary was better. Thus, she sat down on a bench located on the grassy patch of land in front of the library, opened her backpack, grabbed the book from Asad, and re-read the passages just in case she missed something.

***

When the library opened, Amira waited an extra half-hour, so she wouldn't be the "first" person to enter. As it happened the library was close to a community college that was down the street and thus doubled as the college's library as well, so soon enough several overly tired late teen/early twenty-somethings wearing flip-flops, baggy shorts, t-shirts or tank-tops, and baseball caps facing every possible direction entered the establishment allowing Amira sufficient cover.

Amira entered immediately behind a pack of students who were discussing some biology exam they were all dreading and broke off from them once she came upon the nearest stairway. Amira made her way up to the third floor (the top floor), and then looked at the various sections the library contained. Judging from the makeup of the population she had seen, Amira was confident that Middle Eastern Studies was *not* a popular area of study or perusal. Thus, Amira entered down a relatively secluded aisle and pulled out a book on ancient Persian history. Her interest in this particular book had nothing to do with her current situation, nor did it have anything to do with the subject matter or the author. Rather, the lack of cover art and lack of any pictures or drawings within the book made it look *extremely* boring, which is what Amira was going for.

Book secured under Amira's arm, she found a long but narrow, faded-green padded bench along one of the back walls. The bench was long enough to stretch out on when reading a history book but puritanically narrow enough to dissuade coeds from using the bench for anything else; however, neither of those activities concerned Amira at the moment.

Amira sat on down on the bench and opened up her backpack again, taking out the glowing orb and placing it in her front pocket. She then stretched out on the bench and cracked open the book to page 217, which looked *particularly* boring. She then placed the opened book across her chest and closed her eyes. Now, in a library, with a boring book across her body, Amira could sleep relatively safely, likely to be undisturbed by student or librarian alike. For, Amira was just another student bored to death by the thought of learning.

***

Although a Saturday, Davy Crockett Junior High School buzzed with students and several parents. They were there, in part, for an impromptu town hall style meeting regarding the threat of wolves in the area and, in part, for the students to give statements to the police and curiously the Federal Bureau of Investigation, which sent an agent, dressed in a black suit and sunglasses. The man looked serious and forbidding. Although wearing a suit, his sleeve failed to cover the end of a thick scar, which ended in between the thumb and forefinger of his left hand.

As the chief of police and mayor took questions from the audience regarding a much anticipated Wolf Task Force (or as I like to call it, "WTF"), one by one, certain students of Davy Crockett (*The Fighting Crocks!*) composed mainly of the swim teams and the MOP Squad, entered a room to be questioned by the FBI agent and a police deputy. The questioning followed a similar course for most of the students: a quick recap regarding the dance, whether they saw anyone get hurt (no reports of physical injury thus far), and a final question that seemed like a bit of a throwaway query by the agent: "There were reports of one being chased by a couple of wolves, an Amira Masri. I do not believe the student is present this morning. Have you by any chance heard from Ms. Masri?"

Most of the students said they remember Amira being at the dance (who could forget after her "dance grooves" and by grooves I think I mean divots, crevasses, moguls, whatever anti-groove thing you can think of really...hmm, what would be the opposite of "dance grooves"? How about "flail divots"? Yes, let's go with that), but after the wolves everyone seemed to lose track of Amira. No one could remember seeing her.

The above answer both pleased and concerned the Scarred-Arm Man. He had in fact seen Amira post-wolves, so it was good that no one had seen her with him since he was trying to kill her and all. But, Amira also seemed to have disappeared completely, which is *not* easy for a twelve year-old girl to do. Well, there were still swim team members and MOP Squad members left to interview.

The (faux?) FBI agent signaled for the next student. A moment later, in walked a self-confident, obviously good-looking boy with light brown hair, deep blue eyes, and sporting a smile.

"Hello sir (to the scarred man), officer (to the officer)," the boy said.

Calmly, but with a quiet authority the Scarred-Arm Man stared at the boy and asked, "And you are?"

"Kyle Anders."

"Grade?"

"Eighth."

"Were you at the dance last night?"

"I was."

"Could you describe the incident involving the wolves?"

"Crazy, *right*? Not much to say though. When the wolves arrived, I decided it was a good time for me to leave, so I got the heck out of there and went home."

"Did you see anything unusual?"

"Aside from the wolves crashing the party? No sir."

"There were reports of one student being chased by a couple of wolves, an Amira Masri. I do not believe the student is present this morning. Have you by any chance heard from Ms. Masri?" the man asked but waiting for the same tired answer. However, the answer didn't come as quickly as he expected. He looked intently at the boy who seemed to have lost a slight bit of color in his face. This intrigued the Scarred-Arm Man. "Do I need to repeat the question?" he asked.

"No, uhh, sorry. I think I may have seen Amira run from the wolves at some point, but I really don't remember...since again, I was busy gettin' outta there myself, ya know?"

"I guess I do," said the FBI agent, trying to decide what the boy was hiding and how much he could press without the police officer snapping out of his boredom induced coma. He made a mark in his notebook to stop by the boy's house if he didn't find out more information. "Thank you for your time."

"That's it?" Kyle asked.

"Why wouldn't it be *it*? Do you have more to say?"

"Nah, man. Thanks."

The FBI Agent stood up. "No, thank *you*," he said shaking Kyle's hand *firmly* and staring into Kyle's eyes.

"Yeah, it's cool," Kyle said not really sure what he should do to help Amira (my vote would be to get the hell outta there if you want Amira to live, but I'm neutral on the whole thing, so feel free to keep tripping over yourself).

The FBI Agent then had Carlos Ortega brought in. The Scarred-Arm Man already knew that Carlos, Meredith and Karen were Amira's best friends. Torturing had not been authorized by his elders, and even had it been, he likely would not have used it in this situation, not yet anyway since his instincts told him that Amira's friends surely knew something about Amira's whereabouts, but likely didn't know exactly where she was. Thus, his strategy for the questioning at school was just to see if they were willing to lie for her, and later, if need be, he'd reassess what information they could offer him. However, he often found that the best way to gather information from a source was to "inspire" them into talking to other people and use certain electronic devices to listen in on their conversations, much less mess than torture and much less likely to leave a trail.

Carlos, wearing a blue Chelsea soccer jersey, khaki shorts, and sneakers sat in the chair trying not to fidget.

"Name?" the agent asked.

With that question, Carlos nervously began to tap his left foot. "Carlos Ortega."

The agent asked a series of innocuous questions before the reaching the question about Amira. "There were reports of one student being chased by a couple of wolves, an Amira Masri. I do not believe the student is present this morning. Have you by any chance heard from Ms. Masri?"

"Amira? Yeah, she left the dance right about the time the wolves came. She had to leave to go to the airport since she and her family were flying to Egypt because a relative of hers is sick I guess."

So, he knows she's alive. Maybe he somehow helped her escape, the Scarred-Arm Man thought to himself. He cursed himself, even though he knew that killing someone and making it look like an accident does not come without risks. For instance, you may have to leave your victim unattended for a small amount of time, which leaves open the possibility of unforeseen complications. Before he set the fire he scoped out the area around the house. No one was around; no one was hidden. Her friends would have had only minutes to save her once he and Maria left. There was no point dwelling on the decisions he made the previous night. What is done is done, and besides, she still had the Qistone, so possibly it was better she was alive anyway, even though she was not in their custody.

A long silence had filled the room as the Scarred Arm Man rehashed the previous night's events, but he finally spoke again. "Are you aware that a fire broke out in Ms. Masri's house last night?"

"What?! That's horrible!" Carlos said. "Thank god her family wasn't home."

"Do you know how to get a hold of Amira's family in Egypt? The police are trying to reach Amira's parents in order to tell them about the fire."

"Ahh, shoot. I have no idea. Sorry," Carlos said his foot tapping even faster.

"Is there anything you'd like to tell us, Mr. Ortega? You seem like you have something on your mind?"

"Me? Nah man, but thanks. I mean, sorry I could be more helpful. I mean-"

Interrupting him, the agent walked right up to Carlos and extended his hand. "No need to apologize," he said as Carlos stood up and they shook hands. The Scarred Arm Man gripped

Carlos' hand quite firmly and said, "You have been most helpful."

Something in the agent's eyes made Carlos go pale.

"Ye-ye-yeah, no problem," Carlos said trying not to gulp as he finished his sentence. Carlos, used all his concentration to walk slowly out of the room rather than sprint towards the door.

As Carlos left the room, the police officer who was slouched in a generic teacher's chair which sat behind every teacher's desk, asked, "What was that about?"

The FBI agent turned toward the cop, looking at the deputy who likely couldn't catch a cold, let alone a criminal. The FBI agent stared at him for a moment and then turned away, not even bothering to reply with as much as a syllable of recognition. The Scarred-Arm smiled inwardly; he knew he had done enough that Amira's friends would get word to her that someone was asking questions about her. And now he was sure that Amira's friends knew she was alive since they obviously had all concocted a pathetic story together.

The cop for his part sneered at the agent who ignored him even now and went back to dreaming about the various conquests at his disposal tonight after the 3rd or 4th round at the Hunter's Brew, his favorite local pub.

The deputy's eyes were half closed when the next student walked in, but his eyes flashed wide for a second thinking that he was in front of royalty. The girl was so young, but would surely be quite the stunner when she was older; she walked with such an air of confidence it was unsettling, like seeing a young celebrity walk by. The girl sat down without even looking at the officer or agent or being invited to sit down.

"So what lame reason do y'all have for making us students come back to school on a Saturday?"

"We're just trying to piece together the evening, and we would appreciate your cooperation," said the Scarred-Arm Man.

"Nice suit," the girl said to the scarred man.

"Thank you," the agent replied.

"That was my attempt at sarcasm," said the girl who was now staring out the window.

"I know, but unlike you Ms....?"

"Amber Anders."

"Well, Ms. Anders, unlike you, I don't need to use words to hurt others."

Had Amber thought about all the various ways that sentence could be interpreted perhaps she would have dropped her attitude.

"I believe we just had an interesting conversation with your brother Kyle."

"I'm sure it's more interesting than the current conversation," Amber replied "because this conversation is boring to its core," she said through an F-U smile.

The man took a breath. If the cops weren't around; perhaps he could use *alternative* methods to get these students to open up a bit more, but he didn't mind this approach either. His patience had been tested many times while searching for Qistones, so a bit of attitude from a girl who couldn't even drive a car was not going to affect him. "Can you please describe what transpired at the dance?"

"Well, I looked *fabulous*. I wore a designer top my mother and I purchased in a cool, new store in Dallas last week, and I looked *amazing* in it. At the dance, several losers tried to ask me to dance. *As if.* So, I danced with my friends until some pathetic wolves came in. My friends and I left a few minutes later and then went to go hang out without all the lame-o's. May I go now?" she asked meeting his gaze with equal intensity.

"We're not quite done. There were reports of one student being chased by a couple of wolves, an Amira Masri. I do not believe the student is present this morning. Have you by any chance heard from Ms. Masri?" he asked expecting to hear the same tired line.

"Well that sir is the most interesting question you've asked so far. I did see Amira later that night."

"You *did*?" said the Scarred Armed Man, not fully able to hide his surprise.

"It was hard not notice her, she was riding on a *lame* ostrich. I mean, what a freak," Amber said dismissively.

"An ostrich?" the cop asked.

"I *know*, right! I mean how much of a freak can one girl be?"

The agent silenced the cop's line of questioning with a well-placed finger raised into the air with authority. The agent then turned to the cop, "Will you excuse us for a minute? Ms. Anders and I need to have a discussion about telling the truth."

"Take your time," the cop said as he stood up from behind the desk. "I'm gonna go grab something to eat." And with that, he left the room.

Amber glared at the agent. "I *am* telling the truth."

"I never said you weren't.

In a completely neutral tone and his face giving nothing away, the FBI agent asked, "Where did you see her?"

323

"Outside my house. She like totally stalks my brother. It's pathetic really. She was all like, 'Oh, I have to go away for a few days because I'm such a freak and am lame.'"

"You heard her say all this?" the agent asked.

"Believe me, her pathetic voice *carries*. I wish I never heard her, but I guess I'm cursed to be surrounded by freaks," she finished while staring deeply at the agent as she said "surrounded by freaks."

"Indeed. Did she say where she was going?"

"Something about meeting up with her family. She was going to ride there on her ostrich or something. The girl can't even afford to fly like normal people. *Ugh*, it's so annoying being around a girl like that, you know? It's like, isn't my life hard enough? Why do people like her exist? They just pollute your air and annoy you."

"Thank you Ms. Anders. You can go."

Amber stood up slowly, feeling slightly lighter after having been able to vent about Amira. "So are you like gonna arrest her or something?"

"Arrest her? For what? And, Ms. Anders, I didn't appreciate you wasting my time with childish stories. I'd recommend keeping that story to yourself. If you're going to lie, at least create a more believable lie."

His comment disgusted and angered Amber. "I *wasn't* lying. Ugh, whatever, I don't care. Enjoy your life, sir. I'm sure it's *awesome*," she said through another smile, and with that she left the classroom.

"I will," said the agent after she left. "I will indeed." *So that's how she slipped out of town without us knowing. So now the question becomes: where is she going? That question leads to two other questions. One, what is her route? Two, how many miles can she and the bird cover in a day?* The FBI agent had done enough. He thought about waiting around to question Amira's other friends, but deep down knew they would just answer the same way as Carlos had, and now that he knew how Amira had snuck out of town and that her friends would contact her or she would contact them, he knew his time was better spent preparing the details of Amira's impending capture. So, as the deputy returned to the room, the FBI agent said, "You can finish questioning the students that are left. This has been a waste of my time," and then left the room.

"Whatever," the deputy replied. He was more than happy to finish the questioning on his own since he would only ask, "Were you or anyone you know hurt?" and when they responded no, he'd move on to the next student and be done within the hour.

***

Amira slept deeply, but not necessarily well. Again, she was running down a dark, damp tunnel being chased by something, someone. The noise behind her grew stronger. The sound made her skin crawl, and she had to concentrate, so the sound would not create a gag reflex. The sound was a mixture of amazingly quick footsteps and the scraping of metal against stone. Amira came to the end of the passageway and had to choose: left or right. She chose left, *always* left. She continued to run even though the sounds behind her grew deafening. Amira finally braved looking behind her, but in doing so she tripped on a rock and fell to the ground, in front of a large puddle of water, but the face she saw reflected was not her own. It was of another girl, several years older than Amira; her skin was much darker than Amira's; the girl was likely Indian; she had long, straight raven-black hair and dark brown eyes. Suddenly, the reflection took on a life of it's own and in horrible agony *begged* Amira through a heartbreakingly muted scream, *"Help!"* as a pair of purple eyes appeared in the reflection.

"No!" Amira gasped as she awoke with her arms stretched out before her.

Two coeds who had been studying at a nearby table stared at her.

Although I would have advised against it, Amira felt the need the say something, and I guess from that perspective she succeeded...barely.

"Sorry. I had a dream that I was walking in Memphis...but then I tripped...and got scared."

I'm not sure Amira could have said anything that would have made the coeds care *less*, so maybe she is a brilliant fugitive-strategist. Plus, now she got Marc Cohn's one-hit wonder, "Walking in Memphis" stuck in your head. Amira looked at her watch, "3:30." She had actually slept quite awhile, but after the nightmare, she still felt tired. She figured she might as well give the sleep one more go, so she innocently turned the page in a (cough) *shrewd* attempt at making others around her believe she was determined to read and then closed her eyes again.

Amira slept for an additional forty-five minutes. This time when she awakened more students were spread out in the library. Still, no one really seemed to notice her. Amira put the book back and decided the library might be a good place to look at her map and also to find out when the sunset was to occur. Amira's plan was to grab a quick bite to eat after sun down, and then go search for Moha. She wasn't too concerned about finding Moha since the bird always seemed to find her.

After glancing at a map, Amira actually felt excitement. She couldn't believe how far they had already traveled. This plan might actually *work* she thought to herself. Amira then quickly checked a local newspaper to find out when sunset occurred, and with that, she walked out of the library with her sunglasses on and hood pulled over her head. She figured she might as well walk around a bit, look for a park and/or bench to chill out in/on for a spell. That idea lasted about ten minutes as she found herself bored, so she decided to call Karen again.

"*Amira!* I'm sooooooo sorry about yesterday. Carlos and Meredith are here with me. How are you?"

"I'm fine. I'm now in-," Amira wisely stopped herself worried that someone may be listening in. "I'm on *schedule* I think, maybe even ahead of schedule of going to the place where I want to go."

"Oh, good! A bunch of students got called into school yesterday to answer questions by the cops and an FBI agent. The agent was *weird.* He asked about you."

Amira's heart sank. "What did he ask?"

"Well, he tried to be all cool about it and said, 'There were reports of a student being chased out of school by wolves. The student's name was Amira Masri. Do you know what happened to her?'"

"What did you say?" Amira asked.

"The same thing we told the cops outside of your house the night before, that your family had to go back to Egypt for a little bit, and that you left the dance early to catch your flight. Amira you *are* trying to get back to Egypt and now he knows!"

Amira took a deep breath. "That's okay. I mean he probably always knew that. What other choice did I have? But he doesn't know *how* I'm getting from Texas to Egypt, so I still have that advantage."

"But, if he has the FBI after you, he-"

"Do you think he was really part of the FBI? Do you think his badge was real?"

Karen's voice was muffled as she asked Carlos and Meredith, "Do you think his was real?"

Amira could hear Carlos reply in a quite distant voice, "I don't even know what a real FBI badge looks like. How would I know what a fake one looks like?"

"This *isn't* the time for your attitude Carlos," Karen hissed.

"*Guys*," Amira stated. "I need to get off the phone since I don't know how safe it is for me to be on it."

"Okay, well *be careful* Amira, and calls us whenever if you need *anything*."

"Tell her we love her," Meredith piped in.

"Meredith says,"

"I heard. I love you all too. Even Carlos," Amira winked. Then, she remembered she was on the phone so her wink registered with no one but herself, which really made it more a blink than a wink...perhaps a tic.

"Okay, well be careful Amira," Karen said trying but failing to hide her fear.

"I will, and try not worry. I'm safer than you'd think. Bye you guys."

"Bye Amira," "Bye!," "Bye yo!" the MOP Squadders all said over one another.

***

"Were you able to trace it?" the scarred man asked someone over the phone.

The voice on the other end replied, "The call to her friend was too short. However, because we were also tracking her Egyptian family's phone and that call lasted longer, we're able to track it to within 30 miles of where she was calling from."

"And where was that?" the scarred man asked pushing a button to put the call on speaker.

"Somewhere northwest of Memphis."

The scarred man smashed his hand into the desk actually causing a dent in the cheap wood. Amira had gotten farther than he realized, but she was still far, far away from reaching her obvious destination. He reminded himself of that, and took a deep breath. He then opened up the drawer to the desk and pulled out a map of the United States. Scanning it for only a few seconds he said, "Place a team in Virginia. We'll meet you there tonight."

"Virginia sir? But the call came from-"

"I *know* where the call came from, but I'm not interested in where she is, only in where she's going."
***

Amira found a sandwich shop near the diner where she had breakfast that morning. She bought a sandwich to go since it wasn't dark out yet and then found a convenience store where she bought a couple of bottles of water and some granola type bars just in case she wanted to snack at some later moment during their journey. After that, she glanced around the quiet street, and when no one was looking, she ducked back into the woods to search for her fair-feathered friend.

Amira walked around for about ten minutes until she came across a stream. She began to worry because she hadn't seen or heard Moha. She glanced around her: nothing but trees, bushes, and shrubs. Then, something tapped Amira on her shoulder.

Panic stricken, Amira whirled around ready to fight or flee from Maria or the scarred man, but thankfully for her and unfortunately for others (me), Moha had been the one to tap her on his shoulder.

"Oh, *there* you are. What took you so long?"

Moha gave her a "Seriously are you really going to go there after all I've done for you? After I've carried your sorry load hundreds of miles? Oh, and *stop* talking to me!" type look. Moha could convey a lot by just blinking neutrally. Some may say I possibly infused his stare with a certain amount of conjecture, but to that I say, prove me wrong. That's what I thought.

Amira looked around, and no one seemed to be within sight or earshot. "So should we go? Do you think it's safe?"

She had her answer seconds later when Moha beckoned her to jump on and once atop the giant bird, took off deeper into the woods.

The second night felt more difficult to Amira. Even she couldn't dissect the kiss two nights in a row, at least where the conversation would be so one-sided. Further, flashes from the dream sporadically disturbed her and being away from home took its toll. Plus, she had nothing to wear to the pity party being thrown in her honor. I mean seriously Amira. There are worse things than being nearly burned to death, having your house burned down, having a mentor try to kill you, fleeing for your life on a large bird, being separated from your friends, family, and boy-crush, and feeling the weight of the world on your shoulders all at the age of twelve. Okay, maybe there aren't *that* many things worse, but still, grow up. You're alive (at the moment) and if your pursuers catch you, this time I'm certain they'll kill you quickly, so you've got that going for you.

Lacking the ability to remain self-centered for the moment, Amira took in the world around her. She noticed the air was slightly cooler than the night before, the land grew hillier, and that the smell in the air took on a more oaken flavor. She then remembered that she really didn't know what oak smelled like exactly, but the plants around her definitely differed from the plant life in Texas, so it could be *oak* she was smelling, or maybe sumac. Yes, she decided: 27% sumac, 70% oak, and 3% bluegrass filled the air with the current aroma mix. Assigning numbers made it feel true to Amira.

Amira stared up at the stars, locating the Big Dipper, the Small Dipper, and Orion's belt. Okay, really she just found three stars that vaguely lined up and assigned them as "Orion's belt," but I don't have the heart to tell her otherwise. She looked at the various shapes the stars created, thought about how although the stars seemed like neighbors in truth, nothing could be further, for some were millions, nay billions, of miles farther away from Earth than their neighbors, and thus the light from one star was reaching this planet maybe millions of years later than the light from the star next to it. So in a way, Amira was viewing history, but not just any history, millions of different histories all at once.

Okay, fine that's not what Amira was thinking *at all*. Rather, she wondered if her friends were looking at the same stars. (Don't think about it Amira) She imagined Kyle looking at the North Star right now just like her. (Seriously, Amira don't you *dare!*) She imagined he was thinking about her just as she was thinking about him while they both stared up at the star. (No! I'm serious, don't you-) "Somewhere, out there, beneath the PALE MOONLIGHT!," she sang. "Someone's thinking of me and loving me tonight," she blared in a heartfelt and off-key manner.

"And when the night wind starts to sing a lonesome lullaby (F#$%!)

It helps to think we're sleeping underneath the same big sky (must find sharp object!)

Somewhere out there if love can see us through (willing [breathe] to use own finger in attempt to stab myself). Then we'll be together somewhere out there, out where dreams come true." Amira then began to hum the song, forgetting what the rest of the lyrics were. I'm sorry I couldn't join her in a two-part harmony, but I was busy trying to swallow my own tongue.

Amira tried to imagine what it would feel like to actually make it back to Egypt, to succeed through this ordeal, to overcome these obstacles, but the dream felt shallow, felt disconnected, like any daydream that you know *can't* come true. Subconsciously, Amira wrapped her arms around Moha even tighter and leaned against him even more fully.

***

Amazingly, Amira and Moha (well Moha really) covered even more ground on the second night, reaching Charlottesville, Virginia. Charlottesville was much bigger than Munford, but there were still plenty of secluded areas where Moha could drop Amira off and then do whatever he did during the day. Amira pulled a similar routine to her last stop. She found a diner (named "Hoos Watchin' You Now") open pre-dawn, and this time the waitress, a partially hungover/partially still inebriated purple dyed-hair college sophomore who got stuck working this shift because her boss wanted her to quit due to the frequent arguments she had with customers regarding Emily Dickinson, didn't even bother to ask why this young girl was sitting in the diner by herself at such an early hour.

Again, Amira ordered juice, pancakes, hash browns, and fruit salad, and again she asked for a roll of quarters when she asked for the check.

Amira then walked around campus a bit trying to figure out if the college kids she'd see were just getting up or just going home since disheveled fashion discriminates against neither the early riser nor the walk-of-shame-er. Amira imagined what it must be like to be a college student here, wearing a dirty hat with an orange capital "V" on it, joining protesters holding signs with catchy phrases like, "Hoos Against Hooters!" or "Starbucks Star*sucks*!", or "Granolas against granola bars!"

Amira happened upon the main undergraduate library and to her excitement, it was already open, even at this early hour. It didn't occur to Amira that she might need a University I.D. to enter the library, but fortunately for her, the "security" at the moment was comprised of a fully asleep student manning the turnstile who was working here as one of his work-study jobs. Thus, Amira just ducked under the turnstile and continued on. The library was several stories tall, so Amira knew she'd have no problem finding a secluded area. Of course, had she been a few years older, she might have considered that secluded areas in college libraries are often *not* the least foot-trafficked areas. But, naïve, she walked around. To her amazement, there were

333

phone booths on one of the upper floors, so Amira called Karen, again just to check in. She kept her conversation short, but said that she was making good time and tried to reassure Karen that she was okay. Although she didn't want to, she bid Karen adieu, for she knew that a phone call of any length could be dangerous.

On the fifth floor, Amira found a padded bench near a window overlooking a beautiful set of flowering dogwood trees. This time placing an intro book on "Thermodynamics" across her chest, Amira pulled her hoodie over her head and placed her sunglasses on and shut her eyes.

Amira slept soundly for about an hour, dreaming of Kyle. *They were standing in a field where-* actually let me interject for a moment: don't you hate it when other people tell you about their dreams? Seriously, people, those dream recaps have a success rate that's lower than the success rate of a chess team going to a rave. Why? Because dreams generally lack all elements that make a story successful, such as plot, cohesiveness, a beginning, a middle, and an end. The only time someone telling you about their dream is intriguing is when they are dreaming about you and you have a crush on them and you are doing internal jumping jacks because you've infiltrated their subconscious. Otherwise, cousin Kara and friendly Frannie, dial down the dream talk because this guy doesn't care. Anyway, where were we? Oh right, Amira's "field of dreams." *Standing next to Kyle, blah blah, laughing and smiling in the sunlight yada yada. Kyle and Amira lean in to kiss, but suddenly the sky darkens. Amira looks up and sees that storm clouds have rolled in. She turns to Kyle but he is no longer there. She's still standing in the field but now she is atop a hill. She looks down over the grassy landscape below and feels the wind increase around her, brushing past her exposed calves and forearms. Thunder booms all around her, and she looks overhead. The sky darkens even more quickly. Rain seems imminent. She looks back down the hill and at the bottom, a few hundred yards away stands a man. Nothing is around him, yet he stands in shadow, except for his purple eyes. Goosebumps form on her body. She wants to move, but her limbs ignore her. The man seems closer now, but she doesn't see him move.*

"I'd run if I were you," says a familiar British-accented voice that she's never heard before. She turns toward the voice and sees a beautiful girl, of about 18. She's Indian; her skin is darker than Amira's; her hair is equally black, but straight. Amira realizes it's the girl she saw in the reflection when she was being chased in the tunnels.

Amira turns her attention down the hill, and now the purple-eyed man is halfway up the hill. She still can't make out any of his features. He's still covered in shadow, except for the eyes.

"Now Amira. Run NOW!" says the Indian girl.

Amira turns and runs. She's zipping over the land. She calls for Moha to help her escape, but the bird is nowhere around. She glances behind her and sees the man giving chase. She's failed to put any more distance between her and her pursuer even though she's running faster than she knew she could. She looks forward and sees a forest ahead of her, just a hundred yards away. She somehow picks up her pace, but she shivers as his presence feels closer. She's too afraid to look back, so she focuses on the trees ahead. If she can make it to the woods, she can lose him. She hears a snarl behind her; it is soft but deep and powerful. She makes it to the trees and continues on, dodging branches, jumping over tree limbs, zigzagging over the terrain. Finally she dives behind a rock and catches her breath. She's panting. Her lungs burn. She sneaks a glance around the rock and looks for him, but sees nothing. As she looks, she suddenly feels a hand grab her arm. Amira's heart stops; she believes she's about to die, but when she turns, it's the Indian girl again.

"Not yet, Amira," the British girl says trying to smile. "You're not ready to help me. Now is not the time."

"What do you mean? Who are you?" Amira asks as the pain in her chest worsens. She doubles over.

"Amira, wake up. First you need to help yourself." says the Indian girl.

Amira looks up at the girl, "I don't under-"

"WAKE UP NOW!" screams the girl.

Amira yelped as consciousness crashed around her. She bounced upright and realized that she'd somehow tightened her grip on the book and the book's corner was digging into her sternum. Amira's grip on Thermodynamics 101 relaxed, and the pain in her chest that began in her dream and followed her to consciousness dissipated. She took a deep breath and sighed a bit too loudly for a library. Suddenly several pairs of angry eyes were staring at her, but she didn't care because they're just college students. She smiled and thought it's not like they're dangerous. She looked out on the courtyard and thought it's not like she was surrounded by the enemy. It's not like Maria and the Scarred-Arm Man were standing out front. It's not like there were a series of suspicious looking black cars pulling up in the parking lot out front. Well, there was *one* indiscriminate black car with tinted windows pulling in, but one car did not equal an *ambush*. And sure seeing a second, similar looking non-descript black car pull in after it wasn't the greatest sight to see, but again, it was not a big deal. And okay, maybe another black sedan drove by and continued on until it reached the next street where it could turn and take up a position on the side of the building.

Okay, Amira, the dream just freaked you out. Stop being paranoid, she told herself in the most comforting "internal" voice she could muster. *It's not like Maria or that man are going to step out of one of those cars,* and gun you down after making you beg for your life? Sorry reader, I figured I'd finish her thought since she lost that train when she saw Maria and the Scarred-Arm Man jump out of the first black sedan that had pulled into the parking lot.

Amira instantly perked up and pressed her hand against the window, a move that would *totally* leave a smear mark that some poor schmoe will be forced to clean up.

Okay, there are plenty of buildings that share this parking lot, so I've still got time. It's not like they're gonna know to enter-, and with that Maria, the scarred-man and others entered the library. Anyone else get the feeling that perhaps Amira would be better off *not* thinking? I mean she seems to be almost *begging* the universe to do the opposite of whatever's going through her mind.

Amira grabbed her backpack and went to return the Thermodynamics textbook to the place where she grabbed it from before realizing that "book returns" was *not* on the list of important things she needed to do today. She dropped the book on top of a book on creationism and continued down an aisle that went in the opposite direction of where she had seen Maria and the scarred man.

Okay Amira THINK (umm, I thought we established that was a *bad* idea.). Amira made sure her hoodie was pulled tight, which I'm guessing she did due to nerves since it's not like her hoodie could stop bullets, and I'm pretty sure I don't ever remember seeing a spy movie where a government official would say something like, "We almost *caught* him, and we would have...(dramatic pause) if not for that DAMN hoodie!"

Then, Amira saw a slice of salvation in the shape and color of a red "T." Amira inched toward the fire alarm, but even though she was in a dangerous situation it was actually difficult for her to pull the alarm since there wasn't a fire. Though Amira was a bit of an outcast, she wasn't exactly a "rebel." So even though no one was around her, Amira faked a big yawn and stretched out her arm and then "accidentally" pulled the red "T" toward her.

Amira then sprinted toward the nearest exit and ran down one flight of stairs before noticing black suited men coming up the flight of stairs. She was sure they were employees of Maria, so she darted back into the library on the third floor. By this point students were gathering their stuff, swearing about the alarm, discussing whether this would be enough to get an extension on the paper they had been procrastinating on for three weeks (short answer: no.). Amira grabbed a large book (this time a book on erotic art in 18th century India). Amira opened the book in order to make it seem like she was engrossed in the subject matter and that's why her face was covered, but as luck would have, the images inside the book *did* in fact capture her attention/imagination.

I didn't think that was possible, she thought to herself while staring at page 167, and to be honest with you reader, I'm not sure whether the image she saw is possible or not either. Amira's plan was to *blend* into a crowd of students that were exiting the library and sneak by Maria's henchmen who likely were stationed at all the exits. Amira realized though, this plan likely would fail, so still with the book in front of her face, she glanced to her side, and noticed a window slightly ajar, and more importantly outside the window, she noticed a tree that *possibly* was close enough to climb onto.

As students walked toward the main staircase, Amira angled herself toward the window and then made a beeline for it.

Amira dropped her bag and using her forearm strength managed to make the window the victor by failing to even get it to budge. Obviously all the pushups and chin-ups she never did growing up were paying off. She tried again and only managed to let out an "Eek" which emanated from her throat. She grabbed a close by chair for leverage. She stood on it and tried again, but the window did not budge. *But,* from her higher view, she noticed that the window, though open, was still latched. (I know the SAT's are a few years a way, but have we decided whether she's "college" material reader? Just saying). She then tried it again, but this time used too much strength as the window flew upward quite quickly causing her to lose balance and fall forward barely catching herself by extending her arms toward the sides of the window. Had she failed to do so, this would have gone down as a quite lame failed escape attempt.

Amira now realized that the tree was slighter farther away from the window than she hoped. She looked outside though, and no one appeared in view. She grabbed her backpack and dropped it three stories onto the grass below. With the Qistone in her pocket she then stood in a crouching/lunging position along the window pane and told herself that she could make this jump, that she *would* make this jump, that the closest branch wasn't *that far* away.

She then heard *his* voice down the stairs barking out directions.

No time like the present, Amira she said as she jumped for her life. You don't really understand how high up three stories is until there's nothing but air separating you and the ground below. Time seemed to slow, which allowed Amira more time to consider the ramifications of her current course of action. She felt (or imagined) the Qistone's power flowing through her, and then her vision tunneled and she seemed to notice every little detail of the branch in front of her that she still had not reached. She noticed the crevasses and chips in the bark; she noticed the flowers and the buds that failed to bloom, she noticed the gentle rhythm of the limb as it interacted with the wind. She also noticed her fingers reaching out and just barely brushing against the rough bark and the sense of dread that filled her as the branch began to rise above her as gravity asked her if she could "chat." Amira's eyes looked up at the branch wishing they had been able to spend *just* a bit more time getting to know one another.

Fortunately, for Amira, although she missed out on some more quality tactile time with the branch, her hood caught hold of the branch. Suddenly her free fall switched directions and she was falling not down as much as to the left as the branch holding her bodyweight (maybe she was regretting that two-morning in a row pancake breakfast choice) snapped. Her current projection tossed her into several more branches which she grabbed for and this time her grab succeeded.

Yes! she thought to herself for that one second before the two branches she held onto snapped as well.

No! then replaced that "yes," but even though her hands were failing her, she discounted her hair's will to survive, for like an octopus' tentacles, her ringlets clung and grabbed onto seemingly everything. Like a pachinko ball, Amira twirled and bounced downward but with detour after detour. Finally, the ground caught up with her but her freefall turned out only to be "free" the final five feet, so although scratched all over her arms and legs and with her hair full of flower petals, leaves and bark, Amira landed with a hard, but not "too" painful *THUD*.

Amira tasted the dirt in her mouth and then did a quick mental check to see if any part of her body was screaming out in pain. Everything hurt but everything *felt* in tact, so Amira hopped up and grabbed her backpack.

A skateboarder who had been watching her fall failed to pay attention to the road in front of him that was quickly becoming a curb, and therefore his board hit the curb and he went flying onto the dirt.

"Oh my god!" Amira said after watching him take his spill but fifteen yards away. Unable to control her desire to help, Amira sprinted over.

Running toward him, she asked, "Are you okay?"

"Yeah I thin-"

"*Great!*" her philanthropic spirit said as she hopped over him. "Sorry, but I need to borrow your board." Thoroughly concerned with the skater's health, Amira hopped on the board and zoomed down the street. Well, in her defense, he *seemed* fine, and she at least *asked* him how he was feeling before stealing his board.

Now, Amira wasn't exactly a "skater" growing up. Actually, she wanted to be, and as she currently zoomed down the street, she could hear her mother say, "No Amira. Riding skateboards is *dangerous*."

"But *Mom*," Amira said, "I promise I'll be safe. *Please!*"

"You can try to be safe and still fall and crack your head open my child."

"I'll wear a helmet, and knee pads, and elbow pads, and umm *wrist pads*. Please mom. *Please*."

A few days later, Amira had a skateboard along with all of the padding. However, her mother then wrapped bubble-wrap around her knee pads, elbow pads, and helmet, and as Amira took to the generally empty street to practice (since their driveway was gravel), Nara got into her car and followed behind her at five miles per hour to ensure that no car driving down the lonely road would run into Amira because they weren't paying attention.

For some reason, skateboards lost the "coolness" factor and "dangerous" factor as she road down the street dressed like a bubble-wrap monster with her mother driving a beat up station wagon less than ten feet behind her. Thus, Amira left the skateboard in the basement and decided to find other activities to fill up her free time.

Now, as Amira's speed increased due to the increase in the marginal slope of the street, Amira cursed her mother for not letting her master the board, but as the black sedan pulled out onto the street and quickly closed the gap between it and Amira, Amira also wished it was her mother driving the car behind her and not some assassin. Amira felt she was in a bit of pickle: she wished to go faster, but her balance at the current speed was tenuous at best, yet each second at the current speed allowed the car behind her to pull closer still.

The humming of the engine grew louder behind her as the car closed in; she looked back just in time to see that the car was mere inches from her. The car lurched forward, but Amira quickly angled the board hard to the right and thus dodged the sedan, but now she was parallel with it. She looked inside and saw some sunglass wearing, well-muscled man she had never seen before.

The man smiled at her, but Amira was certain it wasn't one of those "happy" smiles but much more sinister. Amira concentrated on her weight distribution and form to increase her speed but the car easily kept pace. However, past the car, and through some trees Amira saw Moha sprinting along trying to catch up. After a few more seconds, Moha zoomed out of the forest and was now running parallel with the car about ten feet from the shoulder of the road. The assassin saw Moha and decided it was time to end this charade, so he jerked on the steering wheel in order to ram Amira and likely kill her.

As the car careened toward her, Amira felt a "pulse" from behind and *knew* it was coming from the Qistone in her backpack. As the pulse occurred, time seemed to slow, and as the car was about to slam into her, a "course of action" materialized in front of Amira's eyes. The world darkened slightly around her as a "lighted path" appeared beginning right in front of Amira, continuing over the hood of the car and ending a few feet past the car on the opposite side. Amira instinctively "followed" that path; she jumped as the car swerved towards her and landed on the hood of car. As she was about slide past the hood, she then jumped again, keeping within the "lighted area."

Moha darted onto the road just in time catch her with his outstretched neck. Instantly, Amira's sight returned to normal. The whole thing had taken less than two seconds. Amira was shocked that she pulled off those maneuvers and briefly wondered what powers the Qistone may contain. Luckily, the driver too was shocked at what just transpired, which allowed Amira time to position herself more stably on Moha's back.

The driver then pulled out a gun, but Moha was too fast and deftly bit the man's wrist causing him to drop the gun. Then for good measure, Moha used his beak to butt the man in the ear in a really hard, very painful way. This caused the man to lose control of the car and veer away from them.

***

Murray Hill was *pissed*. He could not believe what he had just endured. He was a college senior for God's Sake, not some forty-five year old divorcee with broken capillaries around the tip of his nose. Thus, Murray, sporting a scraggly beard, took his pants that showed off his boxers, his t-shirt stained with various condiments, and his dirty blonde hair (dirty as in having actual dirt in it) that was covered with a Baltimore Ravens hat, and walked to his beat up black, Chevy Malibu, spewing curses all the time. He hopped in his car and still couldn't believe his friends had just held an "Intervention" in his honor. His *drinking* buddies held the intervention. Were they not *there* each and every time he got blitzed? Sure, maybe he drank a bit more than they did when he went out, and there were several moments in his life that his mind self-redacted when he was drunk, so he'd have to take their word for it when they said he became violent by threatening strangers, or dangerous to himself by climbing up trees, climbing onto roofs, blah blah blah. But, *Come ON!* he bemoaned internally as he pulled the car out onto the main street that ran through campus. They *all* pulled similar stunts when drunk; that was just college. And besides, he still had his shit together. He still held down a solid, respectable 2.7 GPA and hit the gym once, sometimes twice a week. He wasn't crazy; he never hallucinated or anything like that he told himself as a giant bird slammed into the side of his car.

Holy [beeeeeeeep]! he screamed both internally and externally as he swerved away from the bird and then swerved again towards it while trying to keep car on the street. Now, he and the bird were running parallel down the street together. He stared out the window with his hands now at "ten and two" on the steering wheel and realized that there was this girl with what looked like flowers and bark spread evenly throughout her hair and carrying a Hello Kitty backpack on her back, staring back at him.

"Sorry," she said to him as she and the bird veered to the left and into the woods.

Murray continued driving down the street dazed and confused. He continued on past his own dorm and drove to the University hospital, where he eased his car into a parking spot and proceeded to walk into the Student Health Clinic. He then filled out paperwork and checked the box stating he was a walk-in and needed to speak with a substance abuse specialist.

***

For a minute Amira thought she and Moha were in the clear but the woods were not that deep and on the other side of the wooded area was a dirt path, and on that dirt path appeared a Jeep carrying two men. Amira and Moha couldn't go back onto the road because there too were black sedans zooming down the

345

street gaining on their position since Moha was slowed by being forced to dart in between trees and hop over fallen branches and large rocks, etc. Soon Amira could see that the man driving the Jeep was the Scarred-Arm Man and his passenger was holding a rather large rifle.

"*PHEWT! PHEWT!*" Amira heard as bullets zoomed past her leaving shards of bark flying around, behind, and in front of her. This caused Moha to increase his speed as Amira looked at the Jeep. The man was about to fire again, but there was a fallen tree trunk on the path, which forced the Scarred-Arm Man to swerve hard to the left to avoid the trunk, which then caused the gunman to lose his balance. Amira looked forward and saw that a stream approaching. This forced the Jeep to veer ninety degrees away from them since they couldn't drive into the water. However, the river did nothing for the sedans since there was a bridge up ahead for the cars to pass through. The cars zoomed over the bridge before Moha and Amira reached the water, so one of the sedans then jerked the car to the left in a full stop to the side of the road as Moha launched he and Amira over the river. As they flew through the air, Amira took her backpack off and while holding both back straps with her right hand swung the pack around and down like a polo shot as the assassin opened the door to get out and shoot at them. Amira connected with the door and the man's head as he was grabbing his gun. The force of the blow which sandwiched the man's head between the door and the car frame caused him to crumble as Moha landed on top of the car and then quickly hopped down onto the ground without missing a beat.

Now the other sedan drove over the bridge to keep pace. Amira looked to her left but the Jeep was no longer in sight. On

346

the other side of the river there were denser woods but Amira could see past the woods an open field with a rundown barn and silo positioned in the middle of the field. The woods slowed Moha down, but it meant the car had to keep its distance on the road and that the driver didn't even bother trying to shoot at them. However, the assassin then decided to speed ahead and pull over about one hundred yards ahead of them. He then got out of the car and ran into the woods, positioning himself in front of them in order to take a shot.

Moha began to use a zigzag pattern darting back and forth, left and right in between trees to make it difficult for the assassin to get a read on where they'd be at any given second, which forced him to hold off on shooting at them. Then, surprisingly Moha dove towards the road and out into the open. The look of shock on Amira's face proved that she wasn't quite confident in this move as the assassin tracked their path and through a clearing between he and the road, opened fire. But as he did so, Moha ducked behind the assassin's own car. The assassin mistakenly shot out his own tires and put a few bullets in his engine before realizing what he just did. As he went to reload his gun, Moha charged at him and used one of his long legs to kick the man in the chest. Amira thought she heard the snap of a rib, but couldn't be sure as the man writhed on the ground.

Moha took off once more heading back into the woods and towards a clearing where the broken darn barn and silo were with a smattering of trees between the two.

***

The assassin sat on a broken down tractor behind the barn. He positioned himself perfectly at height to pick off Amira with a bullet if his boss, the Scarred-Arm Man, was correct when he had radioed saying the girl and the bird were headed toward the barn. His rifle had somehow jammed earlier in the morning, but it was not important. He still had a handheld gun, and from this distance he wouldn't need his rifle anyway. From his vantage point he would see the ostrich as it reached the barn and after it passed the barn and reappeared out in the open that is when he'd strike.

***

In a horse jockey like stance, Amira turned her head to look behind her and didn't see anything. So, she and Moha continued forward. The woods were becoming sparser but after one more clearing, Amira and Moha would again disappear into a much denser wooded area in the country side where the assassins definitely would not be able to give chase. The clearing was dangerous but they'd be protected for much of the open fields by darting in between the barn and silo. There were a bunch of low level trees squished between the barn and silo, but nothing that she and Moha couldn't handle.

***

The assassin sat perfectly still. Through his years of training he'd have no trouble knowing exactly when to strike because Moha now was running at an exact speed, so the man through his training could count the exact amount of time it would take the ostrich and the girl to disappear behind the barn and then pop out on the other side. He had several minutes to canvass the land, and he knew this would be the best shot at killing the girl. He'd have a clear shot, and from this position they wouldn't see him, so he stayed crouched down concentrating on evening all of his breaths to help with the counting for the few moments when they'd be out of his sight.

***

Moha and Amira hit the clearing, and there were no signs of trouble. Another couple hundred yards and they'd be in the clear, and by "in the clear" I mean completely covered.

***

The assassin watched them appear out of the woods and began almost instinctively to figure out Moha's speed. He knew the barn was exactly 30.2 meters long. From the time they'd disappear to the time they'd reappear wouldn't be long. He shifted his breathing to match their pace, so they'd disappear on an inhale and reappear exactly when he began his exhale.

***

Amira couldn't believe how fortunate they had been to escape back there. Just another hundred yards and they'd be home free.

***

The assassin watched them reach the barn and disappear as he breathed in.

***

They had made it to the barn, Amira would just have to duck her head in order to pass underneath the trees and then-

***

The man exhaled as Moha's head appeared on the other side of the barn. He would fire at the exact moment Amira would appear. His gun was perfectly pointed at where her chest would be a moment later.

***

As Amira ducked below the branches her hair bobbed up and became intertwined with the tree thereby jerking her off of Moha as she swung 180 degrees backwards before her hair decided to detangle thereby allowing her to do a face plant on the ground.

***

The man fired several shots, but then realized that Amira wasn't where she should have been. The girl had disappeared. How the hell did she do that he had wondered as he hopped off the tractor running toward the area of land between the barn and silo that he could not see.

***

As Amira hit the ground, she heard the gunshots and saw Moha duck behind some trees before Moha realized Amira was no longer on his back. At ground level, Amira noticed a metal object sitting in the grass. She quickly realized it was a horseshoe, and she decided to find out if that old childhood saying involving horseshoes and hand grenades were true. Of course, she would have preferred to test the theory with a hand grenade at this moment.

***

The man reached the opposite side of the barn and sprinted furiously around it.

***

Amira heard footsteps approaching. She held one leg of the horseshoe and cocked her arm back behind her head and then unleashed the throw aiming for the corner of the barn.

***

The man turned the corner gun drawn and was met with a horseshoe that first connected with his gun and then ricocheted off of his gun and hit him in the head knocking him unconscious.

***

"That's how we do it in Texas!" Amira yelled. "Yee-haw!" she continued choosing to forget that she aimed at a spot about three feet off the ground, missed that location by a lot, but fortunately for her the man stood over 6-foot-6. Moha sprinted back, and she hopped on as they continued on their way.

***

"Damn it!" the Scarred-Arm Man yelled as he smashed his hand into a nearby wooden bench. As he pulled his hand back a gaping hole with pieces of jagged wood now existed. "We *had* her," he said, his voice regaining its calm and detached manner. He absently pulled a thick splinter out of his bleeding knuckle and then gripped the top of the bench, lightly tapping his fingers on a green painted, wooden panel.

"Onto D.C.?" Maria asked in a composed voice.

The scarred man remained silent for several seconds. "Yes and no. We split up. Take half the team and head to D.C. I'll take the rest and head to New York."

"New York? Why would she go to New York when she could find a flight to Egypt in D.C. and it's only a few hours away?"

"I'm not sure. It's just a gut feeling, but we can't risk being *wrong*, so we go to both places. The airport, either airport, will act as a bottleneck, and that's where we'll catch her if we don't catch her before she reaches it. Thus, each of us with half a team will be enough to nab her."

"You're sure?" Maria asked.

The Scarred Man remained silent.

***

Amira and Moha zoomed through the woods, up and down hills no longer worried about being spotted by citizens of the

351

areas they passed through. However, although several local residents spotted "something" here and there, since no one was expecting to see an ostrich with an ostrich-rider whipping by, by the time their brains registered something amiss, Amira and Moha were already gone. Soon the sun began to set and in the glare of dusk, they were protected from any distant onlookers. Amira wondered if they might be better off traveling to D.C. at this point and taking their chances there, but two thoughts troubled her: (1) by the time they arrived, the last flight to Egypt would have left thus leaving Amira exposed for potentially hours, and (2) her pursuers likely were to assume she was headed to Washington, D.C. Of course, maybe it would have been nice to share this decision with Moha since he was doing *all* of the running, but such a one-sided conversation never came to be.

In no time, they were covered fully in darkness. However, this night Amira remained on high alert. Any thoughts of Kyle or her family or the MOP Squad were fleeting at best, for she kept her eyes darting around, looking for any signs of movement or flecks of light that seemed out of place. Moha too seemed to glance around more than usual as he ran. Every once in a while, he'd angrily squawk and sprint even faster even though Amira couldn't see or sense anything around them. It was as if Moha was just *looking* for a fight, for the wrong person to mess with him.

Amira got the feeling that Moha was not taking the most direct route to New York maybe to stay away from any roadways, and Amira didn't question his judgment. Late into the night, Amira saw a substantial sized downtown with a few skyscrapers rise to her east, and she realized she was looking at

Philadelphia, the city of Brotherly Love, where every mugging and stabbing comes with a complimentary Philly Cheese-steak, given to you in order to slow the bleeding (the grease acts as a thickening agent).

Amira noticed that Moha's angry squawks seemed to lose their edge and were replaced by a sound more closely related to a cough. Soon heavy breathing replaced the cough, and soon thereafter a wheezing type sound appeared and Moha's breathing sounded shallower.

They came across a small inland lake dotted around the shore by only a few darkened houses, but no lights were on. For the first time since their journey began, Moha chose to take a break during the night's travels. Moha slowed to a trot and slowed further up to the water's edge where he then knelt down and angled his body downward so Amira could easily slide off. Moha then uneasily, nay unsteadily crouched down to drink some water.

"What's going on Moha? You've run so much you deserve a break, so take your time," she said petting him as he drank. His feathers felt soft and warm to the touch, but obviously Moha was working hard because he was sweating quite a bit since many of his feathers felt...wet. As Amira finished the thought in her mind, she realized that birds don't sweat. She pulled her hand away and noticed how dark and sticky her palm now was. A pit grew inside her; it started in her throat but quickly moved to her chest and then stomach. Amira bent over to more closely examine her feathered friend. Gently parting the feathers that were the most pasted down to the side of Moha's chest, Amira noticed three holes that still wept a red substance so many hours after they were shot at.

"*Oh* Moha. We need to get you help. We need to..." Amira's mind raced but ideas were not forthcoming. She *needed* to get Moha to a vet, or at this time at night find an emergency room for animals...not an easy task when you're not exactly sure where you are and are attempting to hide from a dangerous organization.

Trying to remain calm, Amira said, "Okay, come on Moha, there's a town that wasn't too far back, we'll go there and-"

As Amira spoke, Moha stood up to his full height, with his neck and head stretched up as high as possible as his wings slowly folded out. When Moha chose to show his true size, to show how much space he could take up, he was a breathtaking animal. And when Moha looked down at Amira and slowly shook his head, a lesser known saying came to mind and though Amira may never have heard of this saying, I think she'd agree with its truthfulness: you can lead a bird to water, but you can't make him go to a veterinary clinic to make him get bullets removed.

Moha bent down so Amira could hop on.

"Moha, I can't just-"

Moha brought his head down parallel to her eye level. He didn't blink or squawk. He just remained *present*. He then brought his beak to the side of her cheek and breathed softly, and there he remained for what could have been seconds or minutes. Finally, he bent down again, like a knight bowing to his queen, and this time, Amira accepted his gesture and as gently as she could, climbed onto his back.

Surprisingly, Moha took off with a newfound gusto. He sprinted with the same strength he had shown earlier in the evening, with the strength he displayed in each of the previous two nights. However, unlike before, Moha now stuck much more closely to the roads, perhaps whatever internal device he used to take them in the right direction (Amira had planned on doing many course corrections, but found she never really had to) was no longer working as well under his current situation. Or, as Amira saw, perhaps he had another reason. It wasn't until Amira noticed the third bus they passed from the shadows of the trees that ran parallel with the road that Amira noticed where the busses were headed. "To Port Authority" each read. Moha finally stopped about fifty yards from a bus stop.

Amira slid down for what she knew in her heart to be the final time. As tears formed in her eyes, she remained silent but reached her arms upward. Moha bent down and placed his head on her shoulder as she embraced him and gently stroked the top of his head and neck.

Finally, Moha broke their embrace, and as he did, Amira had an idea.

"Wait!" she yelled, pulling the Qistone out of her pocket. Maybe she had seen "E.T." one too many times, but Amira held the stone in her hand and then slowly brought the orb to Moha's wound. The orb pulsed in her hand as she rested it against his matted feathers and exposed skin. He tried to pull away, but she gently kept him there with her free hand calmly stroking his neck. The pulsing grew stronger as Amira closed her eyes and focused her energy on the sensation. After another minute or so, the pulsing grew fainter and Moha slowly pulled away. Excited, Amira looked again at the wound sure she would see it healed, but with great disappointment, if there was a change to its dimensions, she couldn't see it.

Far in the distance, Amira could see headlights from another Port Authority bound bus. Amira knew it was time to go, but she didn't want to say goodbye to her friend. The memories she had of Moha crystallized: when he first arrived to their farm with several other hatchlings, his jet black feathers and how he stood out due to his streak of purple feathers on the top of his head and the fact he was so much bigger than his siblings. She saw Hashim point and attempt to say Mohawk as he tried to imitate his sister. She remembered Moha driving the workers crazy by never quite doing what they told him to do and by never quite following the rest of the pack. She then remembered the day he saved her from certain death. She thought back to their first ride together, to finding the oasis, to Moha interrupting her first kiss with Kyle and later witnessing her first kiss with Kyle. In a short time, Moha became such a huge part of her life, and realizing that, Amira knew exactly what she wanted to say to her friend.

A tear forced its way out of her eyelid and felt cool against her cheek. After taking another breath to compose herself, Amira said, "Moha, I won't ever be able to repay you for all you have done for me, but I want you to know that-"

"SQAUWK!" Moha belted interrupting her. He then winked and took off in a staggered fashion into the woods, disappearing from view moments later. Well, anyway, I'm sure Amira's message to Moha would have been heartfelt, touching, life-affirming, true-meaning-of-friendship "great," etc., etc. Ah well, tough break.

Chapter 9: Crossing Paths

So, dear reader, I know I run the risk of being New York centric since I've dropped hints throughout that the story is pointing in that direction, and now we're on the cusp of the Big Apple. So, I thought I'd take a moment to dispel any rumors about an East coast bias before they spread out of control. Thus, let's spend a minute on the opposite coast, shall we?

A lot of people *hate* Los Angeles but *love* San Francisco. They make comments like, "People are so *fake* in L.A." or "Oh, mah, gawd, there's like totally no culture in Los Angeles because everyone's a transplant."

Now, I don't necessarily dispute either comment, but just because you say something that is true, doesn't make you right. For instance, people in L.A. are fake, but at least they're up front about it. They don't try to hide it. I mean sure maybe their poker faces are impressive, but that's due mainly to botox injections paralyzing their forehead and cheek muscles rather than a deep-seeded sinister nature. I much prefer that type of fakeness over what you find in San Francisco where you've got Granola twenty-somethings driving SUVs and world conscious activists who are afraid to walk around Oakland.

And who needs culture anyway? Seriously, I think "culture" is just code for "crappy weather." Who needs culture when it's 80 degrees and sunny every day? Really, culture is just another word for "indoor activity," like, "Hey, let's get some culture today and go to a museum" or "Hey, let's go to that trendy indie movie theater with uncomfortable seats and a poor sound system and watch the movie about that mute who overcomes all odds to take the mime world by storm!," or "Hey, I really want to go to the Emily Dickinson Café and hear that band that makes all of their instruments out of vegetables play tonight." So yeah, that's cool. Keep your culture. I'll be busy sunning on a beach in Malibu, reading US Weekly, and ogling the self-centered hottie who grossly overpaid for a fabric-lacking bikini while sipping on a Zima.

As the bus carrying Amira (and many other passengers) pulled into the most magical place on Earth, (Disney Land? No, I'm talking about the Port Authority of New York of course!), Amira realized this was *not* how she envisioned her first trip (not counting layovers at LaGuardia or JFK) to New York. As the air brakes went off (loudly) and the passenger door squeaked open, Amira slowly gathered her belongings and made her way out of the bus and into the damp, dark lonely cesspool that greets all visitors who travel by bus to New York.

First order of business was finding an information kiosk to figure out how to get to JFK. Thankfully there were kiosks with the word, "Information" scattered about, so that task was not too difficult. The next order of business was a bit trickier. Amira had to buy a plane ticket. She worried that if she showed up at the airport by herself and tried to pay in cash that would lead to too many questions and possibly detainment by child services while they figured out what was going on, so Amira had to "risk it" and order the ticket over the phone using her mother's credit card, which she had been given in case of emergency, and although likely not contemplated by Nara, Amira running for her life most definitely counted as an emergency. So, Amira found a payphone, found the number for EgyptAir and ordered a ticket. Worried that she would sound like a child on the phone, Amira mimicked an adult voice, but rather than sounding like her mother as a normal daughter would do, Amira ended up sounding Scottish with just a hint of Hungarian for good measure. Strange girl. Anyway, her story was quite simple: she was buying the ticket for her "daughter" and that although twelve, she'd be traveling by herself. The ticket agent asked if Amira would need an airline rep to make sure she got on the plane, etc., but Amira acting as her mother said that she'd be fine without one. Thus, Amira now had a ticket, although to her dismay, she had fourteen hours before the plane took off. She was hoping for a smaller window in which her chasers could find and capture her, but sometimes you just have to play the hand you're dealt, and after several days on the run and several more near death experiences, Amira felt numb, too emotionally exhausted to fear what may await her at the airport.

Since Amira had many, many hours to kill, she decided to go to Central Park since she figured out she could take the A train north one express stop to Columbus Circle and then when it was time to go she'd take the southbound A train in order to travel the longest leg to the John F. Kennedy International Airport.

It was close to rush hour, so the Times Square subway station was rather busy. There were men and women in styled grey and black suits offset by just a hint of color via a collar or tie. Club kids with purple and pink streaked hair with wallets chained to their belts (if male) and neon colored purses (if female) laughed and jumped up and down and seemed all touchy-feely; basically, they looked like all the kids she'd seen in Health Class videos that were locally produced where "those kids" would either get pregnant, overdose, go to jail, or "o.d." while pregnant in jail. Amira always thought a few *too* many of her peers would glance in her direction during the video screenings. Thus, Amira kept secret the fact that she always kinda liked the purses she saw the girls in those videos have. This reminds me dear reader of a theory I have about girls and purses. If you're at a bar or club, you can always tell if a girl's trouble by the size of her purse...*always*. If a girl has a large purse, that means she's generally motherly, protective of her friends, ready for any situation, event, or emergency. She's "packing." Low Blood sugar? She's got a cookie. Allergy attack? Here's a packet of Kleenex and a Benadryl. Iron Deficiency? Here's some beef jerky. Conversely, if a girl's purse is so small that it looks like it couldn't fit a golf ball, that means the girl's basically telling the world, "I brought nothing with me tonight since I can't be trusted *not* to lose everything I would have brought with me due to the fact someone made fun of my elbows today, so I need to drink heavily rather than deal with any issues I may be facing." Wait, what was my point? Oh yeah! So when at a bar or club always and I mean *always* go for the girl with the small purse (end of public service announcement).

Amira's memories of Texas public school videos faded from her as a man, a really tall man with grey hair and ashen skin who wore four coats began to belt out "No Woman No Cry" while strumming his guitar. The man winked at Amira, which made her smile. She then tried to bob her head/body with the music but her rhythm had not improved over the past four days, so the musician just smiled as he slowly but purposefully turned away from Amira. Thankfully, before Amira could feel *too* self conscious a bright light followed by a large, white "A" surrounded in a circle of blue appeared, and then seconds later the train, screeching to a halt, drowned out all sounds in the station.

As the subway car doors opened, Amira followed the club kids and a few of the suits (the majority of suits were waiting on the other side of the track for some reason) onto the car. There were no seats available, so Amira awkwardly reached around and through several people in order to hold onto the metal pole, which was placed in the center of the car and ran from the ceiling to the floor. As the car chugged into motion, Amira noticed the subway warning, which warned you *not* to lean against the door. It was placed right above all the people leaning against the subway doors. Amira didn't judge the passengers though because the warning had a drawing of a person leaning against the door, and the drawing of the person leaning against the door made that cartoon figure seem really, *really* cool. The drawn figure seemed sooo confident as he stood on one leg with the other leg bent 90 degrees, so he basically formed a "4" with the lower half of his body while his upper half rested against the subway doors. Seriously, if this stick figure approached a girl at a bar, you'd expect him to get the girl. If James Dean had to be reincarnated as a warning label, James Dean would *be* the "Do Not Lean Against Subway Door " stick figure warning guy.

Still wishing *she* had been the one leaning against the subway door, Amira reluctantly exited the subway car into a relatively "brighter" feeling Columbus Circle Station. Amira walked up a set of stairs and found herself still in the Subway station, so she randomly picked another flight of stairs to exit the station, and when she did exit, she instantly saw why so many people chose to live in this overpriced, overcrowded, over-attitude-d, city. Although less than twenty blocks from Times Square, Columbus Circle; Central Park; and Central Park South may as well have been on a different continent. Here, the sun shone *brightly*...off of actual *foliage.* People seemed to be *happy*, basking in the sun and each other's company. There was a buzz around the Park; this oasis in a concrete jungle made people believe in their dreams Amira realized. If you could escape all that was wrong with New York while *staying* in the heart of New York, then...then it becomes much harder to use the word, "impossible."

Amira crossed the street and walked along Central Park South heading east. She came upon a huge statue of a man on horseback. She stared up at the monument for a minute. On the front it read, "Jose Marti." She had no idea who Jose was, but the image of him on a horse reminded her of Moha, so she turned away from the statue before her emotions could take over. She noticed stone steps past the statue that led down into Central Park, so she decided to take them. As she walked down the Park steps and looked out past the steps and path and onto the pond beyond, she was amazed at how quickly the sounds of the city faded, replaced again by music. Maybe that was part of New York's charm: music was *everywhere.* As she walked down the

362

wide stone steps, she heard someone strumming his guitar and singing a song she had never heard...

(singing) "Hello Stranger, have you been waiting all these years..."

As Amira walked down a few more the steps, her faith in herself and the world grew, or perhaps *replenished* is a better word.

(singing continued) "For me to find you, for me to wipe away your tears..."

On the second to last step, Amira looked to her right and could see the bridge of the guitar and the musician's left hand effortlessly moving about. She hopped off the last step and onto the paved path and could see the edge of the green bench the musician sat on as he played, but his face was blocked by a tree branch hanging down in front of him. She decided to ask him who wrote that song because-

"Hey! LOOK OUT!" screamed a guy on rollerblades heading straight towards her. Amira jumped forward onto a semicircular stone ledge which separated the path from the pond below. The inline-skater whizzed by her, missing hitting her by centimeters.

Amira yelped as she gulped in a breath of air, frightened by what almost transpired. To escape wolves and assassins only to be taken out by a rollerblader, now *that* would be a pathetic way to die, Amira thought.

(singing continued) "Distance runner, here on the last mile-"

The man who almost bowled her over smoothly stopped a few feet past her. "Dude! *So* sorry. Are you okay? I didn't mean to startle you yo! Wow, *totally* my bad! I thought you saw me."

Amira was ready to yell at the man, to show off some New York 'tude because she wasn't expecting an apology, but since he did apologize, she said, "Oh! Umm, yeah I'm fine. I...sorry, I was listening to-"

"Yeah, babe, I'm not gonna flake. I'm going now. I'll be there. I promise." a guy said passing behind Amira.

Amira looked behind her where the guitar player was, but now the spot was empty. She looked up the steps and there was a guy walking away carrying what she thought was a guitar case. Amira laughed: New York *changed* so quickly from moment to moment. One moment there's music, the next ear-damage inducing subway breaks. One moment there's music, the next a rollerblader is screaming at you to save yourself from bodily harm. Turning back to the rollerblader she said, "Yeah, anyway. No harm, no foul, right?"

"Totally," the man in a "Rudy's Rude!" t-shirt and fabric-torn jeans said. "You rock on today, okay?" he said as he began striding away.

"I'll do that," Amira said more to herself than to anyone else. Amira headed east along the path, which wrapped around the pond located near the southeast corner of the Park. Couples lounged in areas of well-kept grasses while parents watched over their children who stood on the rocky water's edge in order to "interact" with the cosmopolitan ducks that hung around the Park. The path turned northward and Amira followed. As she came to a fork, she noticed an arched-stone bridge in the distance. She chose to take the left fork since it looked like it wound towards the bridge; plus, the left fork continued along the water's edge.

Yellow and purple flowers lined the path between the asphalt and the water. The right side of the path was lined with green benches, many of which had engraved golden plates nailed to them. She stopped to read one of the engravings. "To Bill, November 27, 1998. I'll Love You Always, All Ways. –T" Her fingers traced the black lettering and paused on the comma between "Always" and "All Ways" for a moment. She then took off her backpack and decided to sit down on the bench. She put her arms through the backpack straps and hugged the pack against her chest as she closed her eyes to rest for a minute, hoping to connect to the love she felt emanated from the bench.

Amira slept deeply, and once she slowly returned to the land of the waking, she noticed that long shadows were beginning to stretch over the Park. She popped up off the bench panicked before she awakened enough to realize that although it was early evening she still had several hours before her flight left. She gently placed her backpack on the bench, so she could stretch her neck and then shoulders. She bent her back side-to-side and then forward and backward and swung her arms in large circles in order to get her blood flowing. She then put her backpack back on and returned to walking along the path. She walked up three sets of three steps and came to the arched bridge she had noticed many hours ago. She decided not to take the bridge though because it looked like it would take her back towards where she entered the Park, and she wanted to explore more. Thus, she continued on the path northward. She passed a gigantic boulder with stone steps carved into it and then she came to a promenade made up of hexagon shaped stones. The promenade had an amazing view of Central Park South and she stopped to stare at the buildings she had passed earlier in the day. She noticed a tall building with a rusted green top and to the right of that building another building with huge letters on the top which read, "Essex House." She wondered what it must be like to live on the upper floors of these buildings, the stunning views of the Park the residents must have. She doubted her savings account, which consisted of $729.37 would be enough for a down payment on one of those apartments, so she continued northward. She walked up an incline, passing a broken water fountain as the path curved left to right. She came to a street, which cut across the Park. No cars were on the street, but she had to wait for a series of horse-drawn carriages, the deep "GALLOP-GALLOP" cadence of the hooves hitting the cement, to pass before she could cross. She noticed the grooves the horses and carriages had formed in the dirt and cement over the years; obviously the horse-drawn carriage path that many a visitor of New York had taken over the years was a well thought out and often used path.

She crossed the street and continued walking north. For a second she wondered if she was still walking north and shockingly the Park answered her question, for on the ground were four directional arrows. On the "compass" (sans compass arrow) she read, "Mall Literary Walk, Anne Burnett and Charles Tandy Foundation 1990." She thought a "literary walk" could be fun, so she walked north and noticed that on each side of the large, straight walkway were bronzed statues. She assumed they were statues of writers. To her right was a statue of Walter Scott. *Never read him*, Amira thought. To her left, a statue of Robert Burns. *Never read him*, Amira thought. Next she came to a statue of Fitz Greene Hallock. *Okay, Seriously!* Amira thought herself. *What kind of literary walk is this?! Where's*

Dr. Seuss? Yeah, that must be another path Amira. Somewhat defeated, Amira walked along the literary walk feeling less and less literate with each step, until she turned her focus to the beautiful American elms which created a canopied roof over the walk. Suddenly, several black lamps along the path flickered and then illuminated. She then noticed a few fireflies flashing their greenish light on and off between the elms. What she failed to notice was that the fireflies' pulsing synced perfectly with the stone which pulsed brighter and dimmer, brighter and dimmer within her backpack.

Amira passed a college-aged violinist-cellist-trombone trio who had set up shop halfway down the Mall. Her spirit picked up and she felt lighter as she left the "mall" and entered a large square where roller-skaters and rollerbladers zoomed around to music supplied by a cheap boom box and a series of bongo-playing drummers. On the eastern edge of the square stood an empty, dirty, white band shell.

She noticed that people, without hesitation, walked through the square with the skaters weaving around them, and despite her recent incident, Amira followed suit and walked through the square. Beyond the square were three grass "islands." The islands were surrounded by wooden benches where a smattering of people were sitting and talking to one another (and sometimes just to themselves).

She walked past these grass islands and came to another road cutting across the Park, but here she only had to wait for a few bicyclists before crossing. On the other side of the street a sign informed her that she was about to enter the Bethesda Terrace. The upper terrace overlooked a huge fountain, and beyond the fountain a lake, and beyond the lake a thicket of trees. Amira felt more energetic for some reason, so she hopped down a set of steps to her left, which connected the upper terrace to the lower terrace. As the sun set, more fireflies hovered around the tree-lined perimeter of the Bethesda Terrace.

She stood on the red brick in front of the Angel Of The Waters fountain and stared up at the Angel. She tried to imitate the Angel's pose, so she extended her right arm out and bent her wrist up. With gently bent knees, she moved her left leg forward and left arm back. She wondered what she would see if she could stand next to the angel on top of the fountain. My guess is that she would see a little girl with crazy black hair obnoxiously trying to mimic the angel, but I could be wrong.

Amira then spun around and ran up the same set of stairs taking them two at a time, and then turned right heading west. She quickly came to a cul de sac with a fountain in the middle. She walked towards this fountain that was far smaller than the Angels Of The Water fountain she had just left. Although simpler in design, there was something about this fountain that she really liked. Towards the top of the fountain were eight bulbs, but only seven of which were lit since one bulb obviously had burned out. She watched water fall down from below the bulbs into a larger pool of the fountain for a few moments before she walked beyond the fountain and looked out past a grassy hill and onto a large pond. The water was mostly black now due to the lack of light, but part of the water reflected the light from the buildings on Central Park West. Past the pond was thick foliage. In the foliage, hundreds and hundreds of dots flashed green for a second and then went out and then flashed green again. Amira began to wonder if it was normal for fireflies to flash their "bulbs" in such unison, but the thought quickly faded as she realized she probably should start heading for the airport. Thus, she turned around and walked out of the cul de sac before turning west yet again.

She soon crossed another street and walked up a path she assumed led out of the Park. As she walked up this path, she heard more singing and more guitar playing. The path opened into a circular area. Along the edge of this area, two gentlemen were sitting on a bench strumming their guitars as they belted out "Hey Jude." In the center of the circle, Amira noticed there were candles placed strategically along a mosaic of inlaid stones with the word "Imagine," written in the center of the mosaic. Inside the smaller circle created by the candles was a peace sign made from orange and red bi-colored roses. The image created by the candles and roses that were placed on top of the mosaic was beautiful Amira thought. She wished she could take a picture, but she had no camera, so she continued along and quickly exited the Park at West 72nd Street and Central Park West. She then noticed a subway entrance across the street. She crossed the street and saw that the entrance was for the B and C trains. The C train was a "blue" train, so she walked down the steps and asked an attendant if she could transfer to an "A," another "blue" train. The attendant wearing a bright orange vest said she could transfer, so Amira walked down another flight to catch a southbound train in order to begin her journey to JFK International Airport. She hummed to herself and slowly spun around and around as she waited for the train. Hopefully, she could keep this positive attitude for what was soon to come.

I sense some apprehension on your part dear reader. Would it make you feel better if I told you that she fails to make her flight? Hmm? No? Well, don't get angry. I understand you've watched her survive multiple attempts on her life, travel thousands of miles, show strategy and confidence beyond her years that have all led up to her making it to New York. So, now she has one final step, which on the surface would seem the easiest: hop on a plane. So, for Amira to come this far and fail to make her flight might anger you. I get that, I do. However, at the moment I have two choices: lie to you or tell you the truth, and I choose the truth because I feel we've developed a relationship, so I don't have to sugarcoat anything, not like I was doing at the beginning of this story. So yeah, feel free to stop reading if you want. I feel like I owe you that option. I wish someone had given me that option when I first watched "Old Yeller." So, it's the least I can do. Hmmm, I think I've made things worse for you. Okay, well to boost your spirits, understand she had a pleasant subway/bus journey to JFK. She even got to sit in a seat the entire way. That counts for something, right?!

***

Each airport has a certain set of sounds due to slight differences in the intercom system and acoustics, slightly different shading due to differences in the lighting and color of linoleum tiles all airports employed, and a slightly different set of smells due to variances in the materials used to build the structure as well as due to differences in "food" establishments, and as this unique combination of sounds, sights, and smells of JFK International Airport passed through her sensory systems, memories began to make their way into her head. She had been to this patch of New York many times, at least twice a year since she could remember, but each time she was with her family. Now, she was very alone.

She found the EgyptAir ticket counter and walked up to the ticket agent. The overly mascara-ed agent, smiled way too broadly for the occasion and said, "How can I help you Miss?"

"Umm, I'm supposed to pick up my ticket here. (laying it on a bit thick) At least, I think that's what my mom said."

"May I see your passport?"

Amira handed over her passport. The woman took it and began to loudly click in Amira's information into the computer that would have been considered outdated several years prior to this moment.

"Ahh, here you are. Oh, I see you're traveling alone. Aren't you a big girl?" the woman beamed.

Amira just smiled back. She wanted to respond with a snarky comment about even being able to read, etc., but held her tongue because the less memorable she was the better at the moment.

"Will you be checking any bags sweetie?"

"Nope, just traveling with my backpack. My extended family's over there, so I have clothes already there."

"Well, aren't you lucky having family in such a mysterious part of the world."

Amira didn't quite get the "mysterious" angle, but again she just smiled.

"Okay, well then your flight leaves from Gate 37-A. It's currently on time, so I suggest you get to security since they will begin boarding in a little over an hour."

"Will do," Amira replied. "Thanks!" she said grabbing the ticket. She quickly walked away from the ticket counter scanning the crowd for anything suspicious. She imagined an alarm going off when the woman typed in her name in the computer, but nothing of the sort happened, and as she scanned the crowd no one looked menacing in the slightest, so Amira entered the line for security feeling relatively safe. The line was fairly long, and as Amira stood slowly moving a few steps forward every few seconds, she yawned. Maybe it was the long subway ride, or the fact she'd been sleeping in libraries for the past few days, or the feeling of being emotionally spent from no longer having her protector and confidante, Moha, around, or maybe from missing her family and friends and having her house burn down blah blah whine, whine, wah, but Amira felt *exhausted.* It was as if she abruptly tapped out all supplies of the adrenaline her body was able to produce. She had nothing left.

She passed through security in a zombie like state, walked through the terminal trying to be on the lookout, but she found her eyes slowly drooping closed. She found her gate and saw what she expected to see, mainly Arab families chatting, businessmen reading newspapers, and a smattering of tourists all sitting around waiting for boarding to begin. Amira realized she was *starving* as well as tired. Isn't that the worst feeling dear readers? What's worse than when you are dead tired *and* hungry as can be? This is especially troublesome if you're out of "snacks" which means you'd be forced to actually make something and there's a moment where you ask yourself: would cold, canned soup be that bad? But then you can't find the can opener, so tears begin to stream down as you pass out on the kitchen floor holding an unopened box of macaroni and cheese, 3-cheese blend.

Anyway Amira was still fasting and it was now well into the day, which made Amira sad...*quite* sad. But, then she realized the flight would be traveling east, so sunset would be here much

372

faster than she anticipated. Not sure when meal service might take place on the plane, Amira decided to do some "snack shopping," so she could begin chomping *immediately* after the sun dipped below the horizon.

Amira walked to the store which had everything "On Sale," which meant it cost about 175% what it would cost outside the airport. She considered buying trail mix or a candy bar, but then she noticed her nostrils twitching. The smell of cinnamon, butter, dough and sugar infiltrated her soul. What she really wanted was one of those oversized cinnamon rolls that can be found at basically any American airport. With her nose leading the way, Amira walked down the terminal to the source of the scent.

There between a bookstore and a duty free shop stood a shimmering white-tiled beacon of hope displaying whole pans of freshly baked, warm cinnamon rolls. In that moment, all of Amira's troubles washed away. All her hopes and dreams could be found in a batch of sugary batter. She didn't ask for much, but she would ask Allah for this treat and thank him a thousand times over. She walked up to the counter and found herself speechless, so she just held up one finger and then used her other hand to point at the cinnamon roll display case. The teen behind the counter took a roll out and placed it in a paper box for Amira. Amira threw four dollar bills onto the counter, smiled greedily and walked away from the counter not even worrying about collecting her change. Even though she wouldn't be able to eat it for a couple of hours, just being able to hold the box containing the roll, feeling the heat seep out of the box and the aroma pouring through everywhere else would be enough sustenance to get her through the day.

"We are now boarding EgyptAir flight 2715 for Cairo," came a pleasant woman's voice over the intercom system. Amira sighed and allowed herself to relax for a second, to feel the tension seep from her body. In a heavy-footed walk due to her exhaustion, Amira walked slowly back to the gate. About one hundred feet away, she finally looked away from her cinnamon roll and saw the Arab families and tourists form a semi-formed line as they began to be processed through. Most of the businessmen remained seated, the excitement of beginning a journey leaving them many business trips ago. Although tired, she figured she'd still rather stand in line than sit down, so she began walking toward the gate when one of the businessman gently closed the paper that was shielding his face and with his cold-silver eyes stared at Amira.

Amira's mouth opened but no sound came out. She was stunned. The Scarred-Arm man stood between her and the gate. She looked further down the terminal and noticed another man, a much larger man wearing a black suit spotting Amira and making his way towards her. Amira took a step back and then another before turning around and beginning to jog away. She tried to formulate a plan, but this was *it*. She had no other plan than getting on her flight. There was no "Plan B."

Thankfully the terminal was quite busy, so as she jogged away, she'd duck down in between groups of people trying to lose her pursuers, but they were always within a hundred yards of her. She quickened her pace and bumped into couple which sent her cinnamon roll box skipping down the floor behind her.

"HEY!" the woman yelled at Amira. "What the hell?!"

Amira ignored her and considered, like a soldier going after a fallen brother in arms, going back for the cinnamon roll, but the woman's scream alerted the Scarred-Arm Man and his powerful sidekick of her general position and not even a cinnamon roll was worth losing her life over. Suddenly a door opened next to Amira and a man in a work suit exited. As the door closed, Amira saw it read, "Authorized Personnel Only." The door was about to lock shut, but Amira caught it just before it did. She tip-toed behind the worker who was singing (off key) some song that was blaring from his compact disc player and snuck in the off-limits area before shutting it behind her. Tears formed in her eyes as she leaned against the door. She had come this far! How the hell did they catch up to her when she was so close?! She was standing in some long hallway that turned to the left a hundred feet down. She began to walk down it hoping they hadn't seen where she disappeared to. However, she had no illusions; whatever lock the door had on it would soon be broken, and they would be upon her, so she ran. Her legs felt numb and wobbled horribly with each step. She had barely eaten over the last few days. Her back ached, and she was sore everywhere. The physical exhaustion of the trip had taken its toll on her body; the emotional exhaustion was even worse. On autopilot, though, she ran. She ran as fast as she could. She ignored the ever growing beating of her heart and screaming from her lungs. She ran. She ran right up to the point where she turned the corner and slammed into a man dressed in black who held a guitar case in his left hand. The man had ivory skin; his dark brown hair curled in ringlets and seemed to grow up as much as out. But, what transfixed Amira were his eyes. He had the greenest eyes she had ever seen. Within the green, she noticed tiny specks of gold scattered about. She only stared for half a second before she snapped out of it and realized she was potentially moments away from being caught, tortured, or worse.

"I'm so sorry, sir for running into you," she said while gasping for air and staring at her feet.

"Eh, don't worry about it," the man smiled. "What's an airport experience without some unwanted contact, right?" Amira remained silent still looking down. "No? Nothing? That didn't work for you?" he said now laughing at himself.

With her breath now mostly under her control she said, "Look. I know this will sound crazy, but there are (breath) two guys chasing me, and-" She cut herself off and glanced over her shoulders to make sure they weren't already upon her.

As she continued looking behind her, the man said or rather whispered, "Oh my god, it's *you.*"

Amira's heart sank. Any energy she had left felt like it instantly seeped out of her feet. Maybe it was the loss of Moha or the loss of the cinnamon roll, but she could run no longer. She was spent. She slowly turned her head back to the *thug* standing in front of her and gave up. She realized it was futile to run from these shadowy figures. They were everywhere. She was just a girl after all. What chance did she have? She knew she couldn't win, so she thought to herself, *Well, at least I can look at his beautiful eyes as he kills me. Just let it be quick.*

Amira stared up into the guy's face and what she saw shocked her, or would have shocked her had she the energy to exhibit that emotion. Tears overflowed from his emerald green eyes and streamed slowly down his cheeks. She realized this man dressed in black actually was too young to be a "man." He had facial hair, a type of five o'clock shadow; however, his skin lacked wrinkles. He was probably only eighteen; her fatigue must have played tricks on her before, and she just assumed he was much older.

"But you're so *young*. It doesn't make any-" he began but cut himself off. Then, his shoulders released downward, and he sighed as he came to a realization. "I'm such a fool. Why would I think the future...why would I assume...*now* is all that's import-...(Wow, I think this guy went to the same communication school as Amira. Seriously dude, it's called "finishing a thought." Try it sometime.).

Amira thought he was probably too young to be an assassin, and since when did assassins become so emotional and trip over words like this?

"Why are you at the airport?" he asked, now with a show of concern on his face.

Not knowing what was going on or what to say, Amira blurted out, "I need to get to Egypt, but I can't because they're after me. If I get on my flight, they'll know and be waiting for me."

The teenaged boy smiled, "Maybe I'm meeting you *now* because!...to protect you. Wait, who's chasing you?"

"I don't know...These two guys. One is really, really big. The other guy looks really strong. His skin is like mine, but I don't think he's from Egypt. He has these silver eyes, and he has this horrible scar running down his left arm and-"

"Silver eyes...*Scar* down his left arm? Are you sure?" he asked the color from his colorless face somehow escaping even more.

Amira just nodded, yes.

"Look, we don't have much time. What's your name?"

"Amira Masri."

The boy now beamed, "Well Amira Misri, I'm going to get you to Egypt."

"No, *Masri*, not Misri."

"Ahh, crap. Well I was close, and I have a feeling no one is going to pay that much attention to the discrepancy." He handed her a ticket, "Look, we're flying to Cypres. They won't expect that. From there, I'll get you to Egypt, okay?" he said.

Amira stared in wonder at the ticket, which read 'Amira Misri.' She looked up at him, "Wait, how did you-"

They both heard footsteps fast approaching.

He interrupted her. "There's no time. Continue down this corridor and hang a left. Go out the next door you see. You'll be back in the terminal. Our flight boards at Gate 5," he said as he stepped toward the approaching noises.

"Wait, where are you going?"

"I'm going to ask the gentlemen to leave you alone."

"No! You *can't*. They're dangerous. They won't listen to you."

The teenage boy looked at her intently with his green eyes. "Don't worry. I find that persuasion often comes down to the inflection in one's voice."

"But..."

The boy smiled so sincerely. "We have a lot to talk about *Amira*," he said emphasizing her name. "We'll have plenty of time to catch up on the plane. I'll see you soon. Now *go!*" And with that he took off running down the corridor in the direction Amira came from.

"I don't" *understand*, she said, finishing the sentence in her mind since the mystery "friend" was already out of sight sprinting down to meet up with her chasers. Confused, but thankful, Amira ran down the hall in the opposite direction and then turned left, opened the first door she came upon, and nonchalantly walked out into the waiting area and continued on until she reached Gate 5, which had just started general boarding.

****

Amira showed the ticket to a very pretty looking flight attendant who stood just inside the plane.

"Ooh, first class, Ms. Misri. Your seat is right over there," she said pointing to a plush window seat about midway into the first class cabin.

Amira froze for a second. *"First class? Really?"*

The flight attendant leaned in and whispered, "Would you prefer to sit in coach?" She then winked at Amira.

Amira smiled and said, "I guess first class would be better, wouldn't it?" *What the little princess!* Amira walked to her seat. There was so much space between where she was sitting and the seat in front of her that it felt strange to stow her backpack so far away under the seat in front of her, but after taking the Qistone out of the bag and putting it in her pocket, she adjusted quite quickly.

Amira had a ton of questions she wanted to ask this boy who helped her, and she couldn't wait for him to walk onto the plane, so Amira sat there with her eyes fixed on the hatch. A rather tall family of four entered and gave her an envious look because she was sitting in first class and had a ton of unused legroom. Then, a woman wearing designer sunglasses, designer tracksuit, and a designer attitude entered and took the seat behind (*way* behind) Amira. Then, a man in a 3-piece suit entered and sat down a few rows in front of her. Until the flight

379

pulled away from the gate and was actually airborne, there was no way Amira could relax. Although she was so tired, nothing could keep her from watching the door. The fear of the Scarred-Arm Man walking onto the plane still was just too great for Amira even to consider sleeping, so she...oh, never mind, she just totally passed out.

When Amira awakened, she had no idea where she was for the first few seconds. From being in Texas to riding an ostrich to sleeping in libraries to walking in Central Park to then being chased through an airport all within a week will do that to you. So when she awoke and gasped and then darted her eyes back and forth while swiveling her neck erratically, well you're just going to have to forgive her.

"Are you okay Ms. Misri?" asked the flight attendant who Amira had spoken to earlier.

"Umm, yeah. Sorry, just a strange dream," Amira said as she ran her fingers through her hair and stretched her neck.

"Can I get you something to eat or drink?"

Amira looked outside her window and although the sun was setting, it was still visible. "I'm actually going to wait a little while. If I do that, will I miss the food service?"

The woman frowned at Amira. "This is first class. You can eat *whenever* you want," she finished and then winked at Amira.

"Oh right," Amira said happily, but now wondering if the stewardess was winking to be friendly or whether she just had a tic.

"However, we go around for the main dinner at a certain time. If you're worried, there's a sticker in the magazine in front of you, and if you stick it on your arm rest, we'll be sure to wake you if you're sleeping, so that way you won't miss *any* chance to eat."

"Oh, okay. Thanks," Amira said as the flight attendant walked away to take care of another first class customer. Amira realized that first class was only a third full. It was another lucid minute of thinking before Amira realized the seat next to her was empty. Amira's muscles tensed and she stood, okay well *sat* to attention. She beckoned the flight attendant over.

"Is everything okay?" the flight attendant asked Amira.

"The seat next to mine, isn't someone sitting in it?"

"Lucky for *you*, no. I guess the person didn't make the flight. So feel free to stretch out on both chairs if you'd like," she winked.

Amira opened her mouth to question further, but then decided against it. What could she say that wouldn't draw attention to herself? *Umm, so I think my friend, umm, I'm totally blanking on his name. Would you check that for me? I think he was supposed to be on the flight. Hmm, you're calling the authorities which is likely being monitored by the evil group that is trying to kill me? You know I think I'll just go back to sleep.* So, Amira just smiled at the flight attendant, pushed up the armrest, and stretched out her legs across both first class chairs. She then looked out the window at the sun that wasn't setting quite fast enough. She yawned and decided to open up the magazine and grab the "Wake For Food Service" sticker just in case. A few seconds later and she was asleep again.

Amira stands on top of the plush green hill once again. This time the man with the purple eyes is nowhere in sight. Amira looks around. The hill looks out over an expanse of wondrous trees and flowers; rolling lands that seem untouched by man spread out in every direction. There's nothing around her. Wait, that's not quite true. Far in the distance lays a town. At least she thinks it a town. Amira thinks she sees a tower of some sort and specks of colored roofs of different heights surrounding it. The sun beats warmly on Amira's face. A sense of calm envelops her. But, then there's a flash of lightening followed by a crash of thunder. Clouds roll in far too speedily and blot out the sun moments later.

A shadow appears in the distance and steadily glides over the land. The shadow is in the form of a human. She can't make anything out about "him" but she knows it is the man with the violet eyes.

She hears hollow breathing behind her and turns to find a beautiful girl/woman of East Indian descent lying on the ground. She's dressed in white clothing that's torn and tattered, bloodied in spots. Amira's seen the young woman before. The woman's eyes are closed and she's motionless other than her chest rising and falling ever so finely.

Amira runs to the woman and kneels beside her. She moves the woman's long, straight raven hair gently behind the woman's ear. The woman's eyes pop open up. "Not yet Amira."

"Wait, what?" Amira said as she bounced up and out of her slumber.

"Will you *please* shut up? I didn't pay for a first class ticket to hear you speaking nonsense in your sleep young lady," said the designer 'tude behind her.

At first Amira didn't think the wealthy wench was talking to her, but-

"Yes dear, I'm talking to you, said the woman as Amira peered through her two chairs. "And I use the term *dear* as loosely as a proper woman can."

"Sorry, I'll try to keep it down," replied Amira not all that intimidated after what she'd been through lately.

"I should hope so, but I'll keep my expectations low" said the woman getting up to go to the bathroom.

Amira just shook her head as she rolled her eyes, but then she noticed something. She noticed the woman had placed her own bag beneath Amira's chair and in a side pocket, ever so slightly sticking out was the woman's passport. Amira then had a *thought*, a *devious* thought, a thought I *totally* could get behind. Amira realized her own passport lacked a visa stamp for Cyprus. Amira checked to see that the woman was still in the bathroom. She then quickly looked around the mostly empty cabin and everyone seemed to be in his/her own world. Amira then slowly reached down and grabbed the passport and with as much care as possible tore out the page that had the woman's Cyprus visa stamped on it. She then replaced the passport and put the page in her own passport booklet to be used later. She then pressed the blue "Assistance" button in order to order some first-class food, and she hoped they'd give her actual silverware, so she could be sure to clink the fork and knife together as loudly as possible for the benefit of woman sitting behind her.
***

Well rested and shockingly well fed, Amira stepped off the plane with a clear head. She stood alert and glanced around the waiting area, ready to sprint at the first sign of trouble. But no scarred-arm man, no evil Maria, and sadly no green-eyed mystery helper either. Although Amira lacked the proper paperwork to pass through customs, she already had devised a plan. It was quite uncomplicated really; she was going to use her youth, innocence, and a simple, but elegantly false story that would ring true. As long as she hit a relatively uninterested and slightly decent customs employee, she knew she'd sail through.

Not needing to pick up any luggage since all she had was her backpack, Amira quickly zoomed towards the customs area. Thankfully, it seemed she hit a lull in processing since few people at that very moment were passing through the Cyprus authority figures. Thus, Amira had her choice of agents.

She first noticed this mildly attractive, but probably twenty pounds overweight, female customs worker who seemed to have a pleasant disposition. Amira considered walking over, but then thought better of it. The woman, though nice, likely had to be a hard ass in order to get any respect from her male peers and thus might give Amira a hard time by following proper protocol. So, Amira continued to scan the employees and pre-judge them as quickly as possible. Within eight seconds, Amira found *exactly* what she was looking for.

The man stood about six feet tall and his belly stuck out about half that distance. His lids sagged heavily over his eyes, as if the structures supporting his consciousness could crumble at any instant and raze his awareness into a crushing sleep. Plus, he was old, so he probably had nothing to prove and dreamed about his upcoming retirement in order to pass the days away.

Amira pulled out her American passport (she thought her Egyptian passport might be easier to use, but for her soon-to-be-created ruse it would not have worked), shook her hair a few moments to increase the level of chaos in her mop, and quickened her gait as she approached. Before he could say,

"Passport" and spout out instructions, Amira was already on top of him (practically) and spewing out sentences.

"Ugh! I'm so sorry sir! I'm supposed to visit my aunt who I haven't seen in five years for lunch before hopping on the ferry to travel to Egypt to see my grandparents. Ugh! But, while sleeping on the plane, this stupid...well, I shouldn't call him stupid, he was just really young. Anyway, I fell asleep, and while I was sleeping my passport was sticking out of my bag, and I guess this little kid a few seats over was curious, so he pulled out my passport book and *tore* the page with my Visa *stamp!* (Here comes the genius part) So, all I have is this small section of the stamp with a partial date," she finished holding out the torn paper to him.

"This is SUCH a hassle, and I'm so sorry! I make a promise to my dying grandmother to spend some time with my aunt and *this* happens," she said with raised hands and pointed eyebrows conveying an exasperated and annoyed emotion.

The man looked at Amira's passport book. She had stamps throughout it: some from Dubai, others from Spain, a few from Turkey, so she obviously had traveled extensively throughout the region.

"Where are you meeting your Aunt for lunch?"

Although I'm fairly certain eyes do *not* in fact twinkle, if they did, then this would have been a great moment for the twinkling to occur. Amira smiled and said, "Chattista Restaurant. It's a new restaurant that just opened up. It's near the University." Amira had quickly scanned through the "Attractions" section of the in-flight magazine and found a restaurant. Although unbeknownst to Amira, she had a keen sense about creating a believable lie: the more specific the details, the better the lie. BUT(!), the trick is the *type* of specific details one gives. You need specific details that are close to impossible to corroborate, so picking a restaurant in this "story" was perfect because it sounds believable and it's not like the guard can just call up and ask if they're waiting for a twelve year-old Egyptian-American girl.

The Customs Officer smiled at Amira quite brightly. "My nephew works there! He's a waiter!"

"Mabrook! That's terrific! He must make your family quite proud! The restaurant is known all over the world!" Amira replied. She could not believe her luck.

The man now beamed. "You're not going to cause any trouble during your stay are you?" he winked. *Yeah, what trouble could a twelve year-old bring to Cyprus? I mean other than the apocalypse, but whatevs.*

Amira lowered her head slightly, pushed her lips out just a tad, and then looked up innocently and said, "I will do my best."

The officer tapped his fingers on the table in front of him for a few moments. "Welcome to Cyprus. Enjoy your lunch, and then have a safe trip to Egypt. Next time, be more careful with your passport."

"Thank *you*, sir. I absolutely have learned my lesson." (Score one for Amira! Let's see that's Amira: 1, World: 2,000,343. I'm feelin' a comeback dear reader!)

Amira felt like running outside as fast as she could to the port that housed the ferry that would take her *home*, but she didn't take any chances. She did not want to draw any attention to herself. So, she chose a slow pace for her walk and kept her senses keenly aware of her surroundings.

A twinge of sadness dripped over her as she realized the number of reunions that occurred all around her: a young husband picking up and embracing his wife, a five year old boy running toward his grandfather, a ninja high-fiving a stockbroker (just making sure you're still paying attention).

Of course not all reunions were happy. She overheard bits of conversations that were spoken either in English or Arabic.

"I told you my flight would get in at *eleven*. Why did you make me wait?" said an imposing woman in designer clothes whose eyes were covered by sunglasses in the shape and size of saucers for one's teacup.

"*Seamus!* Where the hell are you? Why aren't you picking up your phone? You better not have bailed on me. We talked about *this*! You told me you wouldn't flake."

Amira didn't realize it but she was staring at the girl, trying to place her ethnicity. She had straight light brown hair with possibly tanned or naturally bronze skin and Caucasoid features. Her accent sounded like a mixture of cultures as well. Although America was the "melting pot," Amira felt that her corner of the pot in Texas had "cooled," and she was always much more interested in the intermingling of genetic traits that occurred in the Middle East. The mixing of Arabs, Persians, Greeks, Turks, Europeans, Africans over millennia often created people who could "pass" for several different ethnicities, and to Amira *that* seemed like a true melting pot. The girl finally noticed Amira staring at her, and although she was obviously annoyed with her phone counterpart, she smiled at Amira and finished her message, "Well, call me when you get this." Now looking at Amira and rolling her eyes, "Boys! Ugh" and then she continued on her way.

Partly, Amira wanted to agree with her, so she could then bring up Kyle and talk about Kyle and his boyish personality quirks, but Amira felt that the older girl probably couldn't care less. So, pulling out a pair of sunglasses from her bag, Amira stepped out into the Cyprus sun to make her trek over to the ferry that would whisk her home.

*C*hapter 10: *Swim Life Away*

Amira had taken the ferry once with her Grandmother to visit Cyprus, and she remembered the ferry ran between Limassol in Cyprus and Port Said in Egypt. The ferry would cost her a couple of hundred dollars, but thankfully Hashim had been wise enough to pack her more than enough money. She knew she may have to do some tap-dancing again with customs' people but the officers around the ferry were much less strict/concerned than those at the airport, so she wasn't too worried. The trip would take about 15 hours, and then once at Port Said, she'd be able to make her way to Cairo relatively easily, especially since she had relatives all over Northern Egypt.
***

The ferry was practically empty. This wasn't the height of the tourist season by any means, so mainly the passengers were made up of retirees wearing similar "uniforms" of tracksuits, fanny packs, travel-guides, and snack packs. No one seemed out place. No one seemed to be on the "look out" for anyone, so Amira felt relatively safe. Amira found a window seat inside the cabin on the second level in an area that was sparsely occupied.

389

She stretched out across the three seats in her row. She pulled a sweatshirt out and put it against the window. She then wrapped her arms through the shoulder straps of her bag, rested her head against the sweatshirt and closed her eyes.

***

Amira awakened from her nap to discover that it was nighttime. She probably could have slept longer, but a storm had rolled in over the Mediterranean Sea, and raindrops began to rap against the window with more frequency and more vigor. Amira yawned loudly, but no one was really around to take note. She decided to see if she could find food somewhere, either in the boat's cafeteria or snack bar. She threw her backpack over her shoulders and walked down the cabin to the staircase, which would lead to the first level, which Amira remembered as having the food locales. Amira walked down the steps and found the food area. Unfortunately it was closed. However, Amira saw a snack machine. She walked over, looked over the various options: peanuts, granola bars, potato chips, a bag of trail mix, and as any mature, intelligent woman who knows she must keep her energy up and her body pure in order to be prepared for whatever comes next, Amira the brave, Amira the wise, Amira the courageous, Amira the- oh, never mind, she chose the Twix candy bar and bag of mini chocolate donuts. Well, I'm sure the world will forgive your quest for Type II Diabetes, Amira. *Look! It's a bird! It's a plane! No, wait, it's Diabetes Girl!, ready to save the world!...just as long as her blood-sugar level remains in a normal range,* and sure maybe if you were forced to swim at this moment, you'd likely cramp up and drown, if you had to run up the steps to make an escape, you'd likely double-over, and if you had to remain alert for the next ten hours, you'd likely scan the horizon super quick for about ten minutes and then crash into a deep sleep, but seriously enjoy those donuts.

Amira ripped open the candy bar and consumed (engulfed) it before she even reached the top of the staircase. By the time she returned to her seat, half the donuts had lost their siblings. Her cheeks were stuffed so full of sugary dough, Louis Armstrong would have done a double-take. Amira stared out the window. The rain rapped against the window with more force. She noticed the boat was rocking ever so slightly as the sea surrounding her in all directions began to energize: rolling waves mixed in with white caps appeared as the storm picked up force.

Amira loved storms. She'd sit on her front porch and stare out into the horizon watching the thunderheads roll into central Texas, watching the storm wall grow higher and higher into the sky as different areas of the darkening clouds would flash with more and more frequency. The feel on her skin as the dry hot air would be replaced with cooler, more humid molecules that would make her hair stand up and frizz out, the smell of dew that the winds would bring to her, the sense of electricity as the lighting would flash in the distance, followed by the deep sounds of thunder that would chase after the lightning strikes, all invigorated Amira, made her actually like Texas. (This trip down memory lane was great and all, but too bad it took her senses away from a small dot of light in the distance) Ignoring her mother's voice which sweetly wafted into her head and told her to stay inside once the storm arrived, Amira opened the cabin's door and stepped into the rain. A symphony of sounds greeted her instantly. The "tapping" raindrops slammed into the deck an octave higher than what she heard from inside, but they also held their notes for much longer it seemed. The wind warmly, but loudly "hooed" around her, seemingly giving her locks the password to some exclusive dance party, for her hair danced in all directions as she stared out into the open water, watching white caps zooming around in various directions, often running into each and canceling each out after creating tiny bursts of white foam shooting upward, like mini-geysers. The whitecaps were like the kindergartners running around the romper room as their parents watched over them while drinking coffee and questioning their own life choices, saying things like "Oh, but I really love my kids. I *do*. No, seriously. Why would I want to sleep in on a Saturday and go party it up with friends tonight?" Hmm, I'm starting to see the appeal of drinking something hot and bitter. The parents in this description would be the rolling waves that Amira saw slowly moving through the sea. Amira tried to imagine the amount of force each wave carried and wondered how "deep" the wave waters ran. Lighting would illuminate her view briefly and then linger for a few moments, giving the scene an eerie "black-and-white" film feeling until the light remnants dissipated as the riotous percussion sounds of the storm and sea would rush in to greet the scene. Amira could tell the storm was strengthening in intensity, the worst of it yet to come, although I don't think she realized she was speaking in metaphor as well as assessing the situation literally.

As the ecstasy driven dance routine that her hair enjoyed with the wind died down for a few seconds allowing the wind to ask her locks of hair for their phone numbers and promising to call even though they'd forget by the time they finished their bottle of water, Amira took the cue from the dance break, and stepped back inside, into the lightly air-conditioned cabin, which felt much cooler now that the storm had dampened her clothes, hair, and exposed skin. A small price to pay, thought Amira, in order to enjoy her friend, the storm.

Amira walked back to her deserted area of the second floor cabin and back to her barely cushioned pair of seats. She tucked the bag under the bench but kept her hand wrapped around a long, loose strap. She then curled up her legs close to her chest, creating a forty-five degree angled fetal position as she leaned against the arm rest and window. More quickly than expected, Amira fell back into a surprisingly restful slumber.

The slight glimmer of evanescent light in the distance flickered and grew, and Amira slept. The light bounced in and out of view through the waves, and Amira slept. The storm intensified; lighting spread its fingers throughout the ocean and sky; thunder bellowed louder and louder, and Amira slept. Through momentary, nanosecond interludes of quiet a slight humming of an engine could be heard. The rain pelted the windows with more gusto, but Amira's body seemed to accept the percussion and incorporate it into her dreams. Yet, the storm grew stronger still; the vitriol that burst forth from the heavens continued unrelenting. Really all that was missing was a an old bearded man with a peg-leg and parrot saying in an Irish brogue something like, "Aye, the sea was *angry* dat night me' friends." Under normal circumstances, a storm like this would *fascinate* Amira for hours on end, and perhaps her comfort level with these storms is what allowed her to so innocently sleep. Hmm, maybe I should keep that sentence handy in case I ever get asked to write her eulogy. Granted, many things would have to break my way, like Amira taking on a heroin/crack cocaine/gambling habit that was so strong it caused her to alienate all her friends leaving her completely alone in the world, thereby giving me the opportunity to speak at her funeral...ahh...oh sorry! I was just dreaming.

Anyway, the storm was becoming so strong that even if Amira were awake, she likely would not have been able to see anything anyway. Visibility approached zero. Lighting would illuminate the world outside her "cabin" window and all that it would brighten was darkness mixed with a bit of the white-painted deck that separated the cabin from the side of the ship. Then darkness would fight its way back into view. Another flash, another glimpse of a wet, white deck followed by black night. The lighting would turn Amira's cheek, which was flattened against window, an odd grayish-yellow color for a second as well, but sadly there was no one around to agree with my description of it. Another flash, another glimpse of white deck/black night, and Amira slept. *Crack!*, another flash of light, another glimpse of a drenched Maria standing outside the window on the white deck that was followed by black night. Another- wait a second, what? Darkness blanketed the outside yet again. Lighting struck immediately to the left of the ship, causing a ridiculously loud crashing of thunder to occur right before Amira. *That* did wake her. She bounced up and stared out the window and saw...she saw...well, she saw nothing: the deck was completely clear. Amira adjusted her sleeping position and cracked her neck ready to go for another quiet spell when suddenly goose-bumps appeared on her arm. She glanced around the cabin, but it was empty. However, several dark shadows moved ever so slowly outside the cabin. Shadows preceded svelte looking/fanny-pack*less* men dressed slowly moving along the outer perimeter of the cabin. These men were *not* passengers on the ship. Amira quickly felt for her backpack below her seat to make sure it was still there, and she slunk down to the floor. The lighting in the room had dimmed considerably, obviously passengers generally just slept at this point in the journey, so the ship saved energy by turning off most of the lights. None of the men seemed to have noticed Amira, so she crawled along the ground toward a staircase at one end of the cabin that led both up *and* down. Amira crept forward ever slowly, but more importantly, ever silently. However, a slight creak in one of the stairs from below caused Amira to scurry into hiding a few rows back from the staircase.

A few moments later a shapeless shadow snaked around the wall of the staircase. An obscured face, long hair, and torso followed soon thereafter. A sinking feeling formed in Amira's stomach and continued to form until she saw the legs, those perfectly shaped legs, ideally colored, proportioned and toned came into view. Amira's leg muscles tightened, then her stomach and forearms, biceps, and triceps tightened. The pressure around her neck increased, and her heart pounded next to her eardrums.

Seconds passed but those perfect specimens of walking-prowess remained motionless.

"I'm impressed Amira. I want to apologize to you. I thought you much weaker than you are. I patronized you, and for that I was wrong." (Not wrong for the murder plot? But for the tone of voice, *that* you apologize for?)

Shockingly, Amira chose to ignore the apology and remain hidden along the floor.

"Amira, I'm going to speak to you as an equal because you deserve that. What's going on is ugly. Sometimes the things we choose to justify are hard to stomach. But, it doesn't have to be that way. Amira, the lies you have been fed by men like Asad must be so difficult to see through." Maria walked towards the left (from Amira's point of view), which "inspired" Amira to silently crawl toward the right.

"However, it's time for you to see through those lies. The Qistone doesn't belong to you. The *stones*, all of them, have a proper owner. They were *stolen* a millennium ago, and the world has suffered for it. Amira, our means at times are *not* wholesome, but understand our goals *are* pure."

Maria walked slowly from row to row scanning the room for signs of any movement. Just as Maria came upon Amira's row, Amira, timing it perfectly, rolled to the row that Maria had just passed.

"Amira, if you hand over the stone, I will let you go. My original orders *were* to kill you, but...those orders came from people who have never met you or your family. I know deep down you are good people. You've just been misinformed. You've been *used*. Amira, please, I'm *asking* you to give me the stone, and I promise nothing will happen to you or your mother, or Hashim. You can even move back to Egypt if that's what you want. I'm sure you've missed your extended family terribly.

"Amira you've born this burden long enough. You deserve to have a chance at a normal childhood, to laugh with your friends, to compete in the swimming pool...to fall in love. None of that will happen Amira as long as you hold onto that stone."

Maria deftly pulled out a gun with a silencer attached and continued, "Amira, it's time we call a truce to this futile battle. Amira, I know you're scared but-"

But Amira felt that was her cue to leave. Then men who had been walking the perimeter had moved on to check other areas of the ship, so Amira moved on the floor as silently as possible before being forced to create noise by opening a door to the outside. As she dove out the door, a bullet hole appeared mere centimeters above her head. Amira now ducked below the windows of the cabin and hugged the wall tightly as she planned her next move, but her attempt at remaining hidden ended quickly as Maria stepped out the door at the opposite end of the cabin and spotted Amira instantly.

"Where to now Amira? This is it. There's nowhere left to go," Maria yelled through the wind, thunder, and pouring rain.

In truth, the ridiculously beautiful woman had a point: Amira was kinda fu-ahhhh/errr in a pickle. In front of her stood a woman, hell bent on killing her, and to her sides and back lay a sea which would be happy to do it in place of Maria.

"It's time Amira. You don't have a choice. You see that right? You can either hand over the stone or you can drown in the water. That's *NOT* a choice Amira!" she yelled more loudly now as the storm somehow picked up even more energy.

"How many Maria?" Amira asked defiantly.

"What?!"

"How many people have you killed? How many lies have you told?"

"The world is not black and white Amira."

"I think that's the first true thing you've said to me." Amira was stalling. Stalling is fine when you have a game plan, when you just need to bide your time until reinforcements arrive, when you're making brownies and are *starving* but still have twelve minutes left of baking time.   However, sans brownies, reinforcements, or strategy, Amira was just another wet Arab standing on a deck of a ship.   Hmm, that sentence sounded somewhat like a discriminatory stereotype, but I'm fairly certain there aren't any stereotypes regarding moisturized deckhands of Arab descent.   If there are, my apologies and may you enjoy healthy skin.   Okay, now I think *I'm* stalling for Amira, and I think I've made it perfectly clear throughout the book: had this story been two pages in length, I would have been fine with that.

Amira stood staring at her nemesis (yes, by now, I think they've reached nemesis status).   Amira stared at the military type men who were behind Maria but slowly moving forward and likely were also circling Amira by walking along the other side of the boat.   Although visibility was approaching zero, what Amira had to do was clear.   Now, Maria was right about something else: jumping into the sea on a night like this was tantamount to suicide.   However, this was Amira we're talking about: Amira of the charmed life, Amira the girl who got every break, Amira the girl who could turn *any* situation to her advantage, Amira of the infinite rainbow, the girl who- yeah, okay sorry dear reader, I can't even finish that without laughing. Truthfully, if *anyone* should *not* jump into the sea on a night like this, that would be Amira.   Seriously, the girl could be given a bowl of jellybeans and somehow turn eating the various flavors into an international incident, and I'm not even sure what that means.

Amira slowly put her right arm through the backpack's shoulder strap and then her left arm through the other shoulder strap. Her fingers slowly ran down the straps to the material that could be used to tighten the straps. Amira stood perfectly still and then said, "From Canada to Cairo, from Seoul to Santiago, fear the MOP, the MOP you can't STOP!"

Confused, Maria began, "What are you sayi-?" but didn't have time to finish, for Amira jerked down on the straps pulling the backpack taut and tight against her back and jetted towards her left, towards the side of the boat, towards the hungry sea.

Fearless, Amira saw the expanse of deck ahead of her decrease as the sea and darkness took up more and more of her view, but she made her decision, and nothing could stop her. Amira reached the railing and without even a stutter, without even an extra breath to ponder the dangerous ramifications, and with the confidence of any good superhero, Amira deftly jumped the railing, closed her eyes, and concentrated on the air rushing past her and the water rushing toward her. Although literally jumping away from danger *into* possibly even more danger, her grace shone even brighter. Her jumping technique and form were perfect. It seemed as if nothing could phase this super girl. Of course, maybe she should have checked first to make sure her jump was clear because it sure looked *less* than superhero-like when she slammed into the tarp, which covered the safety boat attached to the side ship.

Owwwww, Amira thought to herself. Thankfully the taut tarp broke her fall for the most part, or enough at least to prevent her from breaking any bones. Not to be deterred, Amira popped up quickly and ran to the side of *this* boat and she saw something that she thought was actually to her advantage. She saw an orange donut shaped lifesaver hanging from a hook on the inside of the boat. With an amazingly smooth motion, Amira snatched the lifesaver as she hopped over the side of the boat, now even more ready to greet the sloshing water below. So she stumbled on her first attempt, but *this* dive was immaculate, precise, worthy of Olympic consider-

SMACK! Dear reader, that was *not* the sound of Amira hitting the water, but rather the sound of her slamming against the side of the safety boat since she failed to notice that the orange donut shaped flotation device was tethered to the boat.

Double oww, frick frick (beeeeeeeeeeeeeeep) (At times, reader, I'm amazed at the number of curse words she can fit in under four seconds. Seriously, impressive).

Maria and the men jumped onto safety boat as Amira quickly scrambled to untie the floating donut from the boat. One of the men started pulling up on the rope. In about two seconds, Amira would be toast, well soggy toast, toast that's been soaked in soup for instance, but you get my drift. The man grabbed at Amira's hair, which only grew thicker with each minute she stood outside. Her hair was like one of those "magic mops" you see on infomercials late at night; I mean "saturation" was not a word in her hair's vocabulary (and her hair speaks like twelve languages...for reals.). Anyway, his first swipe at Amira's hair missed by a whisker. Thankfully immediately after his attempt what is known as a "rogue" wave hit.

The wave washed over the safety boat and made the passenger ship roll to the side at about a thirty degree angle. Amazingly, Amira held onto the donut through all this, in part, because her much discussed hair became entangled with the donut tethering mechanism. The wave smacked Maria and her men, momentarily throwing them against the side of the larger ship. As the wave retreated, Maria and her men were sprawled on the safety boat, trying to regain their footing. The man who almost nabbed Amira managed to brace himself by grabbing onto to something inside the boat and ducking down, using the safety boat to shield him from much of the rogue wave's power. The wave "pulled" Amira up to the side of the boat. Her likely captor was still crouched down, but she could see he had a rather large knife strapped to his leg. Most people run from men with knives, but in a desperate attempt to turn logic on its head, Amira lunged toward the man.

"NO!" Maria screamed, but it was too late.

Amira snatched the knife and cut the cord just as the man in black regained his balance. As Amira fell to the water, she stared up at Maria defiantly. Even through the rain and spray shooting up from the ocean, their eyes locked momentarily, up until the sea seemingly swallowed Amira.

The water was so choppy from the storm that it accepted Amira freely, and thankfully for Amira, painlessly. Amira thought it was dark *above the surface*, but she realized now how wrong she was. When she hit the water, she lost her grip on the flotation device, so her descent continued for longer than she had anticipated. A surprisingly warm "blackness" engulfed her, shielding her from all noise save for a distant "whirring/whooshing" sound, likely from the passenger boat's motor. She instinctively opened her eyes and the saltwater *burned*, but she kept them open long enough to see the light from the ship growing smaller and smaller and then disappearing altogether. It was at this point, Amira decided ascending was preferable to descending, and I must concur with her decision. Amira spread her arms out and stroked upward with her legs and arms. A powerful, yet gentle force likely from a wave propelled her upward as well, and a few seconds later, she broke through the calm underbelly of the storm and back into an angry surface world with a symphony of sounds all demanding to take the lead in the musical rendition which currently played.

When Amira breached the surface, she couldn't see the ship due to spray/waves/rain. She swore she sporadically heard voices and a slight whirring sound from an engine, but she couldn't tell from where or what direction. First things first though, she scanned (basically blindly) for the orange lifesaver. As she treaded water, she also flailed her arms around in all directions hoping to see or feel the donut. Finally, she did find it...well, maybe that's a bit inaccurate since she "found" it by having it slam into her face after a wave "handed" it back to her.

Ow. The combination of saltwater and a projectile was too much for her nose to take. Her face scrunched up in a rather ugly expression (just keepin' it real people), and then she inhaled followed quickly by the *loudest* sneeze: *"AHHH-chooooooo!"* Okay, keeping it real, I must admit, she has a really melodic and pretty sounding sneeze. Interesting. Have you ever had that happen before, where after hearing someone sneeze or laugh or whistle, your overall impression of the person changes? Hmm? You prefer to talk about the story of the close-to-drowning girl being chased by a secret society to the ends of the earth? That's cool.

Amira used the straps of her backpack to tie it to the lifesaver. A huge rolling wave picked Amira and her life-donut up high and for an instant she could see the boat and more importantly, as the wave dropped her back down, Amira saw Maria, swimming toward her. The wave put the two within twenty feet of one another. Amira immediately began to paddle in the opposite direction, but as good of a swimmer as Amira was, she was no match for Maria, especially when Amira was pushing her cargo in front of her.

"This is futile, Amira. You can't out swim me," Maria yelled. "If you stay out here you're going to drown. It won't be pretty, Amira. You deserve better than to die that way." Maria seemed to magically cut through the choppy water. With each stroke she shortened the distance between them by a foot or two.

Amira tried to ignore Maria. She *needed* to concentrate at the tasks at hand, which in no particular order were: (1) don't drown and (2) escape, and luckily for Amira, those two were interrelated. Amira imagined the feel of the Qistone, the warmth it spread in her when she held it in her hand, the calming effect the swirling colors had on her mood and during this process, she imagined the Qistone giving her strength. But was it her imagination? Amira felt her swimmer's kick suddenly had more force and form to it. She was moving now, actually making progress through this storm. Amira smiled; she might *actually* escap- *oooh*, that was a nice thought she was having, but unfortunately it ended when a silky soft hand (yes, even in the sea) grabbed her ankle with unexpected strength. Maria's well-manicured nails dug into Amira's skin actually breaking through at spots causing the saltwater to mix with her tiny wounds and sting like the *Dickens*. Amira tried to kick free, but to no avail. Then Maria with a violent jerk pulled Amira toward her. In that instant, Amira's grip on the donut which held her backpack and thus the Qistone, slipped. Her head dipped below the water for seconds that felt like minutes. Maria then dragged Amira up by the hair. As she did so, Amira flailed around and her hand instinctively went for the backpack to try and protect the

Qistone, but as she reached for the bag, Maria dunked her back underneath the water. Amira was wasting energy flailing around underneath the water without a plan. Yet, being pulled up into the roaring of the storm was little comfort to her. Maria pulled her up above to the surface again.

"Is the stone on you Amira!?" Maria asked with a look of pure anger on her face. "Just tell me Amira, and this can be all over."

Amira went limp for a second and then with all her strength tried to kick and push herself away from Maria. This sequence actually caught Maria off guard and Amira did in fact break free and take the donut and her bag with her. With her potentially fleeting freedom, Amira decided that maybe if she dumped the stone in the Ocean then Maria would spend all her energy searching for the stone rather than trying to kill Amira. Amira fumbled with the zipper due to the crashing waves and her hands being soaked and what-not, but she did unzip it enough to get her hand in the bag, but right then Maria caught up to her.

"I can search you just as easily when you're dead, Amira" Maria said in a frighteningly calm voice as she dunked Amira underwater once again. Amira's hand was still in her backpack but the rest of her was underwater. This time, Maria held on to the donut with one hand as she used her other arm to push Amira underwater. Maria kept Amira underwater by wrapping her flawless legs around Amira to keep her in place.

Amira jerked her body in every direction, contracting and pumping her muscles while trying to use her hand that was in the backpack as leverage to pull herself back up, but nothing worked; Amira was drowning and death was fast approaching. But then, Amira's hand that was still in her backpack came upon

404

something that was not the Qistone. It was a Ziploc bag which contained a glass cylinder. Amira clenched the cylinder through the bag and did something actually quite frightening: she let her hand and arm, the only parts of her above water, release from the lifesaver and join the rest of her underwater. Now fully underwater, Amira used both her hands to open the Ziploc and grab the cylinder. She realized she would have only one chance at this. Either it would succeed or she would die. There are moments in life that define us and when those moments of life brush up against moments of death, well let's just say a person is not lacking for definition. Although Amira had not heard the "princess" comment uttered by Scarred-Arm Man way back when, if she was going to become that girl, that regal woman, it was now or never.

Amira imagined all of the energy in her body rushing to her fingertips and toes thus causing the rest of her body to relax completely. Now, completely still she focused with as much as she could on Maria's grip, hoping, *begging* for Maria to loosen her hold slightly due to thinking Amira had passed on. A second passed and then another; Amira realized she could be killing herself by no longer fighting, but then Amira felt Maria's legs relax ever so slightly. Amira now imagined that all the energy she had "pushed" to her fingers and toes came rushing back to her heart, and once in her heart, the energy paused and then exploded in every direction. Amira burst to the surface, into the roaring of the sea and the storm and spray and the rain! Amira took in a huge breath of air and as she exhaled/screamed she unscrewed the cylinder and drove the ground up habanero pepper into Maria's mouth, nostrils, and eyes before Maria could react.

Within seconds, Maria felt like her face was on fire. Amira then used the donut and a swift scissors kick underwater to launch herself at the quite pained Maria and then, *no wait! Amira, please don't. Just not in the face! Please, don't hit Maria in the face. It's just too perfect to- ahhh, crap.* Amira totally punched Maria right in the eye with a strength that you wouldn't think possible from someone so petite. The combination of the blow to the head and the searing pain from the ground habanero pepper mixed with salt water forced Maria to let go of the flotation device in order to deal with the pain she was experiencing.

A thought then occurred to Amira. She wondered if her punch would be more powerful if she held the Qistone while punching Maria, so she reached into her backpack, grabbed the Qistone and then went to cock her arm back in order to punch Maria again. However, as her arm moved in a backward motion, the Qistone pulsed and suddenly Amira found herself, the Qistone, her backpack, and lifesaver-donut airborne.

Amira's eyes went wide as she zoomed backward through the air before splashing back down into the sea several thousand yards away from Maria. The dark, angry water engulfed her momentarily; as the darkness and wetness surrounded her from all sides, she realized her Qistone-Punch-Plan must have contained a flaw. Rather than try to decipher the problem though, she realized her time would be better spent reaching the surface, so she quickly popped up out of the water, took a quick breath, and saw her lifesaver with her backpack tied to it. She then realized she was still holding onto the Qistone. She placed the Qistone back in her pack, grabbed the lifesaver and began swimming away from the direction of where she thought Maria and her men were.

***

The storm raged on. The salt stung Amira's eyes for the next thirty minutes until she realized that maybe Hashim packed her swim goggles in her backpack, and somehow through the rolling waves, the spray, the rain, and the thunder, she felt around her pack and pulled out a plastic bag that contained her goggles, so she happily put them on. The angry sea led to near zero visibility, so putting on tinted goggles didn't help matters. However, she swore she saw just a glimmer of light in the distance. She wasn't sure if her eyes were playing tricks on her or not; she wasn't sure if she was actually progressing or if the currents were such that she was just swimming in place, but forward she swam. Several times her left calf and foot began to cramp, forcing her to stop her strokes and do a "dead man's float," remaining quite still with as much surface area of her body stretched atop the water surface as possible so as to remain floating rather than drowning (too bad no one recommended Amira choose healthier snacks earlier in the night....oh wait, I did. High five to me! And, dry high-five at that because I'm all kinds of cozied up on land as I write this...What? I'm being unsympathetic? I have my own crosses to bear, so relax. My typing fingers could cramp at any second too, but I persevere).

Through exhaustion, Amira kept losing hold of the donut handle. A huge wave would power through, and suddenly the donut holding her backpack would disappear, until Amira crested over the wave and "fell" back down towards the bobbing orange donut which still had her backpack tied to it.

Amira always fancied herself a "sprinter" when it came to swimming, but now she cursed herself for not pursuing the endurance side of her sport more vigorously, for she was tiring quickly. Although in her defense, I doubt her nine year-old self thought she'd be dealing with wolves, assassins, ostriches, and world domination before taking her first driver's license test.

Amira knew that even the best swimmers, even military professionals who were trained for these conditions could not last much longer than she already had lasted. Amira asked Allah if he meant for her to come all this way to be soundly defeated not by wolves or ruthless killers or world-domination-knitting-clubs but by water. No one answered her.

She then imagined her father. Her mind traveled back to the calm waters of her youth as a tiny Amira was held semi-immersed in the lake water by her father's strong hands, hands that felt so powerful. She called out to him over the smashing of waves and drumming of raindrops and asked him what he'd do in water like this. The voice of her father popped into her mind and told her to breathe and to concentrate on her form, and Amira replied, "Dad, *now's* not a good time," and he then said, "Now is the *only* time. You're not fully extending your right leg when kicking and-" "No dad *seriously*, I got it." (Amira and her father realized at about age nine that perhaps her swim training would be better left to others, but the anger quickly dissolved and the memories that flooded her mind (was that a poor choice of words?) (is it weird to have multiple sets of ellipses used within an ellipses set?)), and soon she felt herself smiling, if only for a second. Next her mind traveled to Hashim. She pondered what he would say. Well, first she thought: Hashim would be sitting on the lifesaver telling her to paddle harder. He'd then likely say he was hungry. The boy was *always* hungry. But, aside from encouraging her kicking motion and telling her *his* ails, he'd also make her smile. Though young, the boy entertained Amira almost constantly. He was like a walking smile. His energy just infused her and really everyone with positivity. So, she asked Hashim (hypothetical Hashim that is) to make her laugh, but as she asked a wave crashed over her filling her mouth with saltwater.

Finally she imagined the MOP Squad. Meredith would assuredly be underneath her propping her up if possible. Carlos would make a crack about her swimming in clothes rather than a bathing suit, and Karen would sing her some cheesy pop song and subtly or not so subtly sneak in the name, *Kyle*, into the lyrics. Kyle. Kyle. Oh to be swimming with Kyle right now. *That* would give her strength, make her want to impress him and swim with grace. Oh and *how romantic* to take a midnight swim under the moonlight with Kyle. Yeahhh, umm I don't think there's moonlight at the moment Amira, what with the whole ongoing storm-*motif*, but a girl can dream I guess....a girl can also *drown*, but whatever, Amira chose to dream of Kyle as waves continued to crash around her, on top of her, and to the side of her.

Amira knew she was in trouble. She knew she began swimming in the right direction, but at this point, she had no idea if she was swimming towards the Egyptian shore or away from it. She couldn't see any boats or lights even though she looked each time a wave carried her above the surrounding area. The storm had been following the boat, so she tried to "follow" the rain but as the winds began to swirl, this became less helpful.

Just focus on Kyle, she thought. *Kyle and your stroke. You can't control anythi-* a wave crested and crashed over her preventing her from completing that thought.

"Want to go for a swim Kyle?! The water's warm! I could really use some COMPANY!" she yelled into the dark.

"*CLICK-A-CLICKWACKWACK.*"

Amira wasn't *really* expecting anyone or thing to respond.

"Ummm, *Kyle?*" she asked loudly, but I still like to think feebly.

"*Clickclick-wack-cli-cli-cli*"

Amira realized she must be hallucinating and wished her imagination was better so that at least she could be hallucinating Kyle rather than just garbled sounds and- *SPLASH* suddenly a fin sprang up to her left and then another to her right. For a second, Amira thought she was about to act as chum to a few sharks, but then two dolphins popped their heads up and in a high pitched voice, squeaked and squealed at her!

From her MOP Squad required school reports, she realized that these must be Common Dolphins, almost extinct in the Mediterranean.

"You're Common Dolphins!" Amira exclaimed. Yeah, thanks Amira. I think they know that. "Any chance you guys are going to Egypt?"

The dolphins looked at her and disappeared underwater. Once again, it seemed Amira's ability to make new friends was astounding. But then suddenly one of the dolphins reemerged and with its snout shot up in the middle of the life preserver knocking Amira's backpack off.

"Hey!" Amira yelled grabbing her backpack which still floated thanks to all the air filled Ziploc bags inside. She threw the backpack over her shoulders even though the weight made it awkward for her to swim.

"Not cool Common Dolphins! Not coo-" Amira started but before she could finish suddenly both dolphins appeared at her armpits and as she grabbed onto their fins, they took off.

Suddenly she was whipping through the water, and through the spray she could see more Dolphins joining the caravan, at least a dozen if not more. Soon, the rain dissipated and the waves turned from whitecaps to calm, rolling waves. Soon after that, Amira saw lights. She saw the shoreline. The dolphins swam in a V formation to minimize drag and they also seemed to swim into a current that moved toward the land to further increase their speed. Soon, Amira could make out houses and buildings along the shore. About two hundred yards from the shore, the dolphins in front of her suddenly veered left and the dolphins that had been pulling her along dove underneath the water leaving Amira topside. She treaded water for a moment looking for them before they reappeared about 20 feet behind her.

There was a cacophony of sounds from the dolphins that lasted just a few seconds, and with that they then disappeared.

"Thank you!" Amira yelled as she waived her arm over her head to say goodbye. She then turned toward the shore and began the final few hundred yards of her swim.

You know how in Bond films often some ridiculously gorgeous Model/Spy will emerge from the water in a bikini and look so unbelievably attractive that you forget to breathe? Well, whatever the *opposite* of that is, is how Amira emerged from the water. Her clothes were soaked. Her hair was smeared this way and that and somehow wrapped around her face in a way that made it look like she had an Amish beard. Amira made it just a few steps onto the sand before collapsing to her knees. The feel of sand never felt so good. She pressed her palms into the cool grains and breathed deeply, closing her eyes to take in that unique smell where sea air and earth meet. She took another deep, enjoyable breath before passing out due to exhaustion.

Amira stands in a lush green field.

"Amira?" she hears someone say. Amira turns and sees Kyle standing less than twenty feet away.

"Kyle!" she yells as she runs toward him and embraces him. She kisses him and then says, "Kyle, how did you get here? How did I get here? I was basically drowning in the ocean and then some dolphins...Oh no! Am I dead?! Did I die in the ocean and hallucinate being saved by dolphins?" Amira looks deep into Kyle's eyes.

"I'm pretty sure you're not dead, but maybe we should kiss again just to be sure," he smiles.

Amira laughs, leans in and kisses him.

"Amira?" she hears somewhere in the distance.

"Amira?!" she hears more loudly now as she continues to kiss Kyle.

"*AMIRA!*" Hashim called out as he ran/stumbled down the beach toward her. He plopped down immediately in front of her spraying sand everywhere. He then hugged his sister. "'Bout time you got here. Amira, Egypt is *boring* without you. Why are you kissing a seashell?"

Amira opened her eyes to see her brother hovering over her. Now awake, she realized her lips were in fact upon a seashell. "No wonder his lips were so salty," she mumbled to herself. She then hugged her brother back.

As she hugged her brother she looked out over the beach. Less than thirty yards away, she saw a figure, a tall imposing figure whose features were blurred by the rays of the low morning sun. Amira's eyes widened in fear. She thought it was the man with the purple eyes from her dreams, but then Hashim alleviated her worries.

"See Dad! I told you Amira would be here!"

The man began walking toward Amira and Hashim, and she quickly realized it was her father. He was tall and broad-shouldered. He had curly hair like Amira's but it was cropped fairly close to his scalp and bunches of grey were mixed in with the black strands of hair.

Amira smiled at her father as he approached but then turned toward Hashim. "Wait, Hashim, how did you know to find me here?"

"Chetna told me."

"Who's Chetna?"

Hashim cocked his head to the side. "Huh. She said she talked to you lots of times already. You kept waking her up or something."

Amira was about to respond to her brother with another question, but a deep voice interrupted her.

"I am so happy you are safe my daughter, and I am so sorry for what you have endured." With that Mahdi Masri picked up his daughter and hugged her. "I love you so much."

Amira didn't say anything. She buried her head into his chest and for the first time in quite awhile felt completely and utterly safe.

"We have much to talk about," he said offering the understatement of the year.

413

***

Amira walked toward the oasis, the oasis from her childhood. Her senses were fully open, but no danger presented itself. Still, she hesitated before officially entering the oasis. She stood outside on the arid ground and breathed. She felt the Qistone course through her; it seemed to pulse slightly in rhythm with her heart. The stone empowered, yet calmed her. She felt present. She felt the air around her. She felt the sun; she felt the ground underneath her feet, she felt the gentle tug on her shorts. She looked down and smiled at the smaller figure by her side.

"*Amira*, can we *hurry* please. I wanna go *play!*" her brother said through squinted eyes.

"I know Hashim, but we need to go back into the cave first," she said taking her brother's hand.

"Why?"

"Because, we have friends out there that want to help us, and we need to let them know we need their help. *But*, that means soon you'll probably have more friends to play with."

"Okay, but *you* still have to play with me," Hashim replied.

Amira stifled a laugh. "You're going to hold this over me for a long time, huh?"

"Hold what over you?"

"That I said I'd play with you every day after what you did for me."

"What do you mean hold over though?"

"It's a figure of speech."

"What's it mean?"

Amira thought how to explain. "You know what? It doesn't matter." She grabbed his hand. "Come on," she said as they entered the oasis.

"You know playing with me everyday isn't a *bad* thing. It helps us both."

"How's it help us both?"

"Well, I get to practice catching the football," he said as he swung her hand back and forth.

"Okay, but, what's in it for me?"

"You get to hang out with me!" he said sincerely. "I'm fun."

"And humble."

"What's humble mean? It's a pie right?"

"Yup."

"What's it taste like?"

"Hashim, I have a feeling, you'll *never* know."

"I bet I'd like chocolate pie better."

"Probably."

"Amira?"

"Hmm?" she asked as they approached the rock, which would open for them moments later.

"Do you think Meredith likes me?"

"Hashim, who *wouldn't* like you?"

"Yeah...that's what I told Mom."

Chapter 11: G'Day

Tending to the fields was never the most fun task to be given, but the young monk-in-training made the most of it. In his mind, he'd go over the martial arts movements he'd learned over the past seven days. What he enjoyed about his martial arts training was that he always discovered something new, even if he had learned a certain move years before. There was always some new twist your body would teach you, like whether too much of your weight was positioned over your big toe, or if your tongue was pressed against the roof of your mouth during a maneuver, etc.

Faris discovered that re-playing the moves in his head worked toward making him a better fighter, not that he ever used his fighting skills or expected to. He paused for a second to look out at the bountiful land surrounding him. The vegetation formed rings. Each ring represented a different vegetable, fruit, or legume. Depending on the year, they'd be planted in different rings in a pattern that supposedly was specific, but not one Faris had been able to decipher. Currently, he stood at an outer ring containing carrots, staring toward the center of the circular shaped crops. He walked toward the center, passed the cherry trees and orange groves until he had a clear view of the center. The rings did not continue all the way inward until there was a single plant if that's what you were thinking dear reader. Actually, the rings continued in smaller and smaller circumferences until the smallest ring came across the edge of an immaculate green lawn trimmed so smoothly, it's possible some would mistake it for a gigantic putting green, though this green was much deeper and fuller than you would find on any golf course. At the center of the green lawn stood a partially enclosed stone shrine. The shrine was dark, a midnight blue. The texture of the stone varied, at times jagged and rough, in other spots smooth as glass. Inside the structure, one would find a simple wooden bench that no more than three people could sit on at once, though generally only one person sat inside the structure at any given time. The structure, due to its size and location lent itself to solitude, to isolation of thought. Often people on the compound would seek out its shelter to meditate and contemplate about the world outside while staring at the various writings that filled the inner wall.

Faris, however, was *not* one to contemplate, to calm his thoughts. His elders felt this held him back, though his theory was monotony and boredom were the only things holding him back. However, today felt different from other days. The sun had just fallen below the horizon leaving the sky a deep ocean blue. However, the land was lit by a bright three quarter moon.

Something compelled Faris to look inward both literally and figuratively. As he approached the rigid structure while holding the shovel he had been using across his shoulders, he considered the decisions he had made that led him to this very spot. He, an Arab-Australian teenager standing in the middle of a rural

Australian farm, seemed senseless to him, and yet, here he stood. That truth could *not* escape him. The reality of the situation was all too clear to him. So why not take a moment to ponder his life alone, away from the deafening silence that surrounded him at this moment?

Faris reached the structure and put his left hand on the entryway. The stone cooled so quickly after the sun set. The cool sensation transmitted a calmness that began at his palm, traveled through his wrist and forearm, and continued along his shoulder until spreading through his body in all directions. He closed his eyes and focused on the temperature shift in his body and the slowing of his heartbeat. He then couldn't help but laugh and smile. For a second, he thought he was having a "moment" before realizing he was just another pathetic metaphysical sixteen year-old who although believing to be deep, really just made up what likely would be called in a pool setting: the shallow end. He shook his head at his *pathetic-ness* and then opened his eyes. The smile on his faced morphed quickly to a frown and then an open-mouthed look of awe mixed with fear. At first a Chinese character on the inner wall of the shrine seemed to ever so slightly shimmer, but that evanescent sparkling disappeared only to be replaced by what could only be described as a flood of light. The character lit up again and the light spread quickly outward from the character in all directions until all the writings glowed a deep gold that emitted strings of light that looked almost solid.

As Faris watched, without thinking he dug his shovel into the ground, so a second later when he sprinted away to find the Abbot, the shovel remained upright, an inanimate sentry standing guard over the light show that currently played out in and around the shrine, growing brighter and brighter.

Chapter 12: First Book Farewell

And so ends Book One of the Qistone Trilogy. Now readers, I know that some questions have not been answered, but alas, have faith those questions *will* be answered in due time.

Now though, dear readers, we must bid Amira and Co. farewell. When the story picks up again, know that not all the characters may continue on this journey, know that others may disappear only to reappear at a later time, and know not all will make it to the end. Know further that the story may not pick up exactly where you'd like it to. Amira will not grow up fully in the spotlight of the story year after year. For, in truth, life is full of lulls. And sure, some of you might be interested in Amira's "pre-calc" adventures, drivers education, and make-up mishaps, but I prefer we allow Amira to grow from a distance....a *great distance*, like so far away you must squint and think to yourself, "Wait, is that Amira way over there?" and then as you approach you realize it's just some random college kid who discovered Rastafarianism on a whim and thus grew his hair out in a way that looks much cooler on other people but not on him.

Anyway, when possible, I will try to shed light on moments in her life that though ancillary, are not unimportant to this story.

Do not hate me dear reader, for speaking honestly with you. Like Joan of Arc (or maybe just like the Joan of Arc in that crappy movie from the 90s), I am just the messenger. However, unlike Joan of Arc whose only burden was being burned to death, I must soldier on, for *this* message is *far* from over...and I'm all out of matches.

THE OKLAHOMAN DAILY GAZETTE, September 30, 1999

BIG BIRD BOUNDING?...SNUFFLEUPAGUS NEXT?

In an ongoing mystery, ostrich farmers in six different states claim an extraordinarily large ostrich suddenly appeared on their ostrich farms and then just as suddenly disappeared a day or two later without a trace. Interestingly, sightings of what have been described as a "big bird" sprinting along the countryside late at night have been reported recently in more than ten different states. It is unclear whether the above countryside and ostrich farm sightings are related. Further, the motivation behind this mysterious migration remains unclear. Timothy Jones of the Norman Police Department stated, "We take these claims *very* seriously. I have personally requested that the Mayor allow us to set up roadblocks along Sesame Street in order to find answers to this mystery." So far, Big Foot and The Great Pumpkin have refused to comment on this enigma, but...

THE END

Special Acknowledgment

In the scene where Amira walks down the steps of Central Park and hears a guy singing and playing guitar, the lyrics are from, "Hello Stranger," by God Street Wine. (God Street Wine. "Hello Stranger." Who's Driving?. Ripe & Ready Records, 1993.)

$\mathcal{A}$CKNOWLEDGMENTS

I'd like to thank my parents, Michael and Denise, for all of their support, for their belief in my imagination, and for countless, countless, *countless* other things; my sister, Eugenie, the true artist in the family; my sister, Burns, who has taken in her deadbeat brother on several occasions and who has supported all of my creative endeavors; Bethany Geaber, the first person to read and edit my book, whose enthusiasm for the story from the beginning really made the writing of the book possible, and who "strongly encouraged" me to continue working on the story on many, many occasions since I had a habit of sending her story segments that generally ended on a cliff hanger; Lauren Satlowski, for doing the beautiful cover art; Jon Halverson, who so thoroughly edited and commented on the book; Carol Yoon, whose friendship and thoughts I will always cherish; and finally, A. "H.olla At Your Ostrich Wrangler!" F.: thank you for sharing and giving the story its heart; you will always be my favorite ostrich wrangler.

Also, thank you to everyone who has taken the time to read this book. It was a labor of love, and I feel blessed to be able to share the story with you, and I hope you stick around for the second and third book. The best is yet to come.

- Stephen McNamee

3475550